Praise for *Views Cost Extra*

"It was Stanley Elkin who taught us that 'the great gift of fiction . . . is that it gives language the opportunity to happen.' L.E. Smith, in *Views Cost Extra*, has taken that opportunity and given us a remarkable collection of short stories, fiction that exploits the miracle that is the English language. He torques it, turns it upside down and inside out, maims it into brilliant particulars that ask us to downshift and pay fresh attention. Smith knows his world, its physical make-up—'Peel an apple skin with a knife, go all around in one unbroken ribbon, it's like that—driving roads that hug the mountains of New Hampshire.' And he understands the human heart in its mythical quest for 'the quick of significance.' Often hilarious, always original, these are astonishing stories that reshape the known world."
Darrell Spencer
(author of *Bring Your Legs with You* and *One Mile Past Dangerous Curve*, Professor in Creative Writing at Ohio University

❦ ❦ ❦

"A new breed of story-teller is loose in the land: heedless and headstrong, enraged by the fey and the unambitious, dismissive of the wan and merely well-mannered. L. E. Smith is a member of that good and necessary tribe. His are the stories that result when the imagination is blasted from the ancient ice of convention and effete tradition. *Views Cost Extra* is made of rubble and shards and splinters and infernal dreams and splintered hopes--all of it less typed than shouted on to the page."
Lee K. Abbott
(author of *All Things, All at Once*, Professor of English, Ohio State University)

❦ ❦ ❦

"The rich stories in *Views Cost Extra* are filled with rocketing confrontation. L.E. Smith is a ventriloquist with many different voices and dramatic visions."
Alexander Theroux
(author of *Darconville's Cat* and *Laura Warholic*)

❦ ❦ ❦

TRAVERS' INFERNO

L.E. Smith

Fomite
Burlington, Vermont

ISBN-13: 978-1-937677-17-6

Library of Congress Control Number: 2012936689

Fomite
58 Peru Street
Burlington, VT 05401
 www.fomitepress.com
Cover art by Nathania Rubin
Author photograph by Alan Doe

Acknowledgements

Chapter 17 of this book has been published under separate cover as a short story titled "Broken."

Special thanks to Western Reserve Academy and to Headmaster Emeritus, Skip Flanagan, for understanding and making allowances for a writer's compulsion; and to the Kittredge Fund of Harvard University for its generous cash grant; and to The Vermont Studio Center of Johnson, Vermont, as well as St. Andrew's University of Scotland, U.K., for their help with residency grants; and to Bob Watson of Capital Grounds of Montpelier, Vermont, for allowing me hanger-on status at his very fine café to get the writing done; and to Lee K. Abbott, Alexander Theroux, George Saunders, Marc Estrin and David Kaslow for advising and encouraging. Special thanks to my friend Nathania Rubin for her fine atmospheric interpretation of the theme of this book as seen on the cover.

About the Author

L.E. Smith lives in Vermont, writes books and teaches English, has tried to make it as a tennis pro and as a recording artist for Columbia Records, has trained guard dogs, worked as a security guard for the Metropolitan Museum of Art in New York City, delivered mail on the back roads of Vermont, worked as head chef in a restaurant, and for one day sold Fuller Brushes door-to-door in Los Angeles.

Chapter One

Little comfort in a Vermont diner • Patty Hearst abducted • A church burned in Burlington • Travers goes pre-seizure • Coffee, fried eggs or me? • Bisecting circles with a mad Cat on a closed road.

I set down the newspaper, breath raspy, eyes sweaty and smeared with printers' ink, trembles assailing me. I'd been reading the lead story, the Patty Hearst abduction and family history: her grandfather slandered in the movies (a rose by any other name would smell), Patty abducted by the Symbionese Liberation Army, made to feel responsible for America's poor and hungry, probably scratching hives in the airless closet of a cinder block L.A. slum. I felt the itch myself, manipulated by the bully of my imagination. When I read about the burned church in local news, that's what tripped the disease of my brain. This was not an enlightened altered consciousness but a poisoning of my imagination with memory. Nerves heaved like twenty years ago in the boys' choir of Our Lady of the Mount in East Boston, when I had that vision of arson and the seizure that followed, when that church burned with me in it. I was not a well man.

I had steered my Datsun truck deliberately random on back roads away from Boston through small towns in the valleys of New Hampshire and Vermont. Slow and persistent, straddling the center line behind snow plows flashing yellow strobes, a line of cars behind, looking aslant at America, destination Canada. It was my first time outside Boston, my first time down the highway, a failed Kerouac. Ken Kesey wouldn't have let me on the bus. I was going the wrong direction for those boys. I was a loner, over-educated at age twenty-eight, malnourished, disliking but supporting a cat. I was tall and skinny with a sparse black beard and shoulder-length hair like an Olympian on a Greek vase. I thought myself graceful in the buff, a consequence of reading the classics, but dressed in layers of harlequin patched clothes from the recycle shops in Harvard Square. I was taking the thinker out for a drive. Locomotion would help fashion philosophy into practical application for my *Journal of Life Assembly*.

I was tracking the blue lines of Rand McNally, a bogus driver's license tucked into my jeans – too inept to pass a driver's test, too unmechanical to care. I am the same still. Back then I thought the automobile and I could work something out. By the time I found a place to pull over, a comfy diner in a quaint Vermont village, the road had insinuated uncertainty upon my rambles. I thought I had put the granite of New Hampshire and a snowstorm between me and my trouble at Our Lady of the Mount.

I had associated knowledge with comfort, with protection. It doesn't work that way. I thought I had foreknowledged and girded myself against the effects of epilepsy. Stagnating three more years in that old hotel where I'd lived with my uncle and mother, even after graduating Harvard, I made a study of my disease, diagnosing a malady of spirit and perverse imagination. Experience suggests it is an evil inherited from my father, a man I never expected to meet in the flesh, an angel according to Uncle Gerrit, and so a dead man. A man I always expected to see again through seizure and wanted to see, and yet didn't. I thought a new life in another country might render me impervious to the influences of Father Gerrit, a Jesuit priest, and father Jones, my two guardians of misdirection.

I had shaken snow off my patched down parka and taken a seat in a booth and surveyed the litter of someone's breakfast that stained *The Burlington Free Press*, a daily from a town I would encounter farther down the road. The paper had been left folded beneath a coffee cup. On the second page after the Patty Hearst story, local news featured a burned Congregational Church. I read voraciously, despite my foreboding. I couldn't get the boys' choir out of my head – or the homily the priest had read before I drifted into seizure: *the sinner does not hurt the immutable God; he hurts only himself… having failed to attain the only purpose of his existence, he is like a barren tree fit for nothing but to be burnt....* Because I was all dried up back then, at age seven – no color or new shoots, gray stalk only, no sap coursing the vital cavities. I was living Uncle Gerrit's life back then, raised by a Jesuit Priest in a low-rent hotel, and then college and then more hotel time living as a monk. As a reminder that I hadn't progressed beyond this emotional debility, I was beginning to respond in a bad way to the church fire photo-dramatized, a stark image.

My body temperature leapt ten degrees reading the burned-church story. I thought I might combust like one of those Buddhist monks in Nam – doused in the holy oils of self-pity, lit by the short in my nervous system. I tested this theory with another read of the article:

Church fire lights the sky in Burlington. Parishioners in pajamas and galoshes aid pastor, risk lives to salvage artifacts. Twenty yards downwind, to protect parsonage, water-soaked quilts tacked to clapboards, colorful dowries all singed by spark and heat. Male elders weep as bell tower engulfed, reminiscing on Professor Joseph Mosley lecturing in daguerreotype from high up in empty cradle of bell on laws of Greek architecture. His copper-plate likeness hung on wall of parsonage, the marble urn that holds professor's ashes lost in fire, but thought salvageable, likely intact. Church officials plan to rebuild and place urn prominently in new church. Frayed wiring suspected.

Overheating in my long johns, I threw off over-clothes, unbuttoned everything decent I could, uncinched and pulled thermals out at the waist. This was more than flu coming on. I rubbed temples, pressed thumbs against carotid arteries, dropped my head against the frosted window, poked the numbness of my lips with my tongue and almost licked the glass. The green Formica of the table seemed to liquefy. I pulled arms off so as not to fall in.

"Hey, you all right?" the waitress said. "You been sitting here must be a hour. Haven't drank your coffee. Something wrong with it?"

I had been staring into the cup, monitoring my condition, and must have seemed lost in a fit of Socratic abstraction. Ripples in the brindled murk went seismic with a passing snowplow. I looked up at the scrunched red lips and the weepy eyes of the waitress, like my mother's, though in this case mourning extreme ugliness – a face sunk in like un-dentured or sucking a gin bottle too many years. Her body was tight though, dynamic and emotive.

"You sick? How about I go next door, get the pharmacist. She's mostly our doctor. She don't mind. Hey, Oren." One of the men at the counter shifted on his stool. "How about you get Jill next door, would you hon? This man's not well."

"No, really ...I'm fine," I projected past the waitress to the man getting off his stool who lifted eyebrows but resettling with a shrug and said, "Okay, sure."

"Just a bit *wrecked* today." The word wrecked I trailed into a whisper so only the waitress would hear, as this was a shared trait I thought.

The waitress carried my refill to another customer, disgust at my hanging-on while refusing help signed in the turn of her hip, a good, compact motion. No kinship among the wrecked it seemed. I poured more sugar into the cup and stirred, churning through muck, an industry of motion getting me, once again, nowhere. I looked out at the snow obscuring my Datsun truck, thought of the road as a network of escape routes concentric to Boston, the epicenter of my trauma. I hadn't figured I might intersect hot zones radiating out from the place I had left. Burlington, where the fire awaits me, is a town I pass through on my way to Montreal. I began to see myself as a moth drawn to flame, a victim of genetic coding.

The waitress winked to her confederates at the counter, executed a server sashay on gum shoes in the bacon fat of the floor tiles by the grill, showing off a utilitarian shape. "All the handles is in the right places, boys," she tells her regulars, which they have known already since high school. And in her tight, white cotton dress, she is Florence Nightingale of the coffee klatch set, seasonal herpes, china-doll face porcelained over a shrunken-apple pucker, saying in not much of a hush to her audience: "That boy is *ON* something."

Meaning me.

"No question. Hasn't he been swilling your coffee, Katie?"

Laughs seeped from the boys at the counter. The man with a feed cap who spoke stood up, pulled at the bill of his hat as a gesture of good-bye

Besides Ed leaving sour-mouthed out the door, there was the postman, a row of deer hunters musky from the woods, and a highway crew in orange vests to prevent their being shoveled by another crew as road kill. They were pulling jokes on one another (ghost-taps on the shoulder, salt in the coffee), their way of showing they weren't jealous of the happily unemployed, muted, red-plaid hunters. They told stories of draft dodgers some years ago passing through to Canada, while peeking at me over shoulders.

"Remember one-armed Jed the Gooks cut up that was field-dressing flatlanders snoozing in their cars on the highway up to Bethel?"

"Sure, that's right. His own war on them hippie draft dodgers. Thought he was still in the bush."

"Ain't he out on parole?"

"Don't seem likely. He's a bold killer."

"Related to the governor or something ...."

"Oh, in that case ...."

Katie sneaked me a smile, her way of showing I was included in the fun. I began to relax. Body temperature fell within specs; short breathing abated. The sounds and smells of the place linked me emotionally to the old hotel diner in those early days when I curled into the protective care of the assembled neighborhood. I looked again at the photo of the burned church – hardly a tremor of hands, nothing indicating grand mal. "Thank God!" I said much too loud, not an appropriate response for a budding Nietzschean. But I didn't want to flop around like a beached cuttlefish in this small-town cafe somewhere in Vermont, mindless among these strangers, my eyes gone white, lips and arms blubbery. So alien as to be suspected criminal. The road sign that announced the town had loomed Doppler in the snowstorm, had read Northfield Village. What crime had gone down in some field to set compass limits by? Agrarian crime is the worst, family set upon family or friend set upon friend. Secret crimes were a passion of mine, the stuff of Greek tragedy. Church fires are for me both a crime of passion and a thing of fate. The old paranoia was coming back. I was myself again. Hooray!

I looked more closely at the indigenous gathering of this Vermont eatery. There might have been a parking-lot tryst between Katie and Ed before hours, maybe going on for years with Ed's wife Elizabeth ignorant as stone, mainlining morning talk shows at the ironing board. The postman sitting by himself at the end of the counter seemed as lonely as me, but with a hangover from the Elks Club, and with the bad weather, probably scheming to dump bags of mail over a ravine in the woods where used tires and appliances build like scree.

There were also booths that held the more prosperous, those disinterested in the folksy humor of people who know each other too well. These were less-animated citizens I felt creepy about because of their whispers (braying like the men at the counter is better, I thought, more Zarathustrian, more honest), though I heard enough to pin them — a realtor talking rules of disclosure with a lawyer; three college professors sharing in-house politics; a banker outlining estate management to an aging owner of rental properties, something funereal about that one. I looked more favorably on the highway crew boss sharing hunting stories with a contractor. Homemade donuts under a pressed tin ceiling best describe the place physically, and this went down as a mental note of the kind of postcard banter I could send my mother Fiona to calm her worries of our unusual distance in separation.

I got directions to the highway from the road crew, but was then told, after a discussion of preferred short cuts, that Interstate 89 was closed to traffic — "The storm, you know. Wasn't prepared for it." If I wanted to, though, I could "sneak up to Brookfield off Mill Hill," where a dirt road parallels the highway and where a gate for emergency vehicles lets onto I-89. I was told where to find the key to open the padlock — attached to a small magnet underside the utility box. The crew boss pretended not to hear.

"But why get on the highway if it's closed?"

"Oh, hell. It ain't *closed* closed."

Made sense. No matter how stupid the locals might think me for doing this, they would not question my right to stumble into trouble in my own way. Yankee character forbids disallowing a man his own innate foolishness, even should it cost him his life. This I would learn the hard way in coming months.

The Datsun cranked easy enough even under four inches of new snow, though you wouldn't think it possible. Rust held seams together. The engine shook in its braces. The front bumper had fallen off in a low-impact collision with a more substantial American sedan. Tires were bare. My cat named Cat hid with embarrassment in the covered cargo bed among boxes, relieving itself in potted Boston fern as a statement and by necessity. The truck's panels were a jigsaw of colors, so it was impossible to tell which had been factory paint. The original owner, one of several probably, is a black man who bounced drunks in Boston's combat zone or simply intimidated with arms folded like a genie and an Afro nesting a pick. I met him at a laundromat. I was pumping rolls of quarters like a slot-machine junkie. I couldn't stay away from laundromats, even after having graduated Harvard. I was hooked on the rhythm of spin cycles to do my best thinking. The bouncer said the vehicle was powder blue. I reasoned that should I mix on a paint wheel these several colors it exhibited plus the rust, it would all blend to something pastel. Why not blue?

Motoring Northfield Village toward Brookfield Village and the gated highway access was to notice a leaning back to the 1800's: houses unvariously white in clapboard or brick with Greek columns, wrap-around porches stacked with firewood, attached barns in what's called northern ells, and massive chimneys with smoke escaping. Burn apple logs and follow the smoke to the father of the illegitimate newborn. I had dog-eared that passage from a folklore tome once as a kid but wished I hadn't when Fiona surveyed my reading and collapsed debilitated from the guilt and humiliation, which prompted our only talk about my father. Mother said, sunk deep into the cushions of a sprung settee, ignoring teakettle whistling on stove, that spazzing in the choir at Our Lady of the Mount had purchased my first look at my father. She knew this without asking me, and she went all weepy paternoster over it, red hair dripping the blood of Jesus. She said my father, soldier Jones, had come to me in that spasmodic vision of a church fire. She said it had played on the inside screen of my eyes during the seizure like some black & white 35 millimeter news reel from the 1940's ratcheting-up the war effort and crooning over paternal love at the same time. All I could say was "Okay, maybe I saw him." Fiona said, "Aye! No question. He's back." She then confided soldier Jones had gone A.W.O.L. in France in 1948, disappeared entirely after burning a church, after first knocking her up in London. She said soldier Jones had unfinished business with me, though he was through with her.

Those folks in the Vermont eatery where I had stopped didn't factor out to be much different from the usual counter flies at the old hotel diner in East Boston, which is why I stopped. I needed the comfort of something familiar that wasn't a threat. Beyond that, it seemed this road trip deep into the forests of New England with its small outposts of civilization had landed me in the same place I had left behind. I had been moving in circles within the eye of a storm, waiting for a shift in our relative positions to produce the next rough patch of weather.

Then the Datsun drifted out of my control. It would be my first ever experience with "accident." There would be more soon, but back then I was reluctant to recognize improbability. Everything seemed fated to me. And, if you don't know, time slows when you're spinning around in your car during an accident. It afforded me the opportunity to reflect on how I got here before I landed and had to figure out where here might be.

Chapter Two

Exiled to America • Home is a Hotel • Fiona purifies • A Fledgling Travers, a Predatory Uncle • Stories of East Boston • Fiona wears her nakedness like a hair shirt • Uncle Gerrit's heresy • The wallpaper competes with Gerrit's tutelage • Gerrit hanging like a bat from the rafters • Travers' fit and vision in the church choir.

How do you prepare a body to reject Jesus? Surfeit that body in Catholic ritual. That's how. That was Uncle Gerrit's method. An exiled Jesuit Priest, a rough Scot, Uncle Gerrit was too pagan even for Rome. The ordination didn't take. He believed we change gods like we change overcoats, have done so for centuries, one aeon to the next, one civilization to the next. Gerrit thought we humanized and monotheized our gods to feel more secure in a world ruled by star fate, the mysteries, a squabble of gods, organized chaos siphoning down to preordained results. But as I discovered, the toxins left behind in a body indulged and then bled of Catholicism — they could kill you, or somebody near you.

My first recollection is ruderal bloomings in a leaky ballroom in an old hotel of East Boston, my mother's hands raw scrubbing the perimeter like a chastening. Red hair pinned back, mumbling Scots vernacular and church Latin, signing the cross at portals, scoring with lye and vinegar the fungus that grew from water-stained walls. Uncle Gerrit said she rooted after teraphim, tiny heresies some ancient tribe had hidden within the floral patterned wallpaper. I didn't know then he preferred heresy to my mother's Catholic excesses.

In my first sixteen years, I seldom left that hotel. I had come from England in 1945, wet from the baptism, Travers Jones my given name, something of a war refugee.

The hotel had become low-rent rooming years before Uncle Gerrit carried me squirming in a basket across the threshold. He wore the black soutane of the Jesuit order cinched by a narrow girdle at the waist and a jaunty three-cornered biretta sliding on his bald head. My mother, Fiona McDeed, tugged a brocade traveling bag in paisley. "A poor kist," she said to Gerrit, thinking of her own mother that had migrated once with trunk in tow, following the herring from Lerwick to Yarmouth as a fisher lassie. Fiona's kist held all she had taken to the New World from Scotland at the close of the second world war: vials of miracle water, unctions, magic tokens, her Bible and medical books, silver-plated brushes (her one vanity she'd say), a McDeed tartan throw for me, her nurse whites, and an American army uniform, my only inheritance from my father. She felt wind along the hackles as Gerrit opened the door to a cavernous link of rooms, our new home. But Fiona would not lift eyes to survey the apartment before consecrating the corners, there were many, with the water of La Salette.

"You're going bampot idiotic, Fiona. It's a holy wet mess you're making. You're in America now," said Gerrit. "Leave the Holy Ghost in Scotland. Think of the wee babe."

Gerrit placed the basket center of the ruined ballroom. My panting and bleating surrendered to the immense emptiness of the place, suggesting the germinal state of my young life. I smelled dank plaster and heard wind buffet the second-floor Palladian windows. Their fluted columns carried the load of the sky that poured in gray with darts of seagulls skimming the East Boston harbor.

Gerrit lifted me to one of the windows that filled the wall. I knotted fists and pumped fingers in preparation for flight. I did not yet know my element. I shifted eyes for direction onto Gerrit's expressionless blue points of light covered partly by a lappet fold of veiny skin which gave him the aspect of a hawk. The plump, fleshy parts of me felt instinctively like prey. Concern twisted my features. Gerrit spoke again in a practiced baritone to Fiona: "He is a lad-o-parts, Fiona. Regard his comeliness. The absent father will be replaced easy enough or not much needed. But *he* is a skinnymalinkie just now. Can you bring the babe to your breast? This bottled milk is shite."

"I'll not be a slave to the child, Gerrit," said Fiona. "And I'll have the place cleansed to my liking. I'll not be waukrift and festering over lives ruined in this dour place bafore us. And I will have my own sleep at night."

But she never would. Fiona would lie in bed wakeful with aggravation: a failed mother of a fatherless child living among strangers in a strange country. My father had disappeared during the Second World War. She punished herself with the shame of a self-imposed exile, and with the impurities of the place we inhabited. Her worries made a torturous nest for me, but what did I know of comfort? That hotel had ceased catering to its guests long before my arrival.

When the patter of my feet and imagination moved together, I discovered stairs outside our apartment as Fiona jittered in her sheets. I would drag a pillow down the broad marbles once used in procession by a gentry long gone. I would enter the diner that supplanted a gentlemen's reading room. I would sneak in, curl deep into stained booth cushions. I made a nest.

Hans Obermeir was there, broad, intrusive, shift supervisor where flax is crushed for oil, and said, "A man come to see our manufacture of linseed, hair slicked with pomade like just walked in from Pucker Row, like water flies off his back, and we up to our arses in a skarn of flax." A pursing of lips. Tony Palachi said, before Hans could finish his story: "Do you remember O'Connell the shop manager that after fifty years paid a man one hundred dollars to learn his own signature." Heads nod. A story too often told.

One story, repeated, embellished, recognized as omen, tells of a ship builder, a man that had a hand in the James Baines clipper that flew twelve days and six hours from East Boston to Liverpool. But he didn't know to trim his own sails. Became unstable when the Cunard line introduced steam. Stabbed through the kidney a packet captain that invited his wife to dance in the ballroom my mother scrubbed. Back then silk walls, escutcheons blushing pink in gas-lit globes, a gathering of black suits, the packet captain bleeding on the floor.

Building superintendent Tony Palachi, gnarled and bow legged, would spider into the diner, lean against the glass partition, scratch his back upon the chipped gold leaf moniker, The Bottomless Cup (or "the bottoms" customers say, because food slips off ribs, settles on hips). He would survey the clientele, nod away reports of disrepair which was their standard greeting, unscrew the cap of his flask to brace his own bottomless cup. Tony would share his recent ejection of rent-delinquents. Some husband threw a weak punch, children had care-worn eyes, and the wife, "Too good for them all, too good by half!"

Lucy, the waitress, when addressed as "Lucy," tenaciously, ineffectually corrected by nomenclature – tapping with red nails a name tag, LUCINDA. She would scold Tony: "What makes you think you know a thing about family, Tony. You're as bad a hermit as that priest in the attic."

Tony would scuff to the counter, nudge Lucy silent with bony hips as she leaned over a booth table with a cleaning rag. The fry cook, Donahue, scrolls of tattoos on thin arms, gray coils of hair above the ears supporting a greasy white paper cap, he would shake his head sadly, say to me, "Get upstairs, child. These ain't stories for you to sleep by." But his gentle voice contradicted the words. I was soon forgotten, scootched into my pillow upon the vinyl. A good Catholic of the parish would carry me asleep up the stairs to Gerrit's door. Lucy would pack a treat of chocolate cake and fruit pie in a brown sack. Gerrit accepted both with a nod, returned one to Fiona.

Mostly I remained locked away, home-schooled by my uncle, read to from philosophical tomes, regaled with Von Doss choral compositions. Mother nursed trauma cases in a hospital two stops down the "T" in Chelsea. Uncle Gerrit's tutelage was confusing but less disturbing than mother's morning preparations: the bedroom door open because hinged to a cracked frame, wind through broken panes shivering her naked body seated at the vanity, eyes in the pitted mirror spiritless jellies of vivid green. Did she really not see me? My eyes wandered the freckled gooseflesh, the undulant contours. Molded plaster ceiling cupids chunked off intermittently. The once elegant oak wainscoting was mostly ripped away and burnt in the fireplace that had lost its mantle and had been cemented shut. The floor register that once sent heat was now a peep show through which twin boys downstairs tortured my mother with lewd suggestions. Fiona brushed her long red hair, said, "I am justly dunted and tawsed. I welcome the wee devils sherrakin. My soul festers and oozes sin. I am hell's kitten."

Gerrit was a renegade priest among the Jesuits. The brotherhood were not sorry to have his glibness removed from Scotland to the colonies, where brash, cheeky attitudes were commonplace, tiny declarations of independence, obligatory in the Yankee character.

Gerrit's most profound heresy was thinking he could create in me a dark crystal through which the light of truth would shine in new colors to edify a congregation falsely secure in meaningless ritual. He began my education through the catechism in all its ethical contradictions to immerse me, confuse me, and then turn me against Catholicism — mystical vistas of fantastical beauty and salvation crushed by a severity of doctrine to ward off evil. The world wobbled from the effects of my besotted state of mind.

Uncle Gerrit saw the effects of the catechism and my unstable mother were sometimes too much, so he explained that Fiona doused corners of the rooms with holy water and scoured walls with bleach to welcome the spirits of guardian angels locked in purgatory so eager to do good to win a berth in Heaven. Gerrit believed neither in Purgatory nor in Heaven. But he did believe in ghosts. As did my mother.

Fiona said to her son, "Nay, it's spirits from hell that flit and birl about the place. I will have them by the thrapple and out the place bafore they make me dwam," which conjured for me the packet captain murdered in the ballroom. I tossed at night and sweated dreaming of that man crawling in blood toward my bedroom, his hand upon the door, then merciful wakefulness but panting and too afraid of my mother to find comfort there.

Then Gerrit began the lessons of first Communion which demanded a purity beyond my capacity to deliver, which he knew and used to his purposes. How can anyone possibly be worthy of ingesting Christ's flesh and blood in the Eucharist? Real blood with flesh and all its members, bones and parts, skin and hair eaten at Communion, manducare, but not foreskin, though I knew I had one and wondered why and wondered further why Christ would lose his. Christ's foreskin, Gerrit said, has been preserved as a relic for prayer and miracle. All those miracles that must follow ingestion to prevent cannibalized. It didn't help I was teased by Stevie McKay, the Irishman, saying, "Yes, I am a Freemason, and as such I have just here in my pocket a match box with the consecrated host inside – you know, a little piece of Jesus – that I bespat on and prick everyday with a needle as a reminder to him of the way things are going in this world."

During Gerrit's lectures in the ballroom, our classroom, I often escaped through the wallpaper. I saw the wallpaper differently from Fiona. I saw patterns of wisteria curling and loamy woodsy creatures, recurrent as block print, blinking at me from the depths, a spiraling in that moved me to enter this lush forest teeming with animal life. Brown stains from rain slicing off the bay and under eaves formed rivers down which I journeyed past castles and over waterfalls. Other times, learning rote answers to questions posed in the catechism, I would mindlessly repeat the patterned response while channeling the manic buzz of the twins' television in the apartment below. A miracle box of technology in the 50's, as impractical for the working poor of this neighborhood as fin-backed Cadillacs parked in Negro slums said my uncle. I pressed a grateful ear flat upon the school desk Gerrit had placed center of the ballroom facing away from windows. The iron legs vibrated like a tuning fork to the fulsome ecstasies of Lucy Ricardo celebrating disaster (which Lucy I confused with Lucinda of our hotel diner). There were also catchy jingles of Speedy Alka Seltzer relieving and a Jolly Green Giant proclaiming the virtues of his valley.

Uncle Gerrit stood at the Palladian window, hands behind his back locked and leaning against the walking stick – an ecclesiastical tripod counting time as church bells rang, speaking monk words to me but as he looked to the bay, remembering his fisherman father that put out to sea from St. Andrews bay in the district of Fife. Nets winched to a forward spar upon which his father leaned waving to Gerrit in the sunrise until swallowed in the orange slicker that smelled of fish guts. As an American, Gerrit saw the sun warm the bay off Marginal Street in this Irish/Italian neighborhood of East Boston and thought how the West now lights the East. And thank the gods for the American GIs that stopped the Germans, but goddamn Travers' father, which he was sure had already been addressed. Then Gerrit would sneak a look at me glossing lessons and shake off reveries and lean over me with nostrils open breathing anger like stone furnaces out from his long, wide nose.

When he did so, Uncle Gerrit smelled of incense, tooth decay and sweat. I convinced myself Gerrit hung like a bat from the rafters at night in his black soutane. The fluids that ran cold in his body at night would collect in his arm pits then leak a bitter gall that sickened me during my catechizing when Gerrit leaned over my shoulder.

It wasn't until I had my first seizure that Gerrit felt secure in the effects of his tutelage. It came during the third hallelujah in the choir of Our Lady of the Mount on the day I turned seven years of age and was preparing for Communion. The mass was sparsely attended, though Fiona was there, mournful red hair tied in a dark-blue scarf, and the choir, under Father Gerrit's direction, was complete. Working through the hallelujahs, each succeeding "praise ye the Lord" receiving greater emphasis, a response to a prayer the congregation sang in union, I found my own response impossible to subdue. I sprung my jaw in operatic assault upon the third hallelujah. My fellow choristers on the dais, flaxen hair bobbing in black cowls, they nearly tumbled in confusion from their benches. They must have thought they had a banshee seated among them. The tangible mass of sound carried with it so much grief and anger and frustration that it would not be consumed into the great body of the church. Instead, the sound rolled down nave arcade, traveled in ricochet from bulwark to tracery and back to dais where my fellow choraliers sat now in quiet surprise with curious little O's on their faces, tongues still as sleeping dogs.

My tongue had been desperate to maneuver free of strictures placed there by Mother and Uncle Gerrit. I imagined my tongue a chained Samson heaving at the temple of his captors when the vision came: a man in uniform walked toward me bearing the gift of fire like some pyro magus; the gilt and mosaic gaud of Catholic iconography blackened behind the soldier as he advanced upon the dais, as though tar in an oily potash had being applied with a brush; the scrollwork of chiseled pew and confessionals mutated to salamanders tasting the air with tongues before racing away; the large crucifix above the altar ignited. Flame spread to sacristy linen then to decorative tapestries then rolled like lightning balls along the waxed floor, igniting the nave's supporting columns, sending more flame soaring in these six places as though Hell had been drilled into. Beams caught fire and fell as did I upon those seated in front of me. Then came the epileptic seizure.

Father Gerrit leaned over me officiously. He held me with pride, thinking I had succumbed to the emotion of praising a God that promised kindness but had made the world a punishment. As Fiona cradled her son's head, petting the tendons of my neck while spittle leaked from my swollen lips and my limbs jumped like eels out of water, as she looked into my eyes beyond the commotion of parading images, she knew that I had seen my father.

Chapter Three

Travers is conceived as bombs fall • Epilepsy: a perverse potency • Whoring for a soldier's pension. • Martyrs of St. Andrews • Horrors of Boston • The bleedy white soul of Fiona.

Conceived in the London underground, another squiggle in limestone. There's a letter, a confession, an apology from my father poorly written but strongly felt, powerful because no artifice. Sent to my mother, intercepted by Uncle Gerrit before reaching me. The love making was told dispassionate and crude. "Smarmy," Uncle Gerrit said of the letter's tone when handing it to me at a strategic moment this narrative will need some time to get to. The letter said they screwed two days in the train tunnels as Hitler's bombs tumbled Christopher Wren columns like matchsticks, reconfiguring cityscape. The letter excused Fiona's conduct, said a case of "confused morality," meaning she was unsure of surviving the blitz so looked for confirmation of a life that was supposed to touch other lives by touching a healthy stranger. She couldn't help being repulsed by the war-torn bodies she tended as a nurse. The American soldier asked for a cigarette, caressed her hand when offered it. Fiona lifted her free hand, hesitated, a rush of dizziness, then lay fingertips upon his cheek, the corners of his mouth, upon eyes as he closed them. Inhibitions fell away. Water fell somewhere in the black tunnel of the Undergound, steam leaked through cracks of metal and stone, lovers moved hands over warm surfaces and smiled in the overhead flame glow through mullioned glass. Mouths joined as brakes slammed above. A child cried nearby beneath a stairwell. Buttons yielded and bodies arched in rhythm. The pedestaled globe lights painted dark blue flickered briefly from a blast that sent blocks of sandstone from the vaulted ceiling tumbling onto track. The couple exchanged fluids rolling on the tiles of Pimlico Station under soldier Jones' army blanket.

The American took possession of Fiona in a desperate hope to conceive. She let him in. He knew he wouldn't come back from the war. Maybe didn't want to. The First Army corps would soon beachhead Normandy, push toward Germany. Soldier Jones worried about dying, but also worried about epilepsy, gastritis, bad breath, the reliability of the post, VD, and the V-2. Never pregnancy. Should have told her something. Fiona knew his worries bordered on neurosis, but who wasn't jangled of nerves going daily in and out of bomb shelters: pressed up against the stink of drunks, lechers, blathering children, widowed pensioners with cats, in a damp crypt with gray rain falling outside that most, sadly, hoped to see again.

The streets of London, when not bombed, were filled with sinuous nurse rumps flagging in white cotton. Up until Fiona's assignment in the Royal London Hospital at the start of the war, even through the dubious rehab hopes of young men missing limbs and faces, she stayed buoyant and confident goodness would win out. Then her belly grew, and the American soldier, after two weeks of amorous trysts in London, after much death upon the beach of Normandy, he vanished somewhere in France, a village church having suspiciously burned on his watch. She would not hear from him until that letter, many years hence.

The pregnancy would not be well received by family at home in St. Andrews, Scotland, an isolated university town edge of the sea. Fiona's father was one of the few Catholics in a town of Protestants, one of the last fishermen living in the shadow remains of a once great cathedral. His boat, a wooden motor drifter with two masts, a seiner net for white fish, and the rakish lines of a Fifie, worked out of St. Andrews Bay in the time between the two great wars, despite treacherous tides and rocks and winds. He was never in a good mood. He would not appreciate an unchristian pregnancy. Fiona's mother was as irrational in her religious observances as Fiona would become herself, with the added parochial views of a fisher wife that repaired her husband's nets and knit his gansey in the symbolic zigzag pattern signifying the ups and downs in married life. She would think her husband's thoughts.

Fiona found no comfort either way in telling truth or lying to navigate the red tape of maternity leave. But she lied effortlessly to the American consul in London, saying soldier Jones had affianced her before the pregnancy and before his disappearance. Her description of Jones, down to the epilepsy that worried him, convinced the consul the necessary intimacy had been achieved. Fiona wondered, should she bear a son, if the mark of epilepsy would revisit him as avatar of some peculiar Jones destiny. She didn't understand epilepsy. But it did seem Old Testament in significance to Fiona. She tried not to imagine in what way significant.

The consul stamped the Jones dossier MIA when AWOL was understood, rendering senseless any criminal investigation of the burned church. He issued a widow's pension and some articles of clothes thought to have belonged to Jones after a brief romance with the aggrieved. Pregnant women turned him on. This seemed no violation to Fiona who had gone numb anyway, a sensation begun in the womb that spread to extremities. And the consul, he assaulted her like a bluebottle fly: sticky wet caresses, insidious spittle dissolving the sweetness of her body wherever he touched. He didn't leave much. This was to be her final lover – slimy balls slapping at her thighs from a hairless and spindly body, limbs tightening, discharging into the isthmus of creation where soldier Jones had gone before and where nearby I clung desperately as an embryo to the slick, assaulted walls.

Fiona came to Boston when her brother Gerrit sent for her. He had crossed the Atlantic before the war, had settled a niche as choral director for Our Lady of the Mount, an Irish church near the wharves of East Boston. Fiona hugged the deck rail of the hospital ship on her way to America – army boys below decks in bandages vomiting into bed pans, none of them Jones – while she breathed in the good sea air to cleanse lungs and stroked me as I floated new born in the cradle of her arms. She tried to imagine her burdened self and her mother, two mothers, at St.

Andrews bay welcoming her father's boat chugging in past the stone quay. A welcome best never performed. She wondered, also, about the sincerity of the welcome her elder brother would muster when she reached Boston. If anything like the telegram (''come STOP with your babe STOP the gods will provide STOP''), Gerrit would be as ready to support as to condemn.

Fiona arrived in Boston, dizzied from the coastal train ride up from New York City. Gerrit waited at the station, bent more than she remembered from a bad spine, but gracious. He hugged stiffly, took the baby, my wee self, in his free hand, the other held a walking stick, and led her through Boston streets to a ferry bound for East Boston, what he called "a new place, an isle of our own." Fiona was overwhelmed by the colors, the newness and noise of Boston. She had known only an ancient town in Scotland and then the disorienting rubble of a blitzed London. The smell of industry choked her. The self-importance of determined feet displaced her. A people of trite and indiscreet self-confession, idealism mixed with indifference, Gerrit explained, which confused her more. And she would be mistaken for Irish, Gerrit said, even among the literate who would claim, with a relish with which Mr. Leopold Bloom ate, that her countryman's books were banned altogether, the Puritan censure once again.

And there was strange food packed in cans, cleansed of the earth from which it came, cooked in sterilized kitchens. And television everywhere leaking from domiciles, even those with Hepplewhite ladder-back chairs behind white lace curtains. And windows open everywhere with work pouring into the streets from above. Clerks seated by open windows, clacking typewriters, a battery of petty functionaries to get out the orders for Boston's shoe industry. Skyscrapers built to honor the shoe industry. Wealth makes a gentleman, Gerrit said; the mighty rise upon the backs of the common man. Everywhere and everything a commerce of widgets better made than the last, more daring, more cost effective. Ramblers and Studebakers zagged through streets like birds of bright plumage, evolutionary extravagance in a New World. Streets jammed with telephone wires, telegraph wires, power lines, the buzz and flash of neon signs.

Then Quincy Market, through which Gerrit led Fiona and very near the ferry dock, where Fiona hoped for the imprint of farmers and fishermen she knew on market days in St. Andrews. But even here explosions of surplus commodity – festoons of sausage, pyramids of crated eggs, mounds of rabbit, sirloins of prime heavy beef, shoals of halibut and sturgeon, parterres of duck. All antiseptic, as if the glands, guts and organs of these living creatures were impure, useful as cat food or wrapped in newspaper and disposed. Nothing left to recipe the blood pudding Fiona knew. And the boroughs of the apartments she could afford closed doors from habit, thinking she is Irish. Italians and Jews exiled to the same quarter, so Fiona had no choice but to live beside Gerrit in the old hotel of East Boston.

After the ferry, a short walk to the hotel, a different noise and clatter. Here, in this neglected borough, horse-drawn carts loaded with fish bounced the narrow, broken cobble stone – more like home. Tied to docks, small, colorful Italian fishing boats, men walked the streets in Gloucester oilskins and sea boots, oilskin hats rakish as Buck Rogers, odor of tar and hemp. And shop girls dressed extravagantly, boastfully, for the American GI, conquerors on leave from the naval base that inhabits the bay, wavering drunkenly, pulling at their women like Romans did the Sabine. One of these Yanks had conquered Fiona. She was so ashamed. Deep in the blood and tides of her tucked away places lay unfathomable shame. Each GI another soldier Jones sodomizing her most virgin recesses. And there was me, a child hidden away like bad memories, a soldier's uniform tucked in a box in a closet.

Gerrit tried to cheer her as they ferried the bay. She had been chary of words. He joked, belittled himself. Reduced from ecclesiastical research to choir directing, he said of himself, "Forgotten amongst the bishopric nit pickers but perfect in pitch." There was no consoling Fiona. The pregnancy was hard. She cried before delivery, with the babe in arms, and days after. What kind of world had she brought me into? Gerrit prized my red pallor, joked. "Testament to the devil's spawn," he said. "Another Ishmael, wild ass among men, unredeemable Arab." Fiona cried. Gerrit would pray the gods take the child in hand. But he was drawn to my development himself, an experiment in child rearing.

Fiona surrendered me entirely to Gerrit. Her own life ineffectual. Not that she didn't love me. She did, more than is healthy. I was all she had. But Fiona had inside her a tide of emotions slopping entrails, tangling motives, like the River Charles confused in its spinning eddies. She knew she was unstable. Fiona kept a distance from me. Gerrit would provide nurturing. After all, Gerrit is a priest, a clever man, family.

Fiona belonged neither to the old nor the new worlds. Boston scared her. In Court Street a giant steaming kettle above the lintel advertising a coffee stall startled her badly. The glass-eyed locust weather vane top of Faneuil Hall threatened the scourge of infestation. This was a country too jumbled and shifting and strange. She would never fit in. She had begun to understand the expatriate's sentiment: "The best thing about Boston is the five o'clock train out." Home was Scotland. Yet it could not be. Displaced as she was from home as much as from motherhood, a prolapsed uterus signaling the rupture between her virgin and ruined state. Something biblical about this too.

She was young, tall, solid with Norse genes from raiding parties in highland villages where young girls diverted looters. There was no waste to her motions except hands that worried at her sides or together formed a chapel for prayer or picked ascetically at raw skin around cuticles. She seemed always to be bleeding. It came in drips from milk-white skin. She paid no attention. Green eyes had sunk from the world in a tuck of high cheeks. She never smiled though her teeth were perfect. Lips straight and cold. But a high forehead invited onlookers, as did her beautiful, downcast eyes and shapely parts. A handsome combination altogether that drew admirers, whom she never acknowledged. When she tumbled the thick knot of hair down from the pins of her nurse cap it fell like a wall of fire and took my breath away.

Once, in her nurse's uniform, as she pulled loose her hair after a day of work, I called her the prince's bride and received a slap and no explanation. Sadness in the house deepened as I grew older. Uncle Gerrit often took Fiona for counsel into the old cloak room to the ballroom now converted to a kitchen. His words were short, weighted and serious, rising from the murk of a deep well. Uncle Gerrit droned methodically as if chanting from the Psalter on sins enacted from concupiscence. He manipulated my mother through her sins. He manipulated us all. I listened from the thread-worn sofa in one corner of the ballroom. Unease took root in my chest — a bitter and abstract thing that led me down black tunnels of thought away from the silver and green wallpaper of childhood innocence.

Chapter Four

**A recognition unacknowledged • The significance of Travers'
epilepsy • Snakes hanging from the rafters • Gerrit and Paul Tillich
burn a sand castle at Porzio Park • Christ dies in the forests of
France • Tillich will remove Christ from Christianity • The beloved
society of Lucy • The tortures of ultramontanism • Exorcism
empties Gerrit of the spirit of Christ.**

I did not have the normal childhood firsts, still can't ride a bike, but a
cluster of days remembered stays with me like shells from the beach stuffed
in pockets. One day in mid-April, the month of my birth, Uncle Gerrit lay
aside books for a "peripatetic lesson." I was eight, lean as a water rat. It was
a year after spazzing in the choir. The ice beneath piers, a sand-churning
wedge that had girded East Boston island since November, had begun to
flange and melt into woolly crusts. Winter had singed and scraped the island
with ice and wind, oppressed it with degrees minus zero on barometrically
dull days. But it was spring, finally. The sun angled beneath clouds to
nourish obliquely the budding trees. Gerrit draped me in the McDeed
tartan and pulled me roughly down the wet staircase of the hotel. Several
diner regulars beginning or closing their workday waved greetings ignored by
Gerrit. I ran my free hand down the banister, planed it like a wing on a
piston-driven DC 7 that lumbered daily over the hotel, bounced it off the
brass lamp that nippled the newel post, shorting the electric in a brilliant arc
of disconnect. Gerrit ignored my antics. He wanted sympathy between us, a
rare concern for Uncle Gerrit.

Gerrit yerked me into the revolving door off Marginal Street with a
puppy lead of twine cinching the McDeed throw (more caftan than kilt). I

teased for another go round in the scalp-tingling suck of glass cylinder but was pulled back – no go. Then Martin Toussant showed. He had come off night shift at the Great Atlantic Works, refitting boiler plate to war-fatigued vessels, refloating them for commerce. He was pear-shaped with hair hanging four-squared like a mop. His voice projected from a bushy tan mustache singed at the corners from welding torches. He came mornings to the hotel for fifteen cent waffles and shoestring potatoes an additional five cents. He came to chat the waitress. Lucinda's tinseled hair beamed off the chromium grill. Toussant's eyes squinted, soulfully pained. But when he saw my face pressed to the glass door, resolute in opposing Gerrit, he saw the ghost of a war buddy left behind in Europe.

"Jesus H, Father! Pardon me, but the little guy. He's spitting image of my friend Timothy O'Connell, the one with the stunning gypsy mother we all took for a witch. Tim and me worked together in a machine shop before the war. You might of seen him of your parish, Father. He was forever making some to-do of worker's rights and queering hisself with management, which were sadly his own father as supervisor. His mother became some mad over that. I would not expect him any smoother as a church goer."

I ignored the words and followed the whisk bristle Toussant carried upon his lip that danced in a lentigo complexion like sprucing constellations in the Milky Way. Toussant leaned near. I smelled the singed hair. He bent a knee and strained his watery eyes. His scarred hands squared my shoulders, arrested my energies.

"The exact image, Father!"

"Of another cloth altaegether, Mr. Toussant. You see here the tartan that come with him tae these shores from a greener and kinder isle. He's Scots, Mr. Toussant, naught tae do with yer Mr. O'Connell. Now bless our morning rambles, sir, as do we yer morning repast. "

Gerrit nodded from the waist an awkward twist of errant spine, tugged me by the lead. Toussant watched then abstracted away, scratched his head and shook it off as we faded east down Marginal Street through a jam of warehouses then a debris-strewn railway path that swung onto the dead-end of Sumner Street, a broad lane of brick laid by General Sumner. The General had picnicked on flat dunes a century prior and found it vastly sparse. Forty-two stately houses, assorted wharves, lumber yards, refineries and iron works resolved that. As did the hotel I lived in. Porzio Park lay at the butt-end of Sumner.

I hadn't been to church since my first seizure. Gerrit saw these episodes, these electrical storms in my brain, as tiny births under the moon. My first seizure came, he said, with the moon seated in trine with Neptune, a sign indicating keen psychic sensitivity and an unconscious link to and prompting from a family member. The "father," a fire spirit, will replace "our father," he said, and appropriately so, he thought, expecting me to brood over this revelation and mystery.

Gerrit had told me this months earlier, a prelude to Porzio Park. He rolled out the astrodienst natal chart up in his attic apartment. He was a man desperate to find order and ritual in disorder, even as he planned to destroy the rituals of the followers of Christ.

He sat me upon a footstool. Two uncurtained dormers invited shafts of winter light tangible as lead. Under roof beams snake skins hung in shadowed pale light from a hurricane lamp – there was no electricity. But when nosed out these snakes became, unmistakably, Gerrit's soiled stockings. This habit of airing rather than washing Gerrit had obtained from novitiate days dormed with fifty others in an unheated, converted barn loft. Ablutions were done fully dressed and seldom.

The chart had a wheel with twelve houses upon which to plot ascendants and cusps, degrees of intersections and conjunction. He was not surprised that both Jesus and I have Mars rising, a fire sign stained with the rusted iron of forgotten wars, he said, warriors then we two, for a new Jerusalem, he thought, and with Jupiter in Aquarius – water and rust make blood – both progressive thinkers with a strong incline toward radical justice. I will have the potential to wield a righteous sword, he said. But I will not become a religion. I will instead clear heretics off their pedestals on this blighted earth of corrupted religions. Such was Gerrit's astral argument, and my destiny.

He led me down Marginal Street through a press of cursing draymen and bargemen, unshaved giants that supped at the diner now inciting crippling loads through muck and ruts with grimace and sinew through a backdrop of ruin – a ship's chandlery with caved roof, abandoned shipyards with hulks resting on the flats, a gray atmosphere of wood chaffed in salt air and sea, silvery patina like carbon dioxide ice on Mars. It seemed to me a long insouciant stroll beside Gerrit's energetic limp, the walking stick thumping like pontifical mace. Once at the park, Gerrit led me to a narrow spit of sand, sat me on a bench at the grassy edge, walked onto the beach, turned and faced me with arms stretched wide, the stick making circles in air, a gathering in of circumference, something ritual.

"This place, lad, is sacred tae me!"

I looked with confusion at Gerrit's walking stick, which had landed finally on the sand. Gerrit must mean somewhere under the sand.

"It is here that I met a great man that shifted my life and must perforce change yer own. This man's English was more German than mine is Scots. But we soon enough knew each other perfectly. He stopped me as I daundered by poking my stick at the spume of wave and depressed in meditation. This in the year 1940, five years bafore yer mother brang ye here tae me."

The wind shifted Gerrit's robes, ruffled him like raven's feathers. His stick went into the air again for emphasis.

"I was in crisis, lad! And this great, this unco man, he knew and he bid me play in the sand."

I giggled.

"Ah, well, ye might become gleeful in my despite, but I was nigh tae leaving the brotherhood, and a huge blow it would be tae my fisher parents that mistook me, as I did myself, for a larger spirit and force for Christ than their own selves."

"Did your parents moan and scrub as my mother does?"

"Aye, lad. The fisherwife did, though not so mournful as yer own mother. Yet had I departed the church there would have been such a keening and carfuffle as tae madden the devil. But as I say, this great man had started tae build a sandcastle and asked me tae join him. He said he was drawn tae my black robes."

"Who was the man, Uncle?"

"His name was Tillich, named after the apostle Paul."

"Was he a fisherman?"

"Aye. Tillich will be a fisher of souls."

"And did you build your castle, Uncle?"

"Better tae say that together we did hearken tae a music that tumbled the walls."

"I don't understand, Uncle."

"Ye must hearken yerself and trust that what ye do not know today will become clear in future. As I said, he was German, a theologian exiled and a teacher of college that had seen his own folk grow barbarous with Jew hatred and land greed. He had come tae New York City tae teach and scribe and learn about this new land that, as he said, joined action tae thought in new ways. He saw another world war coming and he had lived hisself through the first. He said New England felt to him of Germany, its purling hills and close, small houses and good working folk. He asked me tae tell him of the folk of my parish."

"What did you tell him, Uncle?"

"I touched on some ye know from the hotel diner. Mr. Palachi that shoves his ratton snotterbox intae every unsavory corner of the building, a man jock that flings lives onto the street with the blood thirst of a Covenanter expunging Catholic tenants. I told also of ruchy language used by the fisher trade – my own father would have them by the scruff – and on our street of Marginal, well named, where a boodle of red stocking tarts corrupt our young men. They'll no get ye, laddie," he said roughing my hair.

"The wind is cold, Uncle. Can we go home now?"

Rain had come in gusts of wind from the northeast, a haar of North

Sea damp it seemed to Gerrit, and this mixed with a stinging dust from earthmovers rumbling across the inlet where Logan Airport spread like ink stain over sand hills. A tanker low on its seams steamed into Boston Harbor through the jaws of Fort Dawes and the Long Island.

"Soon we'll go, Travers. But not bafore ye see our sandcastle for itself."

"What's that, Uncle?"

"A stone-blind hinder of new ideas, lad, a torture tae nonbelievers, a rock from which tae launch attack upon our neighbors, a symbol of bumptious self-love!" Gerrit paused for breath and to reduce the ire in his voice. "This will not be the fairy castle in yer wallpaper, boy."

"Why is it not, Uncle?"

"Because too many have died ignobly spitted and wriggling upon the staff that mounts its flag, Travers. Died for naught."

Gerrit told me about the atrocities of the two world wars, which the Christian God, he said, had viewed askance, sadly, then walked away into shadow. He explained my mother's part nursing the wounded that healed in flesh but not otherwise. He told of Tillich's ministry polluted in the first war by young men dying ungraciously in trenches filled with water and rats. He said there are two ways of viewing religion after such destruction – Fiona's way of going deeper into the punishing symbols of Christ, or Tillich's way of thinking the old God is dead, killed in the forests of France.

"Crucified, Uncle?"

"No, boy. He died more quiet like, cowp the creels, my fisher wife mother would say, but this time I hope more useful. He died the moment Tillich opened the prophet Zarathustra's book. Tillich was thirty years old, the same age of Zarathustra's wakening in the mountain cave from whence he clambered down with his words."

"But does Mother know God is dead?"

"No, Travers. She thinks as many do that God bore a son, that one ye know as Jesus, that was sent tae die but fetched back tae life. Ach! There was no such. He was a man, a warrior, aye, but a man only. You will know all in due time."

"What of the sandcastle, Uncle?"

"Aye, the castle. We had built the most wonderful sandcastle ye have ever seen with towers broch tall, walls nebbed and sealed with tiny shell that shined like the crystal drystone of Aberdeen, and with pends and closes in the castle walls, a palace for a king four-squared and imposing. But the most struggle went tae coll the cathedral. We joined sticks like wattle tae vault the roof and set colored pebbles and sea glass tae mosaic the hue of stained glass. The work took hours as we blathered, knotting together hearts and tongues.

"Then he craved me tae run a channel of sea water untae the bulwark of defensive walls. Just then he set the castle roof afire and soon all washed intae brown tide. We had performed the old job-trot, the building up and tearing down, more civil than most history, he said. And thus, besides, Christian symbol shall be restored tae universal potency, tae include all men of difference otherwise. The castle had merged with ocean, that which washes all shores. Tillich talked of fellowship, a 'bund,' he said, an alliance of religions that shall be accomplished when the church itself, imposing, singular and isolated, is leveled tae the ground like our castle. Tillich anticipates a new Christianity without Christ. He expects and prepares for it, as do I, though neither of us yet knows what it will be named. Perhaps you will think of a name, Travers?"

"I will call it Lucy, because it will want to be loved."

"Well, that will be it then, the beloved society of Lucy. We shall go home now."

Gerrit dropped his stick and limped vigorously toward me, grabbed me by the shoulders crying now, then erupted in near song, "Yer epilepsy is a sign, lad, a blessing from the world-soul, a peek at its substance and intent! It is yer message in a sea shell, the sounding of yer own heart that beats in tune with the universe! Ye must see that there needs purification by fire tae bring the new order!"

Gerrit gripped hands together to suppress agitation and breathed heavily into quiet. He had not meant to scare me with his passion.

"Ye yerself were conceived in fire, lad. Yer father has mizzled away in the holy light of a church in conflagration. Yer life will be a pilgrimage intae the light of the new order. Ye must feel that. Ye must!"

Gerrit threw arms around me and gushed and shuddered upon my head. I put my arms tentatively around this pungent Uncle, bathing not a habit he had acquired even in the new world. But he was crying for himself as much as for me and the spiritual confusion of the world. Like Fiona, Gerrit had suffered for his religion. When he was a youth, Gerrit had stayed at seminary in Glasgow despite the tortures inflicted by ultramontanism – attachments obliterated (friends, places, things, memories); forsaking all but God; suffering public humiliations the "eye" of the order (both open and secret censors) imposed to correct behavior; knowing neither sex nor family nor fatherland; becoming a creature without emotion or feeling; threatened daily with magilling (a caning the peasant Rene Magill suffered interminably and so gave his name to the process); and one pale and oily scholastic, a Brother, that condemned comforting hands beneath the covers (Commandment number Seven) unless those hands were his own.

And when Gerrit described to the curate the superstitious excesses of his mother, he was told the Devil is in it. He must do as Aloysius de Gonzaga by not looking too closely at his mother thereby escaping carnal desire. Then put her in a dark room in preparation for an exorcism. Bring Agnus Dei, the holy water. Do not look into her eyes (oculi talium mulierum nocent fascino). Ask how long she has served the devil. Ask what promises she has made him. Ask what kind of witchcraft she is most addicted to (hurtful to children, cattle, or crops). Ask whether she has injured health by special signs. (Examine your father's boat for knots that slip or bind.) Then prepare the sacred mixture of whey, oil, and goat's rue to be breathed in a dish of burning sulfur with asafoetida, resin, and St. John's wort.

Gerrit came to America disaffected, strung-out on the opiate of mock religion, closed-off from the passion Mother Mary once brought him, and exiled, living among strangers. It seemed to him that he and Tillich were the same man.

Chapter Five

Travers' second seizure: *Playboy* and soldier Jones • A classical education imposed • Travers' father declared "guardian angel" • Travers' first solo outside the hotel on Marginal Street, elbows out and ego foremost • Admitted to Harvard at age 20 • Composing a *Journal of Life Assembly* • Travers awakened to Nietzsche, released from Harvard, on the road to Montreal.

At ten I induced a second seizure. That was 1955, Davy Crockett coonskin caps, Albert Einstein's death, Nabokov's *Lolita*, the same year America involved itself in Saigon politics. Shame on us. Pandering to river pirates that manipulated the French and the Communists after them. But my own history isn't spotless. My latest seizure did not endear me to Uncle Gerrit as acolyte of the new religion.

It began as payback for my captivity. I clattered pipes that linked our apartment to Uncle Gerrit's – mournful scrapings on radiator pipes near my bed when sleepless, staccato rapping on water pipes from the toilet seat. Gerrit ignored the noise, took it for steam bullying radiators. One day percussion from the bathroom became especially fierce, niggling enough that Gerrit noticed. I had smuggled a *Playboy* left by the twins on the fire escape landing, anatomy lessons for the boys when they weren't performing ladder-launched acrobatics during Gerrit's lessons to me in the ballroom.

I had my second seizure in the bathroom. Gerrit found me curled and flapping at the base of the toilet, the *Playboy* beside me spread at its bindings, a bird in flight, my fly open to censure – Commandment Number Seven: thou shalt not sex thyself. Gerrit was not pleased. He never told Fiona. He did advise me to avoid "the business of quines and loons altaegether," so as not to become a philosopher married to a Xantippe, so as not to suffer a piss-pot dumped over my head. This new direction in my tonic-clonic convulsions seemed to end his spiritual ambitions for me. He called appalling and aberrant my father's appearance during such an episode, the encouragement my father seemed to bestow upon my experiment. Nor did Gerrit speak again of his mentor Paul Tillich and the "new religion," not until churches burned in Vermont. But this will happen later, after I have gone through college in my unhurried manner, where I will bump into Tillich and Nietzsche in my own way, and a few dismal years hence.

It was the monkish studies imposed on me by Gerrit that got me into Harvard. At the age of twenty, never having attended school, I tested off the charts in high-school equivalency and filled several blue-books of the Harvard entrance exam with esoteric learning that moved the university to knee-quavering scholarship offers. The theology and philosophy departments in particular slavered over me. They must have recognized a unique medieval grounding and wanted a hand in my development, although my development had already been developed. I had had a long stay in that hotel. Aristotle and Thomas Aquinas and Euclid and Vulgate Latin – all that shit paid off, at least initially.

Gerrit said he struggled to reconcile my father's appearance during my seizure in the choir and decided I must accept the American soldier as my "guardian angel." Of course, this was before my second seizure when my father had pimped to the low animal in me, as Gerrit later said. He spoke at first of my father as an angel, a suffering soul, he said, still waiting for delivery from purgatory. Our good works on earth, under their direction, shorten their purgatorial sufferings. In return they give protection in spiritual or physical danger. But Gerrit never did believe this, and there was little comfort for me in thinking of my absent father as guardian of anything – a no-show at my birth and then beyond, he that set the church in Boston on fire while I spazzed out in the choir. My father, my guardian angel, palming orange flame like stigmata, perverse saint, sneering, stretching his arms to me, slouching toward the choir had said, "My gift to you my son."

I didn't trust my guardian angel, for obvious reasons, though at the time I thought I could trust Gerrit. I questioned none of the methods he applied to my rearing, even though it was clear to me he had deprived me of playmate rivalries and loyalties, playground scuffs and the manly transition to sport. So I developed a silent, observant nature through a perpetual state of confusion over the readings forced upon me. He dragged my pre-adolescent mind through Plutarch's *Lives* – livid anecdotes of rogues and super heroes that even Shakespeare couldn't resist. Good studies in character, Gerrit said, and told by a Platonist in the earliest, purest days of Christianity. On his death bed Plutarch imagined Hermes winging him to Heaven. That's the kind of heathen/Christian compromise Gerrit approved.

Gerrit was amused when I leaned over the sill of the Palladian ballroom windows to descry, among the throng, what I took for poisoners, homosexuals, emperors, concubines and barbarians. My friends at the hotel diner began to project sinister traits –the fry cook's tattoos were proof of cannibalism (perhaps gone native when shipwrecked on a tropical island); Lucinda, the platinum waitress that Martin Toussant courted and that stuffed my pockets with treats when I fell asleep at night in the booths, seemed too solicitous towards me, and she and Toussant whispered constantly with heads together (white slavers sizing me for manacles); and Tony Palachi had the hubris and political treachery of an Alcibiades (I double bolted the door to our apartment whenever a ring of keys jangled in the hall).

Gerrit used my epileptic fit in the choir as reason enough for my avoiding church service, though Fiona knew of deeper reasons why we had strayed from the church cavnon. Strayed farther than she knew or wanted to know. And all Gerrit would tell me of Jesus, beyond our similar warrior tendencies, is that he abandoned family, something my mother had done to her detriment, something I surely must not do.

In my teenage extravagances I challenged Gerrit's isolationist practices the way Kennedy had Kruschev's. Gerrit did his share of shoe banging, or cane banging in his case, before agreeing to free me in "modules of time to traverse the countryside" as he explained it, "so long as I would cease my haivering" – stop the nonsensical arguments, he meant. So I began to walk the streets in brief jaunts to the Italian grocer for leeks and potatoes and to the fishmonger for meat. These were my staple diet, and though I got less exercise than a lab rat, I had grown strong and tall enough to want to test myself in the physical world. Once outside in the daytime teem of swap-shop, saloon, warehouse, and fish-market trade, I would race the town bus from the bottom of Marginal all the way to Orleans Street, leaping at pigeons taking air, plowing pedestrian traffic with my elbows. A delivery man with small patience knocked me on my ass one day ending my spree of sidewalk mastery. I had admired from my hotel window Uncle Gerrit's lowered head pacing the sidewalk, aggressive meditation, gesture as orneriness, a singularity of purpose – a severity of character Uncle Gerrit had adopted to keep his romanticism in check, or so I deduced in my freshman year psychologizing in the after glow of Erik Erikson lecturing on Hitler's phobias. That guy was a mess.

I left the old hotel in East Boston for Harvard College, a short distance, but a world away. I was free! singing soulful arias of Parsifal – the guileless fool that finds himself guardian of the Holy Grail, wandering into the domain of the evil Klingsor, enticed by his flower maidens. Strange kind of freedom. But freedom nonetheless. So I thought until realizing Gerrit had burned patterns of behavior into me like circuitry. I spent most of my free time alone, in my dorm room at Harvard or in the laundry room, reading and writing my way toward a system of Life Assembly, a journal in which I collected instructions on how to put together a life — which most guys don't bother to ponder before botching the job, and which I thought would come together nicely, so long as I wasn't rushed.

I had taken up the habit of journal writing through Gerrit's insistence that I write down the Lumina – meditations on and impressions of the ideas and theories Gerrit had led me through. This writing of the Lumina, Gerrit had practiced through the novitiate, one of the few Jesuit methods of instruction he thought held merit. I kept my journal and laundry handy for when roommates screwed girls behind the bureaus and India block-print sheets we had arranged as partitions. I knew every note of Pink Floyd's psychedelic, jazzy Dark Side of the Moon – "a great disk to fuck the chicks, man," advised my roommate. The screamers and name sayers made me nervous. To avoid their climax, and my own, I would run from the room with my journal forgetting my laundry bag, washing only the pair of socks under my feet.

I couldn't forget that *Playboy* episode in the bathroom that had sent me into cerebral dysfunction. I didn't want to stay in my dorm room and risk the stimulation. And I liked the soothing motion of the wash machines, still do, the womb-like churning. I channeled my distractions into obscure philosophical inquiry down in that laundry room, late at night, sorting out the part of myself I understood least – the boy with visions, the boy with the grievous guardian angel. I lost myself within the complex of ontological theory, thinking that's where I would find myself. My roommates and I never evolved past a grunt in conversation – "going to class"/"uh huh"; " seen that new Liv Ullmann flick"/"nah"; "seen my Che Guevara t-shirt"/"huh?" I considered myself radicalized by politics, linked to those of the SDS that got their heads cracked for occupying University Hall, and for holding hostage a recruiter from DOW, the maker of napalm, in a classroom for five hours. I admired their moxie from up in my dorm room.

Then I found Nietzsche's *Zarathustra* in a bookstore remainders bin. I sat on the sidewalk and read, finished the book under streetlights. The whip of Gerrit's cane beat the air above me as I read: "send out your ships to unexplored seas." I could see my uncle on a wintry beach, rapturous, on his knees before Paul Tillich building a sand castle. What a rush! I understood the gift of Nietzsche, poet and warrior philosopher, the man that broke with Wagner over his extolling chastity as virtue in Parsifal. It was Nietzsche that had awakened Tillich: "what can be loved in man is that he is a transition and a destruction"; "dead are all gods; now we will that superman live." I wanted Nietzsche to change me too. Maybe there was something in what Gerrit had asserted, something in my potential to level the towers of Christianity. But not yet. I was then chief among disengaged ponderers.

I carried my philosophical isolation with me into the crowd of Harvard Square. I took Nietzsche's *Zarathurstra* with me to the horseshoe counter of my favorite bar, ordered a Molson, ignored anyone seated beside me, looked soulfully into my reflection in varnish on redwood and waited for my artsy, warrior persona to rise up like a fish – Travers Jones, justifiable poetaster and master of *Life Assembly*, written now entirely in aphorisms. I intended a writer's life. One day my journal would be gold. Paul Tillich would take note.

Although Tillich had become emeritus before my matriculation at Harvard, he had been a presence in Boston for twenty-some years, seduced away from New York in the 1950's, and was still remembered for his heavy accent and inventive phrasing in lecture. My Am. Lit. professor aped him: "Let us drop this futzer-lingual-liquefaction," he would say and laugh and then explain that this was Tillich's criticism of scat-speak that had begun to leak into the lingo of professor-speak. But the voice I remember most clearly emerged from that varnish off the counter top of my favorite bar at Harvard Square during one of my journal-writing forays. He was a presence I could not ignore. "Meet the Herk," he said, and pushed a large, hirsute hand under my elbow for shaking, "direct to you from the executive branch of hippiedom," he said. "Here in the Square to bring some Hate from the Haight." Robert Herkimer was a beat poet, an actor in mime from San Francisco who had recently staged outdoors his "guerrilla theater" in which American MP's beat Vietnam POW's to death right there on the sidewalk in Harvard Square. No one was told this was theater. The crowd coiled and recoiled in fear and confusion. Herk called himself a Digger, a 17th century English-type radical that gave stuff away. The first communists, he called them, with a small "c." "Be a digger or be property," he said. He wasn't too interested in me, though he did give me advice in his encompassing gestures while twirling on the bar stool to watch girls, shaking the long curls of his sandy hair and rubbing temples with his thumbs to assess the range of his voice like judging sound waves off a tuning fork. "If you really believe in it, do it!" he said, finally, and disappeared into the smoky crowd to chase a coed he recognized from the audience of his sidewalk theater. A week later I overheard in the cafeteria at Harvard that Herk had disrupted an SDS conference of the old guard in Chicago with Tom Hayden presiding. Apparently Herk and two others crashed the scene as Hayden was "getting down" on the Vietnam War. Herk thumped a tambourine proclaiming, "I will show you how to free the Digger in yourself!" The SDS never regained control of its meeting. The Diggers ranted for an hour in their compressed and breathy language – "Make your own civilization!" and "Property is the enemy!" and "Don't organize the rabble, organize your head!" and "Chicago is more fucked up than the Kremlin!"

Herk made me nervous. I guess that was the plan – scare enough people and they will act irrationally, even courageously, loosing upon the world a necessary anarchy. Tillich's ideas, once I began to read him, also seemed in tune with the youth revolution, or at least with my own, should I ever get it started. He spoke against the industrial machine; he saw communism and fascism as symptoms of man's longing for a new authority now that the church no longer provided spiritual direction. He thought a new spiritual force would sweep churches out of existence. Uncle Gerrit was right about Tillich. His ideas inspired. I liked to think my ideas would too, at least as much as Herk. I would take a notepad out from the pages of *Thus Spake Zarathustra*, Tillich's bible during his conversion, and conjure up a philosopher's voice in the chemicals of my raging imagination, and fill in the caesuras of my halting aphorisms with stratagem of a Life Assembly that came to me at that crowded bar as if oracular, or so I felt. I would effect change in my bookish way like Tillich; Herk would do his thing in the trenches.

After six years at Harvard I had logged a mass of undergraduate credits that grew like a boil on the registrar's computer interface until I was told to choose something, anything that could be stamped on a diploma to signal the marketplace I had resolved the flux of my unformed self. I had been graduated by the faculty. They had all had me in their classes, watched me stake out the farthest corner of lectures, heard me grunt asynchronous responses to their deliveries, dreaded reading my papers (informed as they were by my study of whale phonemes and Tantric mantra, riddled with obscure references to tribal ritual – I was into Carl Jung – and peppered with aphorisms rhythmic as a Sears Kenmore washer). They felt I had dawdled unconscionably in the undergraduate program, sampled every offering as if Harvard were a safety square on a coffee-table game board. They knew I had audited beyond the reaches of my scholarship funding. They were offended and fed up. They mailed me a diploma and hoped to have seen the last of me. What the faculty did not understand was that I was not at Harvard to prepare for life. To me, Harvard was life, as close as I wanted to get.

But once released, prepared and enlightened, what I wanted from life was to vault upon the rails of discovery, leave behind the epileptic visions. Uncle Gerrit had found Paul Tillich, I had found Nietzsche, but I wanted to be a man of action, not just a man of books. I *was* a thinking man. Philosophy was my thing. But I anticipated the other side of my personality, the warrior philosopher Gerrit was sure would emerge. I felt an affinity to Nietzsche because the philosopher had lost his father at the age of four, and because Nietzsche was haunted by the madness of his father, even heard his disembodied voice in the alley outside his home in Naumburg, and ran from his belief in fate by living unfettered in the persona of Zarathustra. I was looking for the persona that would complete me. I was also looking for my father.

I was "into some heavy shit," my roommates used to say. And I was, until cut loose from Harvard. My research then became formless, my aphorisms senseless, of no use for a *Journal of Life Assembly*. Zarathustra said the random rules in nature. If you were to shoot three arrows into the air, whatever each hits is essential, because it all matters. But I found myself over stimulated living this way. Without the structure of a class schedule, I felt lost. I moved back to the hotel with my mother for grounding, and read philosophy to siphon out the unessential, but instead I spun in circles for three long directionless years, avoided Gerrit as best I could, and got dizzy on the ethers of abstract thought like Socrates ensconced in his cliff-dangling wicker basket.

I got fired from every job I took – pizza cook to landscape maintenance. I couldn't keep my mind on work. Pizza burned. Lawn mowers drifted into flower beds. Mostly I meditated and worried up in those run-down hotel rooms of East Boston where I grew up. I avoided the people I had come to know in the diner. I was in danger of being swallowed by the black hole of my timidity and fear and confusion. A life of the mind without action leads to paralysis.

Then, finally, rescue! Montreal's McGill University offered to legitimize my meditations through grad school. "Hey, parley vous me there!" I said aloud in my best Canadian French during a unique, celebratory immersion in the bars of East Boston among dock workers with little sympathy for tortured souls who sit alone, write in journals, and talk to themselves in French. I knew enough to get drunk quick and leave. I was drunk when I broke the news to my mother and Uncle Gerrit. But I'm a good drunk, a quiet-look-you-in-the-eye drunk, so rather than berate they blessed me. Fiona cried. What Uncle Gerrit shed for tears might have bathed a gnat.

At the age of twenty-eight, the same age of Plato when his master Socrates was given hemlock, a virgin still in many ways, and in the year 1974, I set out to triangulate the back roads to Montreal in a new purchase from grant money, a used Japanese pick-up truck. I was already several months late for the fall semester by the time I had packed crates of books, my stereo, a stray cat for company, and a pair of snowshoes bought at a garage sale (my "manly" image coalescing briefly as a Yukon Mounty trudging the permafrost when I saw those bearpaws leaning on a card table). I didn't know I would arrive in Montreal a changed man. I did sense that I had, finally, gone beyond my usual brief moment of lateral mobility and retreat. If nothing else, I might get swept along in my own inertia and collide into some part of myself that would kick the world in the teeth when necessary while creating aphorisms of *Life Assembly* to heal the soul. Nietzsche still had a grip on me, though I knew enough about myself to realize that real change would take some kind of collision that would unshackle me from my fate.

Chapter Six

Sometimes it takes believing in accident • Introducing Halley Gay • Practicing the Zen moment • Principles of guard-rail extraction • Introducing the Brothers Quebecois • A suspension of locomotion: Travers hands over the keys • King Kong's blonde • The burned church, Professor Mosley and a gruesome discovery.

So there I was spinning in that snowstorm in my Datsun truck. I noticed a yellow deer that had suffered a fusillade of bullets. BEWARE OF DEER hardly addressed the problem. It should have said beware the unfulfilled and the insufficient, or made brief warning of successive accidents pending. Back then I believed in the concept of fate and was unprepared to recognize accident as counterbalance. The end of the day would have me leached and spent, recumbent upon a sofa after an epileptic fit – suffering further the humiliation of anticipation anxiety after caroming snow banks in a Saab, then misfiring an orgasm in the allure of a sexy photojournalist I would meet at the burn site. Her name is Halley Gay. She makes the sensational seem commonplace. Halley would arouse my readiness with her unhesitating leaps of daring. She would study my neurosis like it was public domain. While I lay on her sofa in the dark with a blood-stained truncheon tucked under a pillow, I would revisit the first accident – gyrating down interstate, flattening a deer sign and reflector posts, denting a guard rail, then a too quick stop like cogs locked in a void.

I had fishtailed up Mill Hill to Brookfield from that diner in Northfield, located the key to the padlocked gate and neatly motored onto I-89. There were no tire tracks. Traffic had sensibly diverted. I hesitated, took my foot off the throttle. Voices of dissent second-guessed me. I decided to Zen

my mind free of static by doing a John Cage "happening": I pressed the
accelerator and began counting the mileage posts like hypnotic suggestion
to induce a carefree glide beyond the burned church in Burlington and
deep away into Canada. Make a blank space in time where important
things get done effortlessly, "as efficiently as a Wankel engine." That's
what a college roommate had said, a mechanical engineer in the making
with Buddha aspirations. He and his girlfriend would sit naked, still and
silent, face to face in each other's lap, eyes closed, he in her and she into
him, extending the pre-orgasmic moment indefinitely: Maithuna. He did it
his way, I did it mine.

Nature's winter tantrum decided me in favor of doing it
Schopenhauer's way, negate the "will" and so become fulfilled. Or
Parsifal's way, the way of the pure fool, rather than Nietzsche's way, or
Sinatra's way. But I was not at the moment doing it any way but spinningly,
out of control in my Datsun. Much like my roommate in his girlfriend.
They sat naked together eternally, he unshaved and and she pinkly
excessively flabby, anticipating "the moment" to come. He flunked out of
Harvard in his senior year, having created too many blank spaces in time,
or not enough of them pre-orgasmic. She went to New York City to make
a blank space in her uterus.

The road, I had thought, would efface my seizures and deposit me
cleansed of misdirection at the sacred halls of amnesia, which is Halley's
term for the academy, which is what she will say of my academic
ambitions after having fathomed my disease. But I had no doubt Montreal
signified change. I would assimilate café culture somewhere near McGill
but compose angst-relieving aphorisms in my *Journal of Life Assembly*
rather than challenges. I would replace the wash machine churn of
Kenmore harmonics with a chromatic tinkling of accordion music. I
would turn from Nietzsche to Rabelais – abandon the head and chart the
belly, make the noise of happy frogs. If I speculated further on my
father's pyro-maniacal psyche, it would be from an armchair, maybe an
endowed chair at the university.

But I should have leaned into that curve. With night descending, snow rifling like meteorites, I steered off the planet, my father sneering in a constellation of stars. The truck spun eternally then jolted but still hadn't stalled. I cut the engine after one tire had dug a pit, the other shredded on aluminum guardrail upon which the bumper hung suspended. The truck leaned frontways and oblique, creaking, a drunk horse loose in its bones.

Steam rank with sulfur rose off the engine block and muffler. Green bile stained snow. The burned rubber of belts and tires evoked East Boston's docks, the old neighborhood, unlikely as a memory to ameliorate. My hands shook on the wheel. "Could be the motor's whacked!" I aspirated, assessing both the car's condition and my likelihood of seizure, placing an "h" blow of air between the w & a of whacked, maneuvering sound through pebbles in my mouth as I do when agitated. I sat there monitoring metabolic pressures in my brain like a weather man, expecting seizure. When briefly the storm cleared, as cloud moved in Rubik's cube blocks, I cranked a window to study the emerging stars. But they winked and turned away, embarrassed by my disease and present circumstance. I looked for the planet Venus, daughter of Cythera – an island birth – but not even she, an isolate like myself, gave a shit, not even a wink, though born of foam issued from the severed parts of emasculated Uranus. I had always felt like an emasculated Uranus looking for his Venus. The wind scoured me with sleet. The sky contracted and oozed through the plum-colored bruise of the moon, a leaking gunshot wound. I tried to laugh away tension in my best Zarathustrian, but my most assertive aphorisms echoed diminutively in the cab of the Datsun, a voice at the bottom of a tin cup, a voice like Fiona's – resigned to postpartum loneliness, forever seeking forgiveness. I began to wonder how much of this eviscerated mess of a young man that was me was from *him*, lower case "him" (my father), though I was tempted into sacrilege.

I angled the rear-view mirror to inspect my face. Something of this pulp and gristle must be my father – this bump on the bridge of my nose maybe ("'dromedary saddle back," Gerrit called it, "not likely tae gyang through the eye of a needle"), a narrow face stretched by the weight of its jaw hidden behind a beard and knobby at the chin like the back end of a ball peen hammer. Eyes black as flint. Sometimes, in these eyes, I can see the foul liquid that dilates thin as onion skin fuzzy with veins, hazing out the tactile world, my pre-seizure aura getting busy with the business of staging my father's return.

An aura of witchery attended the scent of caraway, a seed my mother brewed to soothe infant colic and later, she thought, to allay the spasms of epilepsy. I wondered if I would see my father again, and if he had aged much since the *Playboy* seizure, and if Fiona would recognize him. I was briefly hopeful my mother's herbs and magic would fend off another episode. It had been eighteen years since my last. The disease might have gone into remission, my father might have forgotten me – but all this was negated by the burned church in that newspaper in that Northfield café. I wondered how well I would keep, frozen post-trauma, for the highway crew prying me out of the Datsun. I didn't want to shit my pants. Terrible disease. But when I looked again for my eyes in the mirror, I saw reflected back my cat named Cat complaining from the tumble in the capped truck bed and beyond that a dark tangle of pine over the bank.

I considered Professor Staub's natural history, another audit at Harvard. The old man caustic with folksy wisdom, an herbalist like my mother. Staub said white pine were used as incense by indigenous tribes gone eventually flaccid with hallucinogens – another of Staub's slams on the 60's drug culture. I leaned out the window to whiff. Maybe olfactory therapy would reduce the chance of seizure. Should I immerse? There were snow shoes in the bed of the truck, but I would have to face Cat. I didn't know how to attach the damn things anyway. And I was repulsed by the scent of those trees – resinous and loamy, worse than the caraway Fiona had packed into the watch pocket of my jeans, a gram or two, with instructions to brew a cup before bed. Another reminder I carry disease. Hardly a comfort.

What would Zarathustra do? He would exalt in the mystery of Datsun mechanics. I pried open the glove box. The manual fell out. As did a stack of business cards promoting massage in Boston's combat zone, then a rubber truncheon. Massage for the criminally insensitive. Left there by the black man with the Afro and the muscular arms who sold me the Datsun. I hefted the weapon, found it sensual to the touch, form-fitted. A natural appendage of aggression, evolutionary. The manual read surprisingly like a kids' primer, none of the jargon of gears and circuitry and channeled combustion. I thought about radiator pipes I had banged with a shoe to annoy Uncle Gerrit in the East Boston hotel. My soul had expanded through that conduit. When I had seizured on the toilet, aroused by *Playboy*, when I banged the pipes my father had appeared in fiery countenance smiling. He promised the furnace would lug into action, sending Gerrit rusted, thick water like magma. I felt myself, briefly, pyrolagnia, eroticized by a churn of electrons dying in the heat they generated. I was glad my father had appeared in that episode, though I wondered how much perversion I have inherited from him. I shifted uncomfortably in the seat of the Datsun. I breathed on fingers. The cab of the truck frosted. And the manual, as I read deeper into all that could go wrong, began to obfuscate, greased in fingerprints from other break-down strategists, smeared from hands more practiced than mine. The index on troubleshooting had the most traffic, so black with fingerprints it had to be read by Rorschach intuition, by shadowy implications of association. No guardrail extrication surfaced. I resolved next time to assess the condition of a vehicle's manual before buying used.

The destroyed tire, limp upon the guard rail and lofted by its axle, seemed textbook photogenic, but presented a scenario of tire changing undreamed of by manual writers. A diagram took shape in my head pulling me along in vectors of probability, the consequence of a prepared mind, I thought with a philosopher's sense of accomplishment. Then came scraped knuckles and toes numbed in snow that tempered joy with the friction of application complicating theory. But soon I had changed the deflated tire and the frame got jacked up where the other tire had dug a hole. I pushed from behind. The Datsun lurched forward as the jack gave way, dragging the hung tire with it. I slid the other way down the bank toward pine trees. I had left the transmission in gear, so the Datsun bounced a short distance and jarred open a door. Good omen. I slipped back up the bank, mud bespattered but cheerful, brushing off snow, spreading mud at the same time. When I cranked the ignition, the power train commenced to whine.

I exited onto an intersection where narrow roads defined cow pasture somewhere outside Burlington, the whine become a grind of metal shavings. I drove awhile through snow-filled, amorphous landscape then braked hard at a sudden Texaco where two French Canadian émigrés sat outside on milk cans by the restroom, passed a joint and schemed Quebecois separatist politics, snow soaking baseball caps and pony tails. Each wore a dark blue jump suit with a red star on the lapel.

The Datsun slid into the lot. I braked again and jagged injuriously near the attendants who pulled knees into chests while their eyes signaled unconcern. Their disassociation scared me shitless. I smiled in supplication, a guy in a beard as helpless as a teenage girl with car trouble. I rolled down the window and told them, in some distress, voice cracking, where to find the Abenaki's incense trees, how to jack a Datsun off a guardrail (not the x-rated version, I prefaced, which got no laughs), where to find the padlock key in Brookfield should the highway close on them, and then the big muumuu: "Whatever comes," I was beginning to believe, "keep the wheels moving. And run down whatever gets in your way." Still and forever, I was no Kerouac. I sensed my father waiting a short distance up the road with another seizure and a burned church. Then, dispirited, I handed over the keys and catechized them on the color I felt most inclined to think my Datsun presented to the world should it need body work and a paint touch up. The two mechanics exchanged an inscrutable look then several phrases in Canuck. They asked in English for the Datsun's age before offering me a toke of what they thought I was already on.

"No thanks," I said. "Pretty much cuts off the capillaries. But you probably know that."

If they knew they didn't say.

My truck soon had its transmission spilled out over several workbenches. The two mechanics conspired in French over Japanese manuals when they eviscerated the Datsun's transmission. They were maybe, like me, pissed off at Zen maintenance. Sitting on milk cans for hours like they did, making brief effort to gas Detroit guzzlers – lock the trigger down on the pump handle and return to the milk can for another toke, watch the numbers rise into profit. And now a tsunami of tin wind-ups from Japan that almost never break down, all from the same mold as my Datsun, that gas up about as quick as motorcycles – very irritating, very less profitable. And these guys likely sending more than a tithe north to family active in Quebecois secession.

I waited near the hummm of the Coke machine, nothing like a Kenmore wash machine but a mechanical metronome of sorts and small comfort in that. I finished the bottom inch off Mr. Coffee burned nearly to creosote, resisted the *Playboy*, read the captions instead to pictures in *Sports Illustrated* which held my interest as a kind of high school year book my college roommates passed around. I revisited the Patty Hearst Symbionese Liberation Army thing in *Newsweek,* and wondered where this next turn in the road would take her, if in fact it had not already been decided. When I had paced myself out of patience, I leaned through the door to the garage for a report on the Datsun. The two mechanics were still smiling, still smoking marijuana, ignoring customers pulling up for gas, poking through the Datsun's entrails. My face turned chalk. I thought they might have at least told me I was in for more than a turn of the wrench and a paint touch up.

"Will it be ready by the end of the day?"

The two mechanics lifted their shoulders.

"By the end of the week?"

They answered by pointing to the last numbered square of December on a Big Ed's American Motors Emporium calendar tacked on the wall featuring a blonde in a white nightie reclined on a black Gremlin driven by

King Kong. Strange, humorous and sexy. I looked for more telling answers to a corner of the garage where the Datsun lay hoisted on a lift bleeding from a hole in its belly. Cat stared from the tailgate window. Should I suggest a retrofit? Make plans to scrap the vehicle? Cat made the most god-awful noise – retching hairballs, spitting, beside itself in loathing. The burnt oil from the Datsun's transmission case smelled of mortality. I wondered if it were my own. The transistor in my brain that jams signals causing seizures was taking over, processing more of my thoughts lately, shutting down the machine. I was running out of time. I could no longer avoid confronting my father or the burn site. Whether or not I was destined, I felt compelled.

A bus stop kiosk oscillated beneath a street lamp two telephone poles distant from the Texaco. I waited beneath the halo of its light. Once aboard a chugging diesel, I regarded the historic symbol of the red star hovering above its station: last place to rest horses before the western frontier, I mused, but don't expect to take them with you. I was the lone passenger in an overheated bus reading advertisements over the seats announcing commercial venues for medico-spiritual renewal – rolfing and ayurvedic medicine, homeopathy and yoga. The bus traveled west through unplowed streets of tract housing and fast foods and then the University of Vermont and sharply downhill to bars and banks with lake and mountains vaguely suggested by an abrupt cavity where buildings end and layers of blue silhouetted peaks jag in a distant night sky. I was let out a block from the burn site of the church I had read about in the newspaper and followed the acerbic flavor of the air. I walked past an armory then turned up street by the Uptown Hotel with one-day rooming at wino prices that could be a temporary home. It had a fifties linear, alleyway layout and only two floors, appealing to escape-minded drug dealers and students on thin budgets.

I found the burn site deserted, surrounded by candy-striped saw horses. I leaned over the scorched shell of foundation, all that was left of the Congregational Church. The debris smelled of camphor and boiled coffee. Small licks of flame ascended still in a corner. Water from pressure hoses had pooled and frozen in deep recesses. A squall of snow off Lake Champlain unloaded in currents of air warmed by the fire. I lowered my chin into the collar of my jacket, lit a cigarette, pulled on the zipper and hunkered in like backing into a burrow. Behind the hairs of my beard, I twiddled with the idea of man's ineffectual tampering with disaster, laughed scarcely audibly at the thought of parishioners in pajamas and galoshes swarming to help their pastor. My father was working against them, my uncle, even Tillich. I conspired with all three, the urge to burn rising strong within me. It was Nietzsche's antinomies, elemental oppositions, religion depending upon sacrilege to renew itself, what the Greeks knew before Nietzsche. I thought of the urn holding Professor Mosley lying somewhere in church soot. I leaned into the glowing bowl, considered picking a handful of dust to do an "alas I knew poor Mosley" soliloquy but was repulsed by blasted granite block and ferroconcrete with twisted steel rods, steam issuing out like tooth rot from braces on a corpse. I flicked in the cigarette. I was cultivating a callousness in myself toward things ecclesiastic. It felt good. I leaned down and noticed a Sanka can in the window well. And then I saw something else. That was all I could take.

Chapter Seven

Travers achieves grand mal • Overzealous policing • A giant leap into the depths of Halley Gay's scream.

Plato said there are three types of people: those that desire, those that emote, and those that think. The loins, the heart, and the head. At this time in my history, I was a thinker still but yearning to experience the warrior's joy of battle. Uncle Gerrit was a temple of feelings who thought himself a thinker. He took seriously Plato's idea that, for the good of the state, all children must be removed from parental influence and raised by philosophers. Halley Gay was all desire: restless and acquisitive, material and quarreling, chasing the unattainable.

When the photo journalist Halley Gay found me, I lay clonic and contorted with epileptic spasms beside the window well of the church, spittle from my lips gone custardy on frozen ground, my tongue bit bloody and pulsing. I had in my hand an empty, scorched tin can with Sanka discernible still on the label. The sky unloaded snow fitfully. Halley had returned for a follow-up photo shoot of the ruined church. She found me collapsed there and hastened unsteadily through slush and ice to the police station nearby which sent an officer with prejudiced warnings of college students drugged and drunk celebrating, like witchy vegans, the spiritual sustenance of fire, and who were now dropping indiscriminately around town, depleted by the excesses of their behavior.

I fuzzed back to sentience strapped inside an ambulance – more like a paddy wagon – while poked for blood to establish the degree of my criminality. Officer Brady tinkered expectantly the locking mechanism of handcuffs thinking I would incriminate myself as a natural consequence of an aversion to uniforms. A draft-dodger, he thought, sneaking back from Canada, probably cheered the weirdo that crashed a car through the gates of Nixon's White House and held off Secret Service with flares. All long hairs are the same, thought Brady whose formative years as a gear head had polarized him toward the yeasty high of Budweiser and burning rubber at traffic lights in muscle cars rumbling from packed mufflers. Marijuana and draft protest he didn't get, though even he hadn't volunteered for the "police action" of Vietnam, his councilman father having pulled strings, the ties that bind, to keep him home. And me, I had epilepsy.

The paramedic, concerned by the porcelain glaze of my eyes, had recently suffered crisis through a "couples' night" initiated by a husband answering ads in the personals. Unknown hands, some hirsute some perfumed, groping and stroking had rendered her frigid. Her next crisis would be divorce. Small kindness remained for the indulgent sex as she plunged a needle into my arm, though she suspected diabetes and thought Brady a fool. Halley Gay, meantime, had walked to the foundation pit of the church to finish a roll, inspired by the ruins, playing the f-stop to achieve an apocalyptic sheen, aspiring to *Time* magazine's glossy coverage of topical world conflagration, trapping ambulance lights reflected off steam and smoke and falling snow.

When I returned from epileptic vision, odd phrases and shadowy figures in flame played behind my eyes, not the visitation I expected though I felt the presence of my father. He hadn't appeared. The white pod of the ambulance, its tubes and tanks disoriented me, as did the man in uniform otherwise from my father. I whispered to the paramedic: "Mosley is burned. I'm sorry."

"Did you hear that, Brady?" the paramedic said, abetting a high school classmate by reflex, Brady's regime as captain of hall monitors a stain upon her memory. She had admired Brady's vigilance until it shifted toward parking-lot trysts, his gooney boys roving with cameras. She had found herself pinned in revealing dishabille upon the Principal's corkboard among others similarly dishonored.

"Hear what? I'm telling you, Brenda, this kid's ON something. There's a half dozen in custody already. Hey!" Brady leaned into my face, sneaked hands into my pockets. "Is Mosley the dealer, kid? Is he your connection? What's this shit? Seeds!"

"The seed of doubt yields a bitter plant."

"What?"

"I need a shot of pheno."

"What? You asking me for drugs? I'm busting you, hippie shit. Get it? He's a user, Brenda. Don't waste sympathy on him. What about these seeds, kid?"

"I need a shot of pheno."

The paramedic recognized the prefix to phenobarbital, prescribed fix for victims of epilepsy, but I would have to wait for an analysis of blood drawn. She didn't look for medical-alert jewelry, having sided with Brady that a peace sign in turquoise or an ankh cross or love beads or a Jerry Garcia figure of hallowed intaglio is all she would find.

Officer Brady exhibited the expanded chest of vindication, imagining a link farther up the chain of assigned desks in the officer's duty room. Didn't last long. I lifted like the resurrection straight off the gurney when I heard the scream, popped straps loosely secured, and with the ambulance door open, its lights flashing intermittently and parked where they found me, I looked out on the burn site where a poisoned haze obscured the blonde-haired photojournalist who had dropped her camera into the window well.

There was nothing seductive about Halley Gay in a red parka of goose down and chinos ending at unlaced LL Bean duck boots, so I didn't suspect this woman would be my first flesh and blood love interest. With her face contorted, her blonde hair indistinguishable from the yellow discharge of gasses, how could I know? And the scene quickly got more ugly. While the paramedic oxygenated the hyper-ventilating photographer she had led to the back end of the ambulance, officer Brady and the ambulance driver were lifting from the window well a blackened, stiff and withered corpse like found in the lava of Pompeii.

Halley's scream had sounded disproportionately raw, too much pain for the relatively brief length of her privileged life. It had chaffed and scored, nearly corrugated her lungs, folding them like tripe, making breath the overwhelming crisis beyond anything that had set off this response. I was to learn it came from Halley's never confronting more than the form of death, ignoring as best she could its place in weeding out the reckless, careless, and helpless. Halley had always faced danger and odd circumstance and overwhelming discomfort of most sorts with calm, from a distance. As a girl, she had been kept away from caskets parading through her change of bonnets and gingham dresses. The family had sought to protect her from the face of death. But she is from the South, and so lives with paradox, what she calls the "curse of family, a Southern thing," a dance with ghosts. Northerners don't experience this because they charge into the future instead of examining what or who brought them where they are, or at least that's what she thought about Yanks until she met me.

The body from the window well of the church reminded Halley of Willie, her dead older brother, whose twisted form she had seen, though from a distance, and the only other time her scream had impaired her breathing. Ten years in her past, on a childhood dare, her dare, up on Weather Hill butte, Willie had flown out of her life and out of his, leaping for the burnished limb of an old oak grown into the ledge, leaping and missing. This image of her brother's congenital overreaching, as the family calls it, dragged with it an emotional burden of various colors, like the tail of a kite. She felt satisfaction that the sun-browned, meaty hands that rounded her developing breasts were gone. She felt a fever of guilt from excited shivers that had torn the membrane of her innocence and a regret that she wouldn't, in the flaccid days of grand-parenting, shift into numbed forgiveness. She felt self-loathing for letting this bygone trauma resurface after schooling at Bryn Mawr and Vassar, several abortions, several affairs with married men, and a consuming desire for career had failed to beat it down.

For a minute the night became postcard clear, though the stars remained indifferent. I could see the red parka resting near the portable oxygen tank attached to the rear doors, and a nebulae of blonde hair drifting as the generator fans spun furiously inside the ambulance. Halley's wool sweater under the down parka felt scratchy in the engine heat. She unzipped abstractedly. She was still on a trip back home to Rumford, Kentucky. She had taken flight over the ground Willie might have covered had he managed to glide like a bird. She saw blue spruce with deer drinking from the riverbed. She flew over "slag town," where the coloreds live near the landfill and the rail depot, to the town green and Jackson's General Store gallery reserved for the usual old-timers leaning chairs and spitting tobacco. She saw LeFeiver's Café still falling toward the river over which it perches, stilts of 2x4 shored against the bulge of clapboard, and Mayor Cutler in his white linen suit touring the early-morning sidewalks hosed down by shopkeepers. Then she revisited her father's lumber yard a quick jag south down Water Street where, behind Venetian blinds in the horizontal shadows, ceiling fans spin over Colonel Gay's military skull, his one large hand massaging the bristle, the other weighing a stack of yellow receipts, smiling ruefully, pencil behind his ear, flask of Old Duke on its side spilling contents, saying "Girl, this just ain't good enough." Her breathing constricted once again as she looked at her hands. Halley took another hit of canned oxygen. Some part of her wanted Willie to touch her again.

Chapter Eight

Introducing Sergeant Vasari • The effects of Phenobarbital, Travers' drug of choice • Another accident, sperm and vomit • Escape to the overture to Parsifal.

When Halley Gay stormed the police station the night after the church fire and accosted the night-desk patrolman in ruthless agitation to report a passed-out young man beside the ruins of the burned church, Sergeant Vasari expected oddity. He had already met Halley Gay professionally. An excess of parking tickets had led to impounding her Saab, which Halley observed from inside the monikered window of an A&W on the corner of Church and College Streets. She impressed Vasari as hardly contrite though civil by his standards, paying fines with cash to avoid the blemish of collusion by engaging her bank account, and announcing in the flurry of her exit, "Money changers in the temple, gentlemen, every damn one of you!" Strange. What Vasari didn't know is Halley wants no truck with uniforms and no paper trail to remind her how impossible a desire this is, given her profession and family history.

Her daddy's self-defining moment came in WWII: he was the soldier George Patton slapped in the face while touring beds of the wounded presumed malingerers behind lines. Her daddy has been slapping back ever since. And her most recent love affair, Rumford's arbiter of parameters, Chief of Police Monahan, is a hunting buddy of daddy's. The Chief's passion for tracking wild herbs to season, leach and tame the gaminess of wild foul belies his ineffectual role as toady politician ruled by a shrewish wife and hassled by a house filled with kids, although she knew his wandering eye (fond of sampling the rotation of waitresses at LeFeiver's Café).

Halley trends to the vigilante side of the law. She rakes keys against the lacquer of pricey automobiles parked at yellow curbs, shop lifts when prices overreach, wedges pennies in meters for an all-day park, mails letters of protest to members of Congress with upscale return addresses gleaned from phone books when national policy aggrieves her. And Halley would not reveal to police the Sanka can I had pulled from the window well beside the corpse.

As the ambulance ferried me to the hospital for inspection, Halley drove herself and then walked into EMERGENCY beside my wheeled gurney. I had no insurance which facilitated my release. She refused examination. I was still shaken by events of the day – that almost seizure in the café, an accident on the highway, carnage in the service station garage, the blackened body I had found beside the Sanka can in the window well, all finally culminating in seizure. None of which I wanted to focus on even if I could. I had finally been injected phenobarbital after testing negative for recreational drugs, a surprise to Officer Brady. The pheno went through my veins like tiny fish hooks ripping at the secret places I go to when in seizure. The pheno had resurrected and fragmented memory at the same time, overwhelming me with voices I didn't recognize. Release from the hospital came the moment I knew enough about myself to sign my name.

Halley Gay's orientation was admirably direct. She intended chaperoning me until the Sanka can worked into an equation of burned body and church or could be discarded as trash along with me. I had nowhere to go but the Texaco station, I was thinking woozy anyway, so when Halley proposed a drink at Nectar's where a local band gave a tolerable imitation of Elvis Costello, I followed. Halley turned the ignition key between the seats of her white Saab (a graduation gift from Mother), thankful all the coffee spilled down there hadn't yet shorted the system. The defrost kicked in doing just the opposite. "Stupid shitty northern engineerin'!" Halley said rubbing a porthole clean of mist with a mitten.

As Halley questioned my reasons for attending the burn site, suggested relinquishing the Sanka can, I heard the South in her voice, the lingering diphthongs of a southern patrician, and her bossy attitude kind of antebellum appropriate to resisting a Rhett Butler taming. The smell of coffee and camphor became invasive. Residual atoms trapped in nose follicles from breathing waste at the burn site. Or a string of impressions more revealing of me than she? Descartes' primacy of consciousness? Doubt all else but that the mind knows itself best, projects itself as a measure of the external world but is more likely painting by numbers all it sees. I looked to the back seat where the Sanka can rolled around among newspapers. Good! Solid evidence I am not mis-coloring the objective world. There were also a box of lenses, rolls of film, a pizza box, some Tampax sticks, and several winter toques of Scandinavian design sent by Mother. I'm quite sure about that.

"Why do you want the coffee can? Who are you again?"

"I'm Halley Gay, darlin'. I met you at the church fire. I saved your ass. You were a mess, shakin' on the ground and dribblin' like a dog stuck in coitus. When I lose it, sugar, and I have, nothin' but grade-A honey drips from my mouth. I can assure you. I thought you must be a northwoods malcontent lookin' for salvage. Maybe a muskrat trapper short on the next payment to your snowmobile. No offense, darlin', but you were some kind of agitated. Son of a bitch, that's pretty good. Muskrat."

"I'm from Boston. I don't know a thing about muskrat."

"Well I know that now. The hospital profiled your social security number, could not use your driver's license for some reason. I was more or less within earshot. What's your malady? Take some advice, darlin'. Internalize your demons. Those shakes must be embarrassin'. Anyway, son of a bitch if those ladies of mercy don't take you for some college drop-out that has been overtoxined at the burn site. It was pretty comical hearin' that shit."

"I'm no drop out. I had a seizure. Did you say why you want the coffee can?"

"I didn't say, no. But if you spent a quarter on a newspaper you might of seen my work. I take news photographs, darlin', but I am movin' on to

TV presently.”

Not much of what was going on made sense to me even before the next car accident, though I liked the looks of this raunchy-mouthed blonde with the wholesome face and what I imagined to be an exercised body. A tennis player with attitude, a more complex version of those I'd seen in short skirts bouncing down the intersecting paths of Harvard Yard.

We were driving downhill toward the center of town, the Saab burbling from its exhaust, tension locked in Halley's arms. She pulled back on the wheel, reining the power, more than an adjustment to slippery weather. The storm had returned. I was compelled to trope her into theory. Maybe like me she's a fraud as a road warrior, scared shitless of where she's going but drawn to places hard to get at. I wondered how much she knew about the science of arson, how much she knew about the burned church.

My meditations stalled as the Saab spun 360 off ice into a vortex, soundless and weightless, Halley's hands gone to her eyes, the steering wheel looping freely, her arms limp, hands like sparrows fluttering above the wheel, afraid to light, and me whispering “Grab the wheel,” SHOUTING “Grab the wheel – please!” when the jolt of landing threw me onto the dash, Halley onto the horn, the blunt, cute nose of the car tunneling into a snow bank, kicking out of gear and stalling, the radio noticeably lush in Vivaldi then static.

Halley had landed with her face in my lap in a quaint Victorian swoon – with the slightest tremble of limbs, an eternity of silence with the digital clock flashing RESET in green, me tempted to ask, “Is this the part where I loosen the stays?” resisting, as she burrowed into my crotch, the pressure and heat increasing, become rhythmic, and groans soughing then pornographic. And a lunge that hurt in a good way, my hips rising in response. Then the warm, pungent weight of vomit in my lap, my seed aspiring to swim in the paste of Halley's emotional discharge and “O, God, sheeeeeit!” in the diphthongs of Southern patois, sugary spittle leaking still. The Saab's lights bored holes in the increasing snow. The intense heat of halogen gases diffused as it ranged to the double-tiered porches of a white federalist home, cupola looming above the pediment and roof line with an aged woman in white-fluted linen crowing from the second story porch.

"Gawd, Fred, it's an accident. Fred, get the police, Fred!" Halley looked up. The old woman gestured in arthritic cramp, head bobbing like a bulldog brake-light figurine on slinky springs, eyes blazing red in the back window of a Ford Fairlane that Halley had parked behind at the drive-in movie one teenage outing. The driver had fumbled, touched the brake light more often than his date. Not her problem at the time.

"I'm real sorry. Fuck me. I'm sorry. Must be I have the flu. Unless I am pregnant again."

I didn't know what to say. I was still not spliced into the world properly, the pheno coursing my cortex and this orgasm had stunned me as much as the spinout and vomit in my lap. There was a long silence, this time a stationary one, with sexual tension snaking around and jolting our senses like a power line felled on a wet road. Neither could look the other in the eye, until Halley began to laugh. It was a high hiccup, a mule bray, the kind of laugh that turns heads in a restaurant. But it gave me, for the first time, a sign of Halley's vulnerability – it leaped out from her like an apology for what she couldn't help in her behavior. Even more, it brought her eyes to me in what I took as a plea for forgiveness. She said, "Shit, don't go havin' the shakes on me, will you." I lost whatever compassion I had worked up, extracted cigarettes from a button-down flap inside my ski parka and leaned into the rhomboid support of the leather seat to nurse this rare hiatal moment of deceleration, then:

"Look, I think I'll just find my truck and get back on the road to Montreal. You keep the Sanka can. It's not evidence of arson, if that's what you're after, but that dead man is tied to this burn somehow, but maybe you know that. I'll make a phone call so you get towed out of the snow."

The Saab door slammed hermetic, ear popping like a bank vault; my cigarette burned in the ashtray. I brushed away vomit with wads of snow then scoped a path to downtown: porch lamps ermine in the snow attached to houses swollen with prosperity and descending university hill on Main Street lit the way. The ice-box squeak of sneakers pressing snow in zero temperatures reminded me of Tolstoy's St. Petersburg, phaetons on runners creasing the iced roads bearing opera devotees warm in bear skins. I leaned into lake wind, pulled the parka's collar to my ears and summoned the "fool's motive" leitmotif to *Parsifal* – Uncle Gerrit's favorite opera, consequently the background drone of much of my childhood. But I couldn't get it right while trundling past frat houses with torn shutters and lighted crystal chandeliers, because nostril hair froze as I inflated my chest, eyes watered, and I wasn't feeling so great about deserting this woman. Especially if she were pregnant.

Chapter Nine

Alas poor Mosley, bell tower voyeur • Saint Vasari complicit in priestly sins • Dazed by a stein at Nectar's • Introducing Hambone deBoner • Introducing Designer Elvis.

Alas poor Mosley, lost in his urn in the ash of the Congregational Church he had designed, the scorched bell tower collapsed upon him like a reckoning. His ashes merged ignominiously with the burned church, or that's what Sergeant Vasari had assumed. Mosley was the touch of evolution to civic building in Victorian Burlington. He was everywhere in the archives of the town library. He had become, after the fire, a postmortem prosecution witness for Sergeant Vasari, who wanted to know the personal reasons behind this crime. Vasari considered Mosley the true victim of the fire. And like any good detective, he wanted to know his victim. Vasari channeled the idiosyncrasies of the man whose personal vision it was to erect this church. Vasari, like me, explored circles of logic, but in this case to find a track out of the Round House to a town called Clear Thinking. He had a thing about trains. Mosley would be the man to know to understand the Zeitgeist behind would-be church burners native to the area. Sergeant Vasari would distrust me; he considered placing me on a train heading to the town of Bad Intentions.

Vasari was a native Burlingtonian, a Old North Ender, a unique breed I would live among in a neighborhood Mosley avoided. Mosley once taught architecture at the university. He had fashioned the Congregational Church as a knock-off tribute to the Choragic Monument of Lysicrates in Athens with bell tower modified as observatory for summer evening meditations. He was "a low peeper and a romantic both," Sergeant Vasari once told me, because Mosley carried in a vest pocket Byron's *Childe Harold*, which Vasari understood to be a dirty book — all about incest but endeared to Mosley by the beautiful death of its author fighting the Turks in Greece.

Even more, Mosley was an unrepentant epicurean. And he was as unyielding in confessing his excesses as the Spartan youth who dropped dead soundlessly lined up for muster as the wolf cub hidden beneath his tunic ate out his heart. Mosley would climb his bell tower evenings to study the brick Federalist Ryder house below: an oil lamp ascending stairs, the blues and golds of stained glass lilies igniting and fading, pink tasseled bedroom curtains gloaming opaque, Dame Ryder performing in shadow-theater a petticoat and corset striptease from the bench of her dressing table. And then, most provocative, dame Ryder's outsized figure stepping out from the foundations of a Lord and Taylor dinner dress of bronze satin-de-Lyon and brocade that had graced her vigil at the fire.

This for years, more a beatification than voyeurism Mosley liked to tell himself, until red stone from Willard's Ledge quarry peptized in stages through the scaffolding of a Methodist church that asserted its censure rising between Mosley's Congregational Church and the Ryder house. Then Mosley's eye must pierce the circle of a Celtic Cross mounted on the obtruding tower as a pagan cross-hairs view of an embattled God that challenged his passion for the widow Ryder. He fell on his knees to cry his curses. All he had left were Tuesday visits. He would carry a sprig of rosemary to dame Ryder's parlor as tribute to an old friend — Leonard F. Ryder, deceased husband and recipient of Professor Mosley's political savvy who died, nonetheless, from exhausted energies and funds at the age of thirty-eight after eleven failed runs at a congressional seat. At the death of Professor Mosley, the widow Ryder hung with her own hands upon the office walls of the parsonage a daguerreotype of Mosley lecturing in mutton chops on Greek architecture from his bell tower, jaw set but eyes soft and sad with surprise, maybe at the flash of the camera that plumbed his soul, maybe at the loneliness that had eaten at his heart like a wolf cub.

Burlington police occupied the Ryder house a century later after a retrofit in plate-glass cubicles and battleship gray plasterboard. The hearth, positioned dead center as an agent of ambient heat tricked-out in imported marble and teak, initially graced captain's quarters until relinquished to officers on duty because of the moan from lake wind through its chimney. Vasari's boss, Captain John Buss, had learned dame Ryder practiced theosophy and didn't want to exposure himself to the particulars. He thought he heard dirges played on a ruptured bellows from dame Ryder's spinet that he knew to be moldering in a barn loft under a sheet miles away in a neighboring town. This was a relative of Ryder who would tell Vasari, in his detective work, of Professor Mosley's meditations in the bell tower of the church he designed and that Dame Ryder secretly knew of his romantic vigils.

Motes of coal dust rise from heat registers coating metal bookshelves and metal desks like eczema, rising on drafts up the stairs where golden lilies frozen in stained glass choke in the abstract nomina, as Aristotle would say, of their genus. The fireplace is plugged and blanched of personality with gray paint. The mantle has become a display of coffee cups. Sergeant Vasari's cup sits there even now. I've seen it – unwashed and plaque encrusted, a gift from Rotary, stamped with the sprocket-wheel icon, a reminder of sham fraternity during Rotary's courtship of City Hall for the go-ahead on a mini-mall. But city planners had jammed the cogs of Rotary by ramrodding a choke of taxpayer's money into the pipeline, bidding out business for the Ryder house and neighboring property, the Olmsteds, razed to erect a modern fire station. With Church and Main Streets and the proposed parking garage all adjacent on the grid, the police and fire stations had invaded a potential merchants' row. Waterbed purveyors, opticians with Dr. Eckleburg subtleties in advertising, lawyers and realtors and holistic counselors looking for high-profile retail and office space had all schemed for these properties.

Even the Historical Society that coveted the Ryder house was outmaneuvered by the mayor's feint toward waterfront development: the mayor, a socialist, threatened to replace the obsolete coal-burning electric plant with low-income housing. The "hystericals," as Halley Gay calls them, had cut a check held in abeyance for the Ryder property, a sure acquisition they thought, and focused lawyers on protecting views crossing the lake from the Adirondacks into Burlington harbor. Meanwhile auctioneers carried away Ryder velvets and mahoganies and gilts under cover of night.

But all this Mosley/Ryder history was dim and meaningless to Sergeant Vasari before the church fire in the last hour of his shift as he wore away elbows on another shirt and massaged spaniel jaws while dispatching patrol cars by coded message and counting down the months to retirement. Stone-cutter sized like his ancestors, thighs thick as steel girders and splayed, supporting a tuber of beer gut cinched with suspenders, he was educated (beat down Uncle Gerrit would say) by nuns in parochial school, raised in the Old North End where industry built cottage dwellings to root itinerate tradesmen with family obligation, where kids still play ball in streets with brick poking through macadam, and small shops rebuild shoes, recycle furniture, grocer the locals and launder for the uppities on university hill.

When the phone rang, he said, "Yuh?" And got on with police business.

But when the fire alarm mounted next door on its steel tower, third spire after the two church steeples, wailed misfortune like demon celebration, Parson Whitsun of the First Congregational Church, the one now in ruin, prayed to "mighty Gabe," prince of fire and thunder, to delay Judgment Day. Vasari said, "Damnation, plug that gob!"

When the alarm sounded and the phone rang together to announce the burning church, Vasari picked up, said, "Damnation! Yuh? Why call me? You're the fire department, don't you know. Can't you ratchet the noise down? What do you mean next door? Which church? Oh! Well this is one hell of ah night for scorch bandits. Who would carry stuff out ah burning church in ah snow storm with the police so close? Oh – did you get names? I can't arrest the whole damn congregation! I'll send ah couple officers with scratch pads and saw horses. Otherwise, this is your show."

The phone rocked in its cradle.

"Damnation!"

Vasari tensed in the goiter, profile swollen like a Hitchcock wattle. He did not cherish interviewing clergy. He felt creepy around them because he was tagged Saint Vasari by religious Old North Enders for quietly extracting priests naked and disordered from the emaciated arms of alcoholic single mothers embracing nymphomania. But Vasari loved the priests' sins. He didn't know why, but he did. Maybe because charmed by the explanations: exorcising the demon rum, or community outreach, or damn my eyes but she's in need, or quelling the chaos of human affairs. Or maybe Vasari felt akin, deputized by his superiors as they by theirs to "quell the chaos of human affairs." So many good guys in black.

The night following the church fire Vasari logged a call from Nectar's — a foul-smelling Bostonian had mugged a patron and abducted TV royalty. The pungent Bostonian would be me, the TV personality Halley Gay glorying in her commercial success as a television Fay Wray selling American Motors Gremlins. The calendar likeness I had seen where my Datsun convalesced. All this Fay Wray stuff had superseded her debut as news reporter.

So there I was hiking down Main Street, thinking I had escaped the recklessness of another inept driver. Parsifal and I tromped through snow toward Nectar's. Which was beginning to feel less a default destination and more a haven of noise and anonymous crowded bar and cheap beers for meditation and journal writing where I could staunch the passions of my haphazard thinking, which is Spinoza's idea of passion's influence. He also said passions are virtues when generated from sound ideas. I hadn't been generating virtuous ideas for a long time. And I had Halley Gay's laugh swirling through the malaise of my wimpish ciphering. I leaned downhill, gaining momentum as wind sculpted snow patterns on wide lawns. I passed fraternities in degenerate Victorian mansions with fallen porches and rusted cars, heard gropings in an idling Jeep parked in a driveway with "Stairway to Heaven" escaping from rag-top interstices, wondered at a modern brick frat in efficient Burger King style with refrigerator and busted sofa on the porch, waved to brothers in snow shoes climbing a snow bank to dunk hoop. They did not notice me. I passed an armory converted to day care and a natural foods co-op with families of macrobiotics in turbans packing grocery bags.

I smelled again toxins from the burned church as I approached Winooski Avenue, chemical hydroxide woven into the delicate web of pinwheel flakes. They had arrived already tainted, passing over the lake from the ferry dock at Rouses Point, New York, over leaking oil tanks, noxious feed supply warehouses, and the sulfuric power plant of Burlington's harbor to my vomited person. Then Nectar's, its red sign garish in flashing neon, rotating in an electric buzz above a foyer of black glass. An acned face with a black mustache looked out proprietary but kindly sucking a carrot stick.

I pushed through the door to the foyer, shook snow from my shoulders, aimed left following customers toward the deli, stopped, realigned, walked through the foyer again past the cash box, several stationary customers, a fleshy bouncer, and into the bar with pinball dinging when a beaker of glass shattered on the wall at my right ear – a Leyden jar by the effects, my addled brain told me. I fell to my knees, diminished, surveyed the shower of glass with onlookers pressing in, lightning shards like charged electrons filling the room, tinseling it.

"Homunculus in the void...I get it," I said jumbling Uncle Gerrit's lessons, speaking aloud as I was made to in my tutelage, mixing anatomy, physics and religion, a purple face scowling all sense from my fragile intellect, measuring me with mean eyes. "That's me at the positive pole, the place most deficient," I said. "And there's Gerrit at the negative pole, lording it, his usual inaccessible self. And the Holy Ghost...must be my father. He's the electric potential, the spark, and churches burn to the ground. And we are one son, but two fathers, one of the cloth and one the Ghost, and maybe this is the place I go when cloud carries me away, when I seize...maybe...I'm not sure again. "

"Pay up, deadbeat," the bouncer said looming, his mouth a rictus of sound merging hellishly with the industrial wail of an electric guitar, slapped leather, jangled chains, bottles dropped on tables, cans mangled and tossed onto the dance floor, World Federation Wresting above a horseshoe bar where Schlitz flashed and frantic balc aggressive men in jock straps slammed chests. The bouncer thought I had tried to avoid the door charge. "The band don't play for you else!" he said. "And a dollar more on the glass I flung." I smiled stupidly from the floor, same smile I had delivered the Canuck mechanics, a vacuous look I can't seem to outgrow.

"Scrooch yourself down, mon amis. Don't raise up," said a pony-tailed line-cook come from the deli in white apron and checked, meat-stained pants. He had been pouring seltzer by rubber hose into a beer glass when the commotion began and leaned across the bar to address me. His hair curled like jungle vine from the v-neck of his BVDs to the uncharted Congo of his bearded face. Muscles in his arms knotted like rope. His name is deBoner but he was cleped Hambone because of his finesse in a commotion of knives leaning over a spit of meat in the deli. He was equally adept with hot skillets under "Order-up!" pressures, which inspired the bar maids to call him, privately and with affection, simply Boner. They lingered in the archway between bar and deli watching him, gone moist between the legs like the first time a young priest talked to them with passion about abstinence. At the time deBoner was still untouched by the women at Nectar's. Pawed and preened and dreamed on, but not really touched. Not until Halley Gay.

"Keep to yourself, Mr. Hambone. I am resolving a cover dodge."

"Don't be owdacious tempered, Louis, Christly sakes," said deBoner in the same Canuck idiom I had heard at the Texaco garage. "Don't make me speak to you no high-duck language in this company," deBoner said with pique. This man had not laughed at a joke in his life. Louis threatened but deBoner stood four-square prepared for action, a quiet and serious man from a culture slightly askance who knows recipes and will not tolerate cooks in his kitchen. Louis must have felt this too. And because he could not translate deBoner's hunting metaphors, he felt outmaneuvered. Louis shook his spare, waxy blonde hair, scowled beneath the Fu-Manchu draped like a dead animal, the father that beat him as a child hammering at the membrane of his temper as Louis felt again a slap in the mouth at age three from spilled cow feed in the barn, slipping on manure, the family farm a dissolved option from that day.

"Doing my job, Mr. Hambone. This here," Louis said lifting five pounds of fist minus a digit lost to a chain saw, "is meat enough for shits like him." Meaning me.

"You going to *do* him, Louis? " said the band's lead singer. He had sneaked off the plywood stage and stood before us grinning, pointing a middle finger in the air, short legs in alligator boots tenuously balanced, accented in black jeans. He was the Elvis Costello aficionado replete with spiked hair, neoprene glasses and a practiced sardonic voice. I had walked into a Sunday papers cartoon where characters of single dimension exclaimed from dialogue assigned them in circles hovering over their heads. Or maybe I was lost in the circle prescribed over my own head, no clear dialogue yet assigned to me, as yet white space and white noise.

DeBoner wiped his hands on his apron, turned and moved toward the deli assuming I had more problems than beer-stein shock and deserved what I got. But he had neutralized Louis, or at least Elvis had redirected Louis' ire onto a more lively victim. I had still not detected Kerouac tendencies in myself. The road was more menacing than enlightening. Louis, silent and hostile, turned on Elvis. "Hey, man!" said Elvis, backing off, raising hands in the air. He sank into the black leather and spiked, purple-hair crowd contorting on the dance floor, the band tuning-up, calling its leader back to the stage. The beer-soaked native Vermonters remained seated at the bar. They wore flannel and painter pants and John Deere ball caps, long hair and beards. They were there to hit on the college chicks. My embarrassment was of no interest to them. "Don't shoot the guitar player, Louis," Elvis said. "The house loves me." He buddy-hugged the nearest rocker decked in body chains. "I'm in the master plan." It seemed my chance to slip quietly away, but wet sneakers slipped out from under me as I tried to stand. I had been boiled down to nothing but soft tissue and gristle. I was far too relaxed to be of any help to myself.

"Fuck you back," Louis said less volubly than I expected. He was talking less, thinking more, answering short, acting quick to stay in this thing.

I was vaguely aware that I had become entertainment. The pheno had sweated out into my quilted long-johns but was still doing its job – my heart slowed to where I could no longer hear its backbeat behind my ears, my thoughts becoming less fierce. The crowd that had gathered since the stein hit the wall was closing in around me, getting nasty. Except for one short, delicate blonde with a black part in her hair pulled tight by a red beret and dressed in a sweat-stained Red Sox t-shirt. She bounced boyishly on her toes in hiking boots behind the front line with cheerleader thighs flexed in tight jeans and said, "Why don't he get cleaned up? He smells. Hey, what was he *SAY*ing? Somebody tell me."

"Ah, the guy's talking some evangelical shit, like what's on TV after the bars close," said a voice on a bar stool from a man too old for this crowd. "Hey, maybe you and me can share a channel later."

A prior claim snuck behind the girl, short and audacious beneath a Yankees cap, dark-skinned from a tanning bed. He invaded the cheerleader's shirt with practiced hands from behind and beneath and extracted a bra with cheers attending from a table of New Jersey companions who had tracked the snow storm and chartered a Greyhound ride from Hackensack to assault the ski trails of Vermont. He was probably angling for one more dark-corner, leg-over, more for communal back-slapping in the bus ride home than to get laid. Giggles from the blonde. Looked promising.

"Guess not," the man from the bar stool conceded. "Hey, buddy," leaning toward me, "get the fuck cleaned up!"

Chapter Ten

Halley Gay recognized as Kong's Fay Wray • Designer Elvis to the rescue • Halley's breathing problem • Love apples • Truth is a large question • Travers' theory of the arsonist's methods • Burning churches like signal fires • Halley is groped • Travers breaks a face • A formula for assessing culpability • Hambone deBoner, Halley Gay and the groaning quoits.

"The media don't pay, darlin'," Halley Gay said to Louis the first time he dunned her with the cash box at Nectar's. Halley sold ad space for the *Burlington Free Press* before her TV spot as Fay Wray, before making gains as a photo journalist, before moving onto television reporting. She expected Channel Nine to note her potential in commentary. Halley planned to anchor a news desk so used to good effect the after-effects of the church fire: she dropped off at the executive producer's office a hip and cynical video exposé on homeless fugitives adapting to commune life at lakeside Burlington on the lee-side of the power plant where Power Town, a bivouac city, had appeared. The burned guy at the church fire had proved to be a nomad street indigent. The executive producer thought her "preppy and tough, gritty and polished at the same time." He called her interview style a "lip-flap in voice wrap," a phrase he carried to board room rhetoric after a seminar in news media at Berkeley convinced him to trend up the operation at Channel Nine. He said Halley had cleverly shifted the residents of bivouac city into displaying a sympathetic, soft criminality. She has the gift, the TV executive said, of "obverse management." I agree she manages every detail in her life and those around her, up until tangled with Uncle Gerrit. I don't agree this is a gift.

Halley established the compelling arrogance of her personality the first time she stepped into Nectar's, stared down Louis with the assurance of rising notoriety, and extracted a twenty from the cash box as guest fee. Louis numbed with a mux of notions paralyzing his response. On that winter, when Halley entered Nectar's moments behind me, as Louis deserted the cash box and followed the arch of the stein he flung, Halley lifted another twenty and change she clattered on the glass arena over which two pinball obsessives hunkered arguing table possession – "Give over, man."/"No, man. I'm zoning."/ You're fucking that thing."/"No, man, I'm cycling its rhythms, desensitizing it to hip-swivel." The machine responded with colored lights and dings. They pushed aside Halley's gift of quarters with quiet contempt.

Halley found me dazed and splayed on the floor. The crowd become timid shrunk away as Halley leaned to wipe glass shards from my shoulder. Elvis took notice, shuffled closer. She was a beam of light parting the brown air. Beer bottles dangled in wrists thumping thighs came to rest; body chains slipped into graceful ovals, except one purple-spiked slammer whose chain needed oil so jagged like scoliosis. I had been staring at this particular oddity. Black leather creaked and shifted, voices in whisper bent and gabbled through the band's tuning exercise, giggles from the blonde cheerleader at the New Jersey skiers' table squelched silent. Practically everyone recognized Halley from television. Not from reporting, that would come later, but from her Fay Wray impersonation in commercials with some car dealer in a King Kong suit selling American Motors Gremlins. Several payments on Halley's condo by the lake. The greasy calendars tacked on the walls of auto shops she didn't know about, and wouldn't have cared. Not much of her real self had been exposed anyway, presented as she was in country-funk, a Farrah Fawcett doll – rigid loops and waves of hair sculpted by an adhesive green gloop some ad agency had made famous by floating a pearl in its jellied mass. A white satin negligee strained at the knobs of her joints and mounds, nipples opened for the camera, her skin opaque as an unmilked virgin, her back arched supple and inviting upon the black metal of the car to give the set-warmer of that November outdoor shoot uncomplicated access to her curves. Halley stirred the fantasies of her viewers. She stirred some of her own.

Halley had entered Nectar's in a tight sweater and tailored chinos. Her thick hair released from its toque sprung into curl. Feathered tendrils drifted loose around the nodes of her ears. A generous plane of exposed forehead evoked for me one of Uncle Gerrit's more unique lessons. He had once found me in pre-adolescence studying the female form in a book of Praxiteles' nudes. He reached over my shoulder and closed the volume volubly, saying that as a boy he had more advanced notions of female sexuality – he considered nuns God's harem, encased as they are in dark fabric but with the erotic exception of an expanse of skin stark and naughty, wimple pushed to the hairline.

"God's harem will have cleavage of one sort or tuther," Gerrit had said. "Less is more, Travers. What's part hidden haunts in more crafty and deeper ways. What's tae easy tae get cloys in the thrapple. Keep mind of this when flesh is offered ye. Respect God's mysteries. Find therein the abundance ye seek."

I had no idea what he meant, but it wasn't long before the nudes of Praxiteles would, for me, metamorphose into the nakeds of *Playboy*. But in my current state, on the floor of Nectar's, I understood Gerrit's lesson. Halley's forehead reeked of mystery – a fecund oval, mythic, from which my true self might emerge reborn. If there were priestly deviance in Gerrit's idea, it must come from reinventing the self through a woman that must not be touched. And maybe that was the easiest thing, because to actually touch Halley in the physical, I would have to go a distance outside myself, even further removed from navel-gazing than Vermont spinouts on winter roads are from the warmth of a Harvard dorm laundry room. Halley watched sympathetically my struggle expressed in awkward gesture – my hand gone to her knee, then to her face. She brushed my fingers away and whispered, "Be cool, darlin'. Internalize the demons." I must have said something about her green eyes because she answered, "I am a jungle bird,

I am a cockatoo, as Mamma says." Her eyes faded to the gray-blue of her sharp-shooter father. She pulled away and rose above me.

She stood imperious rolled out from an Orkney Islands cable knit, her pulse fluttering in purple artery, her cheeks wide, almost Oriental and bony as a hip, receptive, the skin stretched membrane-thin, pliant, assuming the missionary position of my imagination where Halley moved slowly beneath. Halley had removed the anorak, exposing contours of a body that was, as I had guessed earlier, solid with exercise (all that hustle around town toting cameras), but also supple enough to tease in lingerie. I felt strangely a bedroom familiar, as if there were intimacy between us. Well, and after that spinout on the road, I guess there was. I hadn't yet recognized her as the calendar girl the two Canuck car mechanics had mounted above their workbench, but I was embarrassed, unsure what to say that would sound sincere – misdirected orgasm and puke and bar room violence didn't make for a smooth first date, not that I know much about dating.

"Boys!" she addressed the muted throng. "Will one of you kindly pull my car out from the snow. I blush to say that she has become a difficult extraction, most like a Kotex which has broke free of her string." Halley dipped and swiveled hips to extract car keys from a cargo pocket, the sweater tightening, her eyes teasing. It was impossible not to notice Halley.

Punk rockers on the dance floor and shit kickers on their stools also appeared witless, dazed by the L.L. Bean catalogue seductress they had seen in x-ray in a white nightie on TV. Add to this a resonate, puzzling voice and metaphors more disturbing than deBoner's. For some the distancing of television monitors must have enhanced Halley's status as an icon of abducted femininity. They hadn't counted on being so close to the flesh, and they surely weren't prepared for the voice. But it was the voice exactly and its odd selection of words that completed my journey out from a debilitating interior world. A Lazarus of modern pharmacology (in this case carrying a load of phenobarbital), I rose feebly, hands spidering the wall for support, spirit realigned, directing a request to the Costello impersonator: "Help us out, Elvis."

"Elvis was always a gentleman, my Mamma says, and he had the most prodigious dimples from the back seam of his jeans. My Mamma got close enough to know. Would you kindly direct us to a table in the corner, darlin'...and maybe send a mechanic up Main Street. She's a white Saab with her nose wedged where she ought not to be," Halley said dangling car keys.

Elvis took the keys, smiled winsomely, threw a bar towel over his shoulder and bumped a path through the crowd fading chiaroscuro as we moved to a distant corner. He led Halley and me to a booth moist with wafts of unflushed urinals. He had come to think of himself as the frontier arbiter of "new wave," a New York City transplant bringing culture with him beyond the farthest reaches of that city's most significant radio waves. He was, among other things, a renegade D.J. When the skies of Vermont go cumulus, most common along the damp, mountain-girded Champlain valley of Vermont's western border, he pirated the signal of WEZE, or "wheeze," itself an underground station that spliced into the Chrysler Building's relay from Manhattan. Elvis strengthened the signal with his own mobile relay equipment and sent it out across Burlington — stuff like Barrett gone solo after his break from the Floyd, the industrial-waste Cleveland band Ubu, krautrock from the Machine, Gabriel's messianic break from the bullshit of Genesis after Donavan had floated into the purple mist of the 60's. Elvis kept his equipment in a Ford van, a traveling underground radio station that also served as home, from which he relayed "wheeze" and interjected commentary and added his own selections of "new wave" when the signal from New York thinned beyond his capabilities to rescue it. The amphetamine-primed denizens of Burlington, a growing counter to the counter culture, had dubbed him Designer Elvis, as he promoted all things Elvis on his radio show — everything Costello wrote and sang, everything the true Elvis sung, and every movie he appeared in. Designer Elvis had little talent as a musician himself, but he had the aspiration and drive of a *Rolling Stone* music critic tracking the grooves of self-promotion. He was destined to succeed. A testament to Designer Elvis' influence, the slammers on the dance floor proudly exposed bruises as emblems of the underground initiated. This made for some interesting fashion statements around town. And when Elvis saw Halley, he thought she was more likely seeing him. He couldn't fathom a local notoriety as prominent as his own.

"Lovely fuckin' table, Elvis," said Halley. "Can't wait to see the wine list. Kindly drop the towel here where it may do some good."

I shifted onto the naugahyde bench sticky with beer spills, rubbed the towel over my face after Halley slid it across the table. Dark forms jammed the linoleum dance floor as the band tuned a riff from *Angels Wanna Wear my Red Shoes* telling Elvis he was needed on stage. He had been standing behind Halley's bench seat, wondering if she meant it, if he had really been dismissed so casually. The Schlitz globe pulsated over the bar, condensation dripped from the mirrored mosaic of the ceiling, black paint chunked off walls in the dim light, a Venetian setting in wallpaper reclaiming its days as backdrop to a forgotten spaghetti den. Patrons went back to beers and slamming strangers on the impossibly small dance floor. Elvis went back to the music. He was irresistible with a red Fender in his hands.

I leaned on elbows, weary, head pounding, hands bracing my bearded chin, dark hair matted like a wet dog, features moderately anguished and eyes dull with the calm of resignation – a look Halley somehow found attractive.

"Why in hell did you follow me?" I said, a rare impulse to assert myself which registered just plain rude. The tone and phrasing surprised Halley. Her gestures became rigid, automated. Her lips pursed then folded out as her breathing stuttered. "Fish bubbles," Mamma complained in the days of Halley's alleged childhood allergies. And because I had chosen Colonel Gay's military tone, Halley assembled a defense her shrink had programmed as response to her usual chronic surrender to a man's assertions. But as a result of her deprogramming, she now needs little more than a moment of perceived vulnerability from an otherwise virile man to fasten herself to him. From then on, any direction he chooses, gimped as he may be by the addition of her limp weight, would be her own. She would lose herself in his motion, as she would lose herself in her shrink.

Plowing arms forward on the desk, wrapped in a power suit of narrow-striped populuxe, fingers interlaced with certainty, the shrink chronicled Halley's throat irritations as fixations of sin growing more constrictive with each new affair like the grain of sand from which an oyster grows a pearl. Her throat, he said, must be perceived as an analog to her erogenous conscience, a result of brother fucking, while father waits impatiently for his turn. Halley listened and tried not to listen. She dry-washed her hands breathing through a bubble of collapsing air devoured by the catarrh that plagued her since her brother's death. As we sat together at Nectar's, she felt naked and shrunk to the size of Lilliputian. This was a moment her shrink had primed her for: the professional resurfaced objectified; the mind's cogs advanced on frames of video in anticipation of breaking a big story.

"I want you, Mr. Jones, to tell your truth on the church fire," she said, a small jag in her voice, evidence of her discomfort. "I believe you owe me. Desertin' a lady in time of need is a moral infraction of considerable proportion. You will be glad my poppa resides in a distant county. Besides, you might have stayed long enough after sharin' your salty emissions, as my sorority sisters say, to finish that cigarette."

Halley pulled a cigarette pack from the hip pocket of her chinos and offered one. I felt awkward, and some guilt for having deserted her, but I didn't feel self-conscious, even though Halley had noticed my orgasm while experiencing paroxysms of her own. I was glad some endearing weakness of Halley's had been exposed and shared. Besides, the urine smell and the taint of her vomit on my crotch braided with the musk and honey that emanated from Halley's skin had begun to work on me the way Renaissance women used spiced "love apples" to arouse lovers – peeled and nested in sweaty arm pits, hidden beneath layers of heavy brocade to absorb a flood of female excretions, a preview of salty sheets probably, and presented to their men as intoxicants in silk-lined boxes. Musky, resinous, foul, acrid and sweet all at the same time, the girl and the dark corner came together to make a perfume of romance.

Lighting the cigarette, Halley said, "Now present me the fuckin' truth as you know it."

Truth is a large question. Here's as Byzantine a definition as any: "Truth," I said, "is knowledge of self grounded in its proportionate link to the world at large and issuing, upon realization, grace notes of harmony." This I lay on Halley in extreme nervousness – in addition to a brief life history of isolation, tentative habitations in the mainstream, trauma in the choir, search for self, search for father, even harmony of the spheres. Some in lucid anecdote, some in Nietzschean aphorism, what I could remember from journal entries. I was glad to have an audience. Halley was my first. I warmed up to the opportunity. I had spent much of my life preparing for this moment. And this was the "media" after all. But the words spouted were stand-off intellectual, distancing, similar to the strategy I applied to girls my roommates screwed in the dorm. Halley is the kind of girl I would have run from. I was running still. What do you say to a girl like Halley Gay? Tell her: *I see you putting yourself out there, taking chances in your line of work, taking chances with men, but where to retreat when it all falls apart?* I had the ivory towers of academia. Halley was up a high wire between towers, the rope dancer in Nietzsche's book that fell to his death in the marketplace, after some buffoon tripped his step. Zarathustra carried the corpse out from town and miles into forest, honoring the artist for making danger his calling. Zarathustra walked into the night guided by stars. He buried the rope dancer in the hollow of a tree. I didn't want to feel obligated to carry the corpse of this photo journalist any great distance. I didn't feel up to it.

Halley stared at me like I had taken a fall. She knew I was talking to myself, explaining myself to myself. She is given to neglecting self-definition, said her shrink. She throws herself into work to avoid relationships and memories of the past.

"Jesus! What are you talkin' about, sugar?" Halley said after my panegyric on truth. "Do I just glow in the light of your hermit philosophy? Will you be writin' me a treatise from your grotto? Shit! My journalistic instincts at present will just about wilt Alice Cooper's hard on. But let's try the question again, Mr. Jones, as I still desire what you know of the church fire."

"All right," I whispered into the rim of a third Molson bought by Halley, tacked onto an expense account. "I suspect arson," I said with conviction, too exhausted to contrive. Halley nodded for me to continue. "Church burning runs in my family, so I have become sensitive to the hallmarks of ecclesiastical pyromania."

"Are you sayin' them barbecue ribs, which is to say that old man we found in the window well, was a relative? Oh, sorry...." She saw my grimace. "Pardon me for not bein' the queen of sensitivity. But I called the night desk editor at Channel Nine from the hospital and he said the man found was someone named George Eakins, a known-about-town indigent that has been livin' in the streets for years in Burlington and who was suspected of arson for as many years so made a volunteer fireman after which the warehouse fires" – she took a breath – "stopped. Temporary solution. He fucked up big time lightin' the church, didn't he, sugar. Probably too drunk to get out of the window well."

"No, he didn't do it."

"If that is so, what of the evidence in the back seat of my Saab, darlin'? You found it. You must know something about it. But what's this shit – your family burnin' churches?"

"Yes, my father. He burns churches, or he did. I'm never sure which verb tense to use. I have epilepsy. You know that, don't you? My father did too. Does too? Whatever. When I grand mal I connect with my father through visions. Maybe he is my guardian angel, as Uncle Gerrit says. He seems to be always with me when I go to that other place."

Halley gave me the look of disbelief I expected.

"Look, it's not voodoo. I don't know how it works exactly. No one understands epilepsy. But when I'm seized – it's a disorder of the cerebral function – I have auras with hallucinations, sensory illusions of unconsciousness minutes long that seem to me hours and clonic contractions that disturb the uninitiated. I go into my father's world. The first time, my first episode, that time in the boys' choir, he came to me with fire in his hands. The second time...let's just say he was there again. But this time...strange... he didn't appear. I mean, he was there, but only just his voice, not his image. Look, the guy in the window well was no burner. I'm sure. But I'm also sure there was a burner. I just feel it. And maybe there was more than one burner. I heard a jumble of voices, including my father's, and some kind of argument. It was like being shut up inside a dark closet with people outside making plans to keep you there. I'm still pretty shaken. Can't say I'm thinking too clearly. This has been a hell of a day for breaking the sedentary habit."

"You *are* different aren't you? But I assure you that whatever can be known of the fire, Mister Jones, comes from the physical. The world is physical, darlin', a garbage dump of cause and effect, sugar, enough to set a permanent wrinkle on your nose. That old boy in the window well did not just curl in there to roast marshmallows. He started the fuckin' thing! Hell, you found him with the coffee can that had the combustive shit in it. Right?"

"Yes, but that's not the source of the fire."

"And how would you be knowin' this, darlin?"

"I've studied arson. And I can tell you that one can of camphorated candle, his space warmer probably, won't do much more than scorch a shingle. And yes, I agree, the world is physical, but more subtle and peculiar than our senses can easily perceive. What if I told you the London underground, the subway that is, was carved through billions of tiny skeletons of non-creatures. Look, I know this is a weird illustration, but I've had reason to make a study of the London underground. My mother keens in the dark recesses of our hotel apartment like she's still in the London underground. It's a place where, she thinks, the devil entered her life. Anyway, the whole country sits on this chalky stuff, the Cliffs of ...”

“Dover.”

“Yes.”

“But how do you mean non-creature?”

“Chalk is residue, the condensed shells of non-creatures each a hundredth of an inch in diameter. I’m talking about creatures that shouldn’t, technically, be alive. They are no more than particles of living jelly – no mouths, nerves, muscle, no distinct organs, just a kind of retracting filament for legs and arms. But they feed, grow, multiply, separate from the ocean their small portion of carbonate of lime for protection. They die and pack the ocean floors with their skeletons. Londoners live on what was once the ocean floor. They build their lives upon tiny carcasses, a *FACT* unperceived.”

“Fascinatin’. Truly. You are all brain aren’t you, sugar, a very large organ. It is somewhat excitin’ to be around an organ such as yours that is so well developed. But what can this have to do with our church?”

“The what it has to do is that I can’t see a piece of chalk run across a blackboard without seeing jelly creatures that produced the stuff squirming on the black surface. The words and formulas written there won’t hold still. I get dizzy. Ever since my first seizure, I have become infected with the idea of motion, purpose beneath the surface of things. I see movement as destiny inside the solid. Aristotle thought matter conforms to purpose. Since my first epileptic seizure, when I saw my father with his hands on fire, I can’t sit in a church without going back to that vision. And standing beside that burned church as I did, the first time I have done so, his presence was overwhelming. I’m sure that he is, somehow, the imperceptible substance and truth behind your church fire.”

“Don’t, please, let us discuss truth again. Would your father’s hands have started the fire or does he loan them out?”

“Yes, that’s funny. I’d say your burner probably ran a line of low explosive powder, like potassium and sodium nitrate, or maybe chlorate and red phosphorus if he was in a hurry. Then maybe he packed in several charges linked to the powder that he touched off on his way out, charges that have an oxidizer and a combustible. Maybe several cigarette packs of nitric acid and resin, or barium chlorate and paraffin wax. All this stuff can be concocted in your average kitchen, carried in a duffel bag. Put the charges under furniture or drapes, anything that will burn. And there you are."

"Well, shit. That's pretty good. But can you give me a reason why?"

"I don't know. I really don't know.

"Why does your father burn churches?"

"Maybe something to do with Paul Tillich. I think my mother knows. I know my uncle knows. My father is drawing me toward him – maybe because I'm finally loose from the Catholic influence. My mother is a frantic Jesus lover and my uncle is a priest. It's like my father knows I'm on the road, free of those two. Maybe he survived the war and has secretly watched me grow up in Boston. Maybe he was the street vendor I used to wave to that showed me some kindness when I was growing up. If he's dead, it's not the kind of dead we know. I don't know. But I do think he wants to get to me before I disappear into my books again. He's sending me to burned churches like they're signal fires. And he's making me seize – again."

"Jesus, you really think this fire is about you."

I was considering telling her how much like one of those non-creature, jelly masses I feel myself to be whenever I go into seizure when Halley screeched a second time that night, though more a hiss as of poisoned breath expelled. The drunk from the bar counter who thought I was an evangelist had appeared behind Halley, whispered something in her ear and run his hands under her sweater in imitation of the New Jersey skier he had seen earlier.

"Well, hadn't counted on this. You ain't wearing one."

Halley sat motionless as if nailed to the chair while the drunk's hands moved under her sweater like lab rats circling her breasts. The man showed his crooked, yellow teeth, and I stood up with the truncheon in my hand and let loose. The man's jaw exploded. Raw flesh with tooth root flew off towards the dancers and blood dribbled into Halley's hair as the man's eyes widened disbelieving before he collapsed in a heap like someone had let go the strings. Halley sat there uncharacteristically sedate with a tremble of lips and unseeing eyes, her lips performing fish-bubbles. She seemed to be preparing her own seizure, gone already to some distant world.

Elvis rescued us again. He had been watching Halley from the stage, hoping she would be watching him. He took Halley by the arm and motioned me to follow, kicked the collapsed bleeder in his groin, and led us both to an alley door back of the stage. I was feeling pretty good about myself, still holding the weapon.

We nearly got run over by Halley's Saab with Hambone deBoner at the wheel, urging us in, saying, "Here be your Sab, miss. Not much Christly damage ta speak of that I can see. If you be pretty shook from the accident, deBoner be glad ta drive. I be done work for the night."

Before long I was sitting on Halley's sofa in her condo by the lake holding the truncheon in my hands as deBoner and Halley humped in the bedroom — an all-nighter. I had secretly and ashamedly placed the truncheon under my pillow. There are many kinds of violence in this world.

I wondered if Halley and I would ever fuck like that. I did not grab laundry and head for the nearest laundromat, which felt like small progress. But of course our union would be possible only if one of the two of us, or both, weren't serving a prison term for reckless driving (something we had in common). I began to review Professor Bower's math calculations to assess culpability, my way of counting sheep. The formula goes like this: $T = (PH)/24 + A$ or Time Served equals the number of Persons inconvenienced conjoined with the number of Hours involved OVER the hours of a day PLUS the degree of "asininity of the offense." I figured I would get off with a warning while Halley would likely have her spin-out assessed in its offense to Fred and his columnar wife in the cupola of their home and in its inconvenience to those at Nectar's who had hiked up Main Street through the storm and shoveled her out. Although Hambone deBoner was getting some recompense for his efforts, judging by the groaning quoits of the mattress. And, to be honest, there was something wonderfully vital in breaking apart a man's jaw.

Chapter Eleven

Travers projects his future • A better mouse trap • A church burns in an ash tray • A church burns for real • Halley Gay's NASA launch and Travers' aesthetic, compelling pleasure • Travers a suspect • Introducing the Drs. Needham.

Some read magazines from back to front. Some must know ahead of time the plot resolution of books and of movies. For the retrograde addicted, here's a brief account of a distant future, which is, of course, me in the present: I will become a professor of philosophy. I will earn tenure at McGill University. But my days in Montreal will end prematurely. I will leap down the road again, risk accident, sing arias from *Parsifal*, cultivate a pure heart through the shock of experience.

Winters in Montreal will seem as isolating as those in Vermont – more so when winds gather to buffet from off the plain surrounding this city like an ocean, more so after the death of my wife. I will not propel myself out from that house for months after her passing. But I won't do the Oscar Wilde in Paris thing – match wits with wallpaper –because my wife has rescued me from despair. She was a strong person, stronger than I. Her death will not be unexpected, as she will have gone beyond the doctor's urging to drop the macrobiotic diet, her final eco-political statement, despite my pleading. At our last meals at table together, she will call me "beef" and I will call her "jerky." She was older by ten years but lean, animated, no gray in her hair, kept young I suppose by the vigor of her ideals for correcting the world's imperfections. I miss her spooning me with those long, white legs in the sag of the mattress. I wonder if my wife had leached poisons out from me that caused her death. She would say I had ineffectual mothering. You will notice that beyond that, I had one father missing and a second too much a part of my life. My wife asked me to write this book, for the sake of our son, our one child, as did Uncle Gerrit, though for different reasons. You will understand this better a while later. I tell my son that true freedom is companionship. My story will bear this out.

In those Burlington days, I had taken residence in a gable-end apartment on Grant Street behind the Unitarian Church at the top of Church Street in the center of downtown, but on the rowdy fringes of the Old North End, well positioned to await and attend the next church burn. Several churches fanned out from the top of Church Street like a peacock's tail. I felt sure more burns were imminent though Halley had dismissed my warning. The authorities had dulled her interest by closing the investigation, declaring faulty wiring. And me – the diseased savant – she doubted. Can't say I blame her, though I was trying to feel more misunderstood by Halley than unappreciated. Even at Harvard, Irish sympathizers that teach the poetry of Yeats seldom address his visionary system of intersecting gyres, cycles of predestined history that make you think of Giambattista Vico. Any tweed-jacketed Boston intellectual will be embarrassed to admit Yeats' wife in a sleep trance had pulled out from some dark place like fish from water the voices Yeats applied in his poetry. I consoled myself with thoughts of misunderstood genius, though with epilepsy, I had a hard time seeing myself as more than a medium.

In the next two months of winter in Burlington, Halley and I occupied different planets. There were no points of connection between us once she dropped the Mosley church burn. And cloud cover was eternal. Depression through inactivity and isolation unending. I spent days in that studio rent and nights at Nectar's. The sub-zero temperatures frosting my apartment windows and winds carrying frozen rain off the lake to rattle them never obscured Halley's view of mountains across the lake, given the triple-paned and buttoned-down R-Value of her luxury condo.

I made a habit of evenings at Nectar's with my *Journal of Life Assembly* and *Zarathustra*. I wrote a lot, though not much useful as life strategy I now realize. We each have our own road and our own turns at intersections, our own accidents and breakdowns. Nothing is predetermined. I say this leafing backwards through a distance of time and miles as I motor West through red sand buttes and cacti to no particular destination. There are few places to aspire to. It's not that I have desensitized myself to the unsettling and hurtful days of Burlington. I hope this account tells something of my humanity beyond the zany and absurd that embody more of life than we wish to acknowledge. I remind myself that I write for my son, a promise to his mother, the one that raised him, a necessary distinction as you will see. I want to improve upon the brief note left me by my own father to explain his disappearance and to advise a son he had never known. I'm talking about his second letter to me, his final letter, the one Uncle Gerrit never saw, the one Fiona received in Scotland but never opened. You'll see.

I have read this letter and read "into" it so many times that I have made a world of paternal love where I can disappear, like in the wallpaper of the East Boston hotel. I write this as my son chooses his own path. I write this with the burden of sorrow, palpable but not overwhelming. In my Burlington days, more like a pall that shadowed every thought and every action. But sorrow can bind us to others and to our other selves over time. In Burlington I sorrowed on too many fronts to make good sense of any of my "issues" as Halley called them. But these sorrows did lead me to a woman who would share my life. She took my virginity ruthlessly while increasing the volume of my heart. I had wounds – I still do – but I did not display them around Burlington like stigmata, nor collect bruises on the dance floor at Nectar's. My mother's self-abuse and keening scared me off those practices. I did not let sorrow embitter me, a circumstance that crippled my mother and motivated my uncle to recruit warriors to battle the church.

That Burlington winter I returned to Nectar's a minor celebrity, the beast to Halley's beauty. Good for an occasional free beer. Although deBoner proved the better beast. I had no television except over the bar at

Nectar's where Halley covered local features on the eleven o'clock evening news. Of course, we bar flies all watched as porn slaves to the Fay Wray image of that Gremlin commercial we could not get out of our heads. But I did make friends with Elvis. He became my guide to Burlington, my introduction to the counter to the counter culture – a habit of life I had already adopted, thanks to Uncle Gerrit's influence, but which seemed to need a collection of icons and aggressive tendencies to legitimize. Same can be said for a lot of things. Elvis shared women enough, but I was saving myself for Halley. On especially cold nights, when Elvis wasn't shacked up with a dizzy masochist off the dance floor of Nectar's, he slept on the floor of my apartment in his goose down sleeping bag rather than in his van.

My Datsun truck remained in the shop, got tinkered and partially healed, which the Canuck mechanics noted briefly with bills they mailed: "Come try now! Works pretty good. And please take cat." But there were relapses. They would send contrary mail saying, "Better try later. Needs more work. Cat working pretty good. Very please take cat." Billable hours mounted. I didn't have money to pay for extensive repair. I didn't want Cat back. Not that I told them. He was an alley cat to begin with and could be one again so far as I was concerned. I gathered my things piecemeal, loading them onto the town bus whose service stretched only so far as the Texaco station in Williston where my truck languished. And finally, in a fit of conscience, I stuffed Cat into a pillow case to avoid claws. I collected him on the last bus run of the day, typically empty besides my boxes and me, so I wouldn't be reported abusive to the animal police. I hated that cat.

Not long after retrieving Cat, an arsonist torched the cathedral on Saint Paul Street. It took me a while to realize. I was awake, shaking-off a disorienting daylight sleep, sore and seething beneath covers in my attic apartment. I had been easing pressure through mean thoughts in imitation of the bleed valve in the old radiator beside my bed. A lean diet and impatience, a recent one-sided fight which I had lost, and sexual abstinence in a time of promiscuity were making me fierce. I noticed Cat in pounce mode. "Ineffectual mouser!" I squeezed from tight lips. "Figure you're back in alley trash, don't you?" Cat flicked an indifferent tail and ate a fly that had been buzzing a pizza box lying in a corner of the room. I opened one good eye wider, the other bruised and closed, acknowledged sunset leaking in from a frosted window delineating tumbles of dishes green with slime in the sink, tap water dripping. "A nice mossy scene by a sparse brook. Real Vermonty," I said to the six walls. The path through my room constricted in a sharp turn to the bathroom as dirty clothes accumulated in piles that were "airing-out" in accordance with my system of sartorial hygiene. It had been a long time since I had visited a laundromat. When my clothes became rank, I aired them out or bought replacements at Goodwill.

I had spent so much time at Nectar's lately because I felt it was time for me to know a woman in the biblical sense. My Nectar's evenings were calculated to locate Halley. I knew she roamed Burlington most all night after her studio work looking for exposé, looking for news that would make *her* news. And I thought she might come looking for deBoner. I was also awaiting the next church burn while living off pizza, indulging in beer, cigarettes and sleep deprivation. I was not into recreational drugs, I say at the risk of protesting too much but sensitive to the perspective from a more conservative time into which I have aged. One more church fire, one more seizure might give me direction, I thought, reconnect me to my father, resolve the waiting, the fucking waiting – I hated the waiting! I was determined not to spend another six years waiting. I twisted my good eye to another corner where books stacked in shopping bags climbed like an Egyptian lotus column to the ceiling's expanding bloom of gutter-water backed up from winter ice and dripping.

"Shit, a fucking waterfall," I said to Cat who habitually eschewed nature as hunting ground. He felt more at home in landfills. Flies were his playmates. I decided to help Cat connect to his genetic disposition as a hunter of furry things. I groaned out from bed in the mocking clarity of a street lamp, scavenged from under the bed an empty bottle of Molson beer, jammed inside a thumb-sized portion of sharp cheddar, shoved the bottle into a hole of baseboard Cat should have staked out that had on occasion produced visits from a mouse. I said, "We'll get his little pot-bellied ass before he can shit and run. What do you think, Cat?" Cat looked away.

The radiator banged, my head throbbed. I lit a cigarette tossing the spent match at Cat, free-fell into a director's chair at the head of a card table I had placed by the only window. I tested puffy skin around my bruised eye with fingertips and winced, my hands jittery with tension. I began to burn with the cigarette loose folds of a wadded ball of paper tossed into a brass ashtray, an India import stamped with a prowling tiger. "Tiger tiger burning bright," I said as the paper neared combustion when a painful image jumped out from a partial memory of the beating I had suffered in the alley outside Nectar's. "Where the hell are you when I need you, Cat!" I said stamping the red line of advancing fire. I unfolded the wad to reveal a page from a chapbook titled *Walk Around Burlington*. A pungent, ill-dressed old man had placed this scrap of paper tenderly in my jacket pocket sometime after I had collapsed from a roundhouse fist. There was more, but snatches of memory were displaced by sirens erupting and flames leaping across the street in the window of my neighbor's second-story apartment. I spent a moment wide-eyed and amazed. Well, one of my eyes was wide. The flame reflected something going on a block or two away, a substantial burn.

The neighborhood woke up. Old North Enders with work boots unlaced like slippers slipped into streets from a shamble of low rent apartments, jumped off porches into knee-high snow, slammed screen doors where plastic tacked for insulation tore and flapped in the wind. Some ground ignitions in bondo junkers. All were eager for the chaos and entertainment of misfortune separate from and larger than their own. I intended not to go along. I had chased too many false alarms while Halley screwed her brains out (what she had left) with that French pastry from Nectar's.

I sat at the table sweating in my t-shirt and boxer shorts, scared how I would end up. I wanted another fire, but I was worried I might somehow become its victim. Alas poor Travers! Even if hidden away in this attic apartment, my bones bleached, Cat chewing the marrow, I would be infamous. It seemed my destiny. All seemed fated back then. Travers Jones, church-burner. If I hadn't yet lit a church, I was increasingly tempted to do so. There was no way around this growing impulse. I know something of the folk memory of isolated community, how sins of fathers adhere to the scion. I saw Burlington as an island. All towns are. Consider Malta where Maria called the spaghetti-maker makes gloves. Her great-great grandmother made the spaghetti. And there's Raul the dog-beadle whose nickname comes of an ancestor who shooed stray dogs from the shadow-cooled sanctuary of its cathedral on hot days. My own son may inherit the tag church-burner from his grandfather's sin. Or from my own.

I brooded at the card table, my mind bending around the punishing concepts of guilt and destiny. I peered onto Grant Street and my neighbor's third floor apartment windows with Cat spitting at my worthlessness. Little of what I had scratched into my journal made sense. I had lost the voice. Zarathustra had gone into hiding, meditating in some obscure cave. My father had not substantially appeared since the *Playboy* indiscretions, despite the Mosley church burn.

Nonetheless, from habit I scratched a calculation of distance and direction of sirens aided by the blaze reflected in my neighbor's windows and, to my surprise, went giddy with expectation. It could be the cathedral two blocks down Pine Street. Alarms had wailed since I awoke, wailing like the judgment day, several townships called to the fray. It was a big one. I looked again at the wadded page from *Walk Around Burlington*. The gothic stone tower of Immaculate Cathedral on Pine Street had partly burned from my cigarette. I began to feel a sense of purpose. I crushed the cigarette, threw the butt at Cat and ran into the street in my sleep ensemble. I smelled the lead roof of the cathedral discharging toxins as it melted. I took a heady breath of toxin to open the passages for seizure and to my father.

I ran back to the apartment, stepped into jeans and sneakers, layered on the patched parka, then through slush, stepping between firemen, avoiding police barriers and officer Brady who sized me with mean eyes but heard again Sergeant Vasari say, "Stay on the fringe. This is ah fireman thing. Let them boys handle it." I wanted to be close enough to feel the heat. I got close enough to feel I should step back. The roof went undulant, molten, timbers screamed in turbo-burn as windows shattered in the draft, a kaleidoscope of colored glass filled the air. The 3,000 pound bell came next, shattering floorboards on its descent to the basement. Oh, ye gods, this was heaven! A wave of dust roiled through first-floor windows covering me and everything near. The ground shook. Firemen went numb for an instant, out of respect, fear or fascination. Hoses sprayed placing weight and temperature variance upon stressed mortar and stone, cracking veneer and sending wall tumbling. I climbed into the vacant cab of a fire truck to watch the burn. I was there hours, transfixed, waiting for seizure. It didn't come. I stepped outside once the church had been reduced to steaming rubble. It was pitch dark in early evening. Preternaturally dark, like a moon eclipse – not even stars. I had no idea what time it was, how long I had watched the fire: three hours, seven? I didn't know. I remembered: check the window wells.

Such oppressive darkness. Winter had awaited this burn along with me, had readied itself to consume the townscape in funereal grays of exhausted energies and ruin. But that wouldn't happen. Not yet. A second layer of reality peeled back as though sunburnt skin to reveal in a shock of white light, metallic lightning, stark figures humped over, others jumping on strings, disorienting – like countdown at a NASA launch site. Or maybe a gas leak ignited releasing souls of the doomed priests had locked in the root cellar. Or maybe this was an LSD flashback, or maybe a Nam memory, which I was somehow sad not to have, not being a vet, never having dropped acid. As it turned out, gaffers in ABC logo winter wear, a bit like moonwalkers, had been stealthily laying cable, setting tripods, lugging battery-pack cameras, the turbo hummm of cluster spots issuing white light with firemen disentangling in haste to depart, curiosity seekers already gone, and me trapped in the cold hand of technology. Cable snaked toward me, cameras swayed on the backs of sturdy men, dim voices mumbled in techno speak, and a corona of unearthly blonde hair floated toward me, the body distinguishable below the plane of blinding light as a blue-gray hounds' tooth suit of wool tapered hourglass to flatter a shape that needed no help whatsoever, and as a throwback to practicality, beneath the shin-length skirt, shin-high LL Bean duck boots unlaced. It was Halley Gay.

I stepped precariously back from her approach, onto the lip of the smoldering foundation I had been studying. Legs weakened when cameras pointed, a kind of stage fright I'm prone to since my trauma in the choir of Our Lady of the Mount in East Boston, a youthful solo debut gone bad, with me living solo ever since. But there was nowhere to go. A phalanx of news team had wedged me in. And Halley's face framed in blonde came within arm's reach, smiled in a detached hungry-dog resolve of blue-gray eyes direct enough to paralyze. I thought of talk-show mavens eliciting confessions from unwilling guests, but in this case set up for a thirty-second TV news flash where reluctant interviewees, such as me, unload tidbits of useless information into those eyes.

"Would you mind, darlin', presentin' my viewers a witness account of the fire? Speak into the mike, please. Look into the camera, please .... Oh, shit, it's you!" – the eyes closed then opened then abstracted away – "Cut the juice, gentlemen!" – lights faded and cameras rested on hips – "Mr. Jones, do I impose at an inconvenient moment? What have you been doin' with yourself, sugar? Your eye? You know, Mr. Hambone and I were surprised to find my sofa empty the mornin' after. Did you leave that rubber mallet under the pillow for me? So sweet. Anythin' in particular you wanted done with it? Well, so good to see you. Another church burn, another window well to investigate, right, sugar. Any barbecue ribs tonight? But at least you're not lyin' on the ground dribblin' spit. Some progress there. I am so pleased for you."

I couldn't agree there had been progress. Seemed the opposite to me. Despite the drama of a burn that beckoned, there had been no aura, no seizure, no connection to my father after a two-month wait. This burning church was supposed to be the culmination of all my preparation, and... *NOTHING!* I had wanted my father to step out of the flames, gather me in his arms, purify me, reach me in ways my mother and uncle and the holy Catholic church had failed, make me understand the significance of these fires and send me away refashioned, with a sense of purpose that defied Uncle Gerrit and all his conditioning.

"Now, how about we make you famous, da-lin'? Give us an eye-witness account of the fire. You do still have one good eye. We'll shoot from your least blemished side. I will bet my daddy's best sow that you been here since the start. That right, sugar? Odd coincidence, don't you think? You bein' at both fires."

I didn't know what to say. I hadn't counted on being a suspect, at least not suspected by anyone else except myself. I began to wonder if I could "will" a church conflagration. I looked up painfully from one good eye, mangy beard flattened by the wind.

"Jesus, you're a mess. That's all right. Don't be nervous. This is not lives of the rich and famous, Mr. Jones. It is just a fuckin' thirty second spot."

"I've had no seizure," I managed to say.

"Once again, I am so glad for you. Roy boy, we have a dead one here. Why don't let's pan the ruins anyway. How about go wide angled then narrow to vertical focus on the standin' chimney. God love the irony! No more prayers risin' up the steeple – 'God's dagger pointed at his own breast,' my daddy would say. Don't we just turn on the maker so easy these days. Oh, shit! Lighten up, Halley. Let's say the congregation has dropped its drawers. To think, in all this devil smoke and steam the chimney would expose itself so shamelessly. Shit, that's good. Double shit! Too much steam," Halley complained from the cyclops scope of the viewer. "Anyone left around here that saw the fire? Any parishioners? Damn my luck! Look, Mr. Jones," her voice softened as she returned to me, "is there anythin' you can tell me about the fire?"

"Well, there is, yes. I think I have evidence of arson."

"Look, I had the coffee can analyzed, darlin'. It was nothin' but candle wax, or somethin' like."

"Yes, I told you that."

"You been doin' the Ouija talk with your disappeared daddy again? You are what my papa calls a symphony of loony tunes. All right... pack it, gentlemen! The red satchel goes in my car, Roy."

"What if I told you I was warned this church would burn?"

"And who would tell you that?"

"Some smelly old man with a beard said so."

"Jesus, who turned the key and let you out?"

"I'm not explaining this well. I'm a little wound up. But I'm not wrong. Truth is I've had a difficult two months. I was showing my cat how to bag a mouse in my room on Grant Street when I saw my neighbor's windows light up from this fire. I came down here with the rest of the Old North End losers. If I hadn't been so hung over and sore from someone's fist in my eye – the guy with the loose hands at Nectar's, remember him? – I'd have understood the message I got from that old man in the alley and sat here through the night and caught the burner."

"That pervert from Nectar's did this to you?" Her voice dropped an octave. "I am, of course, in your debt, Mr. Jones. And I must say, you begin to sound more human, but if anythin' you look even more than before a northwoods malcontent. And to be frank, Mister Jones, you confuse me. I don't know, but I think my best option is to stay ignorant of whatever thoughts you harbor. Pack it, gentlemen! We'll go to the station archives for any old fire and dub narration."

"Sure, good idea. Hope you have something in those dusty files on pyros, as you've got a burner in town for sure. And it's a holy man."

I don't know why I said that, maybe because these burns were a spiritual issue with me, but Halley responded with interest. "Someone in the clergy?" she said, the hint at scandal potentially newsworthy. And something in my tone arrested her. She gave me another transfixing stare. My story would reek of fantasy and paranoia from a park bench stranger but given the circumstance of a second church fire, could be meaningful. She hadn't trusted her intuition for a long time. It always got her in trouble. And this was an inconvenient time to be told what will likely be a nonsense tale, and with film to review on the frame-catch back at the studio, hoping to make the eleven o'clock "local round-up" broadcast. But when Halley leaned toward me to better make sense of my odd ideas, she smelled something other than the acrid, smoldering fire, something musky from inside my parka suggesting places burrowed to she hadn't been and that she remembered as oddly attractive back during our intimate moment at Nectar's and in her Saab before. And with my wide-apart eyes, black hair dripping in snow, furtive smile from a boy's beard, all signifiers of some kind of Raskolnikov secret: murder in the family or insanity. Shit, what was she thinking!

"The police station is just that way, Mr. Jones. Talk to Sergeant Vasari. He is a good old boy, by your rather loose Yankee standards."

"I don't think that's wise – seizure-prone pyro suspect blows whistle on pyro. You just know I'll be using the rest of my college grant money on lawyers. Hell, even you have doubts about me."

"Okay then, sugar, how about we play in your back yard. I know a Dr. Needham of Chemical Engineerin' at the University, a crusader for exposin' wrongdoin'. Will he do?"

"I don't know. Maybe. Where do we find him?"

"He's close enough to blow in my ear, darlin'."

Reginald Needham looked over Halley's shoulder and smiled, said, "Oh yes, the Sanka man." He was an admirer of Halley, too shy to make the first move, though she knew. He wanted the TV studio to air his computer-generated time projection of acid rain poisoning the Camel's Hump woodlands. Lugubrious eyebrows is how she knew him, a doomsayer with a voice like Lurch and breathless over the phone like the eco-world is minutes from annihilation. Not the guy for your beach party, but an inspired nose for molecular disorder, a riddle-solver's reflex used lately in bumping Halley momentarily into prime news with a piece on toxic weed spray on I-89. Needham wisely despaired on video tape seated before a stack of books, which had improved Halley's standing with the gray suits and got her promoted to a series of sixty-second fillers which brought me to the TV over the bar at Nectar's – the radical SPCA maven behind a spate of dog kidnappings, opera diva spurns Shelburne Farms Mozart festival, that sort of thing. Halley wasn't yet doing the feature stories she wanted. But she was getting air time, and there were always the commercial reruns of her Fay Wray impersonation.

Needham's wife, Gladys, was also at the burn. She was an assistant professor of anthropology at the University of Vermont. When first introduced to Halley by her husband at a downtown restaurant, she had stared uncontrollably and found nothing embarrassing in explaining that, to her thinking, Halley's mandibles matched perfectly the profile of Cleopatra. Gladys would later show Halley the miniature bust she kept wrapped in cotton in a desk drawer, a 20's B.C. Roman copy from an Egyptian original believed to have come from the Queen's tomb. The first likeness Gladys had unexpectedly unearthed in a rare photo collected from Zulu menstrual rituals (a collection intended for illustration in Frazier's *The Golden Bough* but thought too sexy for its pages). A second likeness appeared in a Nazi casebook from a Prague ghetto census. Gladys had started to think of Cleopatra as the quintessential "everywoman," and she wanted to study Halley, thinking, as do the Chinese, that a map of the face can tell all there is to know of a person – in this case, several persons back to the Queen herself. So Halley had been invited to drink wine at the Needham's house on university hill as the bouillabaisse boiled when the Channel Nine news room had called to send her to the burning church. A camera team would meet her there. Halley insisted that Gladys come along to study what she called "the curious ticks of these backwoods wiener roasters" – which is media speak designating fire chasers drinking beers beside short-wave radio whose earth-mover 4X4's invariably rumble to the site ahead of hook & ladder. My neighbors of the Old North End. Reg came too.

"Well," said Reg, "I am keen on the great outdoors." He shivered and coughed. "But we *are* breathing chemicals you know, in addition to the polychlorinated biphenyls, dioxins, and pesticides of our daily lives."

"Nice, Reg," said Gladys. "Never mind him. Reg thinks none of us will escape unscathed from Love Canal. He thinks we all suffer residual damage. He's not the one in front of which to have a nose bleed." She smiled. Reg did not, but said, "Long way around a preposition, my dear." She studied me with a tilt of her head, dropped a pair of glasses down from her hair to her nose for close inspection. "I have bouillabaisse enough for one more guest. Would you agree to round out the company? We'll just dust you off a bit." She laughed, dropped glasses onto the snow and laughed again.

"Yes, we have the rascasse shipped to us direct from Marseille," said Reg.

"Yes, oh yes, we did, but is the dish a soup, a broth, a brew or is it hotchpotch, as Thackeray says. Wouldn't you know the French would find a culinary use for the ugliest fish in the world. You'll come won't you?"

A short time later, three of us sat formally in the Needhams' dining room around a Victorian gate-leg table awaiting Halley's arrival, my wet sneakers buffing lion heads carved into table legs, a chandelier with rheostat tuning sparkling overhead, bouillabaisse and several bottles of wine easing conversation. Reg slumped in his chair, pulling with his left hand a leg of gray flannel bell bottoms hooked over the other, rolling wine in the glass with his right hand. Gladys knocked her wine glass over, laughed with the ease of the guiltless, leaned over the table toward me in a low-cut peasant dress, chattering about the Cleopatra link –

"Egyptian and African, even a Jewess seems reasonable to me, but to leap from these to Southern debutante – white chicken, you know, after those exotic desert birds. I'm flummoxed, but in a good way. How about you, Mr. Jones. What flummoxes you?"

Gladys' breasts rolled onto the table, warmed to a pink blush from the wine and food. I talked directly to her nipples. For the moment, I didn't miss Halley. She had gone to the studio and then must have stopped home to bathe in patchouli and to weight her neck and arms in massive silver and turquoise jewelry, a kind of armor plate that flashed like car bumpers on her black velour jump suit.

I heard myself speak, and thought I was making sense, but I had exercised the depth of my intellect and found it wallowing desperately in the shallows, uncovering Gladys' breasts.

"I'm disturbed by arson," I said, "I feel compelled to find the burner."

"Mr. Jones has a peculiar way of discernin', Gladys, and he will not be dissuaded. Somethin' of your tenacity, Reg," said Halley sliding open the French doors into the dining room, jewelry spangling beneath the chandelier. Halley can stage an entrance.

Reg smiled, teeth square as a horse, his first smile of the evening. Mostly he eyed Halley in pontifical silence.

"Well I think he's cute," said Gladys.

"Wilt thou now carry thy fire into the valleys? Fearest thou not the incendiary's doom?" I said.

"What's that?" Reg asked, for the first time piqued. "You are referring to the church burning?" Reg had suspicions otherwise as to my valleys reference.

"Yes, that's right. Both of them."

"Oh, I know. It's Zarathustra! Are you…somekindofanchorite…Mr. Jones? Thatwouldexplainalot, wouldn't it?" Gladys' breasts joggled happily.

Halley looked startled. Here was her dinner treat, me, unwrapping myself in ways she hadn't expected. She had hoped to be the demystifier but had to cede to a drunken Gladys.

"No, Mrs.…Dr. Needham, I keep a journal of aphorisms and I guess Nietzsche just worked into the moment somehow."

"Zarathustra…camedownfromthemountains…totelluslesserhumans…

something, didn't he? Doyouhaveamessage…todeliver…Mr. Jones?" said Gladys.

"Despite his earthy appearance, Mr. Jones is quite the fuckin' cosmopolitan, Gladys. A Harvard man, in fact. He thinks the clergy is settin' fire to our churches, and he would like me and Reg to help bring the man to…justice. Is this the right word, sugar?"

"Yes, something like that, but not the clergy exactly."

"Well, Ithinkhe'scute."

A third glass of wine, a spicy red, had begun to tangle my mind and tongue, at the same time Reg had Halley in his study promoting the acid rain show while raking loose hairs in back of Halley's ears with his fingers, at the same time Gladys was giving me a hickey in the kitchen while rubbing her thigh against my crotch, asking, "Sohowdoessupermanfuck, MrJones?" At that moment I couldn't have told you the color of her eyes. Now I can tell you each fold of her body.

Chapter Twelve

Travers gets laid • An angel delivers a warning • A groper returns a favor • Travers nearly laid again • Where's Mosley?

Gladys worked her hand down my jeans – "OmyGod," she said cradling the torus of my infatuation. "Baby, you'resoready." Gladys pulled the dress over her head. White panties gleamed, a bra of half-moons heaved in luminescence, as sincere as the lunette window above the kitchen door leaking porch light. I rubbed palms to warm them before touching Gladys. She seemed glassy, likely to shatter. I looked pathetically like an idolater praying. I surveyed the kitchen to ground myself in ordinary items, but saw instead a sink filled to the rim with clamshells, the fibrous tails of leeks, dirty dishes with a cuisinart poking above the mess, counter tops littered with fennel, bay leaves, parsley and saffron moiling in a spill of clam juice, olive oil and white wine – the scent of bay water at low tide in East Boston. Along the windowsill above the sink strolled cobalt blue figurines of Victorian ladies with parasols, gentlemen leaning on penang lawyers: Thackery's parade of life, Mosley's parade of life. I moved slowly toward Gladys, hesitated, touched the heat from her stomach in the damp hollow below ribs. Unashamedly idolatrous, I gathered and hefted those breasts. I had never been with a woman beyond the mishap in Halley's Saab, but seemed always to find myself in the presence of men and women screwing. Maybe that's why the pelvic thrust came naturally, mindlessly, while she still seemed to be thinking clearly.

"ComtothepantryMrJones. Reg'llnotseeusthere, thepoop!"

We shuffled together across the floor, four legs twined and backs heaving. Gladys stripped the two of us. Urgent pressures stirred the satyr, repulsed the man of culture Harvard had cultivated. Pump and release, pump and relinquish. Surrender to the little death as the French call it. But it was no small death to me. More potent than a seize because Dionysian with rapture, tearing away bonds of the ordinary, but tied to the moon's phases, and to the stars trapped within their planes on an astrolabe of winter sky. Pantry cupboards with lunettes carved through exploded color emanating from the greens and reds and golds of food packaging. I would be going to that place we go to in our death to await rebirth. I was ready, incarnadine behind the eyes and brazen with passion. I was the surge that lifts Venus surfing on her half shell, the big kahuna , the spume from the death throes of Uranus together with the scrubbed and debearded clams, scallops, cod, and deveined shrimp of a bouillabaisse. I had finally got the attentions of Venus. I was her Uranus, and I was glad to sacrifice any part of myself in her service.

Gods! She had her tongue in my ear.

I lunged at Gladys bruising myself on her hip – she pulling me closer to her center; and the moment I slid inside something broke in me, even before orgasm.

Her hands gripped my buttocks.

Call it the end of temerity, the walls of Ilium falling; call it a subversion of masculine hesitancy even as the throes of abandon had opened the door to the horrible truth of our vain and useless existence. What Silenus knew: better not to be born.

My hands gripped her buttocks.

Decorum gave way to the aggressions that lay dormant in me. I suckled and moaned, licked and bit. The daimonic had awakened – potent and directed and wise in its ministrations, oracular. I had not tapped the male desire to impregnate. I had, instead, discovered my own need to give birth, to another self. The Apollonian had perished; the Dionysian had become flesh. Consider that painting by Picasso of multiplex woman seeing many selves in a mirror. The faces of Eve, some playwright calls it. I had at that moment seen the faces of Adam. One last thrust through the bubble of the self intersecting another that becomes a new self. And if Lady Macbeth is any indication, or maybe better to think of Fiona, the drive to deliver some new thing from the depths of a primal need is too potent for a woman to handle, natural conjurer though she may be. It is she who best knows to access the pure life energy – like Fiona McDeed, my mother, naked and lithe and wriggling among the chalky creatures of the London Underground where she tallied my genes out from soldier Jones' salty secretions, like picking rice off the bottom of a pan. But it is the man that brings these monsters to life, these homunculi unchained, pits them against convention. I was, at that moment of release, myself and Gladys and my father become my mother. I had discovered the female impulse to create a new world and the man's place as animator, which maybe Gerrit knew; I had discovered that need through sex. Strange. Wonderful!

Zarathustra defines woman as a riddle whose only solution is pregnancy. The same can be said of man. Zara received advice from an old woman to bring a whip when courting. Misleading. That old woman knew that for her gender to keep the secret of female aggression, a man must fuck and run; a man must think of himself dominant though it is he that is subsumed and changed. I am such a wimp around women that my custom was to run before fucking. But with Gladys in the pantry, there was no thinking to be done. As I say, I was all thrust and nonsense. Until I reached orgasm. At that moment, Apollo returned. I fell to my knees on the cold linoleum, face pressed against the crenellated oak trim of the baseboards with Gladys earnest still in her ministrations, her hair a tangle of sepia in my fingers.

I removed hands from her hair disentangling emotions at the same time. Sadly, almost comically, Gladys moved above me like a boxer punching air after having already lost the fight. I felt the suffering my mother's star-crossed pregnancy had inflicted upon her, how she has looked every day into the blackness of twisted purpose from which I had been conceived and toward which I would journey, and how her fears have shaped me as much as Gerrit's closeting, how the combination of the two had kept me celibate, uninitiated, unaware. I was reminded too of Halley's vomit in the Saab, that moment I realized her paroxysms were different from my own. I dropped hands to my sides, stepped back, found my shirt and zipped my jeans. I was overwhelmed. Nylon underthings and a peasant dress strewn on the parquet floor in the kitchen depressed me. I had come out from a trance. To be sure, sex is another kind of "seize." But Gladys still participated in the moment – she followed me out from the pantry, eyes moist, body luscious and pulsating, exposed and proud, arms reaching, too drunk to know she was being rejected. I asked, in a cold, even voice for a ride home.

Gladys went petulant despite her higher learning. She pushed me away and sobered instantly when offered a conciliatory hug. By the time I looked back, she was dressed and nonplused as rock, smoothing with her hands the wrinkles of her peasant dress in that graceful way women do. We had become too intimate too soon. We had strained and torn what might have become friendship. We were secretly in mourning. When the two of us walked into the parlor to join Halley and Reg, Halley was aware something had gone down between Gladys and me. Reg was oblivious, self-content, ensconced now in a maroon turtleneck and a salmon-colored smoking jacket.

They lounged upon an over-stuffed loveseat, pale blue with beaming yellow sunflowers. Logs burned in the fireplace. Reg poking the embers, tapping his foot in tempo with the Kingston Trio. Gladys and I kept to opposite walls the way magnets of the same pole repel. Halley looked hard at us both. Reg focused on the wall bedside me where he had hung plaques of academic achievement in Latin calligraphy. He showed concern. I had brushed against them with my shoulder. Gladys chirped absurdly for ten minutes – the old fogies of folk music that Bob Dylan refused to acknowledge, how sunflowers go to seed so beautifully. Gladys punctuated her monologue with my request for a ride home. Halley said she would.

Halley squeezed the steering wheel of her Saab. Disgust at inadequate windshield defrost erupted in curses. But there were no accidents. An uneasy silence assailed us once the cussing stopped. She had no patience. I had too much, though exasperation over stalled-out purpose had whittled me closer to raw nerve. I was expected to excuse Halley's bad driving the way Nick had Jordan Baker until Daisy Buchanan demonstrated the wealthy and privileged drive fast while the rest better get out of the way.

We skidded in slush around corners, jumped a curb cutting a diagonal through gas pumps at the North Street Deli to avoid a red light, slid into the curb outside my apartment. The Saab's engine burbled from its exhaust. Halley squeezed my thigh with finger tips like checking a melon for ripeness. She said, "Look, Mr. Jones, ladies can be so delicately vicious. Viprous my daddy says. Your innocence is charmin' to a lady, even seductive, but take my word, sugar, Gladys does *not* want you. She wants you to want *her*. That way she can feel more secure in Reg wantin' her – God, what a thought. Reg is a creep of comic proportion, isn't he? Still, he is her man. She wants to be desirable without gettin' all mussy extramarital. Know what I mean, darlin'? So if I were you, I would find another piece of ass to get you through the winter. Understand? Now, how about I come upstairs and we review more thoroughly the evidence you have of arson."

I wondered if Halley wanted to make herself more desirable for Hambone's sake. My breathing, as Halley squeezed me thigh to knee, had entirely sabotaged the car's defrost system. Halley cursed its inadequacies more violently than before, reached across my lap, the scent of honey and musk, sliding in the watery velour of her jumpsuit on leather seats. She turned her head up to face me, blonde hair spilling into my lap, said "Déjà vu, darlin'? Not quite," then flung open the passenger door. There was promise in her voice. Gladys had been seasoning in the kitchen. Halley invited me to table. But I was not so jejune to know self-interest had prevented her being repelled by the murky undercurrents of my obscure behavior. She thought she still might catch a priest confessing in the confessional with a lit match in his hand. She thought I would lead her there.

She took a seat at the card table. I sat on the bed. Halley drew together elbows and legs, fearful of contamination. Cat looked down from the half wall that separated kitchen module from the bedroom/living room/ everything-and-all-of-a-purpose module (the studio, a single room, is shaped like an L). She accepted a bottle of Molson. I lay on the table the partially burned page foretelling the recent church burn, flattening it with the palm of my hand.

"Where did you get this again?"

"From the back alley at Nectar's."

"When exactly?"

"Two nights ago. I sat at the bar to work through aphorisms in my *Journal of Life Assembly*. I could show you if you'd like."

"Perhaps another time."

"Louis ignores me. He extorts no cover whatsoever, thanks probably to you. I made the mistake of sitting next to the guy whose teeth I busted. I was nervous. He looked awful. But he said he was in the wrong. He apologized. The bartender brought us a round of beers to keep us friendly, the management's idea, not his, and the toothless one kept them coming, a parcel of beers, after which I had to puke. There was nothing in my stomach but cold toast and beer. It didn't look good coming up. He helped me to the alley, then beat hell out of me while I puked. He hit me more than where it shows, because I'm sore in a whole lot of places, some I won't mention."

"That would be blue balls, sugar. You don't know the syndrome? It is a man's way of reactin' to a sexy tease. Blame Gladys. I can see you have been teased. You would surely tell me if more than a good teasin' has been provided, wouldn't you, darlin'? Now this man that left the warnin' on our second burned church ..."

"Yes, the man...but why blue?"

"The second burned church, Mr. Jones, you were sayin', the man that ..."

"All right, shit, the man. As I said, I was retching, lying on my side in that alley, sick and in pain. I zenned myself numb off the frozen puddle inches from my good eye that had trapped a rainbow of oil. The air went static like a beating of hovered wings. I thought Michael Landon had come down as an angel. Like I say, I've been watching a lot of TV lately at Nectar's. Reruns mostly, and sometimes, the eleven o'clock news, because that's when you..."

"Yes, go on… the man."

"Well, a grimy, grizzled beard poked in my face and said, "Shouldn't burn no church with hate in your heart.' He rifled my pockets. I thought I was getting robbed. He wore an army jacket with campaign patches. I thought for a moment I had been 'seized.' I thought my guardian angel had returned. But the world came back too quick for a seize. Awful taste in my mouth: my tongue had wormed into decayed flesh, like I was dying by degrees. Turns out I lost a tooth. You don't want to taste anything like that. But it's in the back. It doesn't really show…"

"Yes, and the man."

"Well, I reached into my pocket for a cigarette and pulled out the page you have here. Funny thing. Your friend deBoner wasn't there to help this time. His deus ex machina is too selective to suit me, or maybe he couldn't find a chariot that day, or maybe he doesn't give a shit unless there's a good fuck as payback."

"Might be it was hotter in the kitchen, sugar. And please mend your language."

"Another thing…you been watching the papers lately?"

"Who reads the papers anymore, darlin'?"

"Sure, I guess, but about the Mosley urn."

"Yes?"

"It's not been found. Dozens of parishioners sifting ruins with shovels and rakes, they won't let the bulldozers in, for two months now, and no urn."

"What urn?"

"Mosley, the guy that designed the church."

"So it melted like everythin' else in that heat."

"No. It's made of stone. There's something wrong here."

"I agree. Listen, Mr. Jones, you and I might need help locatin' the bearded prophet that presented you this page. Might he be a defrocked priest, a man of the cloth that's got lost in the tangles of his mind? Don't burn with hate in your heart, he said? Is he the burner do you think? They say hate and love are twins."

"Who is they?"

"I don't know. Whoever says these things. It would be a twisted kind of love that compels him to burn. Is there any other kind I wonder? Could you, do you think, provide a better description, sugar? I mean there is so much fuckin' pony tail and beard lice in Vermont. Every one of those post office photos of the most wanted looks the same. You ever notice that? Why a person might pick you out, Mr. Jones, as one of those desired of authorities. Uncle Sam's poster boy. The gallery of the woebegone, or is it the misbegotten? I am fuck-me-all sick to death of Vermont. It is a certainty this place will never move past the 70's. There is still disco here. Did you know that? God damned disco! Anyway, we need help scarin' up your suspect. I would like you, darlin', to work with me to find answers to these church burns. I know you have a father to sort out. You are not alone in that – hell, we may be consanguine in that, but with my resources I can get you close to the burner. That's what you want isn't it? Let us work together, Mr. Jones. Reg will help too. He can do his chemical whatevers as we find evidence. Agreed? I need to make a phone call. I know a man that might get us near the clergy. Oh, shit! Here I go again. Can't be helped."

When the phone rang, Sergeant Vasari said, "Yuh," and the voice at the other end said, "Saint Vasari?" and Vasari said, "Sure, I mean no… who's asking?"

"It is Halley Gay, Sergeant."

"Is this the Gay that's been making news on my TV? The one that don't pay her parking meter?"

"I guess you could see me both ways, yes."

"What commerce might I have with ah pretty thing scofflaw like you that's been making herself famous the easy way."

"Well, Sergeant, I am doin' serious journalism of late. And commerce is a funny word to use to a lady, but since you ask, let me say that certain men of the cloth have come under suspicion in these church burns. And, of course, should these burns prove to be arson, we must consider the possibility that that poor man roasted in the window well was a victim of murder. And it is *NOT* so damned easy, sugar, to get known around here."

"Murder? Who are you ta say murder when everyone else says bad wiring?"

"Yes, Sergeant, I agree, of course…*shit, I can't do this*," Halley said off line, covering the transmitter; she looked to me for an answer, but I appeared as stupid as I felt…"Oh, shit, okay, look, Vasari, I am presently with a man that has been trackin' the arsonist and knows where he will burn again."

"No, I don't really."

"Quiet."

"They was set was they?"

"Yes, I believe so."

"Where do I find this man? Or is it 'we' already have? We are 'we' ain't we? This the gist ah this phone call, ta establish 'we'?'"

"That's it, yes, Sergeant. You see, we are several, and I would like you to join our little party, but only you. We feel we are closin' on the arsonist."

"Why take me along if you and your 'we' got it all worked out?"

"You will lend authority to our investigation, Sergeant. To be honest, we may need your expertise. This is an exclusive for me, Sergeant. And a potential career advance for us both."

"I wondered when you'd get around ta poking me for soft places."

"Listen, Sergeant, I am not about to poke the least part of your… anything. I am prepared, however, to bring you to this man that knows more than any detective you may have put on the case, if you are conductin' a case, that is."

Vasri said, "Well, I don't know." He scratched the back of his neck where boils troubled him. He went silent. Halley heard his breathing. She thought of Reginald's nasal flirtations on the phone, but knew that Vasari, despite his rotund glacial speed, was subtle and dangerous unlike Reg. No sergeant of police would have stayed a sergeant so long, passed over for career advance, without having a history of doing things his own way, a certain roguishness which she counted on and knew to be wary of.

"All right, lady, bring on your boy. We'll have ah talk. But I can't say how long I'll let this go bafore I got ta make a report."

"Fair enough. Hey, Vasari, would you know the carpet bag credo?"

"What's that you say?"

"It goes like this – 'Buy 'em out, or burn 'em out, rape the land and Maryann. Then do 'em again the next town down.' Course what them Yanks don't know is the name Maryann we give to our cows. Hope you are smarter than that, Sergeant."

Halley slammed down the phone.

"Your bathroom, sugar. Which of these corners hides it?"

"On the way to the door, but you don't have to leave yet. I wasn't implying..."

"I know."

I heard the shower. Halley was in there a long time. I brewed coffee, put Bob Dylan on the phonograph, scratched it all to hell – my hands were shaking. Cat watched the record rotate, a nervous tick of his tail sweeping crumbs off the card table. I sat down to peer out the window at my neighbor wintering in his attic apartment the other side of the electric lines that crossed the street attached to our two houses. During my vacant moments, when not working on my *Journal of Life Assembly*, I voyeured shamelessly. My neighbor seemed always to be playing either his guitar or his girlfriend, who had just pulled into the driveway in her faded blue VW that swayed on axles in the aftershock of sudden braking. The girl was an exotic Jewess, peasant stock in patched jeans and a flannel-lined jean jacket, a squat though capable body, and wild black hair, black eyes, a heart-shaped face with a peculiar half smile, altogether a geometry of circles and triangles that moved on her frame like water in a glass. I envied the boyfriend. Seduction by a married woman didn't settle much of anything for me. I was still jazzed though, and anxious to give rein to these other selves emerging.

Halley came out from the bathroom naked, said, "May I redirect your attentions, Mr. Jones?" Her eyes watched mine wander so that I felt sneaky and cheap noticing the sway of her breasts as she toweled her hair, and beads of water skimming the wax of her skin, gliding down shoulders, the triangle of her thighs, and dropping to the carpet where the towel fell.

"We have some unfinished business, Mr. Jones. I hope you will not disappoint a lady that has been waitin'."

I ripped off my clothes and trembled standing beside her. Despite what had happened before with Gladys, I had no idea what to do next. Halley took my hand, led me to the edge of the bed where I sat and stared as she lay on her back. I raised one hand and ran it over the mounds and valleys without touching skin, as if some force prevented me. What I did next flabbergasted the both of us – the same motion but with my nose, lingering and snuffling and blowing lightly to stir the downy short hairs; then with my tongue, gently touching skin, leaving a glistening trail in spirals up the mounds and in acute angles at the intersection of her thighs. Halley's eyes closed and she sighed. I had no idea what the sighs meant, but I was too far gone to care. I began lightly to touch, moved nipples with finger tips, traced the lips of her sex, the nodes of her ear lobes, the lips of her mouth.

When she launched into her mule-bray laugh, I raised off the bed, covered my erection, grabbed my jeans and climbed into them. I was about to run out of the apartment when Halley said, "Look, darlin', I'm sorry" – she struggled to catch her breath, pulled the sheet around her – "but I am not used to havin' a man get so close, not since, well, not since a most unfortunate lover that is now departed. I am better at the mindless fuck. You know?"

I wanted to tell her that yes, for once, I did know. I was not now so like Parsifal. But I could see that she was like Kundry, cursed because she had laughed at suicide. She could no longer cry, just laugh. She would find herself subservient to the castrato Klingsor. Her job will be to seduce. I wanted to tell her that I had found the mindless fuck but wanted something else. I asked questions Halley felt uncomfortable answering. She shook her head and said finally, "After my first lover died, I came to feel as if the wind would blow through me, darlin', like I was an empty vessel. It took years to feel solid again. What you just did to me has begun to stir the wind, sugar. I just can't have that." Halley asked for her clothes which I gathered from the bathroom floor. She dressed with her back to me, turned briefly to give an enigmatic smile and walked out. I threw the pillow at Cat and fell onto a chair at the card table with my head in my hands.

"Balls!" I shouted at her through the door. "Blue balls!" I shouted as she went down the stairs. Halley opened the folded sheet of paper that had been ripped out from *Walk Around Burlington*. Not the one left on the card table in my apartment, but the new one she found outside my door on the way out. It featured St. Johns Church that dominates the landscape of the Old North End. "Mr. Jones, she said out in the street, "son of a bitch but you may have the nose after all."

Chapter Thirteen

Travers presents a new face • Reginald Needham picks a fight • Meditations on church arson • The posse takes action • Murder in a bivouac of homeless • Stars that fall upon the ice.

My first love making: it should have been a grotto of white limestone, bodies glistening, muscle kneading muscle in the soft indents and the dry and wet places, Grecian nudes embracing in soft fern, orange newts smiling from the loam. Reality had dictated tangled limbs in a kitchen pantry, and then very nearly again in a ganglia of dendritic offal. Halley must have felt she was basking in a landfill. I looked around me with a new set of eyes. Buried rot off pizza crust Cat had carried away and rejected somewhere in the pile assailed me, as did a cloud of fruit flies lifting off the depressions of his stalking feet. And there was a musty, pungent, gagging odor of mildew from the column of books that moldered in paper bags. If Halley has allergies, she might have collapsed a lung here.

I said a kind word to Cat, which surprised us both, washed algae off dishes in the sink, kicked the most offensive debris into the hallway, showered away Gladys, inspected testicles for blue, found none, and shaved my beard. Even with nicks my face emerged wholesome, youthful, alert. The rest of me was so spare of follicle as to be adolescent, lank, underfed and abused but athletic in proportion, a quick, healing flesh. The vacant tooth from trouble in the alley left a hole too far back in the jaw to notice. The beard came off for Halley, to negate the muskrat trapper association Halley had made that came too near my totem soul. I thought I might be in love. I wanted to be. I had begun to remake myself, at least cosmetically, to please Halley. Her body, the smell and taste of her, even that strange laugh turned me on. Not like Gladys whom I felt an overwhelming urge to ravage. When I thought of Halley, I felt homicidal toward deBoner. What a name. The French deli-man that debones meat, de-boner, debonair he is not, but Halley seemed to prefer blood flowing to the loins rather than to the brain. I wasn't sure what to do about that. My brain was my largest, most impressive organ. But lately it was getting in the way.

When Reginald Needham knocked at my door, I expected another fist in the eye. But Reg was put off by the clean-shaved face that answered. Reg looked paunchy and under-slept. He removed a tweed pork-pie hat, rubbed his head confusedly, gray wisps of hair dancing in the static of dry heat, errant thatch deserting a partial baldness, a comical image had he not appeared so seriously forlorn. He squinted, too vain or forgetful to wear glasses. A camel's hair coat, unbuttoned, hung in folds to the ground. Flannel pajamas and slippers encased in rubbers defined his character dowdy and forgetful – but impressed with itself. Reg must be twenty years older than Gladys. I suspected the usual Pygmalion story: ingénue undergrad marrying all-knowing urbanity. Maybe sexual attraction does come from the brain, despite the circumstance of Venus' birth. There is Athena who sprang new born from the head of Zeus. But I wouldn't describe her as sexy. What other enticement but brain and status could there be for Gladys to love Reginald? I decided that between me and Hambone deBoner, I had the better chance, ultimately, with Gladys. Great, just great.

When Reg placed me as his erstwhile dinner guest he said, "Mr. Jones? Is this you?" I nodded, said "Dr. Needham, hi." He stepped through the doorway commanding, "Be seated. I have a subject of some weight to impart."

I sat on the bed that an hour earlier had supported the weight of mutual intimates, the pillow icy-wet from her hair. Reg stood above me. He had trained an inept body and sallow complexion and quirky sartorial demeanor to render, somehow, a flattering likeness of "professor/ship." I was impressed how adeptly he had fleshed out the semantics of his role, and spooked by how it intersected my own – to profess *ship*, which is from the Latin *navis*, which becomes *nave* (the long hall of a church) from whence I have mis-navigated a path between church burnings and university. By contrast, this would be a man with clear direction that had attracted Gladys. Maybe he had launched into her dorm room in the same manner and with dire purpose (the slightest hint of plagiarism, perhaps, in one of Ms. Sycophant's papers, or a footnote gone astray) and had transformed to juvenilia through his critical assessment the cutesy posters of shapely Mark Spitz, the Disney hair brushes, her collection of Nauga creatures, her legwarmers over tight jeans and Frye boots. Maybe Gladys had surrendered horned-rimmed for stylish granny glasses and Mark Spitz reveries for blow jobs in the office which had evolved to big words in high company over Oolong tea and *House & Garden* parties – her new university hill role. I had to admit the man has force of character.

"Did you know, Mr. Jones, that when two naked bodies unite they become intimately irradiated by potassium-40 in the exchange? This is universal truth. And did you know that most people recognize that Gladys and I exhibit the aforementioned glow of habitual partnering? We are a couple."

This was cerebral sparring. Familiar territory for ivory tower lifers such as Reginald Needham and myself.

"Yes, I see that now," I said. "I have to confess to having been attracted by the glow. But honestly, I thought she was flushed from the wine. I know I was. But if inclined to go scientific, I would have thought she had eaten a bag of Brazil nuts grown from high gamma-ray soil. You can practically license and sell energy off the nuclear reactor churning in your guts from that stuff. I've seen the lab experiments. But seriously, about Gladys, the other Doctor Needham…listen, I'm sorry. We had too much to drink."

"No excuse for a man that thinks."

"Yes. No. I mean I agree. I've come to see that Gladys used me as a proxy. She's really looking for more attention from you. She wants to know you better through teasing you with me. Do you see? It's working isn't it?"

"Well, yes, that may be. (Needham unclenched his right hand, pushed it deep into his coat pocket.) I have been remote lately, but I don't know why I am sharing this with you. And I must say that I find your evidence of arson simply laughable."

"The Sanka can?"

"Paraffin – come on, Mr. Jones."

"I told Halley that was no evidence of arson. The guy in the window well was just burning candles to stay warm, maybe doing his small part to light the darkness."

"Callous."

"Sorry, don't mean to be. I'm serious about this, I mean about the arson."

"Well, what do you have as evidence beyond the Sanka can?"

At this point I told Reg about the page from *Walk Around Burlington* lodged by an alley denizen in my coat pocket, and all I could think to explain of the incendiary methods I felt the arsonist was using, and more –

"... and you see, there is more to it than burning for kicks. There could be personal grievance as motive or a kind of catharsis going on, if our burner is an iconoclast. I know for fact that in every church burn there is passion of some kind. My father was an arsonist, and I have made a study of arson to understand him, as best I can. I thought he was an iconoclast, but now I'm not so sure. And what goes beyond your science, Doctor Needham – 'there are more things in heaven and earth dreamt of in your philosophy,' and all that – is that I communicate with my father through my epilepsy, sometimes, and I mean, these are burns my father does not approve of – I've come to believe this – and that's strange, so I know there is something wrong here. Something beyond the usual case of ecclesiastical arson."

"Yes, Halley told me about the voices you hear."

"William Butler Yeats heard voices, you know. It's these voices that put him in the anthologies."

"Gyres within gyres, the center cannot hold, a terrible beauty is born, and so on."

"Right. Have you studied Yeats?"

"No, Gladys, before I compelled her to adopt a more useful field of study, but I like the fact that Yeats relied on mathematics to anchor his vision."

"Well, look, putting aside the problem of my father's ghostly visits, the aesthetics of the burn are overwhelming. You must see that. Or maybe the art of it can only really be appreciated by another burner, or by someone that studies such things. Look, it's the slow burn that's inspiring: flames trek the walls, hedge and spare the center so that the steeple acts as a kind of wick, draws heat and gasses up in a vortex, with the nave untouched and cold by comparison so that it contains the destructive power until a door is opened, or a window busted, or a blanket of cold water sprayed from a fire hose that changes the balance of heat and cold, and then KABOOM! Up like a molotov cocktail. It's brilliant. It's beautiful! I wish I had been around to see the Congregational Church go up."

"Well, Mr. Jones, this is strange and fascinating, and I must say that I appreciate your good mind, though you lose me with this ghost of Hamlet business. Halley has told me about your concerns for the Mosley urn and your idea that our Sanka can may have belonged to a murdered man. I'm not much of a detective except in chemical analysis. But I am willing to go some distance in this thing since Halley feels so strongly there's something to it. But let us agree to make this simply business, nothing personal. You will not be seeing Gladys again in the fleshly way. Are we agreed?"

"Sure. Of course."

Shortly after Reg left me with a firm hand shake and puddles of melted snow on my floor, a police cruiser with Sergeant Vasari and Halley and Gladys braked outside the apartment. Halley ascended the stairs in a new pair of Timberland boots, another present from Mother, also too small, knocked on my door, leaned down to loosen the ties of her boots and said from between her legs with her butt in the air facing me, "Mama must think foot bindin' is the doorway to heaven."

"What?"

"O, shit, whose face is this? You been pissin' in my Salada, sugar? Hidin' your good looks? Let me see." Halley turned my face side to side with an index finger. "There may be some character to your character. This is a handsome face, Mr. Jones. Why the change?"

"Something you said earlier about beards in Vermont. I don't want to be mistaken for a most wanted poster, unless of course *you* want me."

She had gone back to her shoes. I leaned forward to embrace her from behind. She crabbed away while tying the laces.

"Not much chance of that, darlin'," she said having risen to her full height and placed a hand against my chest. "Get your coat. We're a posse — you, me, the big fella in blue and Gladys. This is so excitin'! It is not a fit night for beastly man so wear your woollies. Vasari has got an idea where to look for your alley man, and Gladys said she had to get away from Reg. She has concocted a ginseng tea to calm herself. She will behave. You will be wise to do likewise, sugar."

I slid onto the vinyl front seat of the cruiser which smelled of dried blood, vomit and teary confessions. Gladys put on glasses to examine me, clucked her tongue critically then stuck it out. Vasari sized my profile like doing a mug shot then pulled slowly into the streets wet with salty snow heading west toward the lake, said, "I heard from Miss Gay here that you be chasing down the clergy. That right?"

"Well, in a way, sort of. I might have misled Halley somewhat, Sergeant…Vasari, is that right?" Halley nodded. "The burner may not be, specifically, a man of the cloth. I just mean that he has the intense passion of a holy man, or at least he should, though there's something perverse about these fires. I mean more than usual for this kind of thing."

"I'm glad ta hear you have excused the clergy, son. I know intimately some large number in this town and they're mostly good folk. Sometimes more sexy than they ought ta be. Sometimes inclined ta shed their vows for ah tumbler ah Jack Daniels and ah tumble batween the sheets."

"That's good, Sergeant," said Halley.

"What's good?"

"Nothin'. Go on."

"Like I say, I can't see none ah them priests burning down the house ah God."

"Well, there is pyrolagnia," I said.

"Ah course. I should ah thought ah that. You trying ta grow ah brain right here in front ah me, mister man? Cause if you are, I am the most unlikeliest one ta be impressed."

"Oh, Christ, Vasari, be civil," said Halley.

"No, no," said Gladys, " I know what the Sergeant means."

"You do?" said Vasari.

"Yes, of course. You want Mr. Jones to define terms. Justifiable. Oh, yes. I think so."

"Now here's ah well-growed brain. Thank you, Miss..."

"Mrs. Reginald Needham. No. Call me Gladys."

"Your definition, sugar?" Halley said to me.

"Right, okay then. Pyrolagnia. It's a pathological condition where an arsonist derives sexual stimulation from setting things on fire. He gets off on it."

"That can't be no priest...why, ta them sex is sex. I know. I have caught them at it. But there's none ah this perverty stuff."

"Well, yeah, I'm sure you're right. But it could be a secular burner with similar stimulation needs."

"Shit!" said Halley. "That would just shoot my story all to hell and back. Network news won't get sweated over some pervert arsonist masturbatin' while churches burn. The whole god damn world seems to be shittin' on me today! Maybe we should just leave this to the police – oh, not that you're not police, Sergeant. But wankin' a dick while lightin' a wick...O, damn, that's good! Well…there won't be enough coverage to make this manhunt much worth my while."

"Don't be selfish, Halley. We can treat the arsonist," said Gladys, "alter his response to stimuli, teach him mathuna for instance, maybe save a church or two."

"For goodness sakes. Here's another brain growing right in front ah me. Won't be enough room in this cruiser with all this new brain growing."

"Sorry, Sergeant. Mathuna. That's intercourse with meditation; sex without stimulation, no orgasm."

"There's ah room full ah fun," said Vasari. Gladys laughed out loud. Vasari looked at her in the rear-view mirror, said, "Them priests might just as well keep ta the vows, don't you think?"

"Well, I don't know, Sergeant. What do you think, Mr. Jones?"

My mouth opened. No words available. I wondered if Gladys had known my college roommate.

"Okay, let's tangle eyebrows," said Gladys leaning forward in her seat, moving hands together like hamsters on a wheel. "Let's talk Pali Kamma."

"Here we go again," said Vasari.

"Mr. Jones is chasing a recurrent problem; the moral energy of the arsonist's deeds is indeed overwhelming. Wouldn't you say? It would appear that way to a Hindu, certainly. Your burner is working his way through karmic issues. An iconoclast is a life form that's been around for a kalpa of time, something like an eon. That's approximately the amount of time it takes for an angel to wear down a cube of iron a hundred miles thick by brushing the top with her wings once every hundred years or so. Someone must come back in another life as fungus, and I'd say an iconoclast is about that low. Anyone that burns a church is fungus."

"Travers' own father is a burner of churches, dear, or so Travers has confided," said Halley.

"Well, that's a shame, because he's fungus. No offense, Mr. Jones."

"How did we get fungus into this?" said Vasari.

"I'm talking about Hindu philosophy."

"You're giving ah lecture," said Vasari.

"Occupational hazard. Now, the problem is Mr. Jones sees our iconoclast a kind of Zarathustra, don't you, Mr. Jones, a holy man come down from the mountains to show us a new way to live. So Mr. Jones is torn both ways – criminalize and incarcerate the burner, or know him better, venerate and maybe emulate him. And to further complicate the issue, Mr. Jones' own father is, or was, a burner of churches. Right, Halley? This is going to be a remarkable study in transference."

"Sure, whatever you say, but will someone please tell me…do we want ta catch the son-of-a-gun or not?" said Vasari.

All were silent. Then Halley said, "Of course we do. Why not? Gladys has brought her ginseng tea. I'd hate like hell to ruin the party."

The cruiser had turned onto Battery Street with Halley's last pronouncement, into a biting wind twisting off the lake from New York's Adirondack range, within range of the power plant that cyclopsed the night with its tower flashing red. The sky was clear, stars frozen in their path. I restrained my instinct to interpret messages from the stars. Vasari parked alongside a hardware store in the Old North End's Battery Park district. A redoubt of castellated native granite wall defined the edge of promontory, a half circle with cannon pointed across the lake since the War of 1812. Bundles of canvas and plastic wedged into the lee side of the wall snapped in the wind. Vasari left the engine running, heat singeing carpet, told us three to "stay put for ah time" while he leaned and tramped into wind toward those bundles by the wall. Gladys dispensed paper cups of Oolong tea laced with something bitter and strong. I drank the potion on trust and to be social. Vasari hunkered closer to the ground the farther he walked, pulled at the brim of his cap, adjusted earmuffs, yanked off gloves and unhooked a billy club upon reaching the first bundle. I saw Vasari's foot prod, hand on billy club, and was surprised to see plastic fly off into the wind and a bearded man sit upright like come awake in his coffin, arms flailing and debris blowing around. Vasari later told me these were crumpled pages of newspapers, insulation against the cold, a custom of indigent wintering, another reason some thought, himself included, that George Eakins had by mistake set that fire in the window well of the first burned church. Vasari grabbed debris, threw it into the face of the vagrant shouting at him. When the billy club came out the man calmed. Vasari kneeled beside the vagrant, talked at length, helped the man re-secure his plastic tent and moved to the next prone bundle.

Five times more this scene repeated. But the sixth time, Vasari uncovered the man himself then leaned to converse in whisper, as the vagrant failed to stir, and then ran circles through snow collecting debris blown off the uncovered man lying stone-still. After five or ten minutes of this, Vasari waved to the cruiser, asking for help. The two girls were deep into their ginseng. I scooted out the door.

Wind pulled at my breath. The snow had crusted with powder beneath. I moon walked breaking epidermal crust while gathering debris that had blown near the cruiser. Vasari shouted something lengthy, but wind stole his words. I heard "sons-of-b's" and "damn knees," something about banshee winds and witches' teats. I crumpled and shoved debris into my parka, thinking evidence, stopped, pulled out and smoothed a leaf or two. Some of these were pages from *Walk Around Burlington.* I crunched over to Vasari who said, "Yuh, I know. Must be your man from the alley. He ain't going ta tell us much." I leaned over the man, dread squeezing my heart. I saw eyes open, mouth open, insulation stuffed inside the mouth. Even in cold the stench of human oils excreted and soaked into layers of unwashed clothes gagged me. I kneeled surveying the dead man's profile, no bumps in the nose, ripped at his collar to expose a throat crusted with dirt, no jewelry, started to rip off his gloves before Vasari realized.

"Jones, what kind ah investigation you doing? You are tampering evidence, don't ya know. Get your hands off that man!"

I had forgotten myself, got lost in the possibility that this shaggy dead man could be my father. But no dromedary bump in the nose (my mother was gracefully aquiline), no dog tags or disease-warning jewelry, and the final examination had been called off by Vasari. I went giddy with embarrassment, stuttered an apology like I had pebbles in my mouth, walked to the cannon nearest the dead man, leaned and looked out onto the lake where the stars had seemed to fall. White lights sparked in clusters expanding into blackness below me on the frozen lake like the sky had dropped its load from the firmament. Maybe this one inconsequential dead soul having soared into the heavens had overloaded and snapped the underpinnings, dropped constellations to earth. I liked that idea. For the sake of the anonymous dead. I had already seen Venus step naked out from my bathroom. Aries would certainly be deBoner, but did that make me Hephaestus? No, that would be Reg. Were Reg and Halley having a thing? Was everyone but me screwing that woman?

I heard somewhere on the ice an engine turn over, saw headlights ignite and recognized the soft light from kerosene lamps of fishing shanties on skids. An entire village of shanties with 4x4's parked alongside materialized as I squinted into wind. The village impulse was also here among these homeless that had come together in makeshift tents, and I knew that even my concept of "soul" was one in which the departed life source lifts off the flesh to join a chorus of the enlightened, a community of the released. Zarathustra had said that the future and the past come together in the soul. Something in this dead-man wastrel with the reedy voice that still sings in my ear —"shouldn't burn no church with hate in your heart" – had plumbed my fear of future events, had recognized the sins of the father that I was increasingly inclined to attribute to my own psyche.

The warning the dead man gave of the next church fire was a care, a hope and a direction. Maybe this man *was* my father. Maybe the autopsy would verify. It was still a possibility. Maybe he *was* burning churches, couldn't help himself, and warning me away from the same fate. I looked to the stars on the ice as a more humble pattern of constellations. From Zarathustra I spoke what I thought was a suitable epitaph: "With the storm called spirit did I blow over thy surging sea; all clouds did I blow away from it; I strangled even the strangler called s_n." I said this in honor of the deceased, whether my father or not, blowing a cheek full of air from lungs that had breathed the dead man's ripeness. I blew him off into the air which never did scud west over the frozen lake but lifted directly off towards the East Coast, towards Boston.

"Hey, what you doing?" Vasari wanted to know. He had begun to extract material from the pockets of the dead man – fast-food condiments and toilet paper and a broken-toothed comb and a tooth brush with splayed bristles and a load of coin slugs and then a letter in French that Vasari could not make sense of but put in his own pocket for perusal at a later time.

I didn't answer Vasari except to look him in the eye for the first time, the long, steady look of a crime victim – a silent surrendering up to invisible forces, a resignation to what is inevitable that Vasari couldn't associate with the radical politics of my generation that had tagged him "pig" and blamed him for everything from the shootings at Kent State to James Earl Ray. Vasari recognized the hurt that kept me a loner, had seen it many times, usually among petty thieves and apprentice confidence men that deem themselves victims, but he saw too that I had little self-pity and a kind of divine afflatus that had been driving me relentlessly into the unknown. Vasari was starting to think he might decide to help me out.

"Hey, kid. I found something here that might could answer ah question or two. Let's get us out from the cold. My wife makes ah week-long stew with enough fat ta insulate your winter. You could maybe use some stew and some talk. We'll fortify and then get on with this church-burn thing tomorrow day first thing. That good for you?"

The stew sounded fine, though I wasn't well-enough practiced in normal family relations to feel like I would have much to offer when we got to chatting-the-fat.

Chapter Fourteen

Vasari's domestic side • The Brothers Quebecois and confessions of a dead indigent • Sexy Salome • Blue balls • Heraldry, eunuchs, a nervous Bishop, and Janis Joplin at the Bucket of Blood • Basic Latin for church arson.

Vasari's house is inconveniently narrow, a ranch of wide asbestos siding and faux brick street side midway to the eaves. He had resettled clear of the Old North End when married to restart a life free of memory encumbrances with a bride farm-fresh. He had married late a Westford dairymaid met on the Ferris wheel at the Tunbridge Fair. There remained but one seat, each was unaccompanied, the man at the gear box was losing patience – "Will there be but one or two? Make up your minds." There had been two ever since.

The house, nestled with twenty or thirty of the same, each on quarter-acre plots to mow and garden, was selected by his bride. Each with a single plate glass window framed by evergreens ten years leaning on gutters, boughs now snow laden. Only the faux brick are various – some mustard yellow, some a checkerboard of black and red, some all red. Sergeant Vasari and I had cruised the bus route toward where my truck convalesced, passed a string of chain motels and gas stations and Tyrol ski apparel labeled "haus," ending near enough airport parking to hear hydraulics off the barrier gate. Vasari drove five miles per under the limit, wedged his down-street vision between washer blades cleaving falling snow. He breathed heavily, spoke only when turned into the driveway, synching gears up and back from R to D on the steering column, packing the new snow. Varsri said, head thrust out the window monitoring backward progress in the red glow of his tail lights: "Tract housing, these here, all come down the railroad in halves ready-made in St. Johnsbury. Assembled together complete right here, so them airplanes can have ah target. You notice the red arrow painted on the roof?" He winked at me, stepped out from the cruiser, groaned as weight shifted to his knees. I told him I had grown up near an airport. We entered the kitchen from a breezeway filled with split firewood. "Sure enough?" he said. His good nature had awakened my communal heart. Vasari had said my brain was growing, but I knew it was my heart.

I rhapsodized for a moment the virtues of airplane traffic that had crowded the horizon of my urban childhood — aluminum arrows in the sky like directions of fate gathering beyond the windows of my hotel room. Vassari nodded as though he understood while groaning off his winter boots. When he opened the breezeway his wife hollered from the hallway: "That you Nicky? It's cold here. Toss a log on would you?" We could see her down the hall. Her girth filled the space. She skidded toward the kitchen in moccasins, bumping elbows on walls, encased in a pink robe. "Oh, company," she said tying off the robe. I had a vicious thought of the two of them, round and solid and naked, bouncing off these narrow rooms propelled by pinball flappers. She sat gracefully beside me at the kitchen table, smiling like I was family. I felt shame for compensating her kindness in secret ridicule, so kept my eyes on hands gathered at the table in front of me. She smelled of Avon pumped from glass bottles of blue bonnets or model-A Fords or some other cutesy conceit. Her hair was thinning badly. The perm meant to hide this fact was flattened on one side from sleep.

"Where was I from?" she asked. "Oh, Boston. I got a Boston spoon here," she said rising from the table and leaning precariously across to the opposite wall. "A good one," she said pulling a glass door to a cabinet glittering with silver and gold miniature spoons. "It's ah patriot, let's see (she squinted, held the spoon at arm's length) oh, yes, Paul Revere, and see here, the top ah the spoon's shaped like ah lantern, ain't that sweet?" She asked was I a university student? Was I clean of drugs? Did I go ta Nam? What was my family like? I wasn't answering. She didn't notice nor care.

Sergeant Vasari was not listening either. He had slipped into the numbness of domestic white noise that filled his off-duty hours. His wide back attended a saucepan on the stove heating stew. I thought of the Cyclops Polyphemus cooking Odysseus' miniature crew one at a time over a fire. Through the isinglass of the wood stove bulldog squat and stout in a corner of the kitchen, sticks of wood burned an intense neon of various shades. We all sweat in our clothes. Sergeant Vasari slopped stew in steaming heaps onto a china bowl Mrs. Vasari had placed before me. He asked me to "gather in" the job he had done himself hanging cabinets – "The best ah Bolivian hard woods, don't ya know. Had ta jig and jag somewhat ta get the right fit around the wood stove, but you wouldn't ah known if I'd not told ya. Ain't that right!" His large hand descended avuncular upon my shoulder. I jumped. Maybe I was going into the stew. He dug fingers under the collar bone which hurt like hell and worked muscles there to knead away nerves. It wasn't working. If anything he worked them in deeper. "Still jittery? Well, there has been ah parcel ah dead men in your rambles lately. That can't settle you much."

He lay on the kitchen table the letter in French he had found on the body and, without explanation, asked his wife to translate. She shuffled to the bedroom for a pair of glasses trimmed in rhinestone, listing side-to-side, then sat back down with an exhalation of breath extending the seams of her mouth and read through before translating, eyebrows raising and lowering.

"Where'd ya get this, Nicky?"

"Nowhere important, but it is part of ah investigation."

"Well, for starters, it ain't finished. But you know that."

"Well ah course, Salome, I knowed that, but what's the gist ah what it wanted ta say?"

"Well, the first part that's done in pencil says about death coming on. Right here it says *douloureux* and *cancer du poumon* and a bunch of *tousser* and something like if winter don't get me, the brothers Quebecois will. Who is the brothers that he's scared of?"

"What? Where's it say that?"

Salome repeated the phrase then said, "And it's a confession of sins." Salome read silently for a moment then said, "Oh my. This boy's been active."

"Never mind, what else?"

"There ain't nothing else."

"Who's it writ to."

"Why, it's addressed ta you, Dear. I thought you knew?"

"I didn't see no name nor address. Where do you find that?"

Vasari leaned over his wife's shoulder. She ran pink nails across the word *policier,* said, "That's you, Nicky."

"Oh, I see. Well, then, go back ta them sins. What's he sorry for?"

"Let's see. He says *bloguer* and *manger créture du parc,* which means trapping squirrels and other such for food. He says he ordinarily likes animals and wouldn't hurt them unless he had ta."

"Well, that ain't no nuisance."

"House pets gone stray?"

"Oh, well that ain't no bother neither, so far as I'm concerned."

I nodded in agreement; Salome smiled.

"There's more. He says *petit voler* which means small stealing, such as early morning deliveries ta the back door of the Pine Street Market. He specially says Pine Street Market."

"Yes, yes. What ah them brothers? Does he say names?"

"Well, no, except he does say the brothers Quebecois has come around."

"Come around? What do you mean come around?"

"Just come around, *arriver.* Just that. And there's a bit of Latin or some such here but its done in ah different hand seems like and in pen."

"Yuh, don't worry bout that."

When morning came I was back at the apartment tossing Wheat Chex at Cat who prowled the corners of his hunting ground (these tiny breakfast cakes were Cat's usual meal beyond cast-off pizza rind). Vasari was at the police station reading the autopsy he had ordered on the dead man from Battery Park. He sat on the edge of his desk in the duty room dousing cigarettes in cold coffee gone scummy in his Rotary cup. Officer Brady, assigned to Vasari's mentoring, was lingering, especially nosy and bothersome of late. Brady sensed Vasari wanted him distant from substantial police work. Brady snooped – riffled reports Vasari had typed and left in the Smith Corona, asked questions in the lunch room of Vasari's temperament and habits. Vasari spotted Brady's immaculately washed and detailed Nova Super Sport with oversize tires gunning past his bedroom window early morning before coming to the station. He had got up from bed to close curtains because Salome had read in her French *Cosmopolitan* (sent from Montreal) how frequency of sex is proportional to expectations of longevity in partnering and mortality. Mornings were for amour. Salome had been feting her husband lately, bounding out of bed to light the wood stove in the kitchen so they could play on top of the covers, sloshing back into bed to make love (she had convinced the Sergeant to buy a waterbed), riding the crest of their love wave back into the kitchen to reward Vasari with scratch pancakes and sausage grilled in maple butter, getting pissed off if he should suggest breakfast at the Arabian Diner on the way to work, plying him with the latest in aphrodisiacs: strawberry incense, coconut oil rub downs, tiger milk cocktails, vaginal flavoring, the BG's sound track from *Stayin' Alive*. 40-D breasts hung pendulous and combustive in lace underwear. Horsy buttocks bulged as she straddled her husband in bed, tickled him in the face with a strand of hair, teasing, "Nicky, Nicky, babykins, what makes ya feel gooood?"/ "How about let me sleep awhile, Salome," he answered. But she would not be denied. So Vasari had squiggled out from under and shuffled to the bedroom window in long johns and pulled at the shades (the sergeant is a private man), groaning on bad knees, when he saw the back end of the black Nova Super Sport slip-tail around a corner two houses down. Despite himself, Vasari had a slight erection. He was pissed! This kid has to be reined in.

Vasari looked around the squad room, didn't see Brady, so he studied the autopsy report which did not fix cause of death. Said no physical signs of violence, though asphyxiation could apply if foul play suspected. "Good call, Doc", Vasari said to himself in reference to paper taken from the dead man's mouth before calling removal. The report further stated so much wrong with this man that almost anything could have killed him: kidneys bloated and rotted, arteries clogged, lungs black from cigarettes and yellow with fluid from pneumonia, not to mention while mentioning angiofibroma of the colon. "Damn, even the taxidermist is growing ah brain on me," said Vasari.

There was no way to ID the cadaver. The army jacket once had a name sewed on, now removed. The jacket may not have belonged originally to the dead man anyway. Pockets filled only with aluminum washers the size of quarters, slugs for vending machines. If there were a wallet, it had been lifted. And Travers Jones wouldn't let up, worse than Brady, left phone messages for Vasari to call back which elicited concerns of the dead man's name, origin, physiognomy:

"Was he...in any way marked up, Sergeant? I mean, any noticeable scars, on his hands?"

"Well, no, but there were something odd,"

"What's that Sergeant?"

Well, it's his balls. They was blue."

"No shit."

"Why sure, what'd you expect. The man was froze, don't ya know."

"Oh, sure."

Weird kid. But even Sergeant Vasari was beginning to credit Travers' thinking that arson, and perhaps murder, were happening in his town. After all, why else would vagrants sleep in unsheltered, open areas at the edge of town, unless circling wagons under fire. These were loners. They fought amongst themselves usually, competitors for the warmest outdoor bivouac and for that cornucopia of garbage bins in alleys back of downtown restaurants. They had been sleeping separately in window wells of the largest buildings in town up until the first church burned and that one vagrant, George Eakins, with it. Then they moved altogether down near the power station at the bottom of the hill. Why then had some gone uphill to Battery Park? And it did seem more than coincidence that this most recent dead vagrant with the tourist brochure for paper insulation would select a page with Immaculate Cathedral, the second burned church, to place in Travers Jones' pocket. And then perhaps killed by the pages of that very brochure stuffed in his mouth. Maybe a vagrant was doing the killing and burning? Something to look into. Vasari could also fathom an errant Old North End priest flipping-out, gone renegade and…what was it Gladys Needham had said, become "iconoclast." But surely there was nothing sexy about these burns, nothing to do with a perverty pyro. Salome might think otherwise. "Oh, hell, maybe I should check where the old lady has been the nights ah these fires! She does enjoy ah hot room," Vasari said aloud and chuckled, threw a cigarette butt into the coffee cup, lit another and gave Brady a critical look as he chatted the little girl with the big voice at dispatch.

That afternoon Vasari drove to university hill and William Street to meet the Bishop of Burlington in his twenty-four rooms of domesticity and chancery office. Religion pays good. Vasari was nervous and the Bishop was nervous. Both for different reasons. Vasari has to change his shirt every time after he visits the Bishop who thought Vasari arranged this meeting to discuss oversexed priests. Bishop Semprebon retreated emotionally into a stockpile of phrases comprising what he named a "rhetoric of assiduous and oblique deflection," phrases he collected in a notebook and then memorized to "keep the barbarian (secular law in this case) outside the holy gates" so to speak.

"Officer Vasari. Nice to see you."

Never a hand shake but always a polite nod from Bishop Semprebon, always fresh shaved, robes pressed: a luster of black trimmed in red with gold cross bejeweled at the crossbars and dangling from the center of his cowl like a third eye. The Bishop's words might have seemed rehearsed to Vasari had he not been too self-conscious to notice (fallen Catholic tattooed on his forehead) and had he not been so awed by the Bishop's resumé and education and, most particularly, by his intimacy with mysteries of the faith. Every Catholic, fallen or ascending, has a chastening respect for the miracles of ritual that bring the godhead's attentions to earth from his distance of cloud and indifference.

"When I was consecrated Bishop," said Semprebon, "two conditions were required for ordination, the male sex and baptism. So you see, Sergeant, you and I, we are not so very much different."

The Bishop twirled his ring as was his habit when seated behind his desk of carved mahogany, stalling to make adjustments in the rhythm and tone of the interview, tweaking dramatic tensions as he knew best to do. The ring itself worked as a talisman in this way – mesmerizingly oversized, embossed and blazoned with his personal coat of arms. The Bishop let the silence work for him and then said, as if just discovering the bauble, "Ah, the ring! Hard to ignore isn't it. In the science of nobles a herald would describe it vert, a boar's head caboshed, and between the attires – just here – a cross fleur-de-lis – and just here – a chief dancette of the same. And Sinister – a catchy phrase don't you think? – which means the left hand side, just here – a sword patty Argent. Do you see? Then overall at the fesse point a raven's head erased Gules... just so." With Vasari's attention directed to the ring, the Bishop spoke further.

"If it were proper to ordain women as priests, well, just imagine. Mary, the Mother of Jesus, would certainly have been the first," said the Bishop.

Vasari kept eyes on the ring twisting on the Bishop's hand, saying, "Yes, that makes sense, but where we going with this, your Excellency?"

"Eunuchs, our most lowly of priests, those who have made themselves such for the sake of the Kingdom of Heaven, will by virtue of their sacrifice be free from the cares and ties, the distractions and hindrances of the natural family life. Tertullian from the third century lauds the practice. Not what we recommend today."

"I spose so," said Vasari.

"And you must know I send my priests out into the Old North End as complete men with a thin line of defense against the impure and unrighteous, with no more than what I have here (the Bishop swept his arms around him in an enclosing circle to suggest his black robes and beads) and the last vestiges of Christ transubstantiating through the digestive tract. But bless them if they don't, some of them, vomit out all at the nearest watering hole that's dark enough to hide their suffering faces. Such a place as Bucket of Blood! God's blood! When you, Sergeant, brought father Dyer back from that odious place in his attack of the pestilence of the worm that dieth not, in a state lacking in grace…well, how could I not help thinking chains, whips and pincers! Sometimes the Middle-Ages got it right! He had that fur hat gambled upon and won from some notorious singer vixen that exposes breast and leaks soul through the most piteous, wailful moan ever recorded on phonograph, and who died in her own vomit…well…pardon me. I am under much pressure from New York to straighten this problem out or be sent to Yakutat in Alaska to die on the ice devoured by the glacier bear or civilize the Tlingit Indians who have already decimated a colony of Russian Orthodox. Unfortunately, there is precedence. Bishop Brice himself lived among the Indians of Northern Maine. And thanks to Thomas Merton's letter to the Archbishop of Anchorage requesting intercession in the wastelands, I could be eating cold beans off a tepid hot plate in some trailer camp on the permafrost. Well, these may be the Trappist ways. But Merton is a writer, and so has become as sacred as the 'word' whose power he invokes. Usurps by my assessment, more likely. So you see, Sergeant, I am Alaska bound if I cannot keep my priests out of the bars, away from women, and out of the papers."

"I hope not, your Excellency. I mean, if that's not what you want."

"Yes, that is decidedly not what I want. I have said as much. But let me direct myself to your problem."

"That would be nice, Bishop. Thank you."

"I have made it clear to my errant clergy that I will be taking a cotillion of brothers with me to Alaska to do penance should I be changing diocese. That should stop their philandering, and give you a good rest in your offices."

"Yes, that would be nice, but I have not come ta talk ah your priests in this way."

"Oh?"

"I have come ta ask what you know ah the church fires."

"Oh, I see. Well, that would be faulty wiring, as the papers say, I'm sure."

"Yes, surely. But…you don't have any kind ah slim inkling ah arson, do you? Some especially ding batty and troubled priest, maybe?"

"Faulty wiring, Sergeant, as the papers say."

"Yuh, ah course. But there's been two fires. Both wiring, do you think?"

"What else?"

"Could you tell me, do you know any priest that's been active in Canada politics, the Quebec separatists that is?"

"We are not a body politic, as you know, Sergeant. We are a body spiritual."

"Well, sure, but sometimes you are ah body physical. That's ah rarity and ah frailty, something of ah design flaw, as you say, not your fault. But why couldn't some one ah you become somewhat of ah body political, just long enough ta get into trouble."

"Yes, I suppose. Perhaps you should speak with father Ruel of your own diocese."

"I don't any longer participate, your Excellency. I mean, I'm no longer ah the flock. You know."

"You know as well as I, Vasari, that you never truly leave the parish where you are baptized and receive Communion. Father Ruel is still and forever your spiritual advisor. Besides, he is French Canadian himself, as you know, and a good man for consultation in this matter."

"Sure, thank you, Bishop Semprebon, for your advice. Oh, almost forgot: what about this language here? What's it mean, do you think?"

Vasari showed the Bishop what had been written in a separate hand on the note found in the dead man's pockets.

"Yes, Latin. It would translate as *We burn all down, let's see, to free the mysteries — the Brothers Quebecois*. Yes, that's it. What is this about?"

"Don't know exactly. Not yet. Well thank you, your Excellency."

"Not at all," said the Bishop as he and Vasari moved into the hallway, a litter of boxes making egress a hip-slider, grime shadows on the walls where pictures had once hung, and the Bishop dismissing the mess with a wave of his hand and this: "Simply a matter of economics, Sergeant. I will be moving quarters to an apartment off the orphanage on North Avenue. This building has been sold to the university."

"Yuh, I see. Better than Alaska."

"Indeed yes, much."

Chapter Fifteen

Designer Elvis' drug connection • Carnage at the Domes of Yosemite • Mushrooms that contract the mind • Cartoon sex and men who wear the red star • Tuning in Designer Elvis and tuning out • Busted more ways than one • Ubiquitous beef stew • Brady's almost apology • A jaunty little priest that knows Vasari • Mustaches on statuary • In church, Travers empties out. What rushes in?

I dozed but couldn't sleep. Thinking about dead men. Sun penetrated my lair delineating the mess that was my life. I couldn't see Cat. Heard his caterwauling. His unhappiness cheered me. There were other reasons to be cheerful. I was drawn to the possibility of denouement, eager to make an end of a twenty-eight year smolder that had finally ignited. Whoever was burning churches and whatever it had to do with me would coalesce in coordinates soon to be discovered, like vectors of Cartesian Datsun truck guardrail extraction on the highway. But I had to get out to the streets, make decisions at the crossroads. The Zen thing, scalars of uncertainty, was no longer working for me. I couldn't wait for enlightenment. If one hand were applauding my decision, I couldn't hear it.

I would locate Designer Elvis. No one was closer to the street than Elvis. He would know reasons behind these fires and the homeless dying. I started with his drug connection. We had been introduced. We had bonded over my dependence on Phenobarbital. I walked into daylight first time in a month. I kept to the north side of Grant Street to soak heat onto bare head and shoulders in the unusually bright sun that poured over rooftops in 20 degrees temperature. Even if Elvis weren't there, the pasha of #6 Uptown Motel might know something. My eyes stung from the searing contrast of snow and shadow, impressions of dark and light burned onto retina like acid on photographic plate, like the burn Halley gave me first time I saw Fay Wray promoting Big Ed's American Motors Emporium, a harlot angel intermittently gracing the TV screen at Nectar's, white night gown floating upon the hood of a black Gremlin.

I passed cathedral ruins on Saint Paul Street, a pile of gray stone misting in the remains of its charred heart. Farther down Church Street, the essential shopping district, awnings dripped from sun melting snow, college students plugged the street in hand-me-down BMers and Volvos motoring soundlessly in the slip-range torque of first gear, conversations out windows, flatlander license plates piquing the ire of locals stalling in clouds of blue smoke in rusted Ford Broncos and Chevy Blazers. But no horns sounded. Burlington, for its out-of-proportion size and pace as a Vermont city, is still small-town polite. I walked past Magram's, Burlington's chic department store, once an opera house, now five stories of house wares and clothing replete with Burlington's only patron elevator, a turn-of-the century cage of wrought iron whose dwarfish but nattily dressed operator ferries customers in patronizing disregard. Magram's window designs were tended by a frizzy-haired, short, doughy man in bell-bottoms studded down the seam and encased in a black, short-sleeve t-shirt too small for his pudgy body. He noticed me on the sidewalk, rubbed with his hand the pelvic bulge of a male mannequin. Was that a leer, a queer leer? I was rhyming as badly as Halley. Some part of me felt sexy from the attention, but thank the gods, not the part that counts. A matron in heels and fox fur swung wide to avoid me on the sidewalk, as if inviting me to make reparations – maybe tuck in the M.C. Escher t-shirt whose design offended her (a salamander eating its tail), or button my parka, run a hand through the greasy curls of my hair. Not my style.

I walked down Bank Street past the Arabian Diner with its artsy/ reactionary political crowd eating lunch, turned at Winooski Avenue by the first burned church, the Congregational Church, walked through the parking lot of the Burlington Police and turned right again at the library, entering the Uptown Hotel's parking lot.

#6 resides second floor at the far end from Main Street with two entrances, one off fire escape. Elvis had taught me to step through the bathroom window accessible from the metal platform, the sill worn smooth from boots passing over. Once inside I bruised shins on the toilet, eyes adjusting to dim light, and rounded a doorway toward kitchenette where gas fires sputtered beneath tin saucepans and cast iron skillets. A large man in a snowmobile suit tended the stove. Spices were hung upside down from the ceiling. Two doe-eyed, teenage girls giggled at the kitchen table, dressed in moccasins and sweat pants, emanating Kama Sutra Oil, ensconced in manly sweaters given to them by the cook whose long, unwashed hair fell back off his forehead in a cock's crow of colic flattened by a headband. Greasy Joe doth keel the pot.

"Hey, it's Elvis' buddy! Mistook me for a pharmacy again have you? Hey, where's Elvis? Haven't seen him awhile," said Joe. "Check out my still, Elvis' buddy."

I followed Joe's thumb to the living room. A crockpot on a coffee table furiously boiled corn mash in a network of copper and rubber tubing, a condenser and a jug where residue dripped. The accumulation significant enough to stew two men dressed in identical blue jump suits. They watched me from their corner of the room, lifted cups as greeting. One walked unsteadily to a print on the wall, a reproduction of a Bierstadt Yosemite landscape. He drew with a magic marker a blood stain on the mouth of a prone man someone else had drawn on the floor of the valley, an apparent suicide from off the cliffs. The whole print was an amalgam of graffiti of a single conceit: carnage from cars gone off those cliffs, bodies strewn in distorted tangles, survivors performing hellish sex upon the dead. The original design seemed an afterthought, as though Hieronymus Bosch had finished the work when Bierstadt stepped out for a coffee break. The two men had red stars on their chests.

"Hey, man, if you don't already know each other, you will soon," said Joe invading the living room, two girls under one arm and a plate of sizzling mushrooms gripped in a free hand, like hosting a dinner party.

"Here's shrooms that'll expand your mind. I have Elvis' crystal ready if you want to bring it to him. Pay later. No charge for the shrooms."

"But I'm not here for…"

"Hey, I make people happy! The whole world needs happy. Happy is as happy does. Am I right, darling?" He squeezed a giggling twin. "Only thing is you have to add something to that masterpiece over the sofa. This is community art. I'm putting in for federal money."

The two auto mechanics that had exacted ransom on my Datsun didn't recognize me. Good thing, since the truck was a sink hole of deferred maintenance, breaking down faster than cartilage in Michael Jackson's face. First the transmission, then the clutch before I got it a block away in a test drive. "Sure, sure," they said, "Canucks do this you think, eh?" Additional bills mentioned leaks and noise and fumes and sags. They kept the thing as collateral against the bill I hadn't paid. I wondered if they had sold it off for parts. When the twins showed, the mechanics handed the magic marker to me, refilled cups from the still, leaned farther into naugahyde chairs, smiled and chewed mushrooms. Cook released the girls, winked, retreated to his kitchen. One hung back timidly. The other made tiny steps into the lap of one of the two mechanics and played with his jump-suit zipper, both hands tattooed in henna. She whispered into the mechanics' ear, pulled the zipper down to his waist and rubbed hair on his chest. I took a mushroom. What the heck. It tasted wonderful – garnished in herbs and braised in animal fat. Slow to take effect. The girl removed her sweater. She was naked beneath. Small breasts, narrow waist, henna patterns of jungle animals racing in a mass ran the length of her arms, parted like rivers at her breasts, disappeared into the waist band of her sweat pants. The mushrooms, I had by now chewed several, un-synched motion and talk, what little came from the cooing girls and silent mechanics. All stimuli traveled through a long pipe to reach me. The girls had both stripped naked and were maneuvering between the two mechanics. I laughed. The sex was cartoonish, a Fritz the Cat porn movie, two-dimensional and impossibly acrobatic. The mechanics sat immobile in their chairs while girls crawled over them like monkeys, pumping and licking and mewling. Walls of the room were painted black with stars pasted on. This I noticed before the shrooms. The two mechanics began to drift like planets in the cold recesses of space with two beautiful moons circling.

Others entered the room and left. Many others. I sat silently smiling stupidly. There was no mind expanding going on – contracting more likely. Someone talked about curing planters warts with voodoo and a Swiss army knife, then about a child kept for a day in a bird cage because he didn't wash his dish. Some talked of commune life, bedpans with turds floating, fucking anything that moves, the hard-asses that want rules, Vishnu will provide, possessions are bad, privacy is bad, money is bad, bladder pains are very bad. Some talked of jail. A black woman with an island accent in a macramé and bead dress danced in the middle of the room happy that Vermont weather will not much bother her once Buckminster Fuller builds a geodesic dome over the town of Winooski.

Someone put on the radio, "Q" something, the usual innocuous pop schlock until Joe said, "Hey, dial for Designer Elvis will you. He's a different place everyday but you'll know when you find him."

Sitting nearest the receiver, I turned knobs landing on the Cleveland band Pere Ubu screaming its discovery of the abyss over an intense drumbeat that shook monolithic speakers standing in corners of the room and tipped a hookah spraying rancid, maybe lethal water across the floor. At the conclusion of the scream, Elvis dialogued the audience: " Nothing like Ubu "Heart of Darkness" from off *Terminal Tower* to gladden your day! Give in to the seismic scaredness of it: look into your heart William Calley, look into your heart Charles Manson, look into your heart Richard Nixon for the monster that pumps insanity into this world and stifle the sucker, stifle, because I am declaring today National Stifle a Dark Heart Day! Surrender your love of napalm in the morning. Release, Symbionese guerillas! Release that poor little rich girl. Let her go home to daddy. Patty, baby, I'm with you, Patty! Follow me to the dissonance of freedom. Anarchy is the only freedom left. Every cause wants to legitimize. Stay un-legitimized, baby. Tell Daddy…Oops! New York is coming back. Returning you now to WEZE, the best of the underground from New York City. This is Designer Elvis signing off, wheeling through your town in Red Shoes with a special word out to #6 Uptown that a big fat cherry sundae is coming your way!"

Then static. Then the slippery vocals of Robin Williamson of The Incredible String Band singing "Earth water fire and air/Met together in a garden fair/Put in a basket bound with skin/If you answer this riddle, you'll never begin."

"Where did Elvis go? I need him," I said to the room, but the room was only me, until police stormed the front door and bathroom window simultaneously, breaking things and barking aggression. I sank deeper into an overstuffed chair, tried to think invisible, head bent ostrich between my knees. Officer Brady was first to find me.

"Well, shit! Look here. I arrested this loser once and nobody would believe me he was criminal. Stand up!"

I couldn't get up. I wouldn't look up.

"I said come here, you shit!" after which I felt a nauseating pressure on the back of my neck and surrendered all my faculties to the law in a hopeless tangle of useless limbs. I went unconscious as Sergeant Vasari ascended the stairs with difficulty cursing Brady for getting ahead of himself (and everyone else) in a bust that was likely a bust for all the damn noise made getting there.

And so it was. All I could be charged with was occupying premises where a make-shift still had produced unspecific quantities of grain alcohol and where marijuana roaches and a busted hookah were found, nothing else: no people, no drugs, just sprays of exotic, legal herbs hanging from the ceiling in the kitchenette and a vandalized print hanging on the wall. There were no drugs in my system beyond hallucinogenic mushrooms that register as plant mold in a urine test. Even so, I was taken to a holding cell for observation as some worried over of my condition, and so Vasari could persuade me not to sue the city over police brutality. I groaned awake rubbing the swollen and tender coils of my neck where Brady had clubbed me. I lay curled upon an army cot. Vasari leaned toward me seated on a toilet, tuberous belly hanging like a piñata between knees, straining a pair of thick suspenders.

"Real sorry, kid, about the baton. If I don't git that Brady in line quick, I swear I'm gonna bury him in paperwork. But that don't help you. Can I git you something? Salome told me bring you stew when she heard, which I got right here, if you're in the mood."

A plastic bowl covered in saran wrap sat on the floor beside Vasari. Maybe it was the effects of the trauma to my neck or maybe the image of Vasari looking like he had just shat out the contents of that bowl that raised my gorge, but in response I ran for the porcelain, pushed Vasari aside for a long, satisfying retching up of whatever poison still lingered in my stomach. As I puked, Vasari stroked the back of my head like I was a favorite dog. Strangely, I felt flattered.

"Tell you what," he said, "let's just git you out ah here. If you're up ta it, I got us ah lead on the Quebecois that was in that letter Salome translated. It's ah visit ta another priest, but there's no helping that. I'll git you released with apologies from the authorities that put you here."

"How about from Brady?"

"Yuh, perfect."

Vasari handed me a kerchief pulled out from a pocket. I flushed the rag down the toilet and followed him up stairs into his office where the blue-gray decor, metal book cases and metal desks, battleship gray plaster board, even the faded blue of Vasari's work shirt placed me in a kind of swan's float down a polluted river, made me think of the powder blue of my Datsun truck that should be carrying me north along the river valleys to my philosopher's tower in the crystal city of Montreal. But that idea soon evaporated. Brady transformed the room with his presence. My neck ached. His pressed black uniform glistened, metal restraints clattered, weapons encased in black leather, all coalesced in an aura of repressed anger. He stood above me. I looked for security into the murk of black coffee Vasari had presented me in his Rotary Cup.

"We arraigning this perpetrator?" said Brady. "You taking his statement? He give you the dealer yet?"

"Well, officer Brady, you should be the one ta know that this man here, Travers Jones by name, is presently charging the department with misconduct and naming you as offending officer."

"Like hell! He's the friggin' scofflaw, Sergeant! Let's get the good guys straight from the bad guys."

"That's what the department is fixing ta do, officer, and presently. Unless, ah course, you'd like ta make a apology. In which case, Mr. Jones here might could be persuaded ta drop charges."

"I can't believe this shit."

"It could git ugly, Brady. You might want ta remember that it was your cowboy show and noise that warned away the real offenders bafore you busted up the place and now have the department paying damages ta the hotel."

"I was doing my job!"

"Yes, badly. Officer, you need ta smarten up."

"That's what you're report is likely to say? Smarten up?"

"Likely, unless Mr. Jones gits his apology."

"Fine. I apologize. But he'd better don't fuck up again."

I never looked up from the cup of coffee, but my smile registered off the seismograph of vindication. Gods that was great! Brady exited wrathfully, showcasing a peculiarity I hadn't before noticed: Brady has a fat ass, like what Marlon Brando tried to keep off film, and it jiggled. Hell, I could outrun that ass with marmalade on my sneakers. Vasari winked at me, said, "So, what say we make ah visit ta the clergy?"

How did I feel about seeing a priest? Vasari had mixed feelings about the Bishop and his minion. He told me, but I couldn't bring myself to explain to Vasari my upbringing at the hands of a renegade clergyman. And I wasn't so sure I wanted to share words with a priest when I had truly been enjoying his discomfort and those brethren of his from these church fires. I told Vasari I would just as soon wait in the car but the cracked vinyl seats of his patrol car had gone pungent in felon perfumery as the heater stirred the ghosts of shattered lives. So I met the priest. He wasn't at all like Uncle Gerrit. He seemed kindly and frail, a soft body sagged from lack of use, a face care worn, Vasari would tell me later, by twenty-some years of Old North End shepherding: chasing the Maplewood Cemetery vandals of Vasari's youth, shooing cows out the nave protestant boys had put there, holding together a congregation become excessively spiritual as more poorly in health and finance. He looked aslant at Vasari and smiled at the secrets they shared. His hands shook and his voice wavered as he removed and replaced glasses frequently, nervously. The soutane draped him like a bed sheet, but the little tri-corned hat gave him a sporty, jaunty look, pulled tight enough for a skull cap, reminding me of an Italian biker's cap — team St. Johns of the Tour de France — and his voice though brittle was sincere and warm in recognition of a parishioner who had strayed.

He had been lighting tapers to fulfill requests for prayers paid by relatives of the departed and the nearly departed. All that's left of indulgences, he said, after Martin Luther got through embarrassing Mother Church. He led Vasari and me to an alcove where the Virgin Mary in a recessed niche of wall holds her dying son, where candles flicker in red glass, and sat us down in a circle of pews designed for private worship where echoes made the most mundane phrase seem profound. I wasn't feeling too good, but managed to assign my discomfort to Brady's baton battering rather than to anything epileptic coming on. This wasn't the time for an episode, though it was certainly the place.

The priest questioned Vasari's health, physical and spiritual, wondered if he had been to confession lately, then explained he must break trust one small time to illustrate character, Nickoli Vasari's that is: he explained to me, in a show of friendship, even pride, that it was he that had enlightened Vasari as to the noble history of his surname (Vasari — a 16th century Italian artist, architect and writer, famous for his frescoes and for

Lives of the Most Eminent Artists and for the Uffizi of Florence). And it's a shame Americans can't learn from Italians, because they make a city habitable, unlike the Levittown craze that has infested fallow land everywhere. I thought back to the Italians of my neighborhood in East Boston. The priest was right if he meant loud and involved as opposed to quiet and private. He said he told Vasari about his famous relative because the good Sergeant in his youth was having a difficult time as an outnumbered Italian among the Old North End's lumberjack French Canadians who floated pine down Lake Champlain to fire the furnaces of glass manufacture that built the small brick houses on George Street where Vasari grew up. So Father Ruel gave Nickoli Vasari reason to be proud, which backfired, as Vasari had snuck into the church one evening and painted Salvador Dali mustaches on all the statuary (was this a sincere artistic endeavor? was it parody? irreverence? he never took it personally, the priest said). Can't you still see the shadow of Vasari's work under the lip of our lady in her grief? Sure enough, Vasari's handiwork had not scrubbed cleanly off. Monseigneur suppressed a chuckle and seemed about to launch into further anecdotes of Vasari's youthful exuberance until Vasari interrupted, deferentially, excusing himself for time constraints and mentioning the Quebecois. Monseigneur went visibly uncomfortable in his clothes, scratched beneath his collar with jittery hands. He tried to shuffle away to chores left underdone. Vasari wouldn't let him.

"Monseigneur Ruel, with respect, I wonder have you heard ah the rumors hereabouts that some French separatist is making life uneasy for the street population? What I need ta know is whether you might ah got news ah this from the soup kitchen?"

After which Monseigneur removed his tri-corned hat, ran a hand through wispy gray hair then explained, yes, there had indeed been some commotion from among the homeless that come Thursday nights to his service and simple repast. The gist of which seemed to be a threat from some group of French Canadians to keep away from window wells of

Burlington churches at night. Make bivouac elsewhere or else — some threats were leveled in the name of Pierre Laporte. This meant nothing to the street dwellers, though the incendiary death of George Eakins did — he was one of theirs — while the Monseigneur explained that Laporte, Quebec's labor minister, had been kidnapped and killed by the Quebecois in 1970. Some 500 people were arrested, mostly the wrong people, and civil liberties curtailed, and the War Measures Act proclaimed. Stores and banks in downtown Montreal with British monarchist leanings were bombed. The priest placed a hand on Vasari's shoulder, said, "Do not take this for gospel, but it is rumored some member of the clergy is involved."

I leaped off the bench behind the two old friends and ran to the chancel lattice where the choir gathers. They watched intently. I was trying not to think and thinking too much. I felt myself emptying out, surprised I had anything left to give over since my first epileptic fit in the East Boston choir many years ago. Churches still affect me this way, those unburned that is. They empty me. It's what Uncle Gerrit called "the tunnel of my conversion, expulsion of the Hollow Spirit leaving naught." And this is *NOT* what I wanted; this kind of emptiness was un-Zarathustrian. Gerrit thought my fit in the choir all those years ago had launched me as a spiritual warrior, but it had simply broken me spiritually. And when up there on Battery Park I thought I had found my father lying dead in the snow — "shouldn't burn no church with hate in your heart," he had said — I had begun to think I had a distinct message, a clear direction what to do, or what not to do. But now, all was flux again and puzzling. Was my father alive? Was he in Burlington burning churches? Was my Uncle here? Were the two working together, drawing me to the flames?

Maybe I should burn churches, burn them with love in my heart. If my father were my guardian angel, maybe I *was* meant for Gerrit's religious reform, like that French Jew Rastibonne, the one William James writes about who converted to Catholicism after following a black dog into a small church in Rome, the dog disappearing as did the church itself, then Rastibonne and the Virgin Mary kissing. Maybe I should burn churches and kiss Halley Gay?

But my walk back through the nave of the church rendered me nearly reverent. Its mass and volume astounded me. If I were to release myself here in this vaulted and medallioned and gilt receptacle of celebrants' hopes and desires, if I were to empty out and burn, I would release myself into the unprotected ethers outside these walls once the church fell. But I also felt strongly I could torch this beautiful building that minute and hold no remorse, no criminal stirrings of self-recrimination, no self-loathing. I was a mess, a mux of contradictions.

I took deep, calming breaths and walked pensively down the isle to where Vasari and Monseigneur Ruel awaited me. I stopped periodically to affect pious self-examination while studying the tableau of stained glass windows. But I was really thinking back to when Vasari and I had approached the church in his patrol car. I could see from a distance a gilded tin rooster surmounting the steeple cross. My mother, Fiona, would be as alarmed by this bestial irreverence as she was by the glass-eyed locust weather van top of Faneuil Hall in Boston. This church had to burn. I knew it, and I knew I would somehow be a part of it. I needed to embrace the legacy left me by my father. I was destined to do so.

The priest and Vasari lost interest in me. I had calmed and found a pew to stretch out on, my eyes upon the medallioned ceiling. Their final words were a mutual complaint of a fire department whose sirens compelled the Monseigneur to, as he said, bless the bells of St. Johns, his church, bless every one: bless Jacque Francois, 4,347 pounds; bless Marie Lamore, 2,200 pounds; bless Antoine Santaro, 1,655 pounds. Vasari mentioned that what he says when sirens go off can't be said in good company or between these walls. I was pretty sure the walls wouldn't much longer be an obstacle for anything Vasari might want to say.

Chapter Sixteen

Halley Gay and Travers naked in the grotto • The shenanigans of Cat • Down the tracks: ghosts and Fisher Cats.

Vasari let me off at the apartment on Grant Street where I found a note pinned to the door: *you busted? that's criminal! hey, I got news — come to the studio — bottom of flynn ave, big red warehouse — follow R/R tracks, listen for brian eno — hey — you got a relative problem, brother, in case you don't know — some old man in god's formal wear with attitude been asking for you as family — see me tonight — Elvis*

What a time for Cat to purr. I kicked the poor thing as it fuzzed my leg. Cat skulked under the bed to feed off something odoriferous it had dragged there that had been gathering potency the last few days. I didn't much care about that, but I did care that Uncle Gerrit was pursuing me. Part of me was scared shitless what this could mean. Yes, and part of me was glad, thinking Gerrit would employ me as an arsonist, purge me of this curse, then place me back on the road to Montreal. I tried to apologize to Cat, but he wouldn't appease. So I shared Salome Vasari's stew with him and sat at the card table by the window to work through aphorisms in my much-neglected *Journal of Life Assembly.* I turned to the chapter on courage.

"Your will and your valuations have ye put on the river of becoming," said Zarathustra, to which I added, "Steer blindly into the storm with a warrior's resolve," and then upon further reflection, "Pay whatever price exacted to master the tides." There was I, once again, with my ear to the ground sounding for undercurrents of information — all those caverns measureless to man that lead down to a sunless sea. All those squiggling sea creatures hidden beneath. I needed to know more before I leaped into the briny mystery. Was that cowardice or caution? Whatever it may have been it didn't matter because in minutes the stew boiled over as Halley knocked at my door lightly saying dimly, "I have brought your truncheon, sugar. Shall we talk somewhat of its usefulness?"

Sometimes a truncheon is just a truncheon. Not this time.

"Come in," I said. "It's unlocked." She opened the door slowly, teasing, slipped a leg in naked to the knee and peeked a smile before stepping in altogether, letting go the wool pants she had hiked up. Halley kicked off Bean duck boots, burlesqued a sashay toward me at the table and fell dead-weight upon her haunches, the hinges of her knees snapping, rested her chin on the table edge and turned my journal around to read it, lips moving silently. "Is this more hermit philosophizing, Travers, dear?"

"Where have you been?" I said. "Don't you know Sergeant Vasari and I have been investigating these burns all over town? There's a lot to tell you, and some I'm not sure I want to tell you."

"That is not why I'm here, Travers," she said, emphasizing the drawl, lugubrious in tone, vanquishing the playfulness she had tried to effect.

"I am havin' a difficult time over some personal involvement at the moment. I need a diversion, sugar, somethin' to take the edge off my goin over the edge. Aren't I just some kind of fuckin' wit."

She began to dry shudder, preserving what she could of an edgy cynicism. I sat there pouting over having been neglected, misreading her emotion because neither of us looked directly at the other. Timorous and tepid and testaceous – all those moiling insecurities we shared seethed beneath our skins. Cat chose this moment to creep out from under the bed to charm my guest with his arched butt-scratch tactics, brushing her leg and mewling his pleasure. The pervert!

Halley was charmed. After patting Cat somewhere inside the silky fall of her hair where they had disappeared together, she stood and brushed all behind her ears and looked at me so brassy that I trembled. I found nothing to say. She dropped her head just slightly to watch Cat move off toward his dish of stew then pause beside my chair for a strategic rebuff when I reached down a consoling hand.

"He hates me," I said hoping Halley would not believe me.

"There is somethin' sexy about a man disliked by animals," she said flatly. "Once again, it comes to mystery. You are a mysterious man, Mr. Jones. May I inquire what qualities of yours repel the dear kitty? Are you, perhaps, more muskrat trapper than you are inclined to let on? No, don't answer," she said with authority and more color. "I have not come to banter words. I have come to surrender myself to you in the physical. I have come to make love, Mr. Jones."

Finally, the grotto and Grecian nudes passionate in green fern. Oh, Heaven! Or at the very least the Elysian fields. Halley had divined and enacted the dream I had of a couple coupling in complete surrender one unto the another. Her skin shone pale white in my arms and slid along the ridges of my excited embraces like a cloud. I couldn't believe I held a substantial woman in my arms. She moved in perfect rhythm to each of my advances. I know this is going to sound weird, but it was like making love to myself. I mean, she knew what I wanted and went there before I could gesture or murmur or whatever it is lovers do when they're new to each other and want to please.

We made love giggling like children, up to the point when I asked Halley what it was that brought her to me. That's when I learned about the father that expected excellence beyond what Halley felt she could give, and the older brother that sneaked into her bed at night so regularly she thought every family played sex together when the lights went out. She told me about finally realizing this was wrong and wanting him to stay away but wanting him still because she had fallen in love with him, with her own brother. He was wonderful, she said. He was terrible. She grabbed the edges of the mattress and pulled and let go and beat thighs with her fists and said, "The shit! The fuckin' shit! He made me love him, and I did, and I finessed him off that cliff, and Daddy knows but he won't ever say, even though I have screwed every damn one of his married friends to make him see. God damn him! God damn them both together! How can I give my heart to a man after that? How can I?"

I put my arm around her shoulder. She shook it off. I didn't know what to say. My *Journal of Life Assembly* hadn't prepared me for any of this.

"Sorry, Travers, so sorry, sorry," she said in stuttering gulps of air that threatened to evolve into the mule bray signaling Halley's incapacity to cope. "I am not much good at this intimacy thing. But I am willin' to try. Give me time, darlin'."

But she dressed and scat out my door before I could think to get out of bed and bring her back under the covers, comfort her as she must have wanted. I just didn't know how to do that. I needed to try. By the time I had descended the stairs in skivvies and sneakers her Saab flew past in its bullet-nosed trajectory toward some other guy, no doubt, who would help her out of a snow bank if not place her there.

I clomped dejected up stairs past the doorway where my spook of a neighbor in #4, crew cut hair and troll like of complexion with a twisted jaw and disposition, played his hallelujah TV at ear-piercing volume (Billy the evangelist favored of presidents doing a God-rock revival meeting in a football stadium), then past the power-shake dieting beauty in #5 with Annie Hall neuroses who dances naked at night with a bald-headed muralist who leaves flowers at her door. I was feeling lonely.

Then a flurry of crashes from inside my apartment. Somebody had slipped into my apartment when I had come around the front of the house to watch Halley clip the side-view mirrors off parked cars in haste to motor away from the exposed self she had left behind. This could initiate another "courage" aphorism in the journal, should I survive. I was beginning to experience the intersect sensibilities of a victim realizing he is likely to be mowed down from any direction because the crossroads is HIM. If not Gerrit, then my father. If not Brady, then this mysterious somebody (or a gang of somebodies) burning churches that have probably painted a red cross over my door so the killers wouldn't miss me.

There I was in my sneakers and underwear, flexing arms in preparation for a defensive move I would have to invent once I stepped inside. Cat spat like the demon he is. Whoever my guest might be, he had stirred the ire of Cat and would be distracted enough maybe to miss my bold gladiatorial entrance. So I entranced. There was no one there but Cat and some damn mouse he had been chasing through the kitchen sink which had sent a stack of unwashed dishes plunging forward off the counter one dish at a time until I had nothing left for meals but shard. Cat thought he had me eating out of my hand. He was right. I tossed a sneaker at the offensive lap-scratcher which toppled glassware in the cabinet having no effect whatever on Cat who looked at me briefly with loathing and wonder at my lack of intelligence then licked a paw like flicking me off.

I was out of there. Cat's testiness had escalated to vindictiveness, and Halley had left before my dick went flaccid. Elvis said something about meeting him, and he was a friend. I walked down R/R tracks by lakefront through the south-end warehouse district of erstwhile ship builders and chocolate manufacture (every Yank in the trenches of W.W.I carried a ration of chocolate from Burlington, Vasari had told me), then lumberers, and railroad magnates who had left material remains along the rocky shoreline from which we may suss the character of New Englander as industrious and stubborn. Like these Old North Enders I lived among on Grant Street – so darn independent as to be aggressively hostile. And it was these small-town, hob-nailed, flannel-shirted illiterates that chased surveyors out from the area in the 1700's when New York tried to annex territory east of its Lake Champlain border. These Vermonters – descendants of mountain men, some that poured into Burlington to find work and brought their cobble-together-a-life values with them, and a rough-edged granite resolve to give life back its bruises in equal measure.

Designer Elvis was a New Yorker, a city boy, but also a pioneer. He had absorbed the frontier inclination to refashion morality with circumstance straight from the pavement of New York City through the soles of his gadabout unshod feet dodging fruit venders with a watermelon pressed against his chest, later in a pair of Pat Boone white bucks that stayed white among friends with less dandy ideas. As his chin hair grew so did his pugnacity, his natty showmanship, and his reputation among the savvy as an inside man. When I knew him better, I learned he grew up on the upper west side of Manhattan – Hell's Kitchen – a place where imagination, wit and sleight-of-hand were applied routinely to keep safe and solvent. The street afforded entertainment and education. All that lamp pole leaning during school hours secured future employment, better than opening a book, unless a bookie's book.

Elvis never gave his true name, but he did say that in his neighborhood, a name was either a lifeline or a liability. In his case, the family name provided apartment living cheaper than rent control, because the landlord wanted pipes, tiles and flooring left intact, and because Elvis' family was everywhere and everywhere on the "con." Numbers and jacked cars, jobs for illegals (immigrants and parole violators), sins of the flesh and protection. He wouldn't say why he left New York City. He did say he decided on the name Elvis partly because he's a nut for shoes: "That Costello Red Shoe tune is way cool as hell," as he would say. Then he got a band started in Burlington and began to "groove" on the two Elvises. On stage he wore black motorcycle boots, alligator boots, or red velvet pulled to his knees over jeans and called his "wonder man satin wonders" that the angels were jealous of. "I mean," he said, "these Elvises got it all covered. The blues gone funky, the babe dynamic, Hawaii movies, the hipster that don't give a shit what you think about him or his music. I'm with *ALL* that!"

So I followed the railroad track, as Elvis had instructed, and knew enough to insulate my skinny body from the cold with layers of quilted cotton and wool and soon got into a rhythm of jumping ties that had me shushing like a Nordic skier and unbuttoning to cool down until I crossed a trestle somewhere near the Blodgett oven factory and nearly poked a leg through the empty spaces before I could think what I was doing. Some old guy in a wheelchair saw me slip from his outdoors perch on a back porch in a row of houses so near the tracks they must lose foundation stones when engines pull their tonnage from Rutland to Canada and scrape clapboard in the shimmy- shake nature of its progress north. I stopped and blew a that-was-close whistle. The old guy chuckled, asked for a cigarette. He was alone on the porch under a halo of overhead light.

"I am dying of lung disease," he said. "The old lady don't give a shit. She pushed me out here because I am a constant complainer. I will admit to that. Or maybe she thinks pneumonia will end me quicker." He chuckled again and caught with a wrist snap the pack of Marlboros I tossed over the chain fence to his porch. He pulled his own lighter out from beneath blanketed legs and took a pull at the oxygen tank fastened to his chair. "You are a mindless clumser, ain't you?"

"Clumser — me? Yeah, I guess so."

"Don't mean no insult, buddy, and thanks for the smokes." He side-armed the pack back to me over the fence. A perfect throw, which I dropped, of course, through the spaces between the ties on the trestle.

"That's what I mean. Too much on your mind. You don't want to end up like Mary Blair at the underpass."

"What's that?"

"She is a ghost now." He blew a long exhalation of smoke and coughed for what seemed like ten minutes. A female voice barked from inside — "It ain't going to work, Curtis. I ain't bringing you back in."

"Ain't she loving? Ah, hell, we are all heading that way, ghostly that is. Some quicker than others. Yeah well, so this Mary Blair, down past the General Electric that makes weaponry... You been to Nam?"

"No, I had a high number in the draft."

"Oh, too bad. I am a veteran myself. I got to tell you them Garand semi-automatic rifles stamped out at G.E. was real sweet poppers when the cross hairs lined up right. Anyway, this Mary Blair, she's a ghost."

"How's that Curtis?"

"Curtis! You know me?"

"No, no, your wife said ..."

"Wife, shit! You don't know me atall. She's my girlfriend. Hell, we still fuck. I ain't dead yet!"

"Glad to hear it."

"That's right. But Mary Blair, she can't fuck no more."

"That's what I figured. How did she die?"

"Oh, I thought you knew."

"No, you were about to tell me."

"Yeah well, sure. She got hit by a train, the 8:40 that is about here now."

"Did you say a train is coming?"

"Yeah well, I come out here every night to feel it skid by. This Mary Blair, she got caught on the trestle walking like a mindless clumser to work night shift in the woolen mill from her boarding house on Lakeside. Killed her instant. Throwed her 75 feet outwards. God damn! I remember as a kid me and my buddies gathered outside the mill's boarded up windows – it has been closed years now – and we heard strange noises wailed out from that place where Mary is sposed to be wandering still. Ain't that spooky. It is a clean way to go though, ain't it, splattered by a train, if you are allowed to go that way. I wonder who makes that decision?"

"What decision?"

"How you are let go to the next place."

"Oh, sure. Hey, I feel some vibration."

"Yeah, that's the 8:40."

"I think I better go."

"Well, that is entirely up to you. Mayhaps I will haunt this here porch for the eternity of 8:40's that will be passing when I'm gone. What do you think?"

"Listen, I think I better go."

"Well, that is certainly your decision."

I got the hell out of there, slipped on snow and banged one knee against a wing of steel girder at the end of the bridge and wondered if this Curtis had meant to talk me to death. But I never did see a train. I looked back around to signal Curtis I made it across all right but he was gone, and the porch light was off, and I wondered if maybe that were a ghost train Curtis had been seeing. And then I wondered if maybe Curtis himself were a ghost. I was thinking pretty insubstantial at that moment, traipsing down a vanishing perspective of track, looking out onto Lake Champlain with twinkling lights moving around on its ice (four wheelers out there visiting shanties again no doubt) and a saw-tooth delineation of granite peaks on the far horizon where New York City moored its Mercedes and Volvos to ski chalets and time-share condominiums for a few days of waiting in lines at the lifts and boozy nights. But at least these are tangible occupations –the kinds of things that can bankrupt you or send you spinning in a coffin of rusted metal to the bottom of the lake. What was I doing? Chasing ghosts? What was it Curtis called me? "Mindless clumser." That's it. He was right. I had hocked the future in order to pay off the past. I was going broke, was spiritually exhausted, with nothing to show for the windfall extravagance that put me there but epileptic fits and a head full of bad memories that regenerated around me like the chewed off tails of salamanders. I was eating my own tail and it tasted shitty.

The animal world responded almost immediately to my irreverence. Before I could tangle myself further in my favorite Escher image, a wraith-like gandy dancer with liquid fur poured towards me through the edge of the woods with ears cocked forward and an un-nervous quivering into stillness of its satiny black withers. It came black on white snow and so smooth and sure of itself among the shadows and silent in its stillness, the healthiest living thing I had ever seen, and gone before I was sure I had been visited. I'm told it was a Fisher Cat. When I got home I asked Cat what pineal degeneration had occurred among the woodsy kitty clan to account for his shabby habits and lusterless, gnocchi pudge of fur. He told me to go lactate myself, that he didn't want to hear it, that my way of life had influenced his. Well, he had a point. This spectral messenger from the woods had placed me solidly among the uninitiated and impure in a loamy rut of tuberous undergrowth and shenanigans that pass for the "superior" race. If Halley thought me some kind of mountain man fur-trapper with mysterious impulses lathered on from a diet of animal fat and gristle – you are what you eat – here was verification from the animal world itself that I was hotel reared and carnivore shy. I guess I was in a bad frame of mind, feeling inferior to a cat, but that's the way I felt.

Chapter Seventeen

Gladys Needham deep in her cups • Words break bones • Convalescing, contemplating murder • Reginald removed, the first Mrs. Needham reinstated, all torn asunder.

Things were getting tense up on university hill. Nested among the mercantile uppity-ups and Brahmans and the academic honchos, the Reg and Gladys domicile was wracked by bickering, especially after Gladys had embarrassed them both at a faculty party (but embarrassed Reg especially). Madame college president pinned to an oriental rug in red heels blathered courtly and numinous beneath a glass chandelier – Ruth Van Patten, cool as paint in her royal blue suit with the ruffle of pink spilling out from a suggestion of décolletage at an intersection of double/breasted lapels, holding a blush of Côte du Ventoux by the stem. And there foundered Gladys, a cow gone loose in the garden in her gauzy summer number of embroidered roses twining like poison ivy a high bodice cinched with a red ribbon – a Bronte throwback that belled-out in a loose fit of the slightest suggestion of pleats. Of course Gladys didn't expect many to get the literary significance, or the personal significance. No one there, she figured, read much beyond the first five chapters of anything outside (or inside, for that matter) the Readers' Digest top ten beach list. If anyone asked, she was Jane Eyre to Reg's Mr. Rochester, having finally admitted to herself that he keeps another wife, one gone mad, up in the attic. Her auburn hair slipped lopsided in a bun stuck through with quills of Japanese lacquered pins that dislodged and fell to the parquet with Gladys kvetching, rueful, picking them off the floor and sliding them back in and picking them off the floor again, carrying an emptied bottle of gin by the neck like atrophy kill.

"So, Gladys, or Doctor Gladys of the Doctors Needham I should say, and that's a lovely dress, I am most earnest in wondering what we may expect by way of published scholarship from you, my dear? I am sure you are working on something ground-breaking. Dean Lussac tells me you are one of his brightest and most promising."

"Nice of him. Thank you, Doctor Van Patten. But I have surrendered my position as tribal griot, yes, no more tom-toms in the night, no more dreaming over desert pouches, callipygian fantasies as we say in the field. I'm working up a fanzine on theories of conjugal homicide just now."

"How is that?"

"Well, shit, Doctor, you've been married and divorced and married and divorced haven't you. What good academic hasn't? Maybe you can tell me – what's new in that since the lusty Wife of Bath changed her men like worn-out panties? Did you kill any of yours? Did you know that in the Middle Ages a nail tapped in the cranium worked excellent well, yes indeedy – tap, tap, tap, just under the hair while he's sleeping. No blood. No muss. Hell, no husband! Ever try that one – huh?"

"Well, no, Gladys, I have not. Reg!" Ruth Van Patten gestured above the nodding press of gray hairs with her free arm straight as a post and an index finger beckoning.

Reginald knew that tone of voice, the implied contretemps, and blanched when he saw Gladys tipping on her heels in a belly laugh of derring-do.

"Dr. Van Patten, how are you? Is Gladys showing off her aerobic jitters again? She is more animated than a scarab beetle in a tungsten lamp, I swear," said Reginald with his hand stretched out for shaking several feet before he reached Van Patten, oozing sang-froid.

"Keep a civil tongue, you damned, you… well!" said Gladys. "That's exactly how I feel around you these days, Reginald, a June bug in January. Ha! Did you think of *that* metaphor man? Did you? Do you even know what damn season it is?"

Gladys lifted the empty bottle to her empty glass.

"Oh, crumb! Time for a refill." And she tilted off into the buttoned-down tweeds and Herrington wools of her colleagues in her loose weave of summer cotton. When she found herself manhandled out the door by Reginald who repeated the phrase "Provost, my God, Gladys, Provost, Provost!" like a mantra with his sour breath fogging her glasses, Gladys knew she had gone too far. She didn't care.

And she didn't care all the way home in the car. Reginald moved tenderly through the gears of his classic '62 Jeep Wagoneer with the oak siding that he polishes weekly in the garage with fine steel wool and toothpaste because it's metal not wood and Reg wants no rust. Gladys lay her feet on the top of the dashboard – "to warm them up in the defrost, husband" – is what she would say if Reg complained, but he knew enough not to complain more than necessary tonight. Keep focused on the one essential problem and meaningful correction may result. God, she is such a child.

Gladys bowed her legs so the dress slid past her thighs, as if to say, sure you can look, you bastard, but you're not getting any tonight. She poked at the buttons on the radio, then dial-tuned her way through schlock and commercials, bypassing all the pre-set favorites, just to drive Reg crazy. He tried not to notice. Reg drove through the lanes past lamp-lit, painted-lady Victorian homes that Gladys had dreamed of owning when she had first started dating Reg, or screwing him in the office would perhaps be the more accurate description of their early courtship. Who knows who Reg is screwing in the office now: all right, leave your brain outside the door and bring that twat to Daddy! Gladys couldn't for the life of her imagine how she could have fallen for the advances of this pusillanimous, self-serving and inflated Mr. Rogers cardigan man with the persistent residue of blackboard chalk. What did she see in him?

"Listen, Gladys, I don't mean to be a munch, but this public acting-out has got to stop if you want us to get ahead in this university? I mean, Provost for God sake! We may never get another chance."

"We, we? What is this, the royal we? What the hell WE are you talking about? There hasn't been a we in this relationship since I let down my panties."

"That's crude, Gladys."

"Yeah, big boy. The truth can be a little raw sometimes. Would you like another dose, or are you already too weirded out?"

"What do you mean?"

"I've been thinking of ways to kill you."

"What did you say?"

Just as Gladys mentioned conjugal homicide for the second time that night, Reg had pulled into the long drive of *his* Victorian lady, the one he purchased during his first marriage as tenure had become assured, and drove around the carriage porch then straightened the vehicle in the direction of the garage and hit the electric eye over the top of the sun visor to open the door – all a matter of routine timing. The slightest pressure on the brake to save the rotors, a gentle motion arrest that's easy on the springs and in this snow a worthy method of avoiding skid, since Reginald seldom uses the four-wheel-drive as transmissions are awfully expensive to fix. And the car would likely never come back the same. But when Gladys said "kill" Reg had uncharacteristically hit the brake which threw off the timing as the tires had gripped gravel beneath the snow and altered the effects of Gladys' usual exit from the car – swinging the door open and stepping out almost before the car has stopped inside the garage, as was her habit. In this case, Gladys' door swung open, her leg went out, the door hit the frame of the garage before entering same and bounced back onto her leg as the car entered the garage. Gladys did not scream. Her leg went numb. Her shoe filled with blood instantly. The tibia and fibula had both broken and punctured the skin as Gladys' leg swung straight down like a doll with joints twisted out of place by a bully.

"Holy shit. Holy shit. I've broke my leg. You've broke my fucking leg, Reg," Gladys said in a near whisper before passing out.

After the operation and pin-installations, Reg spent a month nursing Gladys back to ambulatory once she was released from the hospital:

dashing home between classes (if, indeed, Reg can be said to "dash") with carry-out from The Bronze Gong, her favorite restaurant; back rubs in the morning with cotton gloves because Gladys complained of his cold hands, and sponge bathes in the evening with Gladys periodically succumbing to tickle spells; Reg reading her mail to her with a curious awakening to the large number of friends she has; and Reg condensing and interpreting the lead stories from two out-of-town newspapers and the one local; bringing the latest campus gossip to her evening meal including his closing on the Provost position and any sniping done on that count from jealous colleagues with appropriately mimicked accents and gestures (making Gladys guess the offenders); Reg speaking repentant gracious words to her mother who called regularly to assess Gladys' progress and the damage done to the marriage. She had been waiting for years for Gladys to fall back into the cradle from which she had been snatched.

But Gladys was having good sex now that Reg seemed genuinely solicitous, concerned for her well-being, and maybe some of his own, as having Gladys off campus during this particularly tricky political maneuvering toward that Provost job made the ascendancy almost assured, a kind of primogeniture of the most deserving. And what about that libido! Reg took Gladys with the pneumatic hammering of a man twice his youth, propping her up in chairs, setting her spread upon the vanity, wedged into the hallway stairs, even once in the car on the way to a doctor visit, before they had left the garage. Gladys was getting the best sex of her life, and she knew it – opening her arms to him each time he appeared in her bedroom. But this also worked to remind Reg that he had neglected his professorial mentoring of late. So many nubile admirers and so little time left to enjoy their attentions. Reg started banging college chicks again in the office. He was on a roll.

Gladys played phone answer machine all day while Reg was gone – so many calls to Reginald for office visits, so many girls, ALL girls. Gladys knew what was going on. She began to indulge further in her studies of "illuminating homicide," as she called it, in particular the strange tale of murderers Burke and Hare that she came to in a translation of Jorge Luis Borges. Gladys began to work the case around in her mind. Lord knows she had plenty of time to think. Those two Irishmen had gone on a killing spree in 19th century Edinburgh. They had lured victims from the streets to a garret lodging, gave them whiskey to drink and asked to hear the most unusual incidents of their lives. Once a victim approached the culmination of his life story, Hare would close his hands over the mouth from behind the settee while Burke would sit on his chest watching the last escape of living breath and look into the eyes for the unspoken final thoughts of the dying. It was a reverse Scheherazade, as the Frenchman Schwob has said, where the killer becomes indifferent to the end of the story, having decided that all of even the best tales of human suffering and accident and triumph are endlessly similar. Burke ultimately convinces Hare to take their murdering to the streets, where they cover their victims' mouths with rags soaked in pitch and dispatch them quickly – minimalist artists in their reductions. Fascinating! thought Gladys.

And then, of course, the phone rang. Gladys picked up and snorted, "When is it you want to meet Doctor Needham to fuck, honey. He's got a full schedule today. Could I pencil-dick you in for menstruation Tuesday? He's needing a lot of lubrication these days."

"What? Has Reg got a pimp service now? I'm Donna Massinger. Well, I am now. I was once Mrs. Needham. Is this Gladys?"

"Oh, shit, fuck, yes, sorry, sorry, sorry, the wife in the attic. Shit! It's me, Donna. Gladys that is. It was a joke, really. I'm sorry. Reg and I play these games, you know."

"Yes, I know about Reg's *games*, Gladys."

"Okay, look. I guess we're compadres in a sad kind of way. Things aren't going too well right now between me and Reg."

"I warned you, Gladys. I tried to. Anyway, I'm out of his range, finally. Things are going well. In fact, I'm thinking of remarrying. That's why I called."

"Oh, well congratulations! And, well, good luck, I mean, not that you'll need it. I mean not this time."

"Look, I'm not calling to invite you to the wedding. I want Reg to give me an annulment. It's important to my fiancé."

"Oh, right. Got it. Sure. I'll see what I can do. I mean, I'll pass this along to Reg."

"If you should finally deliver *one* of my messages to Reg, this would be the one most devastating to him. Tell Reg I'll call in a day or two. I *was* thinking about calling his office, but I know what goes on there. Good luck with that asshole."

"Yeah, thanks. I'm thinking about killing him."

The line went silent, no response from Donna. Glady's said, "Donna?" Then she heard a click and a dial tone. What a bitch! Gladys had known she was a bitch from before she became interested in Reginald. Donna's bitchiness had made the affair palatable. And when she caught onto them, banged on the office door with her shoe until half the science department had leached out into the hallway with their petri dishes in hand and protective goggles strapped to their foreheads, no one could blame Reginald for doing what he had to do to escape this banshee from the Bronx who never did fit in around there anyway. And when Gladys had taken over as matron of the house on university hill, she made wholesale changes to wash Donna out of their lives: a complete new wallpaper and paint job in lemons to remove Donna's brooding mauves and pale lavenders; out with the maroon curtain brocades with their gold tassel sashes and replaced by white lace with a flitting hummingbird pattern; many artsy vases fell to untimely demise as Gladys dusted clumsily ("oh, darling, sorry, another accident today"); the painting above the mantle of the Chateau Frontenac of Quebec City where Reg and Donna had honeymooned that Gladys replaced with a Kantoo tribal mask carved of a baobab tree that was supposed to ward off evil spirits (something she never told Reg); and finally, all those phone messages Donna had left with Gladys during the first two years of their marriage that she had failed to deliver. I mean, that woman was unbalanced, wigged out, an uptight P.M.S. floozy going through emotional meltdown. Gladys couldn't entirely get her out of the house, no matter what she did.

But lately, as she felt her wounded body conform to the mattress depression that had to have been made by Donna, as she thought about the wrong done herself and Donna too by this selfish man, Gladys decided to place Donna back in the house and then disappear quietly from Reg's life, leaving him to wonder if, indeed, he really had been married a second time. Gladys began replacing the artsy vases she had broken in the early days of her marriage, pieces ordered through catalogues that looked about the same or that had the "feel" of Donna. Reg didn't notice. But when the interior decorator left Gladys' bedside with a sizable contract for restoring the woodwork and walls and curtains to maroons and purples, when the crew showed up with their steam-heat wall-paper peelers and fresh paint, and when the new curtains went up shedding a blood-red glow of gloom upon the dining table where Reg takes his coffee in the morning, he noticed.

"Jesus, what the heck is going on, Gladys?"

"I was thinking we could both use a change, Reg."

"But this isn't exactly change, is it Gladys? I mean, it all looks vaguely familiar, you know. It's pretty close to what Donna did with the house. Don't you think?"

"Oh, I hadn't really noticed, Reg. Indulge me, will you, honey. I just need a diversion, and you're always so busy at work."

That shut him up, but when she replaced the African tribal mask over the mantle with a new print of Quebec City ordered from their chamber of commerce, Reg had had enough.

"What are you doing, Gladys? It took me forever to get that woman out of my life and now you seem to be inviting her back in. Why? What's going on?"

"Reg, if you must know, I am making a statement here."

"Whatever can that be, darling? You know I don't love Donna. It's been you all these years."

"Yes, that's true, Reg. I'm sure that's true, so long as we don't count the others."

"What others, Gladys? There are no *others*."

"No? Well, hand me that note pad by the phone, will you, darling. Yes, thanks. No, don't read it. Just give it to me. Good boy. Yes, here then: Effy called to say she might be a few minutes late for her office visit. I told her you'd probably start without her. She's a cute number, Reg. I can tell. But there's a slight lisp. I wonder if her overbite might make the blow job a bit difficult. Does it, darling? Let's see. Oh, yes. And here's Joanna who at least had the manners to be nervous with me over the phone. Bless her! Imagine a conscience in one so young. Could she have been a virgin, Reginald? Ah, yes, I thought so. Isn't that just wonderful. Picking cherries at your age. I'm impressed. And now here's ...."

"All right, fine. I can see where you're going with this. You know, Gladys, and I hesitate to bring this up, but you're no saint, Gladys. You know you're no saint. I've seen you in the kitchen with our male dinner guests. I've seen your hands caress the shoulders of strange men. Awfully suggestive if you ask me. In fact, if ever you should want to carry this peccadillo of yours into the courts of law, I'd say we have offended equally. Well, yes, making appropriate adjustments for what's thought appropriate for women. And you know. I'm sure you know. In a court of law, women blemish very easily, yes, very easily indeed. There will be no fleecing Reginald Needham, my dear. Don't you even think of that."

That's when the food hit the wall and some parts of Reginald, the carry-out Thai noodles and kaffir lime and prawns and chopped cilantro, and then Gladys ordered Reg out of the house.

"No, Gladys. That's impossible. This is *my* house after all. I mean, surely you see that. Let's just calm down."

"I don't want to calm down, Reg. I like this anger. It's purifying. Oh, yes, I think so. I want to do some damage. What do you say to my setting fire to this damn place if you're not out of here in ten minutes."

"You can't be serious."

Gladys leaned across the bed and set fire to the bedroom curtains with a BIC lighter she kept by the bedside for her periods of sleepless meditation with a marijuana joint but in this case trimmed to exude a torch-like flame. Reg swanned across the bed to rip down the curtains but landed on Gladys' injured leg. She shrieked with pain and surprise. The curtains disintegrated before Reg could get near them but did no more damage than blacken the ceiling and send a fairy dust of carbonaceous threads adrift in the air.

"Oh, Gladys, how could you! These are radioactive isotopes you've released. We're breathing poisons!"

"Come on, Reg," said Gladys pushing him off her leg. "This is harmless soot. Be a man, will you."

"Sure, sure, what you don't know won't kill you. That's what you're saying, isn't it? Tell that to the women that died of phossy jaw. Did you know they licked the tips of brushes and painted the dials of clocks with radioactive phosphorescence. Did you know that. A slow and painful death. Believe me."

"Preach me no lectures, Reginald."

"I'll not stay here and breath myself into the medical books. I prefer to die of natural causes."

"Good, because if you don't get out of this house soon, there will certainly be nothing natural about your death. Get out! Out!"

Reginald knew enough to avoid a scene with Gladys once she had become so raw. He knew her strength in that regard. So he threw important papers into his briefcase and an assortment of cardboard boxes, pulled out and stacked the dresser drawers that held his clean underwear and socks, rolled up and tossed his trousers and dress shirts and sport jackets into plastic garbage bags and set out for the Uptown Hotel for what he figured would be a brief stay. Gladys saw the blinking red tail lights of the Wagoneer drift out the drive and nearly leaped out of bed to celebrate! The cast held her back, as did the pain. But the exuberance nearly overwhelmed her. Gladys had bested the big bad sophisticate. And she had done it with style. Damn she was good!

Several days later, Gladys had thought about and ruled out the following: a high profile divorce implicating all of Reginald's "little darlings"; burning down the house in hopes the fire would spread and lay to waste all the pretensions that burgeoned there on university hill; going to live with Mother, which is an offer Gladys had already passed up several times since her broken leg; and actually killing Reginald (she had been tempted to try that nail tapped under Reg's receding hair line; she would need an accomplice to do it the Burke and Hare way). Then she thought of Donna, phoned and asked her over for tea, or perhaps some beverage better suited to grease the chaffing of awkward introductions.

Actually, meeting Donna had been easier than she had expected, at least at first. Donna had a soft, round face and bobbed blond hair, a sporty figure and narrow blue eyes that nearly disappeared when she smiled. She was jaunty and healthy and practical in her choice of wardrobe. The two got teary-eyed from the start, regarding each other as survivors of academic chauvinism – all mini-skirt chasers, beneficiaries of the libertine counterculture, metastasized egos, card-carrying members of the White Panthers whose motto reads "Fuck your woman so hard she can't stand up." They compared Reginald's techniques for keeping his wives in line and submersed beneath his radiance – easier with Gladys because of her star-struck wonder at being chosen by the great man of science. Gladys blushed. Not so easy for Donna to knuckle under because of her money – yes, Donna was rich, and it was her lucre that had purchased and furbished the house –and because her Brooklyn upbringing had taught her to reduce human relations to "what's in it for me." And at first, there was a lot in it for Donna – the man she had met at Columbia University had amounted to something; New York City money had bought a lot of real estate in this cultural backwater; and her Daddy was so proud to have a daughter married to a professor.

Then the two Mrs. Needhams began to compare Reginald in bed.

That's when the laughter began. Poor Reginald cut less than a dashing figure with his clothes off. His stomach heaved undulant when he got excited, his breasts sagged nearly as pendulous as a woman's, and Reg never took his boxers off until the moment of penetration, after which he collapsed like a punctured beach ball in a matter of seconds. And on the toilet he sang Broadway show tunes to obscure the clyster wind rush that purged his guts. At meals he talked endlessly of petty triumphs over colleagues while picking his teeth with the butter knife. And finally, babying that damned car that he must see as an extension of his own middle-aged endurance and classical beauty.

They laughed, clinked glasses and toasted "freedom!"

Then Donna said, "Hey, I have a great idea. Why don't we pull this house down a brick at a time."

"Oh, that's good. Yes, I think so. But let's be more imaginative than that. Let's, hold on, yes, let's strip the insides. I mean everything – walls, stairs, pipes, floors. Let's make it an empty shell and then leave Reginald to it. Symbolic, don't you think."

"I like it."

And so they did. Donna brought over a van loaded with rental tools (crow bars, hammers, electric saws, ladders, axes and wedges, coping saws for the hard to get at places), and the two spent four days in face masks and jeans and braids hammering and ripping and plying and bowling over. Gladys kept to the floor, dragging her cast around like a bug with a damaged exoskeleton. She took to calling herself Samsa, a reference lost on Donna, who smiled wryly at her new friend's eccentricity. Gladys clawed away the polished hardwoods of the floor, the baseboard and the wall-papered plaster over the lathe, and pulled apart furniture up to the finials of the built-in corner cabinets. Donna took the ladder around and pulled down the hanging crystal lamps which Gladys smashed, leaving gaping wounds in the ceiling. She scored the plaster ceilings, some with molded medallions of heraldic design. Donna left the curtains up, however, to keep the neighbors guessing. When finished, the two sat down in a pile of rubble to share a bottle of Taittinger Brut Reserve and to make further plans: Donna would sic the clergy on Reginald to get the annulment she wanted and then move to Oregon and buy a ranch for her cowboy husband-to-be. Gladys would leave the university and, and, she wasn't sure. She really wasn't sure.

Chapter Eighteen

Designer Elvis interviews Travers on underground radio. /The scent of Halley provokes a violent reaction • The man in God's formal wear • Violence in a dark room • Light in a Van Gogh vision • Uncle Gerrit confesses: sad news for Travers.

I found the warehouse after first hearing manic rock opera pouring as profusely from Designer Elvis' van as the blue exhaust that coiled out from it in the freezing air. This van was his mobile radio studio and domicile, an old utility van of faded brown with duct tape stitched over rust and an industrial antenna a story tall attached to a front fender that broadcasted underground radio. I walked farther down the tracks. The volume of the music increased. The warehouse looked to be a large red barn with three cupolas on top rising over a clump of scrub pine. The words Floral and Mechanic's Hall painted on a slate roof glimmered dimly in the illumination of a security light. I jagged down a path toward the lake off the R/R tracks. The barn had years ago been an exhibitions hall to a fairgrounds.

Elvis had parked his van on the lee side to buffer the winter wind. The motor was idling, the heat fan churning, a generator cranking power and puffing smoke from worn bearings. I sneaked around and peeked in before knocking. Elvis was there, flourishing an unlit cigarette while reclining in a beanbag chair that doubled as a bed, talking animatedly into a microphone, tweaking a bank of consoles. Quality equipment, Elvis would explain to me: hydrophones, ultrasonic translators, multiplex fm, even vhf and uhf band receivers to snag police and fire reports, and of course, crystal control transmitters with push-pull circuitry to wash out distortion. He tapped occasionally with his index finger the tuning meters that registered the strength of WEZE signals from New York City, which apparently weren't strong enough as Elvis had a cassette tape playing in his most prized piece of equipment, a Tandberg 1600X tape deck from England. I knocked on the side of the van to get Elvis' attention.

"What do you think of the Ford studio? Ain't it just techno-madness in here?" Elvis said as he removed headphones and pulled me up into the van from the sliding door. "You know, the third world does this with a juice can … paraffin wax and a wick. Rising heat. Rising heat is the answer. It makes energy. Pulls in radio waves. Way efficient, but limited. I mean. There's no selection. You gets what you gets. But costs about eight cents. Dried cow dung for fuel. Well, shit a brick, brother, you speechless? I'll end that."

Elvis propped alligator boots onto the vhf/uhf receivers. He winked at me, said: "Omni-directional, " he said, pointing to the mike. "Four-stage pop and blast filter… so," then beckoning me to get close to the mike: "B-Town!" he said speaking into the mike, "give an ear to this man Travers Jones that's here in my studio and that has just got out from a stint doing time with the Man that beat him senseless for no crime at all. Give us the inside story, man? What went down?"

Elvis pressed the mike into my hand, leaned into a cradle of hands behind his neck, smiled at my discomfort:

"Go, on, Travers! You've got an audience," he goaded.

"Well, I can't say much, you understand, because there could be legal issues, and I did get belted across the neck, but I'm okay, and the sergeant was more than fair. He's a kind man, and the stew that his wife Salome makes could have used seasoning but it does set you up for a few hours …"

"Sure, sure," Elvis said, jerking the mike away. "But what about the bust. I mean. You weren't doing *nothing* wrong when the Man cracked you with his stick. I mean, this little piggy whacked you with his righteous fascist incriminations. I say that's about enough! I say it's make your own anarchy time. Evolution needs improvisation. Get out there and make *big* mistakes of your own! That's what I say."

"I guess so," I replied. Elvis had shoved the mike back into my face, then leaned into it himself.

"So, Travers, it's a small known fact that you're doing your own sleuthing of these church fires. Anything B-Town ought to know? I mean, where do you worship when God's under attack?'"

"Shit, Elvis! What are you doing to me? I'm out of here!"

"No, no, wait. Sorry. We've got to talk, you and me. I'll put on a tape. Relax, man, relax."

Elvis slid a cassette into the Tandberg 1600X and hit forward until the digital count lined up a song he introduced as "Brian Eno with the doo-wop vocals on *Burning Airlines Give You So Much More*. This is a l_o_n_g one brothers and sisters. I'll leave you with this thought: Take a break… Listen in total darkness, or in a very large room, very quietly…Ghost echoes…Give the game away. That's from *Oblique Strategies # 18*. Feel it!"

Off the air, Elvis said to me, "Now listen, comrade, you got trouble coming. I'm here to tell you ..."

"What's that smell, Elvis?"

"What smell is that? The generator burns a little, my clove cigarette, maybe. What?"

"No, no, it's Halley. She's been here? This place smells of Halley Gay. What the hell's going on?"

"Well, yeah, she's been here. I mean, free love, brother."

"Have you screwed her?"

"Well, now that's kind of indiscreet, but yeah, I guess you could say we screwed; or you could say we danced the Watusi with our clothes off. Why? You got a claim or something, because I don't mean to step on your action…."

"Well, no, yes, maybe. I don't know. I can't believe you screwed her. That's her smell. I know her smell."

"That ain't perfume. It's Kama Sutra oil. It's fuck lotion. Hey, Travers, every gun slinger in town has bonked that bitch."

That's when I threw a punch at Elvis that had plenty of muscle but a flawed trajectory. Knuckles grazed his chin landing me on the floor beside his bean bag chair where I lay for a minute embarrassed and expecting a boot to the head or something, but nothing happened. I started to cry.

"Oh, Jesus! Get a hold, will you. Look, I'm sorry. I guess I've upset you again. Didn't mean to. Hey, listen to this ..." after which Elvis launched into a panegyric on Brian Eno's psychedelic rock philosophy. He said Eno had started out an artist but switched to music because of John Cage's influence. I said that stuff's what helped me clear my mind of hobgoblins when driving down the highway to here. Elvis said I probably needed to tame what Eno calls "idiot energy," the physical excitement of performance. I told Elvis about my ascetic habits of late which probably hadn't helped calm me much, and he said Roxy music wasn't meant for drugs. He must have thought ascetic was a drug. He said Eno himself doesn't do drugs. He does sex and women's clothes and happy accidents, a Zen thing, in his music. And that's enough turn on for him. "And I've decided, that's enough for me, too," said Elvis. "No more drugs, just excellent ideas and lots of balls and let the incompetence do its work along with the brilliance, man. It's all just one happy accident out there. Make *BIG* mistakes joyfully."

Elvis pulled me up from the floor, gave me a long hug and kissed me on the forehead, said, "But Travers, I've got to tell you about the old man in God's formal wear. He's what Eno would call a Blowtorch. He breathes fire. He makes things ignite. He's a menace, he says he's a relative of yours, and he's looking for you."

It had to be Uncle Gerrit. Elvis switched the radio show over to the fluttering airwaves of "wheeze" and said, "Well, fuck, man, the citizens of B-Town will just have to hear a little fuzz with their buzz, right."

"Elvis," I couldn't help saying, "you sound too much like Halley to have made love just once and parted. What's the gig between you two?" I said in my best cool.

"Man, Travers, will you be thinking women when Rome burns?"

"What?"

"I mean, don't you got a bigger show on right now? This old man going to the prom with Jesus, he's vicious from what I hear, and he's got a plan. Halley said…"

"Halley said! What the hell does Halley know?"

"Travers, she's with the guy. That's what I'm trying to say here. Where do you think I got all that intel that I wrote on your door? Hell, she's banging me all the while playing me."

"What?"

"Yeah, listen. Halley says this old Godly man – your Uncle, right? – he's some kind of Svengali, a crusader for a new world that'll make us all slap-happy – like freeing Aunt Jemima from the kitchen; citizens hotels for free where the sheets get changed every day; no politico over the age of 25 in office; and cars that run on pure sunshine and love. Man! What bullshit!"

"She told you all this? Those were her words?"

"Maybe not the words exactly but definitely the notion." Elvis motioned me to join him in the front seats after which he put the van in gear and pulled slowly into the night.

"But that's her trademark cynicism. Don't you see? She may be with the guy but she's not really *with* the guy, if you see what I mean?"

"Okay, sure. If you say. But what Halley wants from me is some kind of radio plug to the B-Town underground to start something happening. Designer Elvis endorsing some old man in God's formal wear! Burning churches! That's too big a mistake even for me."

"Halley said burning churches? She can't mean that!"

"Yeah, I guess. So, he's your Uncle? That right? Yeah, well, Halley's twisted but maybe she ain't by that far. She's a poor lost daddy's girl. But my guess – this Svengali man of hers is getting used back as much as he's using her. Hey, scan this!" Elvis braked the van to a sliding stop, crossed hands and pulled the bottom of his sweater up to expose a t-shirt with a print of a clenched fist hoisting a fish. The monogram read FISHERMAN. And beneath the fist in small print, You don't need a fisherman to know something's fishy, which Elvis had memorized and recited for me. "You beginning to feel me, Travers?"

Meanwhile we had been slowly poking the darkness with Elvis' Ford van, easing around snow covered slag and scrap heaps in the warehouse district of town. The occasional Doberman leaped out its shelter to the extent its chain would allow to unwelcome us. We could see the dim lights of offices where night watchmen slept. Elvis lay on the horn and fishtailed a spray of snow and giggled us into a parking lot where large, empty buildings loomed.

"Where are we going, anyway?"

"Here it is, the Anthony Lumiere place."

"That's an interesting cultural mix, Elvis. Antoine, maybe?"

"Yeah, whatever. Halley told me to meet her down here and that's what we're doing. Course she doesn't know there's two of us. She wants me to meet her old man Godly man. I figure you should come along too. She said come in through the lean-to at the west side. Never mind the place looks fallen-down deserted. It's not. She said that Lumiere, some French guy, built this place in the last century to develop color film. She knows that on account of her photography interests. Anyway, this guy Lumiere, he built the darkest, driest building in the western hemisphere right here."

"I'm sure I remember he had something to do with motion pictures."

"Yeah, well, I don't know about that, but here's the place."

Elvis navigated around a long box of bricks, turning corners where I couldn't tell we were going around a building. There were no windows, so nothing to reflect the Ford's headlights. The brick seemed, in fact, to absorb all the light we threw at it. Intense darkness from the outside and, once we parked beside the lean-to and pushed through an unhinged door to the interior of the building, an even more intense darkness on the inside. We grabbed hands like kids. Our breathing sounded hoarse and out of control. Echoes shot through the building from an unknown source. I had the feeling bats were flitting above. We stood there a long time trying to adjust to the dim, waiting for objects and perspective to materialize. And they did, but no more prominently than lumps of Vaseline applied to black velvet.

"Is that you, Elvis, darlin'?"

When I heard that voice, I thought maybe I had jumped high enough to hit my head on the ceiling. Elvis became serious and assertive.

"Yeah, it's me. Why all the cloak and dagger? We got something to hide here? I mean, shit, this is creepy."

"Is that Travers Jones keepin' you company, Elvis?"

"The very same."

"This is a infraction of our agreement, don't you think, sugar. This will not be taken well."

"That right? You saying your Godly man won't approve? You think I give a shit?" I could feel Elvis straining with his free hand to catch a hold of anything solidly human in the direction of Halley's voice. There was, or I thought I could see, the slightest waft of blonde hair floating somewhere to our left. I couldn't be sure. "Hey," said Elvis, "bring your old man Godly man around. I'd like to know his plan. Travers here has some interest too, as you pretty much know."

That was the last I heard from Elvis. I felt a rush of air and heard a crack of wood against Elvis' skull as he let go my hand and fell dead weight to the floor I couldn't see that might as well have been a hundred feet down. Then I heard Uncle Gerrit. His voice chilled me: "Bring the lad Travers tae me."

"No, I'm not real comfortable with that" was all I could finesse out from a mealy-mouth (dry tongue maneuvering around pebbles once again); then a flash of light struck from deep away in the dark. My eyes dilated instantly. Pure light. Then a veiny composition of silvers and whites and pinks that ended in a blow to my own head and an explosion of red and me slipping into a tonic clonic epileptic fit, and I swear that I smelled fear. I don't think it was my own. I think it was Halley's. I collapsed to knees as I had done at Nectar's, but this time lost consciousness and flopped and salivated and thought I remembered hearing Gerrit tell someone to bring the Datsun truck around, then I fell deep into my own darkness where a fiery presence awaited me, but not my father's.

I found myself removed to a room enveloped in a yellow-green mist, a poison cloud leaning on the window from outside, a shaving mirror refusing to reflect above a wash stand bearing a basin and pitcher, a majolica jug, a military brush, a drinking glass and apothecary bottles clear as gin, the floor green and alive, crawling alive, photographs of strangers on the loud blue walls leaning toward me in accusatory gesture, the walls also leaning, rush-mat chairs shifting on the slanted floor, all off center and teeming with life, threatening with color and an undertow of violence gathering in the corners, and at the far wall of the room, a fourth wall, too far to see distinctly, shadows, an emptiness, but someone within watching. The four posts of the orange bed on which I lay burst into flame, a kind of ritual immolation and me unable to move. And a tall, gaunt man, first a shadow then emerging from the wild colors of the room, red haired and bearded, laughing at me, but painfully, and walking into view from the dimness, holding up his hands where flames appeared, saying, "My gift to the world," and then the eyes rolling back and him collapsing to the floor, gone into seizure, the room catching fire, and a black emptiness starting to PacMan the room in bite-sized chunks. Only the flaming bed remained with me screaming soundlessly, masturbating violently as if my seed would extinguish the fire.

I jerked back to consciousness, pulled off a tangle of blankets, leaped to the floor, sweating, unsteady, gagging in dry air. I had awakened in another room, my own room on Grant Street. I looked toward the door for the threatening stranger. There was none. I had dreamed, and I never dream. I felt cheated. There was something wrong, I mean, something wrong with the nature of my vision. The world I go to in seizure is not a dream but an illumination, like the private fears and bawdy jokes of Irish monks in those stone towers of Ireland of the Middle Ages. They scratched with cramped fingers their ontological uncertainties in dark stains of calligraphy on vellum. Life back then was brief, and their monk jokes fiercely serious as they awaited the next Viking scourge, awaited the torch and pyre of a breached stronghold, and then gone to blazes like a Roman candle. Dreams are wastelands of impossible symbols, I have always felt. They melt in the daylight like Dali's clocks. Dreams are a waste of intellectual baffling. Jung set dreams to mandala images just to piss off Freud. And Freud thought every dream was about sex. I wasn't about to paint a mandala of the room I dreamed, and I had no sexual interest in the man with the red hair, a poor version of my father, a tortured weakling where my father was virile and deliberate, or so I felt back then. Even Zarathustra pronounced dreams a "terrible mistress," because they sent him back to seclusion, back like a bear to his cave. I was just beginning to venture out from the solitude of all those months meditating in this garret, and it felt good.

Gloom descended again when I heard coming up the stairs toward my apartment, the hobnailed shoes and pronounced limp of a skinny man who used to shuffle and bump furniture with opera leaking from a Zenith radio in the upstairs loft of the East Boston hotel he shared with my mother. There was no mistaking Uncle Gerrit. I remembered that something terrible had happened in the Lumiere warehouse, something beyond the throbbing of my sore head, but I couldn't for the life of me remember what. Not yet. And he would quickly redirect my attentions elsewhere. Uncle Gerrit was good at that.

There he was half through the door, his head characteristically tilted, his body stooped from scoliosis like he'd slid down a knotted rope ladder, his head much too large for his body, and a shock of white hair rising in colic around ears framing a bald head and dark, fathomless pits of nose and mouth like empty mine shafts, the mouth ever open. His appearance reduced me instantly to adolescent subservience under the threat of gargoyle features pressed into my face. But the smell was different. The incense and sweat had been canceled out, neutralized by a scent I couldn't make out, rivers of it. I had a quick image of Gerrit rushing into the arms of lonely perfumed women after erotic confessions. But that ended once Gerrit reasserted his role as the dominant male in my life –

"Travers, lad. How be ye?" came the familiar Scots idiom in the familiar tone of a pontificate. The head bobbed as he angled his face closer. "Don't bother tae answer," Gerrit said forcing a smile then seemed to mean it, avuncular even, deriving proprietary pleasure from memory of me as a pink, scrubbed child he had once roughed behind the ears with a towel. Gerrit now stood inside the door to my apartment, testing the waters with his toes before plunging in. He did, in fact, lift one foot to poke a scatter of litter. "Some things be plain enough, sadly, sadly," he said.

Gerrit walked and rounded the U of the half wall that hid my kitchen. He blanched and rubbed his nose and scurried back to my card table beside the window beside the bed and sat on a chair.

"My God, lad. Yer dwelling in a friar's hovel. Do ye aspire tae sainthood? Do ye pay rent for this? I knew travel would taint yer mind, yer goodly mind. What of those years of learning lavished upon ye from the sweat of my brow, lad? What can ye be thinking tae waste yer scope in this…sloth and refuse. Sloth, my boy, and refuse. Are ye taking drugs, lad? Have yer morals shifted upon the quicksand? By the gods, yer mother has been worried half tae death."

"I'm sorry. I did write."

"Oh aye, a wee jot of a postcard rhapsodizing these hill folk of their folksy humor, none of yer own self. Yer mind's a mystery, lad. Thank goodness for the Burlington postmarks."

"What are you doing here?"

"Well, as much as I would like tae preen yer ego, I cannot cite yer prodigal ways as sole reason for my sojourn. Truth is, I have been asked tae arrange a choral celebration upon the ordination of the Bishop of Montreal."

I was not surprised Uncle Gerrit's talent had been recognized, but I was beginning to remember something was wrong. Something very wrong had recently happened, but this visit of Gerrit's after a strange dream had me off-center and confused.

"Aye, good, and I rang Magill University tae sort out a brief reunion of us two, lad, and tae admonish yer forsaking yer mother. But ye had not matriculated, they said. I have saved yer mother knowing. But I find I must tell her some part of the truth, once I have a tithe's moment tae myself. It is her due. And I met the most lovely man in yer sergeant of police. He seemed tae take large interest in me, and he knew precisely yer whereabouts. So here am I, but shortly gone tae Montreal. And now, what can ye say tae justify yer waywardness, lad?"

"I had an accident?"

"Aye, ye say so. But no loss of limb that I discern. No godly reason tae bury yerself in refuse?"

"No, I guess not. How is my mother?"

"Yer mother, lad, is sound and calm and making grand decisions of late. But more of that anon. Yer father, I fear, is quite dead."

Instantly I knew it was so. And the reason for my having gone through the last church burn without seizure, and the reason for that dreamed-up, red-haired stranger. My eyes began to tear, an embarrassment to Gerrit. Tightness gripped my chest. Then I remembered distinctly what had happened to Elvis and that I had heard, if not seen, Halley Gay, and all the rest. I got worked up enough to challenge Uncle Gerrit for an explanation of events in the Lumiere building. But he countered by placing in my hand the letter I still possess that explains in soldier Jones' own words the liaison with my mother in the underground of London during the war.

Gerrit explained further what he knew of my father. He said it was time I knew all. This information nearly ruined my life, as you will see. He said that soldier Jones was in fact Timothy O'Connell, the man Martin Toussant had seen in my physiognomy – "Did I remember?" – that day Gerrit led me to the park in East Boston to introduce me to his memory of Paul Tillich. I remembered. Gerrit admitted he had been the confessor to Mr. O'Connell. The poor man came regularly to confession near the time he shipped out for Europe to fight the Germans. O'Connell was having a spiritual crisis at the time. He could see nothing godly in a war where the Germans and their pagan gods were said to be fighting the Hebraic Christian God and all his winged minion. "Let them at it then. All them gods! Leave us poor bastards alone!" he would say. He was dissatisfied with the Catholic Church in its silence over Jews disappearing into the ghettos of Europe and then disappearing again. He said his mother was Jewish and much concerned about rumors she had heard of vanished relatives in the old country after cash and jewels and legal documents had come to her in the mail with brief explanation to hold these items indefinitely. Gerrit said to my father that he had spoken to the philosopher Paul Tillich about this very thing – war goes on, God does nothing. Gerrit and my father became friends outside the church. He felt, in fact, that that is where their friendship belonged.

Then Uncle Gerrit told me of the "proposal," one he had been contemplating for a while, waiting for the right man to come along. Gerrit told O'Connell of his plans for a new church, a new world view through a new religion, and that he wanted a child to raise in accordance with these new principles. That child, of course, would be me. Gerrit had convinced O'Connell that Fiona, Gerrit's sister, would make the perfect mother. He arranged for O'Connell to locate Fiona (an army nurse stationed in London) once he had landed there with the American army. O'Connell would seduce the Scots, Catholic virgin with the red hair whom Gerrit knew would turn to himself and away from family and Scotland, the native country, once a child was conceived. Once all had transpired, done absolutely to Gerrit's liking, O'Connell would go AWOL and begin to burn churches in Europe, those that hadn't already been leveled by bombs.

"But my mother knows him as Jones."

"Aye, that's right. Timothy signed his name Jones when he enlisted, bafore the draft sneked him. With the name Jones he was able tae AWOL the army without shaming family that assumed him gone tae cannon slubber on the beach at Normandy, and with the name Jones there would be no East Boston link tae alert yer mother tae the truth of your paternity."

"So, I have been bred to serve this new-world religion."

"No, ye have been bred and educated tae lead it, and yer father would be proud tae have ye do so."

That's when the door to my apartment squeaked open just enough for Halley Gay to peek inside and ask, "Is this a good time, sugar? Have I missed my cue? Have I come premature?"

Chapter Nineteen

Travers projected into the future: Montreal gained, Montreal lost; a companion gained, a companion lost • To East Boston for paternity, grandparents, witchery, adultery, D-Day and churches burn in Europe • Halley Gay fucks away the Zen moment in Travers.

Fathers and sons and fathers and sons again – no matter how many arms and legs and faces grow off the stalk, it's the same puppet dance all the way back to that simpering primogenitor Adam. And sadly, the son rarely develops beyond the worth of the father, usually turns out worse. But which is better, the milksop or the murderer? Imagine how Adam felt about Cain. Fascinating case of agrarian murder, my boy, seminal, first rate job. In my case, as a son, the issue becomes more unclear the more I uncover. Soldier Jones planted me, abandoned me, then tried what he could to change the direction assigned to me. As to my own son – I am hopeful. I tap my fingers on the steering wheel, my companion smiles at me, and something, a cantata, moves me down the highway, two voices in contention, from Bach I think, a theme for my son who is wending his own road, negotiating in the purity of untried optimism those decision detours that define character. I now accept there will be accident in his life too.

After the death of my wife, sitting alone in the drab sanctity of a Montreal townhouse, I think more frequently of my own father. When I draw back curtains of the bay window she would thresh open in her 5 a.m. rush to outpace the advancing sun, the sky chalky at first light, I see garbage cans tipped on sidewalks, wrens flitting between stick branches of urban forestry, soot on Volvo fenders. I grieve for my wife in the shadow of the mountain that crests the horizon from my bay window, the mountain itself too soon outlined in pink and red from a descending sun. I sit at the dining table with a tumbler of whiskey, nod to buttoned-down neighbors that brisk walk past when I part curtains. I suppose they know they are on parade, and they're such conservative farts here in the university borough. I never made it to that Rabelaisian state of mind where belly laughs absorb neuroses.

Before my wife began to fade, when the reasons for her headaches were whispered terminal, she insinuated my return to East Boston to discover what I could of my father. She pushed me out the door with a kit bag already packed. So I flew for the first time into Logan Airport, where the view of my childhood neighborhood outside the plane window washed pastel on geometric shapes that became clear as warts when I stepped out from a cab on Marginal Street and inside the hotel diner where I grew up. The place was more run down than I remembered. And it had diminished in size and impact once my world had expanded beyond its scope. But there stood Lucinda with candy-red nails pouring sludgy coffee, the usual scene, now wearing a platinum wig, her smile a good deal more yellow by contrast, same as her complexion. But her eyes shone clear trembling in recognition of this middle-aged man gone paunchy and pale and a bit hardened from abrasions and bumps suffered outside Lucinda's care. I have to admit to having to work through a case of the fondness trembles myself.

When I told her the abbreviated story of Gerrit and the Burlington church fires, she couldn't have been less surprised. She told me some things about Gerrit she had witnessed that made her feel that way – Gerrit pinching the ears of a dog that had fawned and slavered for his attentions (I tried not to smile conspiratorially at that one, remembering Cat); Gerrit complaining endlessly that vegetables at the diner were served raw (he preferred boiled) and never once leaving a tip; Gerrit eyeing her lasciviously ("and he a man in absentia," she said which took me a while to figure out); and finally the way Gerrit had "nastied" my childhood, as she put it. When

I mentioned Martin Toussant, asked how he is and said I need to talk to him, first she blushed then motioned me to join her at a booth. The red vinyl creaked beneath our weight, held together in a web of electrician's tape. Lucinda twirled the juke box selection panels nervously. I noticed the old standards: Bobby Vinton's blues – "Blue Velvet" and "Blue Moon" – and some other dreamy crooning.

Lucinda said, while pressing alphabet keys on the box, she knew she had aged considerably since I had left East Boston but she still had a young heart. She had fallen for Toussant's romancing back when he bullied the high school basketball team to a state championship (more muscle than skill, she admitted, but the way Martin moved on that court like he owned it, that's what attracted her, like he could tuck the world under his arm and walk away with it if he wanted). He finally gathered the moxie to depart for the big city (Boson proper, that is), where he was offered a job welding vats at a Coca Cola plant. He had waited many years for Lucinda to join him there, had asked often, but she couldn't leave that hotel. There was always the chance her father would return to claim his daughter. Lucinda knew she would recognize him by all the features she had that her mamma hadn't passed to her – a flat bottom, thumbs that flanged like fishing lures, crooked teeth, and something she wouldn't talk about. I said I had something similar in mind as a reason for wanting to find Toussant. I shared the story of my nativity.

When I had finished my story, Lucinda daubed her painted eyes with a napkin, reached across a liver-spotted and veiny hand to pat my arm (thumbs oddly shaped), and gave me the information she could on the whereabouts of Toussant, including his most recent address she had off a letter he had sent, his last, three years back from somewhere in South Boston.

I returned to the cab I had taken from the airport and gave him Toussant's last-known address. It lacked suitability as a tourist destination. I could tell by the driver's questioning gestures, his tipping and fiddling and repositioning a baseball cap, eyes probing my resolve in the rear-view mirror

before cranking the ignition. I had forgotten I had overdressed for this trip –
stepping out from our Montreal townhouse in cosmopolitan professor
garb. Was I morphing into a Reginald Needham? What a thought. Not
possible, I decided, knowing the conclusion to his story, but that comes
later. When I knocked at Toussant's door, he said, "I am about to pay! I told
you that once before already," but he reverted to his freckled, eternally
jejune mix of bewilderment and unquestioning acceptance when I told him
who was knocking: "Why it has been a lifetime since I seen you, the priest's
little man. You're the kid Lucy used to have me carry upstairs when you
falled asleep in the booth. Jesus H. It's you."

He couldn't stay away from "serious water" he confided, so I found
him defending in his retirement a room in a mossy, cedar-shake tenement
beside a row of shoreline oil tanks that obscured the water views but
where Toussant could hear freighters churning and dropping anchor a half
mile off shore to pump loads of fuel into pipes that floated like giant
spigots in the bay. "Defending" because he removed routinely the
landlord's realtor-posted, for-sale signs and flung them across the road
into the rank shallows of the bay. He thought he could out-maneuver and
out-wait the landlord, keep his room there forever. The smell of diesel
pouring through smoke stacks of tankers and fog horns wailing and
broke-down cars and pitted roads and boarded-up houses and porn
businesses deep in the heart of trades-ville reminded Toussant of East
Boston. He regretted having left, asked with those eternally weepy eyes
how Lucinda was getting on, said he wondered should he send a card or
visit or something. I encouraged both, but when he stood to pull more
beer out from the frig, his pear-shaped body having expanded at the
bottom end to something like a giant tuber scraping its way across the
floor, he said, "Oh, this here is the waters settled off my collection of
diseases. I carry a ocean of weight everywhere I go. And let me tell you it
is a Jesus H. bitch to have your thighs chaff together like this." It was easy
to see that he seldom went much farther than the refrigerator. I couldn't
imagine him making it down the stairs to sabotage the landlord's plans to

sell. But, motivation is everything.

When I told him Timothy O'Connell is, in fact, my father. He said, "Damn! That's a fact! I can see it. I can. That priest of yours – what's he pulling?" That I didn't get into, but I did elicit from Toussant all he could remember of my father's upbringing and history up to his disappearing overseas.

Toussant said the Irish of my grandfather and the Jewish of my grandmother had coalesced perfectly in my father. I said, you mean complex artsy showy like the *Book of Kells*, mysterious and darkly humorless like the *Kabbalah*? He said, "Well, yes, I suppose." He said my father, Timothy, and he had worked beside my grandfather who managed a machine shop. They made prototype weaponry for the infantry – masquerading as simple tool & die work. Timothy wanted nothing more than to fire those things at wrecked boats littering the bay (not the job of the shop; the stuff got trucked away to a secret armory in the interior of Maine somewhere to test). But Timothy's enthusiasm for weaponry dampened when he saw the wounded come home from the front. They were so inarticulate and unwilling to share experiences that Timothy spooked.

Timothy's father, my grandfather, was the Irishman I had heard talked about in the hotel diner that paid someone $100 to learn to write his name. As shop manager with a government contract, paperwork consumed increasingly more of the worries and energies he expended on the job. Timothy did the reading and grandfather did the signing, perspiring over every letter so as not to rip through paper or misspell. He loved Timothy's mother with a passion near hysteria. He couldn't believe that eyes so enclosed in Earth-mystery, a Nubian beauty throughout, would settle for a pale complexion and the pale life he could provide. He couldn't believe she would stay with him, and maybe that's why she didn't. Toussant remembered my grandmother's name was Hester, called "witch Hester" by the neighborhood kids.

My grandfather had snagged her away to a remote part of East Boston, all the way to Nay Street, down the end of a dirt lane where the

Chelsea Creek dribbled its wide and shallow windings in the shadow of a toll bridge that crosses the creek overhead. Timothy's mother built beside that creek a paradise of flowers, which Timothy's father had terraced for her in native flagstone. And he built for her a rambling system of porches that were so labyrinthine little Timmy used to lose his way, which was maybe what the husband had in mind – keep his loved ones padding ceaselessly the home paths, which are complicated enough, and keep the world altogether out. Besides decorating the gables and arches of this house with gingerbread, he had built two minarets on opposing ends of the roof, one a tribute to Hester's God that she never had the nerve to explain as errant (it had the Star of David planted at its peak; the other had lofted upon it a Celtic cross). They served as compass points for Timmy's explorations and gave the house an Ali Baba Baghdad look that cars passing the Chelsea Creek Bridge would strain to see, as flying carpets were back then the favored special effects of Hollywood movies.

The arrangement was for Timothy to grow formally to manhood as an Irish Catholic while Mother was free to tamper with his spirituality in her own way at home. And she did, sneaking around Timothy's New Testament stories with folksy concepts of Earth-energy, Gaia the all encompassing. "Earth Mamma" is what Timothy's father called her. She was probably the world's first hippie chick. But "witch" is what Timothy's friends called her. Partly because she kept pigs and butchered them beside the creek where blood runneled down the bank and into the water staining white pebbles.

The carcasses could be seen strung from tree branches with hoists of rope and broom handles, the flesh between tendon and shank bone incised and fixed with small sticks and legs pulled wide apart for butchering. Hester would speak appeasing words to the dead beast through this process, which Timothy explained to his friends was her way of thanking the animal's gift of flesh. A kettle nearby burned fat into soap, so as not to waste. While brandishing tools, she would say proudly: "A good cook changes knives but once a year. I cut with the spirit, not with my eyes. I follow things as they are. I never touch ligament or tendon, much less a main joint. My knives stay sharp." That was spooky enough, but when Timothy's friends learned of his epilepsy, they weren't sure whether he might be the victim of witchcraft. Here Toussant's weepy eyes widened, while his voice modulated expressing humor, while his face with that immense mustache remained impassive.

It wasn't until I heard about my grandmother's affair with an Army soldier that I felt the old familiar dizziness – lost again in those circular patterns. Fathers and sons and fathers and sons again. There cannot be "chance" in a world such as this, or at least in a world such as mine. Gerrit must have been right about the stars and their influence, although things didn't exactly turn out like he had planned or foreseen up there in his attic plotting my life with those arcane charts and mathematical systems.

Toussant said that an Army soldier, a Captain, an intelligence officer, was assigned to oversee my grandfather's production of prototype and modified weapons – .50 caliber machine guns, 2 inch mortars, the Garand semi-automatic rifle that already had 72 parts before the O'Connell shop added more, and a bunch of "unknown somethings" that turned out to be plastic loop antennas used in the Doolittle raid on Japan. Actually, that Army Captain had been assigned to watch over grandfather himself, to assure no secrets were passed by him to the enemy. That's why the Captain became a familiar in the O'Connell home: he was given a room in that ramshackle palace my grandfather had built for his wife, a room the Army compensated generously, and he shared meals and discussed what he knew of the latest war developments with the family. They called him Captain in the home and Bobbie when he put on overalls and carried a lunch bucket to work, ostensibly a machine operator (boring holes in gun stalks, boring, very boring) and ostensibly a good buddy of both my father and grandfather. Until, that is, he began to take carnal interest in Hester.

She knew, and she was flattered and she thought she could change him to a man of peace. She took him down by the creek to the butcher gardens one Sunday afternoon, there where the Tiger Lillies were closing as the light declined. She took his trousers down and performed on him such mind-altering sexual deeds as to make the poor man think he was a wild mushroom growth on dark rotting wood that had been plucked lovingly by a wood nymph and buttered and held over a fire then nibbled and sucked and pulled upon with those full lips speaking his name while praising what she called the "little flower of the sacred light." The trouble came when Hester's husband found his wife gourmandizing upon the young man in that garden and took his boy Timothy with him to live close among citizens of East Boston near the Catholic church, Our Lady of the Mount, and never returned to that house.

That's when Toussant came to know my father best and was told of his mother living alone in that house of witchery. This was also when Uncle Gerrit exerted his influence upon the young man whose life was torn by a mother who would not separate herself from her son nor admit wrongdoing. She appeared in her shawls and sandals each morning seated upon the front stoop of the apartment father and son occupied. She followed Timothy to work and shouted over his shoulder updated news of Jewish relations in Europe, whatever she could discover from sources her Captain friend, as she called him, could discern. Timothy was expected by his mother to do what he could to verify rumors and to aid her family once he stepped ashore on German occupied territory, once he was sent to the war, as indeed he would be. Hester no longer thought she could turn a military response to a spiritual one. Hester had become frantic when she learned that allies had confiscated several teletypes sent by commander Stroop to SS-Chief Henrich Himmler documenting the destruction of the Warsaw Ghetto. Hester's relatives were Polish. **The Jewish Quarter of Warsaw is No More!** reads the title in Gothic calligraphy upon the commemorative volume bound in black pebble leather that was found in Himmler's possession at the end of the war. It documents the mass murder of a city of Jews with terms technical, militaristic, chillingly commonplace: "transfers" said for deportations to death camps, "fortifications on higher ground" for desperate resistance barricaded in second and third story apartments. Timothy promised he would help.

But in confession, he told Gerrit that forces working inside him prevented his feeling obligated to help his mother in this matter. Timothy could feel no remorse for her suffering nor for those of her relatives, and his own by extension. He also felt no compunction whatever to beat the Hun to submission for the evil it had released upon the world. There must be something wrong with him. No, said Gerrit, those forces do not generate from inside you but come from without. And Gerrit explained gradually and with delicacy the precepts of Tillich's evolution toward a new world order and his own take upon the means to achieve as much. Here was a kind of order and meaning and devotion that Timothy could fasten upon rather than the chaos of world war and adulterous mothers and betraying countrymen soldiers.

His own father had slipped too far down a bottle of whiskey to be of any help. Soon he wouldn't hold a job nor pay the rent, so Gerrit took his case to the charities relief. My grandfather died, his liver and heart giving out simultaneously, soon after he thought my father had died on the beaches of Normandy. Timothy O'Connell did join the war effort and shipped out to Normandy, under the name of Jones. The war department had said no soldier named after my father and from East Boston appeared on the roster of the enlisted or drafted, but that they would cross check records for any oversight. My grandfather lost faith entirely in our government – it had taken away his wife, then his son. He figured Timothy had come to an unknown soldier's death on the beach invasion at Normandy. He wondered what his own life can have been worth.

I still can't bring myself to visit the house off Nay Street by Chelsea Creek that embodies my grandmother either in the flesh or in spirit. Or maybe she's gone entirely and the house become an abandoned shrine that I would be sorely tempted to purify with fire.

As to my father's war experiences, Toussant had a couple letters from him, one from before the desertion and one after. Of the Normandy landing, the thing that most impressed Toussant was my father's claim to have never fired his weapon. On June 6th, at dawn, soldier Jones had debarked with a squad of men off an LCVP into the surf where half died before reaching the beach. My father dove behind a section of crossed steel beams intended by the Germans to prevent beach landings but in this case a life saver of armor plate against machine gun rounds fired from bunkers not yet destroyed by allied bombing, or the 16 inch guns off shoals of battleships that blackened the sky with smoke. Soldier Jones looked for the remnants of his squad up on the beach and in the surf but found none he could identify. Allied fighter planes, Grumman Avenger torpedo bombers mostly off aircraft carriers, screamed out of the sky between low-flying barrage balloons; wounded and dying men screamed for their mothers or to their God; tanks chugged off LSTs and sputtered in the surf and sometimes stalled and then exploded as German batteries found their positions; German mines exploded strewing gore among the survivors. Soldier Jones held his breath under water and wished for gills. It wasn't until late in the day as the tide receded, leaving him exposed as well as beaching the Navy's LST's, that Jones realized he numbered among the living. He abandoned his carbine there behind steel beams, crawled slowly to the nearest group of soldiers digging fox holes as scores of German prisoners were hurried down paths along seascape cliffs where an American flag lay stretched out in the dirt to warn away friendly fire.

Soldier Jones was discovered by an officer who pressed him into a squad and in the next few days followed sleepless men over tumbled walls and through blasted farm land that paratroopers and bombers had already cleared of the enemy. When Jones reached Carentan, the first French town liberated by the allies, he found a quaint village church in the precinct he was given to patrol and entered alone at twilight and meditated for a couple hours before setting fire to it and disappearing into the night.

Toussant said he had not kept any of my fathers' letters, but that he remembered them perfectly, especially the one about the church fire. Timothy had fixated on a fresco, somewhat faded and spotted with spores from the damp. That fresco had turned him nearly frantic with despair, and he off kilter still from demons released among the swarming hordes of battle. The fresco that excited his demons you would think might have done the opposite. It depicted a wedding (commissioned by local dignitaries of the 16th century to glorify themselves as much as the church that sanctified their inbreeding). There were maidens riding unicorns, gallants in velvets and leather reining black stallions in a cotillion of hounds tugging and snapping playfully at the entrails of a deer, merchants with fat purses on palfreys, all switch-back descending a castle path with pennants glistening like jewels in the cypress hills to the very church Soldier Jones occupied. The curate in his ceremonial robes welcomed all with open arms outside the doors to his church and the couple to be married rode white barded horses arrayed in heraldic trappings, the couple themselves nearly overwhelmed in billowing white, in silks and satins. All that empty, vapid, barren, and frightening white, soldier Jones thought. The color of expended energies, of explosions on the ground and in soldier Jones' brain, the foggy-bottom river valleys of early morning where enemy lay in ambush, the film that rounds contours of the eyes of the dead, that stretches across the globe ahead of the rising sun. And the lies of virgins who sneak to the river to bleach their smocks, and of the drapery of the tabernacle, robes of the sacristan, the white-washed walls of stucco inside the church. Soldier Jones burned that church in a fever of disgust, stole a new life off a clothesline and vanished into the hills.

My father's ecclesiastical pyromania was explained to me by Uncle Gerrit on the night he first appeared in my Grant Street apartment in Burlington. He said my father had boldly asserted the new order in Europe. He said I must do the same in the New World. Halley had walked silently into the room and sat beside me on the bed looking up at my uncle with simmering expectation, her satiric mind seemingly liquefied to goo. This amazed me. Maybe Elvis was right. Maybe Halley was *with* Gerrit. My father, Gerrit said, had (as Toussant had also said) become pacifist during the most apocalyptic battle of the European theater (what a word, "theater," my father had said in a letter to Tousssant, like we voyeurs have achieved an upgrade from the more mundane parade of highway accidents and public suicide). And in that church in France my father had stated unequivocally his passion for pulling down the old lies, just as much as Paul Tillich had shown Gerrit through setting fire to that sandcastle.

My father, soldier Jones (having abandoned his old life, the O'Connell life), had begun what I must finish. Uncle Gerrit then repeated a childhood lesson – that my father appears in my epileptic fits, a sign of spiritual bounty, as my guardian angel, the one chosen to show my life's work.

At this point Halley ran a cool hand over my hot cheek and gave a nod to Gerrit who groaned off the chair leaning heavily on his cane and scraped out the door, leaving us behind to sort the words he had spoken. I was overwhelmed, guilt-ridden, complicit, trapped in a design beyond my understanding. All I could say was, "Why Elvis?" The only answer I got was, "Not the right moment, Travers."

Halley made love to me, tenderly, speaking all the while, extolling my imperfections, calling them gifts, locking hips on mine and rocking in a rhythm that seemed trance like, her eyes closed and mine wide open focused upon the hollow of her throat that blushed red with passion. I thought again of "love apples" and then of Jesus' sacred heart my mother had hung in a painting above her bed in East Boston. Halley spoke of my epilepsy as a wound as sear and directive as her brother's amorous betrayal that had locked away the love she intended to release there with me. Later I would realize she had been releasing her love wherever a brother Quebecois needed her attentions.

So there I was embraced by the woman I lusted after who had been teasing me blue but now promised tactile devotion. And there I was touted by Gerrit as a warrior prophet (me, the fuck-up, always victim, ivory-towered hermit leading the world to a new spiritual awakening!) and with the blessings and understanding of a father I had never met except in seizure. If Halley thought this was me, maybe it was. It's surprising how much who we become depends upon what others think we should be. I was hooked, high on myself and my potential and looking forward to more passionate love making with this beautiful woman and…what the hell…at least something was happening. Fuck living in the Zen moment. Make the moment. The wait was over.

Chapter Twenty

Vasari investigates Designer Elvis's fiery demise • Vasari suspects cult violence acted upon the Needham home • Brady investigates Dr. Needham's tribe • Vasari attempts to redeem Travers • Make big mistakes joyfully!

The phone jangled Vasari's already taught nerves. He had been lost in gesture, buffing the plaque inside his Rotary coffee cup with the underside fringe of his tie, worrying Father Gerrit into place, and dropped the cup but slapped his knees together in a thew-bruising reflex. "Jeezum!" Vasari blasphemed remorsefully, drew the cup to his chest dipping his tie into the bowl like sopping toast. He needed time to think – another priest had soured his day, this one unsettling in unusual ways, nothing drunken and lascivious, nor razor-edged like Bishop Semprebon's power theatrics. This Father Gerrit was too smooth in the quaint old-worldly way of crafty emigrants, asking in broad a's and deep o's for Vasari to help locate his nephew, Travers McDeed Jones, because of a Burlington, Vermont, canceled stamp on a folksy Vermont post card inscribed with "can't get there from here" clichés sent by Travers to his mother back in November.

The cup polishing had spiraled Vasari back to childhood days of sleepless nights in bed mulling and ordering complication in rhythm with the Burlington Northern and Canadian Pacific that clacked and shook past his house. As mother suggested, and in preparation for a night's sleep, Vasari would tally his concerns and confusions and toss them like freight to the men powering those load-bearing locomotives. He packaged his most serious considerations in bright paper with bows, smaller worries in brown paper secured in twine, tossed all onto flatcars for unwrapping at some undisclosed destination farther down line. That's what his mother had told him to do, when Nickoli lay awake counting sins and others that had sinned against him. Nickoli envied the train crew's scope view of America birling in lamplight down tracks, landmarks dropping away, the train itself glittery blue like scales on a trout, too gleamy and fast to collect a burdock of a worry. For the land bound, a railway through thick forest seemed best suited for escape. Vasari had wanted the night-rider's life until he met Salome and roamed no farther than Newport on the Canadian border where they floated wedged together in an aluminum canoe in the waters of Lake Memphremagog with Salome making one sandwich after another and a twenty pound test line dangled for muskies.

When the phone rang, Vasari had already hooked a fish and reeled it up from the dark water and seen Uncle Gerrit wriggling on the line and lurched and cut the line and dropped his cup again as the terrible fish descended back down to its unholy secrets, blinking red-eyed, twisting frangible backbone, the acid of repressed hostility heating its blood. Vasari had thought to get a writing sample in Latin from my uncle but decided not, but couldn't shake Father Ruel's warning that a priest was rumored burning these churches. Uncle Gerrit had Vasari very, very nervous.

"It's the fire station again," said Brady leaning across Vasari's desk with receiver in hand. Vasari dampered down his picue, gratefully nodded Brady, smiled into the receiver: "Yuh? How you boys keeping? I don't hear no horn. This about the fireman's ball? Salome and me will be there ah course…oh, well, ah course, that's a police matter if it's parked on public… oh, yuh, I see. How bad's he burned? Oh, I see. New York plates? Well, that's a complication…yuh, next ah kin and vehicle collection and such and all."

Vasari put Brady behind the wheel. He asked Brady how he was getting along, made suggestions how to deal with requisitions at the motor pool, and "yuh, ah course" he would get the rattle traps for awhile, the ones busted up rushing to squabbles, the ones bondoed and splayed. The trick is to avoid cars re-numbered then re-circulated — meaning that either the front or the back has been wacked out-of-synch. Brady seemed to appreciate the advice and when Vasari began to comment disparagingly on the increase of cars short cutting through warehouse lots to avoid traffic on Flynn Avenue, Brady jerked the steering on Vasari's patrol car and released the wheel noticing with satisfaction, and some jealousy, the car had straightened its own self on a morning glaze of fresh-plowed snow and un-melted salt crystals. Not much more than grocery store runs has happened with this car, thought Brady.

Brady steered the patrol car off the road and onto one of those pocked-up, bouncy lanes between warehouses, gunning and spinning tail around corners, scraping the muffler as the car bobbed over multiple sets of R/R tracks leading to warehouse loading bays. He wore a serious look on his face that flushes acne scars into moonscape.

"Easy, Brady! The man's already more dead than what we can do much about."

"Yeah, well, I'm just surprised at how good this old car pulls together. What year is it? Got the stiff suspension and all, don't it, and the rack & pinion. Bet it's not been pushed much to its capacity."

"Couldn't say. We're here," Vasari said gripping the dash with both hands and locking his jaw the same moment Brady locked brakes with both feet on the pedal, spun the wheel indecisively, not well-enough practiced in skid control, the patrol car sidling into red-painted brick of the Lumiere building, scraping itself to a stop.

"Jeezum!"

"Not my fault, Sarge! You seen the road conditions."

"Yuh, but I wonder did you? Jest turn off the motor and hand me the key," said Vasari pushing Brady out then shimmying out on Brady's side, which was all he could do as his side of the car had landed flush with the building.

"Nice landing, kid," said Fire Marshal Charley Bushey from inside a red Ford Bronco, idling the engine with the heater fan furious, blue emergency lights shimmering, windows cranked to prevent the asphyxiation he figured had killed the boy in the van even before fire broke out. "Since you police has come, I'll be on my way. Nothing suspicious here that I can see. Died of fumes off his camper heater and then got burned by it. This kid's been noticed parking his van all over in unwelcome places. Probably can't afford the rent around here. Should ah tried the North End. Ain't that right, Vasari. Nobody pays what it's worth to live in the North End. Ain't that right, Vasari."

"I got reasons for moving out."

"Yuh, if it was me, I'd do whatever it was Salome wanted. Hell, she's a bounce on the bed springs my buddies on the farm say. She's worth the nickel to date her prone. That's what they say."

"Keep this civil, Bush! I'm ..."

"I know, I know. I know just what you are – Saint Vasari. Ain't that right? Listen, I'll get a report to you tomorrow first thing. I've called in the coroner but he's away attending a wedding. Ha! Ain't that a tickle. He'd be the first on my guest list. You boys will just have to set with the body till the city morgue comes along."

When Bushey gunned his Bronco out of the path of Vasari and Brady's patrol car, his Bronco being the obstacle that had initiated Brady's panicked braking, what loomed in its absence, twisted and crippled upon melted tires, was the brown and rust Ford utility van with Designer Elvis inside burned to charred tendon wrapped like bacon around the remains of a skeleton that smiled grisly and droll out from its recline on a bean bag chair melted around his body like a giant marshmallow, or such was Brady's observation when he pried open the sliding door and poked with his baton the charred remains.

He hadn't counted on the scent. He hadn't counted on a bothersome reaction to one less hippie shit. Brady cussed a long and clever tirade of disgust (the animal references especially amused Vasari) and spit periodically phlegm that built in his throat as he poked further through ruins until he needed to skip around a corner of the Lumiere building to evacuate the breakfast that had flip-flopped in his stomach. Vasari used his own baton to lift and shift metal and plastic items he took for stolen electronic equipment, including a scorched guitar and amplifiers piled up against the back doors. He noted serial numbers and makes and models. He found no identification on the body, but he didn't look too close, clothes and all having burned away in what must have been a terribly hot fire, any wallet left behind likely burned up or melted. He opened the glove box for a registration but found only stacks of cigarettes hand rolled that smelled like mouth wash. "Jeezum, must be the guy's humidor," Vasari decided. Under the passenger seat he found a metal box discolored but unlocked with goods inside well preserved: a clip of cash, a scatter of foreign coins, a roll of vintage winged Mercury American dimes and a magnifying glass, a tin of suspicious pills that will turn out to be aspirin, several cassette tapes found to be bootlegs and a notebook with monthly expenses tabulated (food and entertainment and gasoline and flopable pads in the area). Among the names of pliable hosts listed were Halley Gay – crossed out – and Travers Jones. Not surprising this guy would have Halley Gay in his black book, thought Vasari, but Jones? All roads lead to Jones, thought Vasari.

But what disturbed Vasari about this open-and-closed accidental death was the position of the key in the ignition – notched full "on" which means an engaged engine. Vasari noticed a generator mounted on the backside of the van, what the kid must have used to power his guitars or something, but that thing has its own gasoline tank, so why idle the van? Judging by the position of the key, the van's engine would have been engaged when the fire broke out, and the heater control was also full "on," so why have the camper heater going? Vasari checked the propane tank of the camper heater and found it half filled and unexploded. The more Vasari pondered, the less what he saw made sense. This was more than a curiosity. He told himself to have patience, that he was circling trains in the roundhouse presently and simply needed to find the best way out to that town called Clear Thinking.

Was it the husband to Gladys Needham that had helped Halley Gay do chemical analysis investigations on the TV? Mayhaps he could have a look here at the van, test materials for arson, estimate the incendiary origins. And be quiet about it until Vasari could figure out what's to do. Yuh, maybe so. He told Brady to wait in the Lumiere building until help arrived to remove the body. (''Break ah window ta get in if you have ta.'') Of course Brady would discover there are no windows, but he would find the access door inside the lean-to and he would find within flashlight range a board with a nail on the end, blood everywhere and dribbled in a line on the floor out the door he had entered.

When Vasari parked beside the Needham house on university hill, he knew something was wrong. No one had plowed the drive for quite a while or driven up it. When Vasari scraped with his steel-toe shit kickers the snow-laden stairs to the front porch to knock, the door swung open before he lay a hand on it. Wind had tossed it and a pile of snow had drifted into the foyer and reception rooms and frost had laced walls and stalactites had pinned the ceilings where pipes had broke and water froze. Salome would love to see this: she had snuggled him for days after and cried all the way through that Zhivago flick where the good doctor had shucked the world for a Siberian hideaway with his lover deep in sleigh-bell snow and they had made love and he had written poetry with the wood stove singing. Salome had wanted Vasari to chuck the job and sell the house by the airport and build a cabin deep in Westford sugarbush where even the lumberjack's Clydesdales had not stepped. The wood stove had signified love to Salome ever since, the hotter the better. These memories forestalled Vasari's discovering the house had been gutted. Which he noticed, finally, and thought perhaps rent asunder in a cultic way, a way that ideology got stated like Eat the Rich, Nuke Nixon, Roast the Pigs. That last one Vasari was particularly sensitive about. Vasari began to think that he had some kind of sinister movement afoot, that church burners had perhaps moved on to the houses of the uppities. He half expected to find the Needhams ritually dispatched in the basement or attic or something. He rooted around for slogans left behind (something from the Brothers Quebecois) and for the Needhams, but found only one hell of a lot of anger released on walls and furniture.

Back at the station, Vasari phoned the president of the university where the Needhams teach. She spoke to Vasari from pressed lips and other anatomical tightness. She said neither of the Needhams had attended classes for days. She didn't mention concern for their welfare but did suggest that this absence had damaged Reginald professionally. When Vasari described the condition of the Needham domicile, she dried up like a vacuum pump had collapsed her orifices altogether. Small soughing noises escaped lips in what was becoming an impossible conversation. Vasari offered several scenarios, from kidnapping to insurance fraud to commune life gone bad. All received murmurs and sighs from Dr. Ruth Van Patten up until Vasari mentioned that he needed to find the Needhams to clear up their involvement in a series of arson/murder episodes that may be cult related. That's when Dr.Van Patten opened up and expelled all the ill humor Vasari felt she had capped, a veritable windbag of "you must" this and "you must" that, all having to do with unwarranted suspicions and the ineptitude of the Burlington police in dealing with local crime that she was sure must expand exponentially as political complications arise – "Political aggrievement of the nationally affiliated, well beyond your expertise," she said. And "Keep the university well *OUT* of it! The Needhams, for all their savvy and academic acumen have (she was sure) acted independently of the university in whatever misdeeds they may have erred into. They are an odd couple, after all." Vasari had to agree with the oddity of their having been a couple at all.

Not long after Vasari's conversation with Dr. Van Patten, Brady walked tandem into the station with one of the twins from Midtown # 6 handcuffed to his wrist.

"So, listen, Sarge, you'll never believe. Oh, and remind me to tell you of the blood I saw at that warehouse. Somebody is maybe in pretty rough shape. So but I'm there at the hospital to see that the burned hippie shit gets tagged and tucked away proper and would you believe – this hippie chick comes shaking down the hall in her pretend Indian squaw getup saying she's being chased by the ghost of Jim Morrison, whatever, and she's chased her own self by a couple nurses, one with a syringe and I'm thinking, shit, must be a transfer from the mentals at Waterbury, but then I get it: this chick is having a bad trip. So I tackle the bimbo and make her look me in the eye and ask what's the shit she's on and where'd she get it, and she says he's with her sister, and I say where, and she says Midtown #4, only it came out scrambled but I figured it out, and that makes me remember the bust at Midtown # 6 and some bunches of hippie chicks that was supposed to be there but wasn't when we got there, and then she goes off again on the ghost of Morrison and so I clamp her and bring her here despite nurses accusing police brutality and such."

"By Jeezum, Brady!"

"Nothing I can't handle, Sarge. Now listen to this – sit down, damn it – okay, tell the nice Sergeant what you told me about that professor that's giving you the shit."

"Papa teach, need-a-pig, papa need-a-pig."

"What's she saying, Brady?"

"I'm not sure, but wasn't you working with a university professor called Needham? Need Ham – get it?"

"I'll be darned. That's good work, officer!"

"Sure as hell!"

So officer Brady and Vasari motored off once again to the Midtown Motel, Vasari driving this time, a replacement car from the fleet, one of the re-numbered variety. It pitched and rocked with each crimp in the road, but Vasari didn't drive fast enough to lose control. A lot of people said that about him.

When they reached the Midtown Motel, Vasari insisted Brady remain behind in the cruiser with the drugged out twin that Vasari didn't know was a twin until her sister answered the door of #4 Midtown: same sharp angles of the face, same cat-green eyes, same peroxide streaks, same lithe body dressed in Indian garb: a head band of glass beads, suede moccasins laced to the knees of skin-tight jeans, but in this case small breasts poking through the black rayon of a halter top rather than sequestered in a jean jacket like the twin in the patrol car, and as she flapped her arms animatedly, Vasari thought she was making an attempt to fly in her bolero jacket of white ostrich feathers, and the same tiny voice, this one saying, "Shit, it's the pigs. Why can't you leave us alone!" Vasari explained that her sister writhed in the back seat of his cruiser in some kind of mind conniptions that he figured was drugs and that he wasn't looking to arrest nobody but that he needed to speak to a Dr. Needham, Dr. Reginald Needham of the University. Did she know where to find him? That's when Reg came to the door.

"Well, officer…Vasari is it? Italian. Oh, yes, I remember. Vasari the artist! Something about a famous door in Florence. Do you do doors Sergeant? Those painter genes managing to hold together the matrix, yes? Deformities galore, dear me – the bowels the pancreas the bladder. Lead poison you know. All you Italians. Murder incorporated, murder in the family. Moody, very touchy. All that lead you know. Come back to finish that masterpiece of a busted bust, have you? Ha, glorious!"

"Well, I don't know. What bust might that be?" said Vasari trying not to breath too deeply as clouds of marijuana smoke welled out from the doorway. This was not the Reginald Needham that Halley Gay had introduced him to. The man had gone native, Abnaki Indian or some such – his thinning hair oiled and tied into a pony tail, love beads, jean overalls and shirtless, his hairy chest flabbing as he chuckled, as he did mostly throughout their brief talk.

"You know very well what bust. I was right here, right next door when you goose-stepped into room # 6 and scared these two darlings half to death (Reg placed his arm around the one twin standing by his side who nuzzled). Why, that debacle of traduced citizens who were minding their own business, of course. Did you know that the native population inhaled herbaceous concoctions regularly, all spiritual and medicinal, and I do not mean native Vermonters as you call them, those sons of Canadian trapper refugees, I mean the feathered and animal-skin bedecked and proud warriors of, of, something or other. Oh, shit, what was I saying?"

"I can't say I know my own self, Dr. Needham, but I'm glad ta find you well. Your house is not so good, howsoever."

"Oh that, sure, I know. My wife, you see. She has had a terrible attack of nerves. Can't take the politics at groovy university. I simply walked away. I have no desire to litigate or to, or to, oh, hell. Anyway, I am chucking it all – vanity, ego, materialism. Relocating to Maine with my tribe. Homestead deep in the bush."

"Your tribe?"

"Why, yes. These two lovely Indian girls." Reginald hugged the girl at his side again, then said, "Or this one anyway. How now powwow? Ha! Reg loves it in the middle, darling! Where's your sister again?"

"With me, Dr. Needham, in the cruiser."

"Oh, that's right. Will there be bail? You know anybody else that might want to make a tribe? Apart from Gladys that is. She's well *OUT*. Imagine her gutting my house. Well, desolation is liberation. I mean, what's a domicile anyway but a wind break, an assembly of indigenous materials anchored temporarily to the earth. I shall be living in a teepee and eating from the bounty of the earth, Euell Gibbons, you know, beating off invasions of blister beetles by tromping furrows and waving magic sticks. All else is vanity – empty show. I have had enough of your life, a life of, of, shit! Where was I?"

"It strikes me ah good many folks have been asking that question, professor. But what I need ta know is did you and Halley Gay come ta any conclusion on these recent church fires. Any arson involved that you know?"

"Oh, that. Well, Halley said to drop the whole thing. And then, of course, she dropped me. The bitch! She will *NOT*, no, certainly *NOT* be among my tribe. Will you tell her where to find me, though? I mean, should you run into her. We have some unfinished business."

"Yuh, but professor. My question."

"Your question?"

"Any evidence ah arson ta your way ah thinking?"

"Well, all right then. Here is my last contribution to your troubled world, Sergeant. Then you must leave me to my new life. Agreed?"

"Yuh, sure."

"All right then. In my estimation there *is* deliberate burning going on, but it is too clever to make itself known as arson. I would watch that Travers Jones bastard if I were you. He is connected to this burn business somehow. And I would not mind seeing him pay for his crimes. Of course, yours is a judicial system I have abandoned and am presently contemptuous of, but he has transgressed against his fellow citizens in unseemly ways. His criminality will unravel under scrutiny. Of that I am sure. Now, will you be releasing my, my ...."

"Your little Indian?"

"Why yes, that's right."

Vasari decided to keep Needham well out of the burned-van investigation, but he did take Needham's advice so far as to stop at my apartment on Grant Street. I answered the door inhospitably. Vasari noticed discomfort in my weak hand shake and jiggling eyes. I combed a hand through my hair and dodged around the room to find cigarettes, lit a match and blew it out and ditto again still looking for cigarettes – avoidance tactic number 909. Vasari must know something of my involvement. My brain raced with vanishing options. The floor seemed to give way under my feet. Vasari had been a friend but as he asked about my health while lowering himself slowly with bad knees onto a chair by the card table, the jangle of his keys and handcuffs reminded me of Tony Palachi of the East Boston hotel. Vasari seemed likely either to evict or lock me up. He told me Salome said hi, told me he would have "brung another tureen ah stew" had he known this visit was imminent but that "something last minute had come up." Sweat began to bead on my forehead. He asked again about my health. He asked was I still interested in investigating the church burns, asked was I still working with Halley Gay (more blush and sweat, Vasari did not ask again about my health), and he asked had I seen Gladys Needham. I told Vasari my Datsun truck approached road worthiness, that I planned trekking north soon to Montreal. I said I hadn't seen Halley Gay in a long time (not his business), but the disappearance of Gladys edged me toward system overload, especially after what had happened to Designer Elvis.

I mumbled from Zarathustra, "O that falsified light, that mustified air, where the soul may not fly aloft to its height," and burned trash in the brass ash tray on the table with a shaky hand, tried not to freak out as the table had begun to liquefy, moiling and bubbling in a mass of detached molecules. Vasari launched into a circuitous assault on my nerves with his oblique approach to the death of Designer Elvis. Half way through I said "What?" so he started over: did I know the guy that lived in a van with some kind of electronic warehouse and that played music regular at Nectar's? /did I see him often? /was I a friend? /did I know his other friends? /and finally, did I know about the accident? I can't blanket-lie effectively, especially when observed so closely. I'm just not equipped that way. But I can edge around a topic nearly as well as Vasari, and knew I had to, so I folded hands together beneath the table and squeezed until joints cracked me wakeful and ready and told Vasari, yes, I had heard Designer Elvis had had an accident in his van, a fatal one, told me by Halley as a news flash, I said, when Vasari asked. And yes, okay, I had seen Halley last night but it was a "spontaneous free love" kind of tryst that Vasari didn't need to know about entirely. He hemmed and guffawed a bit but let it go. Then Vasari said my name had been found in Elvis' address book and that the accident may not, in fact, have been entirely accidental. He said officer Brady had found blood on the floor of the Lumiere building near where the van was parked.

I hadn't counted on being implicated by Elvis himself but I did know about the nail in the board that had struck Elvis in the head. Halley had told me after our love making – "Pure accident, sugar, the kind my daddy would call a sow's poor lot become more regretful when the knife's gone dull." She told me to be thankful the nail side of the board was not used on me, and that the epilepsy had collapsed my knees and not the nail, and she asked me what explains my uncle's motivation? Did I understand him to be far-seeing and visionary? Will these church burns alter ecclesiastical history, did I think? Did I understand these church burns as symbols of purification? "Well," she said, "certainly more effective in a world of excesses than posting a list of complaints on a church door." And she asked did I accept that some innocents must suffer as a consequence of the fall out from as large a blast of reformation as the world has yet to see? I trembled naked in her arms as she spoke. I couldn't help responding favorably to Uncle Gerrit's vision, his mission and his methods. But this might have been conditioning. It was certainly said in a time of distraction.

Vasari's questions weren't so easily handled. Vasari asked did I know Designer Elvis may have been murdered by the same people that had murdered street indigents and that had been burning churches? He asked did I know of a cult calling itself the Brothers Quebecois? Had I seen my uncle the priest that's been asking for me? I gathered myself for one last repulse, said "Shit no! I don't know what the hell you're talking about. And I don't know what makes my family your business." I knew I had just sided with my uncle and my father and I felt both ashamed and liberated at the same side. Vasari avoided eye contact, seemed embarrassed, eager to leave. He said he was sorry for my response, said now he was truly alone but bound to see this through, let the chips fall and so forth. He groaned back to stature, placed a hand on my shoulder and squeezed while saying, "Careful, son. These Quebecois devils play for keeps." He ambled out my door having aged several years in front of me. It had been a long day and I had let him down terribly. I knew he wouldn't survive beyond the third church burn, which saddened me, as he stood directly in the path of my fanatical uncle. But what Elvis had said to me in his van kept playing through my memory as weird justification for his death and maybe for Vasari's too: It's make your own anarchy time. Make *BIG* mistakes joyfully.

Chapter Twenty-One

Travers among the Brothers Quebecois • A raven shares its black • A deserted farm house; a forgotten Christmas • Travers re-employs the truncheon • Halley confesses to a purpose, fulfills a purpose, purposes otherwise • To what Gerrit truly believes Travers truly commits • The Fisher Cat returns • The urn of Mosley discovered • The death of Designer Elvis detailed.

I sat in the dark in my skivvies at the card table by the window, Cat batting my cigarette pack through a mishmash of floor debris. I shut the nasty moppet in the bathroom, returned to the card table to smoke the pack, Cat tossing himself spitefully against the bathroom door. Wind snapped telephone and power lines that weave together like a dream catcher the houses on Grant Street, silvery windows glittering sequin in a mesh up and down the block. My window was a dark space where otherwise and in other windows domesticity exploded in felicity and St. Elmo's Fire. My dream was arson. Directly across the street, my neighbor's lone table lamp shadowed tangled limbs on a sofa, male and female, sockets and joints embracing and separating, souls fusing at the first decision to launder together. Or so I imagined. I wished Halley would gather me in her Saab and fade us, spin us out into the winter landscape. But instead she appeared at my door at my uncle's behest. "Won't you come with me to an intimate gatherin' of the brothers Quebecois," Halley said, her voice dry, ironic, emotions steeped in the pit of her stomach, but even lackluster her eyes produced an emollient wherein I gave myself away pansy-assed and thumb-sucking.

Out on the street, Hambone deBoner sat behind the wheel of my

Datsun truck all manly hirsute, black hair spilling down a white BVD t-shirt tucked into bib overalls, his toothy smile like chicken bones braided into his beard. What I hadn't already ceded to Halley, I gave to deBoner and to the fates anything I might have ordinarily called my own. Halley sat between us.

That truck slipped through Old North End Burlington with none of the hesitancy of its previous owner, and it smelled otherwise from me, like oil and sulfur (or as I imagined gunpowder might smell) and damp wool and rope and hay, and then marijuana as deBoner lit a joint passing it to Halley who toked and passed to me, probably thinking, any friend of Designer Elvis … I motioned it away. I didn't mention what Designer Elvis had said of drugs, what Brian Eno had said. No distractions. I wanted to stay grounded through this segue into the new person I was to become. If I were to burn, I wanted the wherewithal to bear witness. And I didn't want to risk another seizure. Not then.

We drove through the town of Winooski beside the river of the same name that translates as onion then past Saint Somebody's college and on through the five-road junction of Essex, then into woods over dirt roads plowed as single lanes. DeBoner bubba-spanked gears like driving a semi, churning wheels, one-handing the steering wheel while rolling another joint with the other, letting go the steering to shift gears, the THC jazzing his language with sex talk directed at Halley, the truck skipping over ruts. My brother in arms, my comrade of the revolution, deBoner diminished in stature as we drove deeper into the heart of his woodsy element: no longer a minor god of the underworld, he seemed now more trailer trash with an exotic accent and musk appeal. But maybe that's what revolutionaries are, what Patty Hearst responded to so fervently — unwashed romantics, visionaries with a death wish, lives brief as orgasm. Halley sat mannequin-like, silent and regretful, collapsing deeper inside herself with each mile as deBoner slid fingers up her thigh. I dug the truncheon out from my parka and placed it back inside the glove box. I thought I heard a stifled cry when the latch grabbed and looked to Halley, but she had abstracted away, dry as salt, fixed on a large bird clinging to barbed wire at the end reach of our headlights – a rampant profile heavy with beak, a foam of chest feathers, Cro-Magnon skull, and a mouth soundlessly opened releasing black into the world.

"Thou art a bitter bird, said the starlin' to the raven."

"What?"

"Nothin'," said Halley, "just another sayin' of Daddy's."

"Non temere est quod corvos ... "

"What dis shit?" said deBoner.

"The rest of it goes Cantat mihi nuance, ab laeve manu... it means something, that raven cawing on our left just now. Parsifal would take it out with an arrow."

DeBoner glanced at me with scant interest while slamming gears, so I said, "Hector's wand, if you want to know, Mr. deBoner, that I have placed in the glove box" and smiled and got no reaction, and said further, "Persuasion for the grout heads among us." DeBoner stroked Halley's thigh a bit higher, she pliant and he splenetic saying: "Musheer booktionary, he." Halley remained silent and distant.

We steered off the main road, which of itself would daunt most not bred to the mud and ruts and dust of Vermont's interior byways, deBoner gunning the truck up a steep incline, spewing gravel and snow, jouncing in and out of ruts, then cresting the rise of a granite outcrop and swinging parallel with a beaver pond glinting in our headlights at the edge of a pine copse. Once inside those pines and a distance gone alongside a brook heading back down the crest on the other side, deBoner braked the truck after a bend that hid a weathered clapboard farm house with attached barn, all leaning somewhat with busted windows secured in plastic. A toothless hound slack and cataract blind slunk toward us from the gallery porch, barked once then lay down exhausted from the effort. Beside it a dark form moved in the dim light of a single bulb dangling from a cord. One of the Canuck auto mechanics had stirred, sitting cross-legged on a crate in blue jumpsuit with the embossed red star, smoking a joint, pulling on his ponytail. His presence would explain why deBoner had my Datsun truck. I reached inside the glove box for my truncheon, which deBoner did not see, as he was spinning the wheel and gassing the truck into a doughnut turn. Halley noticed, concern registering in a stealthy shake of her head. Maybe she was more sensitive than I to the violence around us; maybe she was feeling guilt for having led me by the genitals into this den of madmen. Oddly, I found myself stepping fearlessly into the house, truncheon warming in my hand, both pushed deep inside my parka.

The one Canuck mechanic had remained on the porch; another sat deep in a torn sofa inside the house. Despite his slothful demeanor and dazed stare, he snagged the car keys deBoner threw, sneered at me and stared away. He had in his other hand a broken kid's toy, a battery operated space ship dented and chipped. I wondered what he might be doing with a toy until I kicked with my own feet articles from a scatter of toys and cast-off clothes: dolls and building blocks, a candy red ballet shoe, a ripped cowboy hat, and in the corner of the room a skeletal Christmas tree leaning in a mangle of denuded branches and disjointed 2x4 supports. A sad house. Halley went up the stairs to somewhere. I stood there looking at the auto mechanic on that sofa, determined to bring his eyes to mine. And he knew, and he ignored. So I walked up to him, looked down on him, noticed for the first time that our breaths steamed out our mouths (it was icebox cold in there). When he finally sneaked a look at me, I said, "What made you think you could give my truck away?" He gave no answer, so I decided to be more provocative: "Did you burn Designer Elvis in that van?" "Oh," he said, "must to know do you? Well, yuh. He burned real good." I pulled the truncheon out of my coat pocket, swung for his mouth, struck the sofa, found myself on the floor with a boot pushing my face into pine boards and a scuffle above me, one saying "Let go!" and another saying "He be mine by God!" and "Not now! Let go!" and "Soon, by God, soon him be tinder in that Jappy truck."

DeBoner yerked me off the floor, screwed my elbows behind my back, pushed my face into a wall and held me there until Uncle Gerrit stumped to the landing top of the stairs and called out to leave go, for I was, as he said in his scratchy, Scot's voice, the true light in the chapel where we do our work, the spark of an enlightened one.

"Him be spark right enough, soon enough by God," said the Canuck auto mechanic whose smirk I had tried to deface. I don't think deBoner knew what the hell Gerrit was talking about, but he did release me like a reflex, like Uncle Gerrit's own fist. deBoner shrugged in the direction of Gerrit to indicate where I was next to locate, and seemed so dispassionate as to have forgotten that we were rivals for Halley or that I had attacked one of his kinsmen but might have preferred attacking him. His sober, mechanical response to violence unnerved me. I couldn't help feeling that deBoner's adherence to an old man's dictates was tentative, symbiotic, easily dissolved and likely to turn on its master when it does. Well, perhaps deBoner thought the same of me.

I joined Uncle Gerrit upstairs on the landing where he pointed me which door next to enter. I went ahead with Gerrit clumping behind. There was Halley curled into herself on the edge of a cot, a knot of tight jeans, Nordic sweater and unlaced Bean boots. She looked away. She looked out of her element. The room crackled with green wood burning in a cracked-maw fireplace, the only source of heat discernible in that house and so Gerrit's room. My uncle moved directly to the fireplace, hung his cane on the mantle after pushing aside a pile of books, asked me to join him there and drew me into his arms for a long, sincere hug. I can't remember having ever been hugged before by Gerrit. There were tears in his eyes, which he wiped away quickly and by apology explained having lived these many months among strangers and cutthroats and seeing me from a distance often and yearning to draw me to him but the time not then propitious. He spoke disparagingly of the Brothers Quebecois. He knew these were hired guns, in for their own purpose, but also passionate in their own way as French patriots among the English, which he understood, and so long as their needs matched his, "ours" he corrected, they would follow loyally our directives.

I turned to warm my backside and saw that Gerrit had transformed this room into a kind of walk-in astrolabe with star charts pinned to the walls and ceiling, a brass gnomon and a lyre-shaped systrum on a makeshift table. He said to me that Halley had been revealed to him as the receptacle of the next great reformer, after himself and Paul Tillich of course. Gerrit said that his charts had cast her fecund and willing, not to worry that she services the brothers entire, because it is my seed she prepares for to conceive the child. With this, Uncle Gerrit pulled his cane off the mantle and moved out the room without looking back. The latch of the door shot through me like a promise. As I turned to Halley she sat naked on the edge of the bed, shivering, her clothes having melted away, shoulders squared, blue-green eyes defiant and ceremonial. "High-priestess primed, darlin,' " she said and called herself Isis, and said further, "Won't you come help me put together the pieces."

I could have been put off by her cynicism, but the love making drew my brains away. But soon she stopped, pushed me back with a hand on my chest and spoke Gerrit's chart language, telling me of ecliptics and decans of 10° that insinuate the minutia of her planet influence relative to the horizon. She knew I wasn't listening. She complied with my urges and we exhausted ourselves like randy salamanders in the salt ponds that filled our hollows. As we breathed love's pants, she asked had my uncle spoken to me of mystery, of *the* mystery? I said yes, derived from the Greek verb *myien,* to close. She closed her eyes and momently closed her mouth, then smirked, then giggled. She called herself *mystes,* the initiate. I said, yes, that's right, and Gerrit will think himself *mystagogos,* leader of the mystes, and me he calls *dadouchos,* the torchbearer. She hugged me and sped away to the bathroom. She returned naked still and danced around the room, thighs and breasts jiggling, singing the names of stars that Pythagoras viewed as soul origins – she ran a finger across the charted ceiling – she sang of stars falling to earth – she dragged her finger from the ceiling to her chin then traced a line down her middle to her womb – and sang further, "thus ever the soul strives to return." She sat on the bed, put arms around my neck. "Yes," I said, "from Plato's *Timaeus* wherein the case is made for each individual having fallen direct from a particular star."

I laughed.

She laughed.

She removed her arms from around my neck, said, "Travers, what do you make of this star business? Does your uncle believe this shit? Elegant as it sounds, it is shit, is it not?"

She smiled. I said, " I don't know anymore, but I have heard all this star business before. It filled the hours of my captive youth in East Boston. And, well..."

"Well, what, sugar?"

"Well, if I were you, I would be skeptical."

"Yes. I have little room in me for belief, though it does sound pretty. I am, however, earnest in reportage, darlin'. I am not without professional ethics."

"You're on assignment? You'll have us all put away!"

"I am only here to record facts after the fact, sugar. You and the Brotherhood shall be long gone before the exposé."

"You can't do this."

"Will you quote me the alternative? I have missed the stormin' of Disneyland, sugar, the invasion of Tom Sawyers Island and the flag raised there of a new world order. The Vietnam War is over. Communism has become its own religion. God has gone into exile. How about should I change my name to Hilarious and rob banks with the Symbionese Army, go up in flame like Patty Hearst's abductors?"

"What's that? Patty Hearst has been burned?"

"Where you been, darlin'? Look, celebrity works for me. I am not likely to anonymously protest a nuke plant. But I will be there to cover the arrests. Your Uncle has begun somethin', sugar. I want to see where it leads."

"Why not go back to your shrink? Read a self-help book."

"Do you really think, sugar, I might benefit from gestalt, from encounter, biogenitcs, Scientology, meditation, massage, rolfing realignment. Fuck all! Do I live in the present, darlin', go with the flow, give myself permission, free myself of shoulds, get in touch with my body? Will you be surprised to learn I have grown accustomed to keepin' the company of thieves? Look, it is the debutante's curse. Raised on taffeta, prone to khaki. Is it not enough I have found myself here with you?"

"But I'm foundering. Can't you see that?"

"Yes, darlin', and so delicious to watch."

She hugged me and we made love again.

As we lay on the cot with legs and fingers tangled, Halley gave reasons for a sympathetic assessment of Gerrit's vision: his hopefulness even in thin odds, his endearing and childish acceptance of this vision that comes to him engendered of his greatest disappointment, the holy Catholic Church, and his belief in the stars which had sorted this moment as a time for me to spawn Gerrit's next experiment in the womb of Halley. Laughable, she said, but also endearing. She said Gerrit was not entirely wrong, and his methods were not more criminal than most world-altering agendas. She said history will judge Gerrit fairly if the facts can be presented objectively … or, let's say artfully. She was here to present that perspective over and against the outcry of his victims. She said the larger issues were intriguing and important – burn away the illusion of a sympathetic Christian God and pry open the opiate eyes of parishioners washed in the kaleidoscopic light of the stained glass lie. She said it is nice to think it is not our destiny to tend garden in a senseless, weedy world.

I leaped off the bed and ripped from off the walls all those star charts with points of light like spikes that had fixed my wriggling soul and ripped further and tossed all into the fireplace where it flamed and roared sending jabs of light out into the room like tiny fists. I leaned a moment on the wall to steady my dizziness, closed eyes and breathed deep before I could finish the job. Halley said, "Internalize, darlin'. Don't lose control, sugar, not here, not among these jackals."

I took from off the mantle one of several volumes of the Hermetica and nearly flexed it into the fire as Gerrit pushed open the door with his cane. He looked at me, then at the book I held over the fire. He thumped slowly toward me, took the book from my hand, asked Halley to leave us for a while. He examined the book briefly then set it on the mantle.

"Aye, Travers, so ye must do. This is just as I want of ye. All goes tae flame. All must burn tae free our destiny and reassert the ancient wisdom. It shall arise of the ash, no text needed in that regard. But do allow me this one indulgence. Old men love their books."

"But what of Halley? Why involve her?"

"Ach, she believes no more than what's useful tae her ownself. No thing more. But she will take yer seed as yer mother did of Timothy O'Connell."

"You've got Halley pantomiming Greek mythology. She's not right for the part. Don't you realize how senseless this all is? You're working with thieves, murderers, an unscrupulous journalist. And I'm not sure what I am anymore. Shit!"

"Ach, yes, that's right! Is it the Tabernacle Choir ye would have me work with? Blaspheme as ye like and traduce me tae dust, but mind that ye step upon yer own father's bones as ye do me, and upon the bonnie man Tillich. And has not Nietzsche worked tae free yer mind and soul and yer hand for business. Ye cannot simply curl intae yer mollusk shell and float with the tide. I am ashamed of ye, lad."

Gerrit then reminded me of the Catholic lie that had sprung from the "mysteries" Halley had spoken of — saying further it was first the gods of the mysteries that ruled stars and planets. He said Christianity had stolen from and then stamped out the mysteries by demolishing the Sarapeum of Alexandria, a repository of ancient tradition, and then in the year 394 crushing Roman aristocracy, who clung to the old beliefs, in the last battle at the River Vipacco. Then Mother Church taking for its own the baptism that erases sin, the great festival of the sun god of December 25th, Isis and her son suckling mirrored in Madonna and child. Even the emperor

Constantine wavered between Christ and Sol – the Syrian sun god that nearly became chief god of the Holy Roman Empire. The true power of the church comes from its historical figurehead, Gerrit said – Christ, the biography of Christ as warrior philosopher; the worship of man by man being a most potent drug. But he was just a man, not a god.

Thus and to legitimize Gerrit's plan, Tillich's theories, we offer up our own torch bearer, "yer own good self," said Gerrit, "tae burn away the dross and light the path, and it will have come from Tillich tae me down tae ye and finally tae yer own son."

"But you use the same symbols as the church. Don't you? What then does this church burning accomplish?"

"Oh, aye. We use symbol. We must. Symbol lends potency. But our symbol is a purification, a baptism of fire. We burn all material back tae expose the true spirit that is trapped within. We light the way of the philosopher's quest. We burn that a new spirit formless and pure may root in a reinvigorated, prepared soil."

So Uncle Gerrit really did believe in this star-chart business. And he wanted to tear down organized religion. Mad, utterly mad. But that's why I liked it. There's no question the Church needs reforming, reminding that what it has become, the bully on the block with hangers-on, little resembles where it began – a democracy of gods from the "mysteries" and elsewhere. It had been easy for me up to this point to vacillate with impunity – yes, I'll burn, I say, while making plans to escape to a philosopher's perch at university. When you're accountable to your own self only, it's easy to imagine yourself engaged in meaningful polemics with the world. Oh, yes, I had limned the rules of engagement in my Journal of Life Assembly, and Gerrit was right – Nietzsche had helped. But I could see patterns of thrust and retreat, thrust and retreat again back to my den of moldering books and voyeurism once I had bloodied myself or that which I had bumped up against, briefly. It was time for me to commit to something large that lays its hands upon the rough edges of life and won't let go.

"OK, I'm in," I said oddly comforted, resigned to my fate.

Halley entered the room and joined us beside the mantle wrapped in a sheet from the cot, hugged us both and as she did so the sheet fell away. Halley laughed in her nakedness. Gerrit blushed radishy. I noticed then my own nakedness. But I was most handsome in the buff, and the fire felt good warming loins and buttocks after Halley's warming. She picked the sheet off the floor, wrapped the two of us as Gerrit once again shuffled out the door, saying, "There will be a fair carfuffle among the brotherhood for me tae settle, I'm sure."

We dressed, sneaked down the stairs and out the door onto the gallery porch where the dog slept that Gerrit had named Sirius. He came with the abandoned house. The house itself overhangs a decline of hillside verdant with giant white pine, live with water flow, the beaver pond emptying out in a rocky cascade of brook. What noise there was otherwise, and there was plenty, leaked out the seams of that twice-blasted house (a family thrown untoward into the un-sheltering ethers, a brotherhood of icon destroyers pissing on the last Christian observance this house may ever know). The Brotherhood were squabbling again. Gerrit could be heard banging his cane to tame those voices, ordering that what remained of the Christmas tree be taken to his room to burn. Halley and I walked off the porch, down the hill in snow, alongside the brook through pines and juniper, naked poplar and maples, all shaking and clacking, graceful as Balinese dancers in the wind. A powdery avalanche of snow fell upon us from off pine branches. We laughed and brushed away the dusting. A sharp animal cough surprised us from above, a mewling, throaty greeting, not un-approving. The frost-tipped fur of a black Fisher Cat, my old friend, moved liquidly overhead through dense branches of pine, as much at home there as slinking on the forest floor. It stopped in the crook of a stunted branch, regarded us in amusement before springing across the brook into a new patch of pine then away.

"I've met that animal before," I said.

"A weasel is it?"

"No, a Fisher Cat, a marten if I remember Professor Staub's natural history. They're rare and rarely seen. He must like us."

"Maybe so but not me him. Have you never seen a weasel take its prey, Travers?"

"Speaking predatorily?"

"Predatorily, yes. Outside my daddy's chicken coop, it dances and flops on its back and carries on until chickens stick their heads out wire mesh then BITES their heads off."

"Clever."

"Yes."

"Why are you telling me this?"

"I'm sayin' don't be the chicken that is mesmerized by the dance, darlin'."

"But you are!"

"Yes, but will this not be one hell of an exposition in reportage?"

"You're playing a dangerous game, Halley."

"It is a dangerous age."

In the clear night a narrow band of smoke from Gerrit's fireplace weaved and stitched all together like a quilt. Follow the chimney smoke back to the source to find the father of the child. But that would be Gerrit or one of his murderous minion. Halley brushed snow off a stump beside the brook, sat and looked up through a gap of otherwise dense branches. "Shit, Travers, what if you have knocked me up, darlin'," she said in wispy good nature, nothing sarcastic, reached for my hand and pointed with her other a point of light darting the black sky at great speed then disappearing.

"What if that star is the soul of our child, Travers?"

"Road to hell is paved in what if's."

"I suppose so. And I am just the one to drive us there."

"Yes, I think you are."

We followed our footprints back to the house as the moon settled over an east hill. Chickadees and waxwings pecked at pine-seed exposed in loam at the base of trees. A flock of chatty starlings broke in a wave over the roof of the house. One settled on a gable end mimicking a raven's caw. Halley reached for my hand again, but I had noticed light in the basement window and kneeled to brush away the snow for a clear view. Halley said, "Travers, leave those Canucks to themselves, darlin'. Come with me into the house." But there was something odd going on down there. One of the three labored over a small, intense fire in a Franklin stove; another hacked at something with a small ax; the third picked through a pile of debris that I eventually understood to be loot – chancel crosses and Eucharist cups, Latin inscriptions scraped off marble fonts, countless statues (some scraped clean and smashed in a corner). And there on a workbench stood the marble urn of Mosley.

It was that urn, the ash within of a man with faults but with vision and passion, that called most eloquently for me to support Gerrit – oddly, a man that built a church sending me to the aid of one that would destroy all churches. Mosley, like Gerrit, had merged the past and the future into one cohesive plan of a life's work. Mosley had borrowed from the Greeks for his church design and had kept his pagan spirit intact through his Christian observances. I admired that. I knew Gerrit would too. Vasari loved the man for his romantic obsessions and political savvy. Mosley too had suffered the imposition of an upstart church growing in the gap between him and his one true love, the widow Ryder. And as I thought more about Mosley, I began to think that I understood Gerrit better, coming from Scotland as he did, a country at war with itself and others over religion. I knew from what my mother, Fiona, had said of St. Andrews that she and Gerrit had grown up among grim reminders of martyrdom and in the ruin of cathedral stone collapsed cairn-like. A harvest of stone gathered from the four corners of a kingdom and piled ziggurat-high, leveled in high winds, piled again, imposing, imperial, but tumbled altogether finally in the words John Knox had spoken. And lying deep beneath this weight of stone, the Pictish race, those that Caesar feared, and then invaders that came quietly to stay, the first believers who shipped west from Greece to grow a religion greener than the shores that received them.

Gerrit wanted to strip all back to spirits that inhabit the air we breath, free those tiny heresies my mother had tried so fervently to wash clean from off the walls of our East Boston hotel. I decided I would take the urn with me, return it to the parish that planned to rebuild near Dame Ryder's homestead, appease Vasari in the process. I owed him that. But of course whatever they might rebuild, Gerrit would certainly re-burn, but each was a worthy, a necessary gesture. I wondered – would Gerrit replace the bones of St. Andrew in their reliquary if he could rake them off the sands of the bay where they drift in the tide? I think he would, yes, then burn the church that held the reliquary. Shit. Life's a complication.

I decided to confront that cellar of thieves, demand from them the urn of Mosley, since it offered nothing valuable to the coffers of the Quebecois, unless a gold or silver-filled molar or two, which I determined to save from desecration. I did not share my plan with Halley, said I would meet her in Gerrit's room. I did look forward to getting back under the covers with her. As I opened the door to the basement, a roil of acidy smoke escaped up the stairwell as did voices in pidgin Canada/French, bitter and stressed, with deBoner asserting order as best he could. I dug a hand into my parka but the truncheon was missing. I descended stairs that cracked with each step. At the first sound of trespass, silence issued from below. Scared shitless hardly describes my condition. I mean, these guys had murdered Elvis and would do for me the same without raising a pulse.

They eyed me motionless and edgy. I walked directly to the workbench, gathered the urn in my arms – "Father Gerrit said," I said, lifting what must have been a hundred pounds of marble, polished to gloss-black with tiny veins of green. Something Italian imported, nothing like the milk-white of Proctor home-grown.

"Monsignor Gerrit – him say dis? Him say what?" said deBoner sliding an iron pan over the top of the Franklin stove like cooking eggs, prodding with tongs a glint of precious metal dissolving with heat into pus-like globs then smoothing out like butter and poured into a second pan that held a make-shift mold the shape of a fleur-de-lis.

"Gerrit said…take this urn back to where it may be honored. The dead must be honored, he said."

"Him say no thing of dis to me."

"Yes, well, you're not the torchbearer are you?"

"Don't make dat Christly god talk. You be not so much crazy as dat monsignor upstairs. Why you be here anyway? We be no god-blessed brotherhood. We share gold and blondie bitch is all."

DeBoner smiled meanly, stretched arms over his head ending the motion with a flex of abdomen that appeared more impressive because he stood bare-chested and sweat-drenched, farmer overall bib dangling below the waist, feet dug for purchase in a dirt floor. He threw another block of wood into the stove, isinglass deviling the features of all these hairy brethren of chaos. One of the car mechanics, the one with the ax, tossed morsels of gold into the pan and retreated back to his corner for more chopping.

"Dat one wid the ax, dat hansome, you shall not trust. Him take you heart out by you nose wid a clothes hanger. I seen him do dis thing. Him the one you shake dat silly stick at. Dat other dere, him wid bad teeth and rat breath, him be maybe crazy like you Uncle. Him blow up banks in Montreal to kill the English. Him say death just a idea, so it easy, like you crazy Uncle say. Him and dat hansome kill together you friend, but want boots too, but take more fun in killing of him."

"No! It's you, Hambone, that swung the nail into Elvis' head. I know that for a fact."

"Yes, indeedy, but him still alive – bleedy like pig, but groan and open eyes. And you…, you be gone into you fit dat brother Seymour him whisper you ear dat him take you heart out you nose wid clothes hanger but you too frothy. But him whisper anyway in you ear what we going to do to Elvis and we three take groany Elvis to him van and burn him good."

"That's murder!"

"No, it be more. You Uncle him speak of heretic *martyr*. Him say burn alive in van so him know us and why, so him know his own death and why. And by God, him die beautiful! Brother Bousquet, him pass a joint and you Uncle him say no hashish! Him say hashish mean 'assassin' in Araby. Him say we no assassin; this not who we are. And him say snuff joint and say Elvis must know why him burn, so too must you, and we take you feet and arms and drag you from dark of Lumiere to nearby burning van. And you Uncle, him say crazy god words and speak to bleedy Elvis in van but him grin and nod and move him lips and say 'make big happy mistake' or something, and grin more again, and you Uncle, he rage and kick away Bosquet that wants take Elvis boots. And you be groany and writhey and brother Seymour him pull you eyelids open and you Uncle him say 'we be poets of a high order' or some such; him say 'we transcend earthy dull and stop clocks and rage rip and dash to pieces tablets of law,' or some such. And you, you eyes roll and you frothy still, and Elvis him burn like shadow in white heat and then all *STOP* when night watchman of neighbor warehouse him stand on chair and pound inside glass window and shout so we hear, finally, him dim voice, and stop and all slow down, all pale shivery and lusty and dreadful, and drop all and all walk away. You see?"

"I don't know. Maybe I see. What about you, Mr. deBoner? Do you see? Do you know what you have done?"

"Oh, yes, sure. I hire out, fulfill contract."

"But you have committed murder!"

"Fulfill contract is all."

"Why *this* contract?"

"What make you think I so picky? You Uncle, him find me and these two else that was tinkering cars, and him say we be a brotherhood for God and Gold. And him say, we put back the letter "l" in God dat always dere, a cross wid arms broke off and sold off, just hide someplace, and we be a brotherhood dat bring the "l" back to the word God. I be no philosopher, but I know what gold buy. Why be you here?"

"Born to it, I suppose."
"Born to Christly martyr if you take dat urn."

Chapter Twenty-Two

A room of 50's avant-garde and schmaltz • Gladys unburdens the weight of her very large brain: the ritual of human sacrifice; life among the homeless of Power Town; Travers Jones medically and otherwise disposed to burn; death threats at Power Town • Salome and Gladys share a sisterhood of certainties – Gladys might be in love with Travers • Reflections on Henry Adams' dynamo: smoke stacks, the steeples of industry • Darnell Hoover, guardian of Power Town, Psy-Ops released from Vietnam, indicates the next church to burn • Gladys wonders, can epilepsy be, as Dostoevsky believed, the origin of life, the first touch of God?

Once reciped and griddled, if not eaten, and if Salome hasn't given it away, it goes spread on snow as animal slop – no Tupper Ware burps in the Vasari kitchen. Farm habits die hard. At 6 a.m. Salome scatters breakfast scraps out the front door for squirrels and scavenging house pets, which Nickoli Vasari peppers with beebee shot, which neighbors ignore, though they know. At 6 a.m. Gladys muscled Reginald's Jeep Wagoneer into the driveway as Salome discharged the remains of breakfast out the front door thinking sexy, recharging the amorous engine for a second assault after having banged then fed her husband breakfast in bed.

The Jeep had lost its gleam – mud bespattered and salt stained, headlights cracked, fenders dented, the power steering torque-bound and grinding.

Thinking another turn around because having overshot the airport, Salome was backing inside the house before the driver revealed herself. Salome hesitated, snapped cast iron a second time as if to de-lard by brute force, her wrist the equal of any Russian plowgirl. She calculated with her free hand the spring of her permanent and prepared to greet a stranger as the car swayed to a stop, Gladys emerging ungainly, bumping the horn which scattered critters winged and earth-bound but anchored Salome in speculation. Gladys had little to recommend her as a house guest: hair bandannaed like a ZigZag rolling papers sketch, boots grimed, woolen socks pulled to the knee over sweat pants torn at the pockets and rust streaked, several pilled sweaters bulging a jean jacket, a dirt-smeared face. And withal as gadabout and unselfconscious as a child. While slipping on packed snow, pulling on the Jeep's antenna for stability, Gladys addressed Salome.

"Salutations!"

"What can I do for you?" Salome said rehearsing directions to the interstate, the back roads to Bristol, and other usual misplaced destinations.

"Oh, well, you won't do much if you don't know me will you?"

Salome giggled. "Who might you be?"

Gladys placed her sore leg on the cement stoop, gripped the iron rail for balance, looked up at Salome but went deeper inside herself than necessary for an answer, self-assessment having become a habit of late: "I am perhaps something undercover," she said, "a vigilante of sorts with stenographer habits, I suppose, and something vengeful, even gainfully bitchy at long last. But I should probably say police work, shouldn't I? It's about these church burns."

"Oh, I see. You might could want Nicky, Sergeant Vasari. That right?"

"Well, yes, that's right, yes, but I will talk to you."

"At present you will be talking ta the neighbors."

"Then may I come in for a moment, if you don't mind."

"None whatever."

Salome leaned open the storm door, reluctantly belted the pink corduroy robe that wrapped a confection of French lace corset whose rocket bra bestrode wedge panties the size of Idaho. Gladys caught her breath and limped into a 50's living room, Scandinavian spare and jaunty geometric, impossibly insubstantial for these two most substantial people

— in one corner a tea cart of teak and rattan displayed a collection of plastic dinnerware in gaudy Bakelite colors; cozied alongside that a coffee table of glass and spider-leg iron; then two chrome loungers with green synthetic upholstery and black oaken arms; also rattan end tables abutting; three fragile butterfly chairs of molded plastic in burgundy stuffed the remaining corners of the room. Gladys walked to a low sideboard of blonde oak with brass knobs on pull doors and curiosities on top dusted and beckoning. She switched on a leopard skin lamp by a pull of its tail and the odd assortment lit up like candy.

"Who you talking ta, Salome?" said Nickoli Vasari leaning out the bathroom, shouting down the hall, water splashing out a tap, WSKY's Tod Banyon listing birthdays while inciting locals to phone in controversy off the granite blasting in Barre, his voice avuncular though tinny, trapped in a portable speaker.

"Don't know, Nicky!" Salome shouted back, her voice unsure and somewhat whiny, as morning talk between the two had over the years pared down to nonesuch. "She's one ah yours I believe, come here ta inform you, or ta see our furniture mayhaps!"

"Yuh, sure. Undercover did ya say? What undercover?"

"She's here about the church burns, Nicky!"

Gladys rocked the heel of her gimp leg, smiled, nodded that's right while placing glasses on her nose and picking through the knickknacks.

"Oh, it's Jackie!" said Gladys lifting a head vase in ceramic of the x-first lady, turning her wrong side up, surprised by the red and white Inarco label. "Japanese?"

"I suppose," said Salome.

The president's wife waved the royal wave in black gloves, eyes wide open and empty, mouth cherry red and closed tight as a fist. Gladys replaced Jackie then hefted a Fiestaware milk jug in water-blue plastic, deep-water shell organic in shape.

"That would be out ah mamma's frigerator. Must ah been dropped a hundred times. Bounces in a singe piece."

"It's beautiful. Oh, yes. Hey," Gladys said, "is this Snappy the Snail?"

"Yes, papa's cigar repository."

"And this?" Gladys said pointing to a doll in a grass skirt.

"That would be ah Kewpie doll on Hawaiian vacation."

"Yours as a little girl?"

"That's right."

 Gladys fingered the skirt. "Celluloid is it?"

"Might could be."

"And a dump truck?"

"That's right. Buddy-L, ah ten wheeler with hydraulic lift. Still works. Mine too in my tom-girl days."

"This stuff positively gleams!"

"I keep good care ah what belongs ta me," Salome said possessively.

"Tell her I'm there momently," said Sergeant Vasari. He snapped off the radio with pique, compelled by circumstance lately to tread wrong ways from retirement, and said to his gauzy image in the steamed mirror, "You can't hardly hand pick that stuff out the ground, Bob, jeezum." The taps quaked from water-tower pressure exerted close enough for Vasari to hear all summer long the neighborhood snot noses ping rocks off its bulk. Vasari set off down the hall in his uniform, knotting his tie to assert "unperturbability" as he saw it, and rounded the corner into the living room.

"Why, Mrs. Needham! I been looking ta see you. Your house and husband will be ah surprise if you don't already know what's what."

"Oh, I know what's what, Sergeant. I mean, I know very well, what with this very large brain of mine."

"Yuh sure, if you say. But you do look somewhat street worn. You been living hard times of late?"

"Well, no, actually not, no. I have been engaged in fieldwork."

"You working on a degree, Mrs. Needham?" said Salome.

"Oh, no, not that, no. Real Life101, non-credit, enjoying every dismal moment."

"Can't say I get the gist," said Nickoli.

"Okay, let me say I have just about solved your church burn mystery."

"How's that?"

"I have been living among street dwellers and refuse gleaners of your fair city, Sergeant. They are a fascination in ego misintegration, role confusion, clannish cruelties, distantiation. They are stagnant, unregenerative, despairing, and positively endearing."

"You will be growing a brain on me again, Mrs. Needham. I will be needing ah interpreter."

"Yes, well, sorry, but my interest in the behavioral sciences set me after your little problem. And, but may I ask … we are still a posse, aren't we?"

"Why, sure. Ah course. But what can you have discovered, Mrs. Needham?"

Vasari remained in the doorway of the hall that attaches kitchen to living room and shotguns the length of the house with bathroom, closets, and two bedrooms branching off right and left in the un-clever but worthy symmetries of tract housing. He rolled his hands as if warming them, gestured to Gladys to take a seat. She was too wound up so examined further the bibelots on the sideboard, then chirped, "Gladys, please call me Gladys. And take a seat yourself, Sergeant, if you'd like. I don't mean to reject your hospitality, but I'm much too filthy dirty for refined company."

Salome blushed and smiled standing beside the front door, hands pulling at the straps of her robe. Gladys blushed too when she looked for a seat the Sergeant might occupy, discovered there were none convenient to his girth. Strange phenomenon – a room kept exclusively to show. Where can they spend their waking time together? Then she remembered the lingerie and redirected her thoughts.

"That *Mrs.* stage is over for me, you know, well over," said Gladys. "Yes, well, first an irrefutable truth that men are pigs – oh, beg your pardon, Sergeant; no pinko politico dig intended – and second that revenge is a necessary ingredient of the healing process."

"That would be meaning you had gutted that uppity hill mansion you have once occupied?"

"Oh, yes, well, symbolically, perhaps, I mean, no confession intended but when the imagination unfettered confronts the solid immoveables, you know, something has to give, but what clued me to your burn solution, Sergeant, was the obvious murder as statement implication. I mean, the Battery Park assault, stuffing that poor man's mouth with the instrument of his betrayal. It's all symbolic. Don't you see? Everything: the church burns, the Elvis songster burned alive in his van – yes, alive, I believe so. I am quite sure of it. Heretics are burned alive. And that man was pop culture's apotheosis and so hedonistic and heretical. The church burns heretics, Seargeant. And so doe these church burners. They are spiritual in their own twisted way. Oh, yes."

"Yuh, I see. But what of that man burned in the window well of the Methodist church. What's that mean?"

"Nothing at all really – unfortunate accident, collateral damage. But it gets the ball rolling, like what that terrorist says in a Malraux novel: 'A man who has never murdered is a kind of virgin.' He wonders what it's like. He ventures beyond imagination when desperate, and the results surprise – murder is easy, but it doesn't displace what I take to be the original intent of these burns."

"What's that?"

"The ritual destruction of our most powerful symbol – the house of God."

"But why?"

"Retribution. Justice. This kind of act is always personal. Some wrong has been done him by the church. Yes, you see, catharsis builds in the psyche of the degraded and explodes in acts of retribution."

"Sounds messy."

"You are a funny man, Sergeant."

"Much misunderstood if I am."

"It's like this, Sergeant. Usually one finds single episodes of violence, but in this case we have a prolonged series with a third church in jeopardy.

Strange – using symbol to efface symbol, like the master planner has his own order he wishes to impose on the Church. Don't you see? A third church burn, a magic number, the holy trinity, the sacred pyramid, the triangle, that most perfect of geometric shapes."

"Yuh, I see. And all this you learned from them Battery Park citizens? They must be some smart."

"Yes, they are intelligent in their fashion, but no, not from them. Rather from months of research on aberrant crime while recovering bedridden from this lapwing pin-job" – Gladys slapped her thigh and winced – "yes, reading and pimping for Reg."

"What's that?"

"Answering the phone. That's all I did. Well, up until the end, that is, when I made my own statement. But don't you see? It's endemic to our species, these large statements, unavoidable really for some that have turned too far inside themselves that they think no one knows or cares what they think. Like our friend Travers Jones."

"Yuh sure, but what all do you know of Travers Jones in all this?"

"It's his obsession with these burns that got me wondering. And his association with street life that Halley Gay told me about."

"Yuh, Halley Gay, the posse initiator. What's come ah her?"

"Don't really know, Sergeant. Following a lead to somewhere I suppose."

"You was saying about street life?"

"Yes, Travers knows intimately Designer Elvis, the man that came to a bad end that held court at Nectar's. Him and the denizens of Power Town that Halley introduced me to when she wanted my input on some reporting for the network news. I was intrigued. So I lived among them for awhile."

"I can see that. What's it like."

"Oh, well, it's like nothing ever. I mean, how keen the senses when rendered guardian, when half starved half the time. I mean, that's why the booze, to deaden the senses, because they strain so to be so alert and watchful edgy all the time. I mean, sussing which busybodies will dial the cops – oh, sorry, a lovely bunch of boys, mostly."

"I ain't so sure my own self."

"Yes, well, so you say, but you learn quite a lot."

"How so?"

"Well, things like which of the blue-glazed foods dumped outside restaurants will stay in the stomach, or which laundromat attendants will let you snooze in the steamy warm and which will call in the Old North End toughs to beat you like a stray dog, and you learn to hide yourself in the brambles and dense hedges of out-of-the-way places."

"Out of the way? What ah that hobo camp at Battery Park that you and me and the other posse poked into? Them indigents had worked theirselves up ta tourist status seems ta me."

"Yes, but these people live on the fringe ordinarily. That Battery Park bivouac came together in the open from pure fear. You know that. They were once loners inhabiting back alleys and hedges and window wells, until George Eakins' fiery death, then they gathered at Power Town. That's when Halley and I investigated this unique little community. Then the threats, after which a splinter group gathered in Battery Park where we found them, Sergeant, and that poor dead hobo, then soon all disbanded and regrouped down the hill by the power plant where eventually a deal was struck."

"A deal? Who with? What do you mean deal?"

"Yes, well, this is where it gets interesting."

Gladys placed Snappy the Snail back on the sideboard, removed the glasses off her nose, backed against furniture like leaning on a chalkboard, glasses folded in a fold of hands. She began to lecture.

"You see, once I had collected my share of bruises and puked up dinner regularly and had begun to show the obligatory paranoia, I became part of the community. I was told the deal."

"What's the deal, if you don't mind saying?"

"It's this: a priest and some threatening Quebec brotherhood, they will leave all to their natural state of destitution and eventual organ malfunction once the third church is burned, so long as all information pertaining to these burns is kept to themselves. Or they could die at the hands of those mad dog Quebec fellows such as that one dispatched at Battery Park."

"That so?"

"Yes, and it is the priest that is the master planner, though that boy Travers Jones is up to his elbows in this, sorry to say."

"How so would you say?"

"Well, what clued me initially was the epilepsy, some research I have done on this fascinating disease. It's the shakes, the Johnny Shakes we used to call them when I was in school."

"What's that?"

"Yes, because Johnny Trahern had them in fifth grade, and most likely still has them."

"Oh, sure, I see."

"But what I learned is that the nature of this disease equips one who suffers it with personality traits befitting your criminal arsonist."

"So it is ah disease that is doing the burns?"

"Well, yes, in a matter of speaking, could be, though the master planner has some other disease I would say. Anyway, it is the Johnny Shakes that programs its host to exaggerate – mythomania it's called – and to go hyper-religious – meaning spiritual issues overwhelm the psyche – and to sometimes go antisocial: consider Travers' habit of isolation and waiting for Zarathustra."

"Who?"

"Not important. But here's the kicker: it seems arson is one of the most observable of antisocial traits among the afflicted."

"So, what you are saying is that Jones has got all those reasons to burn, not that he is the one."

"Yes, that's right. Innocent before we lock him away, right Sarge?"

"Yuh, sure. But I must say he does appear at all these burns, and that was some odd behavior the day Travers and me visited Father Ruell at St. Johns in the Old North End."

"How's that?"

"Well, he up and parted our company smack in the middle ah large matters that come up in the conversation and he meandered at the tabernacle like in ah trance that's seen devils cavorting thereabouts and when he got there paced about like possessed. I tell you ... it was some strange."

Gladys walked thoughtfully to a corner of the room and fell into a butterfly chair beside a Lightolier floor lamp, her voice scaled back to near whisper.

"Yes, that's it – hyper-religious, like I said, Sergeant. And there are family issues I have heard about from Halley and didn't pay much attention to but now see very clearly."

"What would that be? I have met his priest Uncle. Don't like him much, but that's not so different from many other priests I am blessed ta see in professional relations."

"Yes, well…fascinating. But there is him, the Uncle, for sure. Well, and Travers has not got a father at home, did you know? The one he had he thinks has been somewhere in Europe burning churches, if not here doing the same. And his mother has been a neurotic and superstitious and a primitive fatalist non-factor, and there is the priest Uncle like you say that has raised the boy at home with suspicious intent. And then there is the epilepsy. That's a lot of baggage."

"Yuh, sure, but what's it all mean."

"It means unresolved Oedipal complex" – Gladys' voice ascended steadily upscale, colored by discovery – "it means mystical experiences from seizures, it means the duality of the sexual and the spiritual self have got all confused together in him, it means some emasculating priest has destroyed his boyhood fun and planted the idea that suffering is good for salvation, yes, and it further indicates ..."

"That boy is ah mess."

"Yes, that's right," Gladys said, once again diminutive in tone and become introspective, "but he is a good lover."

"What's that?"

"Oh, nothing really."

"You can't for sure say he is guilty."

"That's right too. And I hope he's not. I have a soft spot for him, and I am trying to sort out what that means."

"So what's to do now?"

"Well, I'm going back to my field work" – Gladys said expressing determination to do so by slapping the handles of her chair –"and I'll come by here again tomorrow morning same time with more of what I have found out, if that's okay with you."

"Yuh, sure. Okay by me."

Gladys extended the goodbyes by poking obliquely as best she could into the lives of Sergeant Vasari and his wife Salome, the Sergeant's brief responses orphaned in Salome's expansive delectations, airing the Labrecque family linen and the Vasari intercession, telling farm life (pulling the fledgling vegetable plants and keeping the weeds, assigned to baking ever after) and married life (going to the big city with a professional man, saying fuck all to gardening and taking to opening cans from the A & P). The two women had become intimate on a level both superficial and deep. Vasari watched with interest as each offered intimacies of a life history and each received the same like pulling on the teat of a sisterhood of certainties. After Gladys told of her failed marriage and career and roll around in the kitchen with Travers Jones, Salome said: "You might could be in love with that boy."

The Jeep Wagoneer cranked haltingly, which Gladys failed to notice, as Salome's parting statement on Jones coursed through her veins and jabbed at her emotions. Two pistons responded, others engaged fitfully, reluctant chorus, blue smoke belching from dual exhausts, then a backfire and a very high rev with Gladys leaning on the execrator, pulling the choke. "Do you like how I yank the old man, Reg?" said Gladys bemused, not altogether kindly. She thought about Travers – what a good lay, but just that, no more – and backed out the drive in a slip of tires, braked, got out to lock the hubs 4x4, tromped the gas again. She didn't slow until miles later, down the hill from Burlington, the power station by the lake came in sight, brick tower blinking red, white smoke emissions pluming. Down beneath Battery Park she went, where gorse bush, cedar and pine hug cliff side and hide a network of trails and burled nesting places, a complex not unlike the Viet Cong tunnels where hordes of gollum-like creatures withered and pale bunkered in the F-4 fire storms of Nam.

Gladys motored across R/R tracks onto a washboard strip of road rippled by heavy trucks delivering wood slabs to the power plant furnace. The smoke stack loomed once again, monumentally ponderous, cyclops-eyed and burnished in the first sunlight sneaking over the crest of hillside upon which Battery Park lay. The plant itself presented a ziggurat silhouette of brick and mortar, windows glowing urgently in the serious business of throwing steam at turbines. Gladys made for a community of shanties, make-shift lean-tos stacked like cards against the west wall, nearest the hillside and its labyrinth of underbrush paths, catching ambient heat off the giant furnace.

Gladys braked, intending to hide the Wagoneer behind a quonset shed, but lost direction temporarily in considering the imposition of the power plant tower standing like an obelisk and shining at the top with the sun like electrum, a transmission of energies from beyond, as evocative in message as a cross rising above a cathedral. She had entered the world of Henry Adams, his broad shoulders atlassing the new faith, turbine tower emitting rays of faith, the mysterious power of radium, a churning of dynamo, more suitable to American sensibilities than Virgin Queen, Mother of God. The Virgin and the Dynamo – images of infinite power. What was it Adams had said? One centripetal, pulling toward it all chaos and exerting order. The other centrifugal, accelerating latent energies outward toward chaos – Salome Vasari snapping an iron pan in an iron wrist, Gladys disassembling Reginald's house, Travers pumping her on the floor of the kitchen pantry. The new religion in America had always been industry, expansion and release. It became clear to Gladys that these church burnings had something to do with effacing landscape and releasing latent energies. Must tell Sergeant Vasari. Level the church steeples in Burlington and what townscape do you have – the smoke towers of industry. Yes! All that raw energy pouring waste and heat into the ethers, which Reg would certainly appreciate, the pud. Whoever was doing these burns was ceding the spiritual world to the secular drive for power. Why? Was this too part of the statement being made? Or was it an unintended consequence?

Gladys parked the Jeep, traipsed the lot through a scatter of orange and yellow mini-dozers, full-sized graders and bucket loader earth abraders helterskeltered about like dinosaurs collapsed in a graveyard. She meandered ridges of frozen mud puddles squeezed out of earth from truck tires the size of Ford Pintos. Darnell Hoover, first citizen of Power Town, met her at the opening of a path leading into brush and toward the backside of the power plant. Self-appointed sentinel, erstwhile Nam infantryman, nut case with a heart and a blasted right arm, babbler and sometime savant, draped in poncho with hair pomaded, slicked back like James Brown, moon-faced, tall and lank as his Bantu ancestors, Darnell stepped silently behind the diminutive Gladys whose habit of whispering to herself he thought charming.

"Damn it, Darnell! Shit! You spook! I was just talking with my buddy Henry Adams (Darnell sneaked a look behind to see if he had missed somebody) and he was saying about the Virgin, yes, and about the Dynamo, yes, about these two."

"Who's that you been talking?"

"No, I have been thinking, Darnell. Symbols of force, Darnell, symbols of energy. That's the key."

"Ain't nothing to me. But them wheels maybe could be? You got the key to that?"

"Listen, Darnell," said Gladys, taking him by the elbow of a withered arm, leading him in a low crouch beneath pine boughs, through an undergrowth of juniper, sumac and spruce like strolling a park. An unlikely surprise to an intruder, Darnell smelled distinctly of wood smoke, sweat, sweet cologne he had somewhere procured and poured down his collar. His one natty habit. "Darnell," said Gladys, "another church burn is imminent. And you know, don't you, Darnell? I need to know which church."

"Why you want to bust your cherry on that? What you should do is silent yourself and keep down your head for after the smell of death clears out the air."

"You won't tell me?"

"No, I'll tell you. But if only you pass me them keys."

"The Jeep?"

"I got somewhere to be that needs wheels like them."

"Well, all right, Darnell. But promise me not to baby that thing."

"I ain't too much practiced with machinery."

"Good! And the church burn?"

"That will be coming, likely this night."

"Tonight! Where?"

"Up there upon the hill where the Old North End gathers on Sunday to make a noise less godly than a wahwah riff of Hendrix. Everybody say a-men."

"Why, Darnell, that's poetry. The Old North End you say, the big stone church? But that's a French church. The Quebecois burning a French church? That right?"

Darnell stopped walking, stared trance-like, inspired if wooden, pointing over the top of Gladys' head with his blasted arm west in the direction of dark woods hugging the cliff-side rock of Battery Park, said, "The church that next burns stands somewheres there awaiting the deep and everlasting."

"Yes, well that is very clear. Thank you, Darnell."

Gladys and Darnell stepped out from the tunnel of undergrowth that let out at the west side of the power plant. Camp began to stir. Moans and exhortations from inside lean-tos greeted morning, its clear sky, rag traces of cloud, chilly, way cold. Shadow was eternal in camp, hillside blocking rising sun, the power plant itself blocking sunset, though hoarfrost silvered everything. Several grim figures emerged from cover, shuffled the path that bends to lakeside, un-cinched upon a fallen tree for communal relief. Uncharacteristically un-hassled by authorities, this camp seemed like permanence, a new thing for these usually loner types, and like any piece of real estate suitable to a particular clientele, it had developed of its own accord in a kind of organic evolution as its use and purpose deviated. Gladys looked to Darnell to explain the unusual communal spirit (or maybe dispirit in this case) of these sidewalk sleepers that mostly keep to themselves from paranoia or misanthropy or just to hear their own voices inside their own skulls. Darnell said little that didn't tag end with a Nam or Jimmy Hendrix reference. As self-appointed keeper of paths, he had also deigned to tend fire (roaming paths at night in Nam guise, hauling dead wood into camp to boil the kettle). Darnell had organized a 24 hour feed whereby Power Town residents tossed food refuse gathered from B-town restaurant bins into a cauldron to boil out disease and dirt. Food became water bloated, tasted of cardboard, but was safe, warm and plentiful. A ladle lay on one of many stones ringing the perimeter of the fire – warming stones that residents gathered to sit upon while eating and heat layers of clothing, so skin would thaw, effluvium separate from attached layers of insulation. A kind of renewal.

Darnell had told Gladys of a night some few weeks back when a devilish priest and a death-dealing Quebecer had invaded the camp and threatened violence should anyone speak to authorities of these church fires. Some had scattered after that, gone uphill to Battery Park until another death, then most returned to camp. When the priest and the Quebecer had descended upon Power Town a second time, Darnell shimmied a tree, cradled his head, bit his hand to stop the scream that came all the way from Nam – he saw again hootches burn and water buffalo oozing blood, children crying, mothers rifle-butted, a village of mud melting in rain, blood mixed in swirls like color wheels of paint that spin masterpieces in town fairs. He saw himself alone, out on flank, crawling with rifle cradled through the haunting incense perfumery of a Nam village cemetery. The platoon caught up, made laager there among grave stones while he crept into a sniper's tree, awaited daylight, expecting a gook patrol sidling into town, chatting and shuffling loosey-goosey. Then it did. The Americans attacked. Darnell with his two years of high school education had sat in the crook of a tree to snipe and direct mortar fire, black face poking out from branches like a Cheshire cat, smiling grotesquely, conflicted because he had opened his heart to this country of green paddies and lush mountains so far removed from home. So had his flesh – rosette sores blooming in the mud, algae, mildew and manure, in straw and cattle and decay, pustules bubbling and bursting, adhering the leather strap inside his helmet to his skull. But he also took comfort in familiar night skies: there shone the Southern Cross, his Tennessee touchstone. No stars that night but what he had caused to rain down on that village. Gooks and villagers ran from and into bursts of artillery, limbs flying off, faces unbelieving, a canister of Stokes mortar fire, friendly fire, struck his tree, exploded, burnt and killed nerves in his right arm.

Back in Vermont, he thought to jump out from his tree in that Nordic jungle, engage the hostiles invading Power Town. Knife in his one good hand, Darnell could have done damage. But instead he clung, cried and shook for the turn his life had taken that day in Nam. He could never again belong with his own kind after watching his black brothers butcher and rape – his good, best friends that had passed the weed, lionized Malcolm-X and Ali, made plans back stateside to make rock music, diddle white chicken, marry a black sister that baked corn bread. He became more of a loner after that. He cringed, shook, blathered when a black brother approached.

Discharged as antisocial, Psy-Ops said, though he had countered that by saying killing villagers was maybe a scooch more antisocial if they cared to know. He rode the train from Memphis as far north into whitey land as army money would buy. He slept some, ate infrequently, felt relatively sane up until the first church burned, after which he found himself founder of Power Town. Then hostiles appeared with odd ways of talking, warnings and murder. These two had kicked out the fire, thrown brands of smoldering wood under lean-tos to route out inhabitants, said death warnings to those that "held Mother Church tae near in their nestings," the priest had said, which Darnell later interpreted to the throng as unhealthy sleep habits. Many had vacated that night, had followed the rail lines south to Rutland after threats of hearts removed through noses. The name Travers Jones had been spoken as chief in retribution, one who had burned his own friend in his own van down by the Lumiere warehouse (which these street dwellers already knew about and more about who really did the killing). Vasari's name had been spoken as likely to want information that would land them in jail or place them in opposition to the Brothers Quebecois, which would be more dire than angering police.

Darnell stoked and fed the fire with scrap wood. He sat beside Gladys on the warming stones, peered silently into carbon orange and sodium yellow at the fire's center. Gladys tried to pull together her feelings for Travers. She had betrayed him by meeting with Vasari to explain what she learned of these church burns. She might have been more generous. That night in the kitchen, when they made love, Gladys had left Reginald forever – not from a sense of guilt, not because Travers was a better lover, but because Gladys realized she had been working up the nerve for a long time. Travers fascinated her. Interesting case study, to be sure. Beyond that a man living in another dimension –because of epilepsy, which Gladys studied more thoroughly once she and Travers had become intimate. Dostoevsky had the disease, thought his words became somehow crystalline and pure through the effects of aura; because voices and visions and smells and color all assail the brain during aura; an electrical storm the body creates, pure energy from the origins of life, the first touch of God. Gladys was not inclined to religious observance, having worked through a multitude of rituals and beliefs practiced by a multitude of cultures, rejecting all as inapplicable to her own nature, but just now, sitting beside this fire in a sudden slurry of snow, and beside the fractured psyche of the Nam vet whom she knew to be sweet on her, staring into fire, Gladys felt something stir somewhere where spirit resides with the sexual. She thought of John Donne's love elegies, sex and religion, Donne's poem "Autumnal" justifying an older woman attracted to a younger man. Despite having bad eyes since birth, her teeth were good, her body tight still. And the fires of longing burned, would certainly moderate over time, but never extinguish. Gladys became spongy with affection for Travers, and for the strange man beside her, feeling as generous as a sex goddess invoked.

Chapter Twenty-Three

Flowers from hell blooming • Preparations for a burn • Monseigneur Ruel's perilous vigil • Travers once again in tonic-clonic land • The burn goes bad; the posse reunited; Vasari pulls his gun; blood, blood, and a purifying fire • Mosley's urn rescued.

No one slept that night at the farm house: anxiety, impatience maybe, the Brothers Quebecois kicking empty Budweiser bottles, arguing, laughing in pidgin French, and me nattering away at no one, scratching nads through jeans, fully clothed, in fact. I lay on a blanket on the floor in what must have been a child's bedroom, the wallpaper a tableau of Disney, goofy stuff, daffy stuff. Halley lay with Uncle Gerrit in the astrolabe, doing her best nympho gun moll impression, but in the early morning, pre-dawn hours, looking too awful to have been mutually pleasured – her eyes puffy, her mood herky-jerky, brooding, edgy. Squirrels got busy on pine boughs hours before the sun, chattering, dropping pine cones upon the old zinc metal roof under which I twisted with a hard on, resentfully, regretfully, getting no sleep whatsoever so logy and loose in limbs, finally roused by Halley, told to come downstairs. A tension headache gathered behind my eyes.

The brotherhood were downstairs scuttling between rooms, pulling on beef jerky. Uncle Gerrit, oddly domestic and contented, scraped a pan of gruel in the kitchen with a wooden spoon in the light of an oil lamp, his skinny self presented in stamen-red winter undies, his black robes unhooked and draped, a fan of petals. Okay, that's a stretch, but for some reason I did have flowers in mind. I could smell them, in fact. Uncle Gerrit made me think of something exotic pushed up from the underworld, something mythic, nourished off the corpse of religion, a poisonous bloom. Halley sat on a milk crate leaning against wainscoting in her spotless khaki. Hardly blithe, she watched Gerrit nervously, second-guessing, digging out with fingers the pasty remains of breakfast from a cup.

"That's not the Uncle Gerrit I know," I said crouching beside her. "He never dresses other than priestly."

"I guarantee you have not missed a god damn thing, sugar?" Halley whispered in some portion bitter, otherwise bemused.

"He looks like a flower from hell. What was that French poet's lament, the one that lived off bat turds and absinthe in a Paris garret, flowers are evil, or something?"

"Yes, or something. Bawd-lay-her would be the poet's name, sugar, and from what I know, his overarchin' theme." She blushed, eyes teasing, leaned off the milk crate to hug me, ran a hand down my trousers to pat my tush. Cute, but hardly compensation for a cold bed. A brother Quebecois, Bousquet, smirked at the two of us, spoke Canuck to his fellow brother who grimaced and spat at my feet through crooked teeth and blue gums, then laughed outright. I acknowledged his machismo with a homo wink, which increased the ire in his blood and raised his middle finger.

"So, Halley Gay, you may now officially be addressed gun moll to the underworld flower king. Is that right? You're a kind of Persephone aren't you. Tell me" – I pushed her gently away – "how does your garden grow?"

"Let's see, I am inclined to say cocks and balls all in a row. Did I get that right, darlin'?"

I was so hard up for affection that abuses from Halley fell on me like endearments, while Uncle Gerrit had gone positively efflorescent in complexion and agility and attitude – youthful, spry, caneless even, his spine a notch or two straighter, a dancing flower of death.

The brothers thrashed by again with flashlights and crowbars and boxes of gear, a gallimaufry of argument and violent gesture propelling them through the kitchen to the attached barn then back again, splintering door frames with their shoulders, kicking holes in the plastered walls for fun, dusting us with the gray monads of extinguished life, a psychic toxin more potent than lead paint, the brothers generally overtaxing and assaulting the integrity of that old house. "Gathering taegether the wares of our trade," Uncle Gerrit explained, unconcerned. You would think by the commotion that Allied Van Lines were clearing us out. Not much got packed from our end, but plenty was anticipated from the other, a sum that might enrich us, so the brothers thought, should windfall invest in bad pennies. We were going to burn and harvest precious metals in Old North End Burlington, St. Joseph's Church, the one where Vasari had left evidence of his youth in mustaches painted on the saints.

It seemed odd to me that no significant planning had taken place before the excursion — nothing like what you see in movies, no charts drawn up or police routes timed or tasks assigned. There was no plan, at least nothing he wished to share. Uncle Gerrit made that clear. It is the only thing he did make clear. There seemed no initiative beyond Gerrit's implacable will, a resolve to burn too refined for any of this to be haphazard. I knew he had a plan. The brothers went about their business in restless fume, bumping each other, cursing, grinding dried beef with yellow teeth. No one was having fun. No one was in a good mood, except Uncle Gerrit. He cleared mist off a kitchen window, leaned his worn and channeled but somehow also fetchingly winsome face inches from the glass, identified several star clusters, whether keying on their associations with war, love, hubris, I don't know. He said "propitious, verily, most propitious" and winked at me so emphatically as to have developed a facial tick.

Uncle Gerrit collected the breakfast dishes he had sullied, wiped them clean with a rag in a deep lead sink, asked me to muscle the pump to draw the spring water. Two or three primes and it gushed, so cold as to have spilled off a glacier. Halley giggled cynically at Gerrit's husbandry. Gerrit splashed water on his face, stripped off the soutane, unbuttoned his long johns to the waist, splashed the cold water on his torso, the silver chest hair glistening, the white skin slimy as snails. "Ah feel most alive!" he said. "An old fish, surely, but thankful of the North Sea that hatched me." He stood silent a moment, looked out the window again at the morning sky, dried himself with a dish rag, sighed, replaced the soutane, hooked it tight against his thin body, the robes leveling his shoulders, beveling his waist, flattering with folds and tucks, a contour of illusory muscle. Gerrit stumbled while retrieving his cane as if suddenly burdened with two-thousand years of priestly shenanigans. He thumped lopsidedly, delicately placing dishes in cupboards lining the old farmhouse pantry, still lively and optimistic if off balance. I have to admit, the ironies of a man about to destroy a church washing cracked and chipped dishes in an abandoned home both unsettled and inspired me.

The brothers backed vehicles out from the barn. The Saab stuttered and skipped, its carburetor mis-tinkered by hands less than judicious. We heard the Datsun's tinny horn and knew to gather ourselves in winter coats for the long drive into town. The brothers sat rigid in the Datsun, deBoner expansive in farmer jeans and a stained, white t-shirt, overlarge for Japanese machinery. He smoked weed. The other two gristly, lean and sober in their Texaco jumpsuits, pony tails tucked under collars and blind-man wrap-around sun glasses. Halley drove the Saab cussing windshield defrost with Gerrit beside her and me hugging myself for warmth in the curve of the back seat, sliding on beige leather among magazines, soda cans, empty chip bags, a box of Tampax, the Sanka can from the first church burn that had drawn so many of us into this mess in the first place. This seemed a prime moment for a visitation from my father, guardian angel, truly departed, truly angelic, Holy Ghost. It was quite literally Father, Son and Holy Ghost conspiring to burn, renew themselves in the ash heap. Be Zarathustrian, I thought, make large mistakes joyfully!

Uncle Gerrit became pensive then nit-picky about Halley's driving. There were to be no "vehicular infractions," he said. We followed my Datsun truck through snowy farms lumpy with fence posts and manure piles, the occasional John Deere or Nuffield cripple buried deep in shadowy moonlight, then along the Winooski River past tire garages, beverage wholesalers, low-rent housing in Old North End Burlington.

Halley steered with her shoulders like pacing the Indy 500. Burlington lay asleep in flashing yellow traffic lights, beneath a low cloud of ocher. A Coca Cola delivery truck crowded our rear bumper, appeared as suddenly as a comet, its headlights pouring light into the cab of the Saab. We looked like x-rays of our selves, coruscating in an outline of corona, beatification of the heretics, our thoughts leaking from pores, the car noxious with the scent of pent emotion. When those headlights turned onto a side street the dark enveloped us again; our thoughts went secret again. Uncle Gerrit went acerbic cautioning Halley's driving, his bald head dimpled with tension. Her hands blanched on the wheel, lips drawing breath like a fish pulled out of water. Gerrit fixed his eyes on some vanishing point on the horizon. A smile trembled on his lips. Halley said nothing. I said nothing.

We almost missed Monseigneur Ruel when we entered the church. deBoner had crow-barred a side door into the sacristy. The brothers were already bagging items when we found him – wakeful, eyes rheumy, etiolated, bloodless, altogether a soft mass of tissue and bone indistinguishable from the paunchy cushions of a worn leather chair where he sprawled with a book and eyeglasses in his lap, a study in sedentary and pampered intellectualism, but his face iconic like carved in mahogany and placed reverently among chalices and beads and candle sticks and cups and incense burners, a glut of shiny stuff. He nodded a greeting as though expecting us, said "Bless us!" rubbed his eyes and explained further that everything of value had been gathered into this room. No fire was necessary. He would not say a word of our malefactions. He said it would be as if we were never there. He said those that tread the rock of Peter and build no foundation will leave no footprints thereafter. Did he mean evermore? Interesting theory. Pretty much anti-Zarathustra though, unsuitable to the moment. Ruel must have sentineled a number of days in this room. He had been sleeping there. A corner of the room had been separated by a Chinese screen and tricked out for his person, ensconced as he was in home comforts behind the screen: a small T.V. asserted its black eye upon a lamp table, a plate of supper leavings lay upon a ladder-back chair, his feet rested upon a low cushioned stool. He was dressed in a white night shirt, covered with an afghan, its selvage of fringe squaring him in like a picture frame. He had been tucked in at night by the matriarchal presbyter who most certainly occupied the guest chair for evening chats while Monseigneur nibbled his meal.

Uncle Gerrit told Reul his chatter would be of no avail. Gerrit's voice seethed in mistrust and condign loathing at the sight of a brother embodying what he might have become himself, were he to have thrived in the spiritual compromise of material embellishments that distinguish monkish grace. But he found himself crying, staring down at Reul's wispy fluttering – weak and pudgy, pale and frightened. Reul said, "Ah, you have the melting mood upon you."

"Aye," said Gerrit. "I slubber that ye leave yerself tae hollow out and wither, a dried thing, empty of passion. This material which ye guard is mere surface, stagecraft upon which the spirit flits and glides but takes no purchase."

"You are welcome to all you see, including my life. But please leave the church as it stands," said Reul.

Gerrit stepped onto a plane of prismatic light streaming down to the stone floor from a stained glass window overhead catching fire with dawn breaking through cloud.

"Aye. A man's life be essentially immaterial. Ye know this. A spiritual man would know this. I once mistook the colors that float upon yer foot stones as the true spirit of Christ." The two mechanics, meantime, packed valuables, opened cabinets left unlocked and bursting in silver and gold. "And," Gerrit continued, "there be moments when I have shucked the abrasions of ultramontanism by the prism of refracted hopes and dreams, the un-solids of God's promise." Reul had no chance to respond as one of the brothers had begun to wrap him in duct tape, closing his mouth, attaching limbs to the leather chair. "And," said Gerrrit, "it took Paul Tillich tae redeem me, tae rebirth me; the evils of this world that he expressed opened up tae me a view of the deepest levels of truth." I stood in a corner of the room, my tongue numb with expectation (a visitation of pebbles in the mouth), passive, horrified and excited. Gerrit said, "I shall purify all in Fire; I burn tae free spirit, tae reassert the mysteries this church and others of its ilk have bottled up." Monseigneur Reul sat wrapped in duct tape, mummified, his eyes resigned, maybe even sympathetic.

Uncle Gerrit gathered himself to accommodate a storm of ecstasy, Druid blood heating, eyes abstracted, aggressions aligned, cane lifted crozier-like striking the stone floor as if expecting to sunder and crack the underpinnings of Christendom, then a moment of orison with Gerrit seated in the ladder-back chair beside Reul and wordlessly moving lips, slipping into meditation until Christ intervened. Suspended overhead in a corner intersection of facing wall and ceiling bleeding upon the cross, he leaned toward Gerrit, forgiving, offering himself in Gerrit's despite.

"Thou bloody whelp of Mary's lie!" said Gerrit. "I deny thee. The true miracle will out! Travers, Travers, where be ye, lad?"

He searched for me with his hands as if blinded. I hesitated, took the hand as Gerrit wept openly, said, "Do ye see, Travers, son, the deference this poor misguided priest pays tae the false prophet. Ach! This too shall burn."

Having been for years free of the closet of my mother's demons and the classroom of my uncle's perversions, I prided myself immune to this mumbo jumbo. But the moment had overwhelmed Gerrit and through him agitated everyone in that room, including me. The two mechanics that had disappeared into adjoining rooms, rooting through lower chambers, reappeared in the sacristy as Gerrit took my hand. They stopped, kinetic and fidgety, angled heads at me, then with a nod from Gerrit leapt on me. One pulled me to the floor. The other sat on my chest. Gerrit turned his marble eyes away, said, "Bring the lad tae the altar. It is he shall set flame upon the dais."

My head throbbed. The brothers pulled me to the tabernacle in the main body of the church and taped my arms and legs. Gerrit shuffled in speaking low and husky some incantation that sounded like a dirge. The brothers went through the altar and nave niches taking what seemed of value. Gerrit sat beside me on the stairs by the offertory rail, brought to me Eucharist wine and wafers, said, "Eat, lad. The poisons shall course thy veins and change thee. Ye shall enter through thy epilepsy the world of spirit to battle the false prophet." Bless me! I ate and drank. Gerrit turned to face the empty pews, addressed an absent congregation: "Soon enough we release the spirit of the torch bearer upon thee that he may dazzle the obscurities, whisper in the silence, teem in the desert." Strange words but to me the message became clear: I was not to light the fire. I was to *be* the fire.

Maybe there was something in the wine, or maybe it was the thought of that Irishman in East Boston who tortured Christ in the host he kept locked inside a match box, but I began to feel the epilepsy coming on. The attending aura, an invisible breath, diffused strangely redolent of flowers and dark, fecund earth, a place where gardens thrive. Gerrit said to me I must initiate the burn. But he saw I was going quickly into seizure. He was not upset by this. He expected as much. Like my last fit in the choir back when I was a boy, Gerrit took this as a sign. He said he welcomed my moment of vision. He said Halley would give birth to a son who would grow in his care to be the next torch bearer to free more souls in my name and in my father's name, release all to the "mysteries. " I wasn't listening. I was sinking deeper into tonic-clonic dysfunction.

I saw my father again. It had been a long time. The reunion was joyful, summery, the air thick with spores and humidity. My father busily happy, smiling and peasant-like, hoed a walled garden, sweat drenched in a rocky soil, the wall ancient and of stone. One side of the stone wall formed the facade of an old church with a stained glass window in blues and greens, with Christ in white robes, his hand raised in a blessing. I thought maybe I had seen my father's spirit in Heaven, until much later when I found in Fiona's possession a photograph of his lost years and realized my vision was of a Heaven on earth, a place my father had discovered through the kindnesses of strangers applied to heal invisible wounds. A village curate had befriended him in an isolated river valley somewhere in Europe, a haven for the transgressor from America whose silent industry among the curate's gardens had won him acceptance among a generally exclusive parish. He made things grow even in the shadow of hillside and stone wall. He had his mother's gift.

I awoke, seemingly hours later, in the arms of Gladys. She was rocking me in her arms. I had gone completely into that place where visions of hopes and dreads dance behind my eyes, and I had released body fluids while in her arms. An unholy image. She and Darnell Hoover had sat deep in the front seat of the Jeep Wagoneer, backed into the parking lot of a laundromat Darnell knew to be friendly to indigents, a place that had zoned me Kenmore rhythmic in my aphoristic journal writing during a more peaceful time. It was a place near enough to St. Joseph's Church for Gladys and Darnell to observe comings and goings. The Jeep had gathered more dents, a cracked windshield, a slow leaking tire, a sprung leaf spring, a couple bullet holes. Darnell had abused it as Gladys had requested, bouncing it over construction sites to collect material for Power Town security: wire to string ankle high, sharp metal scrap, panes of glass to lay on the forest floor, nails. No one would sneak past his night perimeter again. He had even driven across the frozen lake to Plattsburgh Air Base to procure ordnance but was shot at and so forced to turn back.

Halley Gay had seen and recognized Reginald's Jeep from her Saab, rubbing with mittens a porthole of misty observance, had seen the flash of street lamp upon window glass which Gladys nervously rolled up and down repeatedly despite Darnell's insistence she remain silent and unseen, which he had learned as a sniper in Nam. Halley lay on the horn to warn the brothers of intruders. The horn sounded shrill and insecure in blooming daylight, but the brothers heard it, dispatched Monseigneur Reul dispassionately (nearly took his head off with a deep cut to the neck; he spilled his life at the feet of Jesus, having no time to prepare for death, yet feeling as if he had been preparing all his life). The brothers gathered valuables and Uncle Gerrit and transported all to the vehicles. deBoner remained behind to set burn charges in four corners of the nave to separate the material and the spiritual in another church and, apparently, to do the same for me. He had dug holes with the crowbar through plaster and lath walls to expose dry support timbers and in the air space between walls had stuffed hymnals and religious tracts of offset print from the archives he had ransacked. But he hadn't counted on Hoover landing on him in a fury of Nam flashback. Darnell fell upon him from behind gripping deBoner by the neck, intending to spin and detach the spinal cord, but he had forgotten about his handicap and gave deBoner a severe neck wrench instead and scratches from the talons of his blasted hand. DeBoner sent Darnell into the pews with a back arm, drew a knife but found Darnell recovering quickly with a knife in his one good hand, so deBoner cussed in Canuck and ran out through the front door where Halley had bounced the Saab up over the curb to the broad, processional stairs deBoner slipped down in his haste.

In the final shakes of an epileptic fit, as my senses begin to distend and synch again with the outside world, there is a process of crawling through tunnels of dissociation. Then a series of aftershocks, tiny electrical brain storms where something of my vision and some of what's real blend in misshapen images. Flash! and there's my father tilling the earth, amused at me shackled and made to swallow altar wine that spills out my mouth in overflow like a fountain. Flash! and there's Gladys naked caressing me on a kitchen floor, and I'm vomiting bouillabaisse all over her lap. I crawled out from that tunnel with sore knees, burned maybe on the pede-cloth carpet of the altar. I had a severe headache and the taste of rust from having bitten my tongue. I had been cut loose of my bonds. My head lay in Gladys' lap. The fact I had pissed myself didn't matter to her. She had been looking at me with a curiosity bordering on wonder. Her first gesture was to ask what it was I had been dreaming? Had I touched God? or some such silliness, and –

"My God, Travers, did you know the good Monseigneur has been murdered? Did you acquiesce to this? How could you? I mean, you were nearly burned yourself. Did you know? How can your own kin want to burn you alive? It's Greek tragedy in here. Awful!"

There was little I could say in response that would make sense, given my condition. But I wanted her to understand that Uncle Gerrit had intended me a sacrifice like Jesus, a martyr. I felt oddly flattered. Gladys would take the secular view and ask me later how I think Uncle Gerrit had expected to get away Scott free without leaving behind a who-done-it. But at that moment, Gladys' attentions had made all this personal. She had gone beyond her usual clinical jargon. There was kindness and deep concern in her voice. Gladys rocked me in her arms, hugged my head to her chest, rocked me some more, said again, "Awful. Just awful."

When Gladys and her Nam friend plunged me into daylight, hooked their arms through mine, dragged me the length of the basilica past colonnade and pews, I was surprised by all the white, still so very white — no potash blackening, no shimmering heat off corrosive flame, nothing burned. My eyes ascended to the vaulted ceiling. It stared down at me through donor inscriptive medallions, a community I had betrayed, harsh and unblinking, the eyes of a tribunal of the richly righteous judging me, finding me guilty, the praetor shaking out his robes in indignation upon a chair of gold behind me as I was led away. "Buck up, Travers, buck up," said Gladys sensing my flagging morale. So I did. I raised my head again to where organ pipes on the balcony gleamed. Flanked by columns and beneath a fan window, they gleamed like angel wings. Those wings spread to enfold and embrace me, to forgive me, though I could not easily forgive myself. The air smelled of flowers. It was my father, it had to be, my guardian angel. It is the last vision I was to have of him, it is the one I carry with me now. That was to be my last epileptic fit.

We pushed through oak doors where the morning air undulated in cherry lights beaming on police cars and shattered with threats, beads on gun barrels conjoining eyes, theirs and ours. Officer Brady celebrated in agitated arm gesture. Here was I, chief on his wanted list, smack in the middle of this church burn. He warned fellow officers I was dangerous beyond a doubt, possum docile. Gladys and her Nam buddy appeared too scruffy to be the good guys. We were made to lie face down at the top of the stairs where deBoner had recently slid away before the police arrived. So we were it – arson suspects, murder suspects. Had I not been too spacey to know what was being said, I would have confessed to every accusation, despite having been forgiven by a higher court. Vasari worked his way into the circle as best he could on bad knees. He waved back his brotherhood of the law and explained the nature of our vigilante investigations, which raised eyebrows and elicited cynical recognition for the odd way Vasari does his job, he with the rapport with nutso priests and street indigents. Vasari said he would debrief the posse and assign martial response back at the station. Nothing more to do. False alarm. The circle broke. Brady kicked off toward his car. Others followed as if tethered. Brady did have leadership qualities it seemed. No one as yet knew about the dead priest.

Vasari asked what happened. Gladys said it's happening still and that I knew where and that if we don't get going soon the dead priest will be found and hold us up so that the Brothers Quebecois get away. Vasari frowned, sighed, said, "The good Monseigneur?' Gladys asserted yes, afraid so. "Damn," said Vasari, regretting his association with us, I'm sure, but knew a convoy of police cruisers would sneak up on nobody. Vasari said for Gladys and her friend to follow. I stepped into the police cruiser and led us all back to that house in the woods. Come what may.

The day started exceptionally warm, false spring in mid-winter, snow melting in rivulets and veins, sluicing in ruts off the dirt roads, that dirt the consistency of taffy, mud splashing side windows of the cruiser. Vasari knew not to slow down in the morass so we scraped bottom, bounced in and out of ruts all the way to Westford. Gladys and her one-armed militia followed in the Wagoneer, Darnell driving, zigzagging, bouncing off snow banks like a bobsled, the massive chrome, baleen grill of the Jeep threatening to swallow us ahead in the police cruiser, mud from our wheels spattering their windshield. Vasari wheezed, coughed, asked was I involved in the Father Reul murder? Said, "Damnation, that's a low crime!" Asked had I joined the savage brotherhood? Asked whatever can it be that motivates my uncle to kill and burn? Salome would be sorely disappointed, he said, which upset me. But I never said a word, my emotions roiling and actions unsure, not until I cautioned the turnoff where that same raven, Uncle Gerrit's totem, pointed the way again, this time in daylight. I wondered did Halley see our bird and if so what can she be thinking?

As we entered the thick, dark woods, winter returned. The road went slick with packed snow, sun shied away. We had plunged back into night. When we rounded the corner leading through pine alongside the flow of a brook, the house was already on fire. We could smell it. Halley's Saab was parked beside the porch, burbling and skipping, unsteady in its RPMs. Halley was nowhere seen but heard screaming inside the house. Vasari braked alongside Halley's car, nothing subtle about that man. Gladys' Wagoneer stalled and slid into us, pinning us, which would later prove to be a bad thing. Vasari swung his door open, swiveled in the seat to plant both legs for a painful alley-oop. Halley came out the door onto the porch with deBoner in tow slashed and bleeding, holding together his guts it seemed, the blood rich and prodigal, spilling through his fingers and in a wide trail down his pants onto the floorboards. Halley shook and bobbled like a puppet, but was all business nonetheless, her lips puffy like she gets. She looked at Vasari, then at me. She said nothing. Vasari said nothing. I said, "What the hell is going on, Halley?" "Manson fuckin' vibes, sugar," she said. "Helter-skelter all over the place, more damn knives than a butchery, bloody, all bloody." She wedged deBoner into the Saab and drove off past Darnell and Gladys who was reactive enough to wave arms and shout, "Hold on, Halley, stop! Where you going?" Which did no good whatsoever. I wouldn't see Halley again until a year later, and many years again after that.

Uncle Gerrit occupied the house, as did two remaining Brothers Quebecois, with knives certainly, and smoke pouring out the basement windows.

"That's where the brothers melt gold," I said. "There's a wood stove down there used as a smelting furnace."

"Might could be faulty wiring," said Vasari.

Gladys walked over quietly, lay her hand on Vasari's shoulder, said, "Not so very likely, Sergeant."

Vasari said, "Yuh, could be not" and drew his gun and stepped onto the porch and entered the front door as Darnell sneaked into the house through the attached barn directly into Seymour loading the back end of my Datsun truck. His face was slashed and bleeding which he daubed periodically with a rag that he dropped to the ground to lift milk crates of substantial weight, his black eyes flashes of mica discerning Darnell's shadowy movement opposite the truck, then himself entirely flexed as one knot of muscle dropping the crate, spinning low, drawing a hunting knife attached beneath his pant leg that struck at Darnell's knees springing away but too late to escape hamstringing, the Canuck's knife whetstone sharp both sides like a pike. Before Darnell recovered, the brother leaped on him in a madness of abandoned self-concern that Darnell had not even seen in Nam.

I followed Vasari through the front door, chattered instructions where to find the basement door, and where Uncle Gerrit kept the astrolabe antiquities he would certainly be collecting as smoke coalesced in furry lumps between warped slats of floor boards until the cellar door burst open in a storm of smoke with one of the Canuck brothers coughing, hauling a corn meal sack of heavy material up stairs which he dropped that scattered back down the stairs. Vasari said, "Don't ya move, mister man!" The Canuck unfazed rushed Vasari, slid a knife smoothly into his ribs, twisted and pushed Vasari against the wall while extracting the blade. Vasari said "damnation" very quietly, never shot his gun. Vasari collapsed slowly, like his knees had finally given way to gravity entirely and not reluctantly. I bent over Vasari, said, "Why didn't you shoot?" "I ain't never once fired this thing," said Vasari wheezing and squeezing my wrist reassuringly. Said further, "Get yourself gone." The Sergeant's eyes had gone milky. Seymour had pulled out the knife and wiped it on Vasari's shoulders. He looked disdainfully at me, made no motion toward the gun that hung useless in Vasari's hand. He walked back down cellar stairs, protecting eyes with a forearm, holding the knife at his side. I twisted Vasari's gun from his hand, which had a more urgent grip than I had expected, but which I resolutely wrenched free like robbing a corpse and followed Vasari's murderer into the fiery cellar.

Gladys had been told by Vasari to wait in the police cruiser. Not in her nature. Gathering smoke and silence from a house filled with opposition had her too worked up. She closed the cruiser door with care, opened the front door off the porch with as much care, bit her fist when she saw Vasari bleeding, breathing heavily, focused on some world that lay behind that stained and flowery swirl of wallpaper. Gladys whispered his name, couldn't break through. She screamed when the gun discharged beneath her feet. One time, I thought. Several times she would later tell me. There was no response to the gunfire from any other part of the house. Darnell had lost his life in a struggle with the Quebecer who had gone unscathed and was packing the Datsun, waiting for his Canuck partner to fetch a last bag of loot. Fire now licked baseboard molding in the living room. Creaking floor boards overhead indicated Uncle Gerrit active in the astrolabe. Gladys strained eyes to see what might emerge resolved from smoke rising up cellar stairs. I emerged unsettled and shaky from having taken a life, and from having stumbled over another body (that night watchman missing from the warehouse near Lumiere who had seen the Elvis immolation). I was thankful to have in my arms the urn of Professor Mosley.

Gladys and I dragged Vasari onto the porch. She ran for the Jeep, over-revved in her haste burying wheels to the hub in mud having finally yielded to the false spring as a fine rain worked down through the frost line. The police car was wedged between house and Jeep. She returned to me and Vasari on the porch, said, "I'm sorry. I'm so sorry." I don't know how many times. Gladys placed Vasari's hands in his lap and held them. I sat beside him but could not from shame touch or look closely at him. He was beyond caring. Vasari had found a depot somewhere deep in the north woods where he was unwrapping packages dressed in bright paper and bows and some in brown paper and twine he had wrapped in his youth, all come off a flat car that had dieseled fifty years through mysterious woods on rail lines. His sins flew out of each opened package dissolving in the smoke-thick air. Nickoli leaped on that train, spry and unburdened, and began the night-rider's life he had wanted as a child.

The house began to heat with the fire. It wasn't until glass shattered and books and instruments of astro projection clattered on cars below that I remembered Uncle Gerrit upstairs. He was still in the house, up in that astrolabe. His voice crowed what I assumed to be apocalyptic hysteria. I moved around to the cars, looked up to the window where Gerrit smiled at me. I listened more closely. He said he saw now at last that his prognostications were off kilter, that he now had me and Halley together raising a son and how glad he was that I was well but that it was all foretold and how my account of all this would justify the Brothers Quebecois and himself and Paul Tillich and that my son too would sojourn in the land of spirit and that it was my job to place the torch of illumination in His hand and to show Him what had gone before and that he trusted me to do so. Then he walked back into the house as flame broke through the roof, starlings diving across the sky. Gladys dragged Vasari off the porch as the house had become too hot even to lean against. My Datsun truck exploded backward out the attached barn, braked and accelerated shimmy-tail away from the house. Gladys keened as Vasari passed. I walked down the mud road with Mosley's urn in my hand. I felt a hand on my shoulder, nearly jumped out of my skin. It was Gladys. She looped her arm through mine, pulled me around to face the house, said, "Look at that, Travers!" I swear I saw constellations dissolve and planets break free of their orbits and shoot off into the ether from their fixed places upon the astrolabe. We walked away from the burning house through pine alongside a brook and away, far away.

Chapter Twenty-Four

Travers on the road again • Suzanne Norber(t) née Halley Gay discards her son, takes up a life of crepe • Travers and Fiona in St. Andrews, Scotland – her final days • The Citroen that almost could • A final word from Travers' father • Revisiting the scene of the crime • Into the sunset.

As options diminish, I find myself participating more fully in the past. I have built rooms in an expanding house of memory well beyond its capacity to sustain growth: foundations tilt and shift, doors close of their own accord, walls crack and furniture leans. I pass through these rooms bearing the dim lamp of philosophy. I embellish my journal with accounts you presently read. But on this day, the future begins. I will open a door onto my father's world and find there a letter, one I have already mentioned but not shared, his final words to me sent to Fiona that she could not bring herself to read. "When you are alone, you are not free." Those are his words. Without my lovely wife, Gladys, I am very alone and very un-free. So I have abandoned my house in Montreal before it tumbles. The front door slaps my heels in a back draft – a matter of winds snaking through stressed joints, or the ghost of Gladys good-riddancing me. Yes, I have married Gladys Needham, but she is gone from this house and expects the same of me. She was the care giver. Even Cat benefitted from her attentions, having been saved by Gladys from my apartment in Burlington and taken to Power Town to live there with the indigents of whom he was a kind.

Sometimes we wish to escape our memories; sometimes we are made to. The empty chambers of my home echo dry as the tomb. I have switched off lights and mailed keys to a realtor. I am leaving behind Montreal and McGill University. No more students. No more pretense to answers to questions that will never have answers. Parsifal takes his nose out from the books that have made a desiccant of his soul, poured silica into his heart. Zarathustra has closed shop, bought a ticket out. I am jobless, homeless, widowed, a middle-aged man with more memories than friends, but I am no longer inclined to despair. As I have said, Gladys worked me through all that.

My son sees my recent urge to hegira a good thing, inclined in his youth thus to assess all radical change the old guard initiates. He is gone to university in one of the southern United States. Thankfully he has no interest in religion whatever. He is busily happy, studying the bricks he treads of Jeffersonian architecture, diddling his girlfriend in the dorm, embarrassing his roommate no doubt. He sends out his laundry. It is a Sunday and he is sleeping in.

As for me, the church bells of Montreal peal a warning that I am loosed onto the community. They think me spiritually infirm still and aberrant as all get out, in need of a cure – on the road again, torch bearer for the unclaimed, the forgotten old gods. They can't know I am weightless, harmless, emptied of malice, troubled only by echoes in this house I have occupied with Gladys, all those memories that work their way out from the wall paper when I can't sleep at night. If anything goes up in smoke it will be me, spontaneous combustion, come to the end of my wick, but no more than a snap and fizzle, a light bulb weary in its tungsten. Pfffftttt! and it's done.

As I have said, this is not despair – more like one self all used up waiting for another to evolve. Gladys has for so many years defined me. She brought me into the daylight as best she could. I am inclined to shut myself away behind doors. There's nothing left for me here. I am going back on the road where memories collide with the present to shape the future. I am courting accident once again, but oh, ye gods, please, not so crazy as before. After twenty years a university stooge, I haven't the balls for large statements. No more philosopher warrior. I am more concerned to get right this one, single life.

A taxi will shuttle me to Dorval, to the airport outside Montreal, but first I go to a riverside address where I meet a friend for dinner in the old city on the Rue Le Moyne. I avoid the underground because I still feel too intensely the humm and buzz of secret things beneath the surface. I still can't use chalk in the classroom. My friend you will know as Halley Gay. She now answers to Suzanne Norber(t), a Gallic patronymic typically prodigal in throw-away consonants. I first noticed Halley in a newspaper article featuring a flagship restaurant in the tourist district of Old Montreal. She has established herself a successful entrepreneur in the eateries business. She has made crepe a gourmet concoction. The proprietor shied from the camera in sunglasses and a trendy silk scarf. The blonde hair has been died auburn, but the forehead and wide cheeks and attitude are all Halley Gay. The irony of Halley's having gone from news breaker to fugitive to media darling once again has made me giddy. I mean, for Dionysian urges to reappear to the balding and paunchy encased in chinos and loafers —well, it's too much. The paper had her a mademoiselle, single, or widowed like me, de-coupled of deBoner in any case.

I have sleuthed her restaurant a year ago in the spring in the evening, a warm rain spilling onto cobbles, staining blocks of granite four stories tall and two centuries old built for river commerce — warehouses, counting houses, customs. Tourists jostled for room on the slate sidewalks, dodging rain beneath arched doorways, the gaudy eye candy of art galleries glittering, the gaily-painted boutique and restaurant signs elbowed and swinging in wind above my head. Halley was there seating tables, tall and gracious, officious, efficient, stunning in black parachute silk pants, a strapless pink tube, a sparkling choke collar flirting in an expanse of skin. Hair trimmed short and angled to frame her face. She had grown into her skin, still sexy, self-confident, a modern French woman. I couldn't walk in on her then. I was too nervous, and it hadn't been long after the death of my wife — too weird. But now that I am leaving Montreal, in the fall of the year, and have made reservations by phone for Professors Gladys and Travers Jones at a corner table, I have given warning I will approach Halley for the first time twenty years after she has given birth to our son and surrendered him to me and Gladys and burbled off in her white Saab.

On that night of the burning farmhouse, she drove deBoner to Canada on a dirt road to bypass border police. He directed Halley to a small town of red tin roofs in a farming community outside Quebec City. His wounds were dangerous because of blood loss. Seymour's knife, scimitar in its lines, had peeled back abs but left viscera untouched. According to Halley, deBoner was the one true Quebecois among the three Canadians, thus the tussle over melted gold and silver. She will tell me deBoner dreamed of a free Quebec. The two auto mechanics dreamed of Monte Carlo and fast cars and faster women. Halley had lost her dreams entirely but clung to deBoner's romancing hopeless causes. I still think he is a low thief and a murderer.

When she found herself pregnant, again, and was sure conception had occurred in our brief time together in that old farmhouse, she wouldn't abort, not this time. But Halley couldn't raise the child either, not as a fugitive living with a fugitive. Once deBoner healed, a discrete veterinarian having stitched the wound, he and Halley relocated to Quebec City where deBoner found work cooking in a restaurant. Halley waited tables, polished her French and borrowed a name from off a street sign. She gave birth to our son as deBoner chased Seymour to Labrador and disappeared. She took our son to Montreal, found me attending grad school at McGill University, phoned and asked to meet me at a tourist information off-ramp south of the city on highway 15. She was a wreck when I saw her, breathless and weepy, gaunt and disheveled. Her white Saab had begun to rust, had lost hub caps and a side-view mirror, had gained a cracked windshield. She told me the boy's name was Emile and that he was mine and that I must raise him. She handed Emile to me through the window. I stood there flummoxed, my tongue sorting words through a mouthful of pebbles. She drove away, braked, backed up, trembled out from the driver's seat and took the boy from my arms and hugged and rocked him for several minutes that seemed hours then trembled back into the Saab, cursed the defroster and sped away. But she had remained in Montreal and had parleyed her good intelligence and her trust fund into a thriving business.

How can she not know me now? How can this be? I walk into her restaurant. She looks past me, or through me. Halley distances me further with flawless Parisian French, seats me, asks do I expect Madame. I say she has died, bravely and horribly. The only thing that gives Halley away, this charade, this travesty of memory, is a band of moisture glistening above her lip and a quavering voice. She tells me Michelle will be my waitress and "bon appétit" and somehow expects me to think it's over. Well, it's not! Not by a long shot. I turn in my chair and announce in plain American English: "Hey, Halley, Suzanne Norber-T née Halley Gay. I know you!" She stops, her back to me still. Her legs begin to shake. She reaches for the nearest chair back, nearly collapses onto a customer seated there. She still doesn't look at me. Scullions and servers leap to her aid. She brushes them off with a wave and laughs a mule bray, gains control, apologizes to customers so gracefully I want to cry. Halley never looks back. She stands, brushes hands down red palazzo pants, pulls at the waist of a Chinese quilted jacket, adjusts the jersey scarf that wraps her neck, walks away into the kitchen. I don't see her again that night. I don't expect to see her ever again. I am amazed at her composure, so determined not to unpin the life she has so expertly fashioned for herself. I withdraw feeling empty, despite having worked through a Florentine crêpe, a desert crêpe, an entire bottle from cru classé. I order coffee to put me right. It shakes in my hand, dribbles onto my chin. I ask the waitress to phone a cab, lay out a generous tip, and write Halley a note on a napkin: *I am flying to Scotland today to resolve the accident of my birth. Were we two yet another accident? May I see you when I return?* I move to the street where windows of the restaurant spill light in puppet tableaus of teeming, complete and loving lives. I stomp out what I can of these images with loafers, vow to resume the hermit life of my youth, tell the taxi to get me to Dorval to the airport quick!

Unfortunate choice of words. That driver shakes my guts hopping traffic, working up a tip, I'm sure. My emergency is metaphysical, not literal, but I haven't explained myself. I don't feel like making corrections. That would be too much work. So I ride it out, go deeper into memories of Halley with each correction of the wheel. Once at the airport, my stomach refuses to settle. I don't like airplanes. I once saw them as arrows of fate tearing the fabric of sky I used to watch as a child from the Palladian windows of my hotel rooms. I now believe in accident, which plays further on my nerves. Certainly as vehicles airplanes plant me uncomfortably in my past, remind me of my visit with Toussant in South Boston where I learned of my father's hellish family life and of his complicity with my uncle. But this time, I am off to St. Andrews, Scotland. Fiona McDeed has written me in an infirm hand asking that I come to her family home by the bay, a stone cottage in the shadow of a ruined cathedral. This will be a trip further back in family history than I have yet undertaken.

I arrive in Edinburgh with a lengthy train ride to St. Andrews ahead of me. I'm frazzled, care-worn, drunk as a lord, a hot pistol of imposing epithets leveled at customs to bull myself through (not my best side, but it doesn't surface too often, or so I like to think). "Settle yerself, Professor. Stay the night in Edinburgh. A wee nappie perhaps afore trekking off tae the low highlands," says the polite but irate customs officer. I know this is good advice. I secure a hotel room near the train station, surprised I get past the doorman – aristocracy certainly built this place. I'm guessing old money still floats it. I dine guiltily upon venison liver glazed in a sweet mustard sauce, the grisly heads of elk and deer separated from their guts and mounted on the stone walls of the vaulted dining room.

In my room there is a stunning corner view of a hilltop acropolis and on the opposite hill Queen Mary's palace and beyond that a boxy mountain called Arthur's Seat. I suppose it's the title "professor" that gets me these accommodations. There is a shelf of books, all Scots literature –

Sir Walter Scott novels, of course, or his monument would shed tears, and a book of Edinburgh ghosts chased lately by tours, a history of wars against the castle, some poetry of Robert Burns whose jilted lover appears in cameo all over this town, and a Robert Louis Stevenson biography. I choose the Stevenson, discover him aimless, bohemian, estranged of his father, enamored of married women, another mirror to my soul. I close the book, switch on an electric fire that plugs the hearth, open a pygmy bottle of Famous Grouse among a selection of Scotch whiskies and liqueurs that line the mantle, and fall steeply to sleep despite trepidations of Fiona's condition.

Early morning I escape kidney pie and kippers, finagle a coffee to go, nod to the supercilious doorman and find myself shunting down a rail line, Brit Express, perpetual chug-a-lug whose unforgiving and everlasting motion will eventually deposit me at the same depot where Vasari unwraps packages, somewhere deep in the primal woodland. But first I have my mother to meet at the end of this line, not Vasari, and she's alive but not so happy though on her own ground rather than exiled to airport island, which is what East Boston has become. The terrain north of Edinburgh is all Firth-of-Fourth shoreline with islands nesting ruined castles and abbeys, small villages with harbors packed in the fishery trade, graceful and colorful wooden fifes giving way to Norway built trawlers of steel, all pulling out to sea in a diesel fog. Sheep look to have had legs dipped in ink, and carry pink or blue or red blotches of paint on their backsides. They cling to rock side, pull grass inches from rail lines and motorways, risk their mutton blithely. All here seems gentle and unhurried.

I am in a taxi again, shortly, wending narrow coach ways to the walled, seaside university town of St. Andrews. More cottages by the sea and then a famous golf course, wind-swept and barren and royal, although not always so much favored of kings, says my driver, and so once, very long ago to be sure, the university compelled by King James II in the century of the fourteens to abandon links and take to archery fields instead – war pending, as always – "Gowf and football to be utterly cryed down and not usit!" said the King, my driver says, as we pass through a castellated archway into the walled burgh. I ask to be let out, shake hands with the burly Aberdeen taxi man that married a lass from the south highlands. He's been awake all night delivering train passengers from the inland train station to this seaside town, sipping from a flask and historicizing customers. I tell him my mother is Scots and Catholic. He says that's a hard combination any day. I get a recommend of a foot path to the harbor and send my bags along to my mother's house.

I want to get a sense of this place myself, minus the history and morality lesson. I want to feel the weight of Europe as it has shaped my mother. There is a lot of stone here, a lot of gray, but despite the early morning hour, there is cheerful bustle – bakeries stocking pantries, a butcher hanging sides of beef, men in orange jump suits sweeping streets, art galleries scrubbing windows, gentlemen in dark suits muscling briefs to the finish line, mothers racing perambulators while shepherding older siblings to school. The sky is sterling blue and tumbling with cloud, seagulls perch the crow-stepped gables of pantile roofs, some of the stone housing is covered in white harling. Lovely town.

Sidewalk denizens will not look me in the eye, but they smile and say good day, aware of my otherness. I am feeling good about this place, even as an outsider. I am thinking my mother will be healing in her soul among these good people. But that's not the case. After finding my way past the cathedral, the colossal and symbolic ruin of which shames me, I walk down The Pends alongside medieval defensive walls and through the Mill Port gateway where I know I am about to cross over to my mother's world. I cast a look down a length of stone wall before committing: a short road with fishery cottages; my bags lie beside the door of one house central to the street; an old rag-top Citroen the size of a golf cart and with flat tires squats at the curb. I wonder why my bags reside street side until I stand foursquare with the doorknocker in hand and hear from inside: "Devil me none of yer deviltry. Gang yer ways off ma door!"

I tell Fiona I have nowhere to go if not here. There is silence, then,

"Ah, my God, you will be Travers, my son, or I am dreaming, or the devil has shapen you."

"No, it's me, Travers. I promise. Just, please, open the door, Mother."

The door sneaks open. One giggly eye scans the middle-aged man I have become. The door closes abruptly. There is silence. I say, "Mother, won't you let me in?" There is no answer. I knock and tell family secrets to the door to assert my identity, but still nothing. I investigate the back of the house leaping short walls that delineate the back yards of adjoined houses and bend limbo under clothes lines until I find the blue trim of my mother's house. I look in at a small, recessed window. My mother in a white shift with long white hair races about the place, tosses water on walls, talks to herself. I find a back door that opens easily enough and step inside the tiny dark cottage with fisheries gear everywhere and daguerreotype photographs and chipped dishes lining walls on a strip of wood mounted near the ceiling. I smell disinfectant. Fiona has scoured the walls. Then commotion from an adjoining room off the kitchen into which I lightly step.

"Bless me, God, ye have trekked fair through ma door. I am lost tae the devil. God bless me!" She falls to knees in front of me, closes her eyes and prays. I fall to knees and wrap her in my arms and rock her and weep and tell her that I am home, that I may be a devil but that I am a mortal one and that I would never harm her. When she does finally look me over, run her hands over my face, when she knows me, she un-tenses and collapses into my arms, a sack of bones, brittle hair, bleeding cuticles, gaunt and sallow. She can't have eaten in weeks. Her voice cracks and slows to a staticky moan like a gramophone winding down. There is a coal fire lit that keeps out the damp, but otherwise the place is old-clothes musty, animal-fat oozy, and coal-fire acidic with walls stained in the waters of La Salette.

I gather Fiona in my arms – she smells dry and buttery like a baby, like my son Emile that I carried to his bed and loved to smell his hair. I carry Fiona to a batting-torn and nappy sofa beside the fireplace decorative in cathedral architrave hearth inset and am reminded that a grand old religion has eaten the mind and guts of my mother with guilt and grief. I sense myself drifting back to iconoclast. I feel shameful, shake off the bitterness and consider I must bring my mother out from this place into the restorative sea air. That would make a difference.

I ring a mechanic who agrees to tinker the Citroen, my mother's vehicle. It seems the two stroke engine needs little more than a battery and a crank while the tires leak but will hold air long enough to putter about town. The mechanic teases the Citroen back to life – it sputters like a lawnmower and pollutes about as much, and yes, I still have no driver's license. I steep tea bags in hot water heated over the coal fire (there is a metal appendage on a hinge for such things, and luckily so as the gas won't flow, nor will electricity, all expired accounts). I gather my mother in a wool blanket that smells of wet dogs and drive her along the coast in the Citroen with the top down. She smiles in the rush of sea air, but she sinks far into the seat and opens her mouth but cannot speak, cannot lift her arm to push hair out of her face. I know I must get her to a hospital.

When I have got Fiona settled into white sheets in geriatrics, and as she seems restful and receives nourishment from an I.V., I find the Citroen collapsed upon its rims and bleeding oil. I phone a taxi to get me to the house and shiver myself to sleep on a sofa. I dream of war, armies in kilts and then in khaki. I dream of the glory of dying for a nation, for religion, a sense of belonging so keen as to have overestimated its place in the universe. I see planets regard each other with envy and misunderstanding, wobble and nudge then pile into each other like marbles in a boy's game. I am awakened by a loud crash and believe the earth has taken a knock by the moon when I see outside those narrow windows her majesty's sanitation crew bouncing trashcans off the side of a green truck.

I wash in cold tap water, shave as best I can, hire a taxi to the hospital where I am told my mother has passed in the night. I know it's me that killed her, that abandoned her, that caused her complete surrender to grief and isolation. I am told I must speak to a minister that will be here shortly or see a priest if I prefer, but I run out from that place pursued by demons. They think me crazy.

I leave Fiona's house to the National Trust. It's a treasure of late century fisheries trade I tell them, the gear loft jammed with rigging and nets and tools of carved wood, or rent it to golf enthusiasts, I say, fed up with their bureaucratic suspicions. Either way I'm done caretaking rooms still greasy with lives. I take with me a photograph of my mother and her family in her youth, Uncle Gerrit less imposing in this one than any other, smiling and playful and hopeful, the way I should like to have known him. My mother sits beside her father and has thrown an arm around his shoulder. I take also a bag of clothes the hospital handed me as well as one more item from the closet, and there is a discolored envelope unopened and addressed to me in a faded typeface that was left on the mantle for years, judging by the postmark. I decide not to read the letter until I am on the plane back to Montreal, shortly after a run in with constables over a moment of alcohol poisoning and an unsuccessful attempt to push over several of the walls left standing of the cathedral on the hill above my mother's house. The letter says this:

Travers my son: April 28, 1976

    I have never seen you though your mother tells me you are a smart boy. I do not have too much education my self. I was born into the trades. I have a trade now. I am a gardener though probably not much of one except for the common kind of vegetables and some flowers I know that put off the bugs. More to the point is I come by this gardening when I left the army in some disgrace. Your father you see is not so good a man. I send this letter to your mother in scotland because I know nothing of your whereabouts. Maybe she will send this along to you in the states. Maybe you will find yourself in the same room again. Either way I hope so. I was a foolish young man that got pretty early in my life fed up with all manner of things and so become desperate. There was the war of course which was horrible that I ran from in disgrace. That is bad. But it is doubling your mother with a life I ignored which is most bad. I was led wrong by your uncle. But that is no good excuse. You must by now know the odd ideas that has corrupted your uncles mind and heart. The man is dangerous Travers. He has ruined me and your mother. But I must admit to doing very bad things my own self. Every day I ask forgiveness in my new life. It is a humble way that I recommend to you if the world becomes overmuch. I tend a parish garden in a mountain valley in france where two rivers meet together. I have a small cottage and enough to eat and I burn peat to keep warm. I enjoy my life here. I discover that I have inherited my mothers gift of making things grow. I treated her bad when I was a young man. What I want to say is that I hope you can understand your mother and forgive her sadness that must have made your life difficult. But mostly I want to say that to be truly free in this life as I have learned you must be partnered. I hope with all my heart that you are not alone in this world. If you are alone you are not free. My friend Father Pierre Cousins has taught me this. He is a kind and gentle man that wants to know nothing of my wrong doings though I tell him more every day. He wants me to make right what I can. Which is why I garden and why I write you. I find myself becoming short in breath and the dampness that goes into my lungs at night has rooted there. I write you to say that I hope you will become a better man than your father which may not be too hard to do. Take care of your mother as best you can. Forgive your uncle though from a distance. I know you have no reason to honor these words as I have never been a father to you but I send you my apology for what I am and I feel that some day you will understand and forgive me in some portion. Here is a photograph of me with my friend Father Cousins. I hope you will remember me as I am in this photograph.

 Your father

 Timothy Gould O'Connell

Embrace companionship, he says. That is the meaning of the Holy Grail that Parsifal discovers. Freedom and isolation, he would say, are not the same. I judge myself loose and rambling but fettered in memory. As I find my mother, I lose her. As I find my father, I lose him, though I possess this photograph of a middle-aged man who had found a way to bring new life into the world after having abandoned me, and I carry with me my mother's obsession for what lies behind the wallpaper, and I possess a house filled with Gladys that has cast me out. I have lost much recently, too much. I spill my Scotch as the plane bumps into turbulence. What I should do, I tell myself while signing the steward for another, is plant myself somewhere near Emile, buy a ranch in the hills near Charlottesville and trot into town on horseback, or maybe chuck it all and ride that horse west into the sunset. No, I will do well to make my son more a part of my life. As I look down the isles of middle-aged passengers on this flight, all these gray and tonsured male scalps scare the shit out of me. Where am I in Shakespeare's seven ages? Five maybe: large-bellied and smart talking. Or six: muscles lean and ropy, shrinking in an expanding world. May the gods save me from "second childishness." What of Halley Gay? Can a woman's heart mature in good health absent a child? I don't myself have the glands for nurturing. I have kept an emotional distance from Emile. Perhaps I don't have the humanity, the heart. But the more holes that anger has augered in, the more sadness, or angel wings, Gladys would say, that in their gentle violence have worn away at this rock in my breast, the less mass, the softer it has become. I take soldier Jones' army uniform out from the bag at my feet, crush it into a ball, bury my face in it. I smell his fear, his uncertainty, his anger, and the ocean depths he sought as protection from enemy fire at Normandy. At this moment, I am glad to have given my mother a last taste of the ocean before her antiseptic death.

I land in Boston, hung-over, locked into pattern, going down, riding my arrow of fate like Peter Sellers astride his A-bomb. I am moved to change flight plans and pay a penalty for that as we all must in moments of abrupt complication. I book a flight to Burlington, Vermont. It's a short way. I land as the sun plunges into Adirondack Mountains. I have never been here when the weather is other than winter. I'm surprised by the lush green, Edenic, loamy air I breathe, remembering having to suck teeth down my throat to take a breath in dry sub-zero degrees. I take a cab to Nectar's. Stupid idea. The place has changed. I have changed. I collapse in jet-lag stupor at a table near the same bathroom and beer-drenched corner that produced erotic aromas when I sat here last with Halley Gay, twenty years before. The place is clean of urinal and beer spills. And the lighting has spiked, the same with beer prices, and the band lays down improv jazz, the crowd affects artsy, the Schlitz sign has disappeared and a large-screen TV airs mute MTV videos. There is no cigarette smoke, there are no threatening bouncers, the pinball corner displays a plastic fern, and no one dances. The edge is gone. Even the down-staters, the flatlanders, seem to have found other dens of misbehavior. A young girl in a very short skirt and cowboy boots sits at the table beside me, props her legs on a chair so that her skirt gathers at her hips. She wears glasses and jots furiously in a journal. Christ, another writer wannabe. She finds me watching her legs and moves the next table down. Dowdy, middle-aged professors aren't supposed to notice nice legs. This is not my town anymore. I guess it always was a young person's town.

I decide to get drunk. The epileptic fits have abated. So why not? Or should I score a joint? Drugs complement your lifestyle in mid-life one way or another. At least the waitress is kind, young and flirty. This makes me feel a little better. I settle in for another round of Scotch which becomes a few more as I fool myself into thinking the waitress has designs on me. The bar is jammed with people who know each other, who hug extravagantly and share volumes of anecdote which draws laugher which draws more laughter which all leaves me very depressed. Why did I come here? I wear my past like an impenetrable bubble; there is no point of intersect with the present. Maybe that's the lesson. Maybe I need to resettle into the tweeds and elbow patches, resole these loafers and find a quiet New England town to retire into, maybe up in the hills outside Northfield where the highway access lets onto a dirt road, complete the circle of my life that way. Maybe some backwoods podunk will tolerate an eccentric professor pacing with a cane the back roads, head in the clouds. I will have a pension to draw from, my son having received college tuition

benefits (all very incestuous, this college game), so I have no expenses
beyond tooth repair (that alley whomping I took in the mouth outside
Nectar's having begun to shift into bridge work). How can I be thinking I
belong here in Burlington? The jazz band modulates to jungle boogie which
incites the room to finger tapping and head bobbing. I need a nap. Young
people in tight clothes, short hair, tattoos, goatees, piercings, they look at me
like I'm a footnote in fashion history while what I see are recycled beatniks.

My head dizzies with the noise and alcohol. I make preparations to
escape with my duffel out the back way through the deli when an
imposing blonde – nothing girly about this one, nothing trendily mutilated
or lispily chatty – she parts this cognoscenti of art on the hoof with an
entitled stroll in khaki hiking shorts, L.L. Bean deck shoes untied, a
beaming halation of white Oxford tucked and rolled at the sleeves. I must
have disappeared again into the illusions of cerebral dysfunction. I didn't
see this coming. Must be all this booze and heartache. Will I soon be
writhing on the floor in tonic-clonic convulsions, grossing out the
waitress, that cute girl in cowboy boots? There will certainly be, once
again, a gathering of disaster groupies standing over me.

A ring of keys flung brattles on the tabletop. I am exposed pinned and
wriggling in the shallows of my divining soul. I have not dived through to
the unconscious but have instead bounced off the shellac of impenetrable
surfaces, or I have emerged only so far as a patient might from ether. The
blonde places her palms to my cheeks, draws my face to hers, floats me in
the blue of her eyes says, "My automobile resides street side beside this
salt buffet in which you wallow, sugar. Would you, Mr. Jones, kindly assist
a lady grateful to locate a drivin' partner that has survived the sometimes
bump or two. I seek the man that will introduce me to my son. The most
I can offer, darlin', is a soft place to land. But don't that seem quite a lot
these days?"

Halley has tracked me from the skies where I rode my partiular arrow
of fate back here to Burlington.

"Yes," I say, "it does seem like a lot." There is no need to mention I don't have a driver's license. That's more than she cares about. She has always been a reckless driver herself. We both know ignoring the rules of the road is the best way to find our place together.

Fomite
Burlington, Vermont

Fomite is a literary press whose authors and artists explore the human condition -- political, cultural, personal and historical -- in poetry and prose.

A fomite is a medium capable of transmitting infectious organisms from one individual to another.

"The activity of art is based on the capacity of people to be infected by the feelings of others." Tolstoy, *What is Art?*

AlphaBetaBestiario - Antonello Borra
Animals have always understood that mankind is not fully at home in the world. Bestiaries, hoping to teach, send out warnings. This one, of course, aims at doing the same.

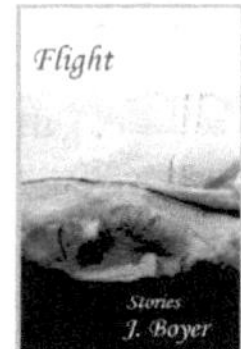

Flight and Other Stories - Jay Boyer
In *Flight and Other Stories,* we're with the fattest woman on earth as she draws her last breaths and her soul ascends toward its final reward. We meet a divorcee who can fly for no more effort than flapping her arms. We follow a middle-aged butler whose love affair with a young woman leads him first to the mysteries of bondage, and then to the pleasures of malice. Story by story, we set foot into worlds so strange as to seem all but surreal, yet everything feels familiar, each moment rings true. And that's when we recognize we're in the hands of one of America's truly original talents.

Improvisational Arguments - Anna Faktorovich
Improvisational Arguments is written in free verse to capture the essence of modern problems and triumphs. The poems clearly relate short, frequently humorous and occasionally tragic, stories about travels to exotic and unusual places, fantastic realms, abnormal jobs, artistic innovations, political objections, and misadventures with love.

Loisaida - Dan Chodorokoff
Catherine, a young anarchist estranged from her parents and squatting in an abandoned building on New York's Lower East Side is fighting with her boyfriend and conflicted about her work on an underground newspaper. After learning of a developer's plans to demolish a community garden, Catherine builds an alliance with a group of Puerto Rican community activists. Together they confront the confluence of politics, money, and real estate that rule Manhattan. All the while she learns important lessons from her great-grandmother's life in the Yiddish anarchist movement that flourished on the Lower East Side at the turn of the century. In this coming of age story, family saga, and tale of urban politics, Dan Chodorkoff explores the "principle of hope", and examines how memory and imagination inform social change.

Fomite
Burlington, Vermont

Still Time - Michael Cocchiarale

Still Time is a collection of twenty-five short and shorter stories exploring tensions that arise in a variety of contemporary relationships: a young boy must deal with the wrath of his out-of-work father; a woman runs into a man twenty years after an awkward sexual encounter; a wife, unable to conceive, imagines her own murder, as well as the reaction of her emotionally distant husband; a soon-to-be tenured English professor tries to come to terms with her husband's shocking return to the religion of his youth; an assembly line worker, married for thirty years, discovers the surprising secret life of his recently hospitalized wife. Whether a few hundred or a few thousand words, these and other stories in the collection depict characters at moments of deep crisis. Some feel powerless, overwhelmed—unable to do much to change the course of their lives. Others rise to the occasion and, for better or for worse, say or do the thing that might transform them for good. Even in stories with the most troubling of endings, there remains the possibility of redemption. For each of the characters, there is still time.

Loosestrife - Greg Delanty

This book is a chronicle of complicity in our modern lives, a witnessing of war and the destruction of our planet. It is also an attempt to adjust the more destructive blueprint myths of our society. Often our cultural memory tells us to keep quiet about the aspects that are most challenging to our ethics, to forget the violations we feel and tremors that keep us distant and numb.

Carts and Other Stories - Zdravka Evtimova

Roots and wings are the key words that best describe the short story collection, *Carts and Other Stories,* by Zdravka Evtimova. The book is emotionally multilayered and memorable because of its internal power, vitality and ability to touch both the heart and your mind. Within its pages, the reader discovers new perspectives true wealth, and learns to see the world with different eyes. The collection lives on the borders of different cultures. *Carts and Other Stories* will take the reader to wild and powerful Bulgarian mountains, to silver rains in Brussels, to German quiet winter streets and to wind bitten crags in Afghanistan. This book lives for those seeking to discover the beauty of the world around them, and will have them appreciating what they have— and perhaps what they have lost as well.

The Listener Aspires to the Condition of Music - Barry Goldensohn

"I know of no other selected poems that selects on one theme, but this one does, charting Goldensohn's career-long attraction to music's performance, consolations and its august, thrilling, scary and clownish charms. Does all art aspire to the condition of music as Pater claimed, exhaling in a swoon toward that one class act? Goldensohn is more aware than the late 19th century of the overtones of such breathing: his poems thoroughly round out those overtones in a poet's lifetime of listening."
John Peck, poet, editor, Fellow of the American Academy of Rome

Fomite
Burlington, Vermont

The Co-Conspirator's Tale - Ron Jacobs

There's a place where love and mistrust are never at peace; where duplicity and deceit are the universal currency. *The Co-Conspirator's Tale* takes place within this nebulous firmament. There are crimes committed by the police in the name of the law. Excess in the name of revolution. The combination leaves death in its wake and the survivors struggling to find justice in a San Francisco Bay Area noir by the author of the underground classic *The Way the Wind Blew:A History of the Weather Underground* and the novel *Short Order Frame Up*.

When You Remember Deir Yassin - R.L Green

When You Remember Deir Yassin is a collection of poems by R. L. Green, an American Jewish writer, on the subject of the occupation and destruction of Palestine. Green comments: "Outspoken Jewish critics of Israeli crimes against humanity have, strangely, been called 'anti-Semitic' as well as the hilariously illogical epithet 'self-hating Jews.' As a Jewish critic of the Israeli government, I have come to accept these accusations as a stamp of approval and a badge of honor, signifying my own fealty to a central element of Jewish identity and ethics: one must be a lover of truth and a friend to the oppressed, and stand with the victims of tyranny, not with the tyrants, despite tribal loyalty or self-advancement. These poems were written as expressions of outrage, and of grief, and to encourage my sisters and brothers of every cultural or national grouping to speak out against injustice, to try to save Palestine, and in so doing, to reclaim for myself my own place as part of the Jewish people." Poems in the original English are accompanied by Arabic and Hebrew translations.

Roadworthy Creature, Roadworthy Craft - Kate Magill

Words fail but the voice struggles on. The culmination of a decade's worth of performance poetry, *Roadworthy Creature, Roadworthy Craft* is Kate Magill's first full-length publication. In lines that are sinewy yet delicate, Magill's poems explore the terrain where idea and action meet, where bodies and words commingle to form a strange new flesh, a breathing text, an "I" that spirals outward from itself.

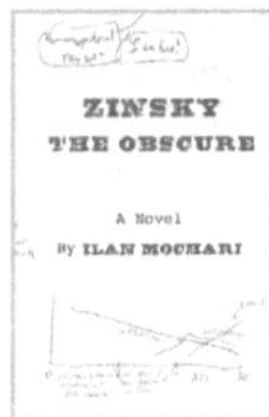

Zinsky the Obscure - Ilan Mochari

"If your childhood is brutal, your adulthood becomes a daily attempt to recover: a quest for ecstasy and stability in recompense for their early absence." So states the 30-year-old Ariel Zinsky, whose bachelor-like lifestyle belies the torturous youth he is still coming to grips with. As a boy, he struggles with the beatings themselves; as a grownup, he struggles with the world's indifference to them. *Zinsky the Obscure* is his life story, a humorous chronicle of his search for a redemptive ecstasy through sex, an entrepreneurial sports obsession, and finally, the cathartic exercise of writing it all down. Fervently recounting both the comic delights and the frightening horrors of a life in which he feels – always – that he is not like all the rest, Zinsky survives the worst and relishes the best with idiosyncratic style, as his heartbreak turns into self-awareness and his suicidal ideation into self-regard. A vivid evocation of the all-consuming nature of lust and ambition – and the forces that drive them.

Fomite
Burlington, Vermont

Visiting Hours - Jennifer Anne Moses
Visiting Hours, a novel-in-stories, explores the l ves of people not normally met on the page---AIDS patients and those whc care for them. Set in Baton Rouge, Louisiana, and written with large and frequent dollops of humor, the book is a profound meditation on faith and love in the face of illness and poverty.

Love's Labours - Jack Pulaski
In the four stories and two novellas that comprise *Love's Labors* the protagonists Ben and Laura, discover in their fervid romance and long marriage their interlocking fates, and the histories that preceded their births. They also learned something of the paradox between love and all the things it brings to its beneficiaries: bliss, disaster, duty, tragedy, comedy, the grotesque, and tenderness.

Ben and Laura's story is also the particularly American tale of immigration to a new world. Laura's story begins in Puerto Rico, and Ben's lineage is Russian-Jewish. They meet in City College of New York, a place at least analogous to a melting pot. Laura struggles to rescue her brother from gang life and heroin. She is mother to her younger sister; their mother Consuelo is the financial mainstay of the family and consumed by work. Despite filial obligations, Laura aspires to be a serious painter. Ben writes, cares for and is caught up in the misadventures and surreal stories of his younger schizophrenic brother. Laura is also a story teller as powerful and enchanting as Scheherazade. Ben struggles to survive such riches, and he and Laura endure.

The Derivation of Cowboys & Indians
- Joseph D. Reich

The Derivation of Cowboys & Indians represents a profound journey, a breakdown of The American Dream from a social, cultural, historical, and spiritual point of view. Reich examines in concise!detail the loss of the collective unconscious, commenting on our!contemporary postmodern culture with its self-interested excesses, on where and how things all go wrong, and how social/political practice rarely meets its original proclamations and promises. Reich's surreal and self-effacing satire brings this troubling message home. *The Derivations of Cowboys & Indians* is a desperate search and struggle for America's literal, symbolic, and spiritual home.

The Empty Notebook Interrogates Itself
- Susan Thomas

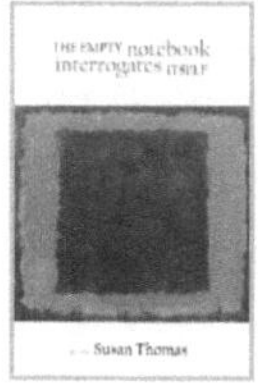

The Empty Notebook began its life as a very literal metaphor for a few weeks of what the poet thought was writer's block, but was really the struggle of an eccentric persona to take over her working life. It won. And for the next three years everything she wrote came to her in the voice of the Empty Notebook, who, as the notebook began to fill itself, became rather opinionated, changed gender, alternately acted as bully and victim, had many bizarre adventures in exotic locales and developed a somewhat politically-incorrect attitude. It then began to steal the voices and forms of other poets and tried to immortalize itself in various poetry reviews. It is now thrilled to collect itself in one slim volume.

Fomite

Burlington, Vermont

Kasper Planet: Comix and Tragix - Peter Schumann

The British call him Punch, the Italians, Pulchinello, the Russians, Petruchka, the Native Americans, Coyote. These are the figures we may know. But every culture that worships authority will breed a Punch-like, anti-authoritan resister. Yin and yang -- it has to happen. The Germans call him Kasper. Truth-telling and serious pranking are dangerous professions when going up against power. Bradley Manning sits naked in solitary; Julian Assange is pursued by Interpol, Obama's Department of Justice, and Amazon.com. But -- in contrast to merely human faces -- masks and theater can often slip through the bars. Consider our American Kaspers: Charlie Chaplin, Woody Guthrie, Abby Hoffman, the Yes Men -- theater people all, utilizing various forms to seed critique. Their profiles and tactics have evolved along with those of their enemies. Who are the bad guys that call forth the Kaspers? Over the last half century, with his Bread & Puppet Theater, Peter Schumann has been tireless in naming them, excoriating them with Kasperdom. …from Marc Estrin's Foreword to Planet Kasper

Travers' Inferno - L.E. Smith

In the 1970's churches began to burn in Burlington, Vermont. Travers' Inferno places these fires in the dizzying zeitgeist of aggressive utopian movements, distrust in authority, escapist alternative life styles, and a parasite news media. Its characters – colorful, damaged, comical, and tragic – are seeking meaning through desperate acts. Protagonist Travers Jones is grounded in the transcendent, mystified by the opposite sex, haunted by an absent father, and directed by an uncle with a grudge. Around him: secessionist Québecois murdering, pilfering and burning; changing alliances; violent deaths; confused love making; and a belligerent cat.

My God, What Have We Done? - Susan Weiss

In a world afflicted with war, toxicity, and hunger, does what we do in our private lives really matter? Fifty years after the creation of the atomic bomb at Los Alamos, newlyweds Pauline and Clifford visit that once-secret city on their honeymoon, compelled by Pauline's fascination with Oppenheimer, the soulful scientist. The two stories emerging from this visit reverberate back and forth between the loneliness of a new mother at home in Boston and the isolation of an entire community dedicated to the development of the bomb. While Pauline struggles with unforeseen challenges of family life, Oppenheimer and his crew reckon with forces beyond all imagining.

Finally the years of frantic research on the bomb culminate in a stunning test explosion that echoes a rupture in the couple's marriage. Against the backdrop of a civilization that's out of control, Pauline begins to understand the complex, potentially explosive physics of personal relationships.

At once funny and dead serious, *My God, What Have We Done?* sifts through the ruins left by the bomb in search of a more worthy human achievement.

Fomite
Burlington, Vermont

As It Is On Earth - Peter M. Wheelwright
Four centuries after the Reformation Pilgrims sailed up the down-flowing watersheds of New England, Taylor Thatcher, irreverent scion of a fallen family of Maine Puritans, is still caught in the turbulence.

In his errant attempts to escape from history, the young college professor is further unsettled by his growing attraction to Israeli student Miryam Bluehm as he is swept by Time through the "family thing" – from the tangled genetic and religious history of his New England parents to the redemptive birthday secret of Esther Fleur Noire Bishop, the Cajun-Passamaquoddy woman who raised him and his younger half-cousin/half-brother, Bingham.

The landscapes, rivers, and tidal estuaries of Old New England and the Mayan Yucatan are also casualties of history in Thatcher's story of Deep Time and re-discovery of family on Columbus Day at a high-stakes gambling casino, rising in resurrection over the starlit bones of a once-vanquished Pequot Indian Tribe.

Views Cost Extra - L.E. Smith
Views that inspire, that calm, or that terrify – all come at some cost to the viewer. In *Views Cost Extra* you will find a New Jersey high school preppy who wants to inhabit the "perfect" cowboy movie, a rural mailman disgusted with the residents of his town who wants to live with the penguins, an ailing screen writer who strikes a deal with Johnny Cash to reverse an old man's failures, an old man who ponders a young man's suicide attempt, a one-armed blind blues singer who wants to reunite with the car that took her arm on the assembly line -- and more. These stories suggest that we must pay something to live even ordinary lives.